JILL TRESEDER was born in Hampshire and lived all her childhood in sight of the sea on the Solent and in Devon, Cornwall and West Wales. She now lives in Devon overlooking the River Dart.

After graduating from Bristol with a d͡e͡---   ͡n, Jill followed careers in social work, manage͡r͡---   ͡cial research, obtaining a PhD from ͡t͡͡'   rsity of Bath along the way.

Since 2006 she has   ͡ction, and has published five full len͡g͡

ALSO BY JILL TRESEDER

The Hatmaker's Secret
A Place of Safety
Becoming Fran
The Saturday Letters
My Sister Myself
The Birthday House
Blackthorn Winter

The Red Chair

Jill Treseder

SilverWood

Published in 2025 by SilverWood Books

SilverWood Books Ltd
14 Small Street, Bristol, BS1 1DE, United Kingdom
www.silverwoodbooks.co.uk

Copyright © Jill Treseder 2025

The right of Jill Treseder to be identified as the author of this work has been asserted in accordance with the Copyright, Designs and Patents Act 1988 Sections 77 and 78.

All rights reserved. No part of this publication may be reproduced, stored in a retrieval system, or transmitted in any form or by any means, electronic, mechanical, photocopying, recording or otherwise, without prior permission of the copyright holder.

This is a work of fiction. Names, characters, places and incidents either are products of the author's imagination or are used fictitiously. Any resemblance to actual events or locales or persons, living or dead, is entirely coincidental.

ISBN 978-1-80042-307-7 (paperback)
Also available as an ebook

British Library Cataloguing in Publication Data
A CIP catalogue record for this book is available from the British Library

Page design and typesetting by SilverWood Books

NO AI TRAINING
Without in any way limiting the author's exclusive rights under copyright, any use of this publication to train generative artificial intelligence (AI) technologies to generate text is expressly prohibited. The author reserves all rights to license uses of this work for generative AI training and development of machine learning language models.

To Hugh, still with me in spirit

1 2010 *Naomi*

Late spring, bluebells an indigo wash under the trees, in places so intense it hurt. An acid-green light filtered through the canopy of new beech leaves. It made Naomi thirsty. Her old Land Rover nudged forward at walking pace, sinking into the ruts, clambering over roots.

Always further than she thought, this trek through the woods. One more gate than expected, each with its side gate for walkers. Each one closed today. Stop, get out, breathe in bluebells, almost peppery, open gate, drive through, get out again and close gate. Those spring-loaded catches, long metal stalks like snail tentacles, so satisfying to operate and reminding her that this track was mostly used by people on horseback. Each time she went through the ritual, she felt her pace slowing, threshold by threshold. Tiny things caught her attention – a rustle in the ditch, the clatter and blue-pink flash of a jay, and lichen on the crossbars of one of the wooden side gates – a kaleidoscope of grey, green, yellow ochre, tiny eruptions of brilliant orange – a microcosm of glorious technicolour. The last gate.

It was always further than Naomi had thought, back then, when she went to fetch milk from the dairy at the farm. Swinging the little churn, being careful not to spill any, humming along through the enchanted woods, happy as the day was long. Enchantment always carried danger, of course. But she hadn't known that then. Found out the hard way when the days turned out to be longer than they were happy.

But all that lay behind her now. A new life in the bracing air of the rugged north Devon coast. South Devon, where she'd grown up, was very beautiful, but too cosy, too busy. Here was wildness, solitude, the ocean and a chance to take stock in an old haunt that was dear to her heart. She had her state pension, which should easily cover the modest lifestyle she planned. She'd dig a vegetable patch, get horse dung from the stables. In a year or so she could be halfway to being self-sufficient. She would walk and swim and forage, make her own bread – and, maybe eventually, find the courage to write her story. But that would be a bonus.

There lay the trunk of the fallen oak, covered in moss and ledges of creamy fungus, where she used to pause with her milk churn. She would lie down, feeling the grain along the length of her spine, and gaze up through the canopy at the leaves fingering the sky. Nearly there.

As she came out of the wood the light changed, rinsed clear to the far horizon. There it was. Scoop of valley like a glass brimming with Atlantic blue, and that wonky roofline nestling under the towering shoulder of the cliff. She turned off the ignition and yanked on the handbrake. She had to walk.

She stood at the top of the steep track, breathing seaweed air, listening to the silence. Just the tick of the cooling engine, the drone of a bee in the gorse. There were the two chimneys and the window she'd used to escape. More than twenty years ago. A love-hate relationship if ever there was one, a volatile see-saw. She'd stayed in it far too long. Be that as it may, it was generous of him to make the place over to her. Unexpectedly generous. She'd been in a fever of anticipation ever since she got the solicitor's letter. Typical Wilson, only managing to be kind from beyond the grave. Unpredictable, ever since that first meeting.

It's 1982. London is spread before you on a double page of the A–Z. From the Isle of Sheppey in the Thames estuary to the edges of Berkshire in the west. A vast unknown territory. You consult the index, follow the gridlines from the top and the side of the page until your fingers meet. Why does it always have to be on the join of two pages? You can just make out the two halves of the road name, bisected by perforations. Can-ford Pl.

You parade in front of Fay's full-length mirror in your outfit. Fay's told you, 'Not the ethnic look,' so your favourite floaty skirts are out. You've opted for what Fay calls your safari suit with a white shirt. Cool, unfussy and not quite beige. But safe. You've never followed fashion, but anything goes these days. Sandals will do. Far too hot for the patent sling-backs. Relax, you tell yourself, hitching your black patent bag over your shoulder and swinging out of the door.

Outside the Tube station, you look around. The A–Z is in your bag but you've memorised this bit of the map. That should be the road. Lined with plane trees. You cross to the shadier side of the street. There it is, Canford Place, set back on the right, halfway down. Substantial houses. Sleek cars parked discreetly in drives.

You're shown into a conservatory used as a waiting area – three wicker chairs in a semi-circle, smothered by a jungle of tropical plants.

Which chair to choose? How long will you have to wait? If you sit by the door, he may come upon you too suddenly. You opt for the furthest seat and snag your leg on the corner of a low bamboo table as you cross the steamy space. The midday sun is pouring in. No blinds. No ventilation.

You sink into the chair, gobbled by cushions covered in oversized peonies, and feel the perspiration trickle between your breasts. You rub your leg, no blood, thank goodness. The long view of the garden – lawn bordered by shrubbery and tall trees – is partially obscured by condensation. Attempting a casual pose, you cross your legs and your thighs slither against each other. Now you're grateful for the peonies. Embarrassing to stand up and leave a damp imprint on plain fabric – your backside for all to see.

From here you can see the doorway and a passage leading away to the cool and shadowed hall. Doors click and slam in the depths of the house. A telephone sounds and a woman's voice calls out. A toilet is flushed. But you are left alone to swelter.

Minutes tick by as drips of condensation break away, creating tiny channels of clear glass on the window. The plants aren't all tropical. One looks the same as the two-foot pot plant in Fay's living room. But this one is a tree, already bending its tip into the high arch of the conservatory. Your appointment was for twelve. Ten, fifteen, twenty minutes past the hour come and go. Just as you're convinced you've been forgotten, there comes a soft click and a current of cool air across your back.

'Naomi Osborne, I believe?'

A wealthy voice, like chocolate with a bitter edge in the inflection. As if it challenged your very identity.

That was the moment, wasn't it? The clench in the belly you should have acted upon. You felt ambushed, as if he had stalked you. Imagined him observing you from the cool of the garden while you simmered like a frog in a pot. Those were your first thoughts, weren't they? Admit it. That little bunch of nerve endings flagging a warning: this person is not to be trusted. You shivered, didn't you? In all that sultry heat, you shivered. You should have walked – out of the house, into the Tube, back to Fay's. Deep down in your belly, you knew it.

But his smile is warm, he flings his hands wide in a generous welcoming gesture and his handshake is firm. Tailored shorts, a loose white linen shirt. Thick dark hair, cool grey eyes.

'You will be glad you came,' he says.

Now, here she stood, a middle-aged woman – some would say elderly – poised at the edge of the wood facing the sea. Crossing a threshold. Starting down the hill, her feet wouldn't wait. She skidded on loose stones, jumped over tussocks of grass until she was running, running, down, down, along past the cottage and up the slope, across the wide expanse of springy turf to the bench. She threw up her arms and yelled into the roar of surf breaking on the rocks below. 'I'm here! Here I am!' The wind swallowed the sound of her voice and she dropped down onto the wooden seat. Could it be the same weather-beaten plank? It certainly looked the same; the grain and the grooves felt the same. Comforting, yet carrying memories that went against the comforting grain.

Naomi shook herself. It might be the same bench but the salt wind and rain had scoured it of memory – just as the ancient hills were immune to human goings-on. Like the centuries-old cottage. What were a few sordid months compared to the generations of workers' lives those walls had witnessed? And, before that, the life of the stone before it was quarried? No, she didn't fear the intrusion of memories.

In any case, she wasn't the same woman. No longer that submissive person, dependent on Wilson's approval. That was the old Naomi. She was her own person now. To give credit where it was due, she probably would never have come this far without Wilson. He'd taught her a lot, revealed her potential before deciding she should not be allowed to step into it. He'd played cat and mouse with her back then, but now he was being benign, helping to launch her into a new phase of her life.

The breakers rolled in, hypnotic. Every so often one towered over the others and took her breath away, along with all sense of time or tiredness. Eventually she remembered the car and walked back up the track, inhaling the honey smell that floated off the gorse as the day warmed up. She coasted back down the hill and parked alongside the little shed, the wood-store.

Shouldering her bag, she followed the cobbled path to the door and fitted the huge iron key into the lock.

As she tried to turn it, a voice called from inside, 'I don't know who the hell you are, but you can bugger off out of here.'

Naomi froze. The place was supposed to be empty. What on earth was going on? And why did that voice seem alien and yet faintly familiar? Why did she not feel afraid? The door was already unlocked. No wonder the key wouldn't turn. She dropped it into her pocket and lifted the metal ring. Pull and twist, that familiar action. The door swung half open.

'I thought I said, bugger off.'

That voice again. Gravelly. Harsh. Bluffing. The memory teased and vanished. She stepped inside, into the dimly lit passage.

He was standing in the kitchen doorway against the light from the window. But it was enough. Memories slotted into place. Wilson's brother.

'Hell's teeth! It's Naomi! What the devil are you doing here?' He stepped back, steadying himself against the table – still that scrubbed pine top with blue paint peeling off the legs.

The light fell across his face. Heavy-framed glasses, ginger moustache. He'd had a beard back then. A strange jutting affair, the colour of carrots. Barbarossa, they used to call him. Yes, it was Gordon, all right.

'I'm taking possession, Gordon. That's what I'm doing here.'

'The hell you're not. I live here. It's my place now.'

'Wilson left it to me. He left it to me in his will.'

'The hell he did not! At least…'

She took a breath. 'We'll see about that. But meanwhile, I need a wee. You're not going to bar the way, I hope.'

He gestured graciously. 'Be my guest.'

She sat on the toilet, head in hands. His guest! The devious toad. Bad memories flooded in. Wilson's neediness, Gordon's saccharine hostility. Days of barbed comments and innuendo flaring eventually into a bitter row. Wilson storming off, the sound of the key in the lock. After the first lyrical months of love, Wilson had been unpredictable, one day almost worshipping her, the next manipulative, punitive. But when they were alone it had worked, even if it felt like walking on eggshells. When Gordon visited, he needled and provoked, looked out for cracked eggs and made sure they got broken.

So what had gone wrong? Why was he here? She ran her hands under the tap and dried them on her trousers, avoiding the grubby towel.

'Scotch?' Gordon said when she emerged. 'For old times' sake? Good for shock.'

She shook her head. 'Nothing for me. I just want to know why you're here.'

'I'm guessing you didn't wait for the second letter.'

'Second letter?' She paced to the window and looked out on the path that led to the waterfall where she used to watch salmon leaping. Second letter. Doubt crept in, knotting her stomach. That phrase at the end of her letter. *Further information to follow. Await our instructions before taking action.* Something like that. She'd assumed it was lawyer-speak for nothing much.

'The second letter containing the small print,' Gordon said.

She paced back to the table, staring at him.

He gulped his whisky. 'They said I might get a visit.'

She escaped back to the window.

'For Christ's sake sit down. You're making me twitch.' Another gulp. 'Look. We'd better have a civil conversation.'

She swallowed a retort and sat down. 'What do you mean, they said you'd get a visitor? And what small print?'

'A visit from the other beneficiary. But you see, I wasn't expecting you. I'm in shock too. You see, he always said you loved this place more than him. So I knew he wouldn't leave it to you. Wouldn't give you the satisfaction. I was expecting one of his other women. Penelope, for instance. Or the dreaded Deirdre. But I was wrong.'

He was appraising her across the table. That teasing look.

'You've worn well, Naomi. The years have been kind to you.'

She wasn't rising to that one. The years, she noticed, had not been kind to him. Bags under the eyes, the whites turning sepia. She repeated her question. 'What small print?'

'The bastard. He's playing us off against each other.'

She swallowed her impatience. 'But he couldn't leave it to both of us. Could he?'

'That's in the small print. You own it, but I have lifetime tenancy. The right to live here until I die. He giveth with one hand and taketh away with the other, Naomi, my dear. I might be the wrong side of eighty, but as far as I know, I'm in perfectly good health. So put that in your pipe and smoke it.'

'I will have a Scotch, after all. Just a finger.' How could she have been so naïve?

He splashed out a tot and pushed it in her direction, refilled his own glass. 'The party's over, Naomi.'

'Party? What party? There never was—'

'Poor Naomi. I feel quite sorry for you. He gives you your dream. I bet you were thinking how generous he was. And then he turns it neatly into a nightmare. For me too. Clever really. You have to hand it to him.' He smiled across at her and chuckled.

She downed the whisky and stood up, the heat of it giving her the edge she needed.

'I'll be in touch. I—'

'Off to call in the bailiffs?'

'Oh, Gordon, grow up, for heaven's sake! There's no point behaving like that.'

'So you're leaving me here in peace?'

'I'm not such a fool as to think I can get rid of you easily. I need to think. So do you, I imagine.'

Shouldering her bag once more, she left, the key still in her pocket. There had only ever been one key. Wilson must have gone to a blacksmith to have a duplicate made.

She drove back through the woods. No bluebells now. Nothing but a gallery of images: Wilson, Gordon; Gordon, Wilson; Wilson closing in, walking away, charming, demanding, devious.

She found herself at a standstill, gripping the wheel, staring at the smeared underbody of an insect that had met its end against the killer windscreen. Would she never be free of him? Oh, the shame of that. She shook her head violently and shifted focus to the five-bar gate ahead of her. As she closed it behind the car, she made herself pause to inhale the leafy breath of the woods.

More than anything she wanted to ring Fay, her best mate since she was four years old, whose house and mother she'd known as well as her own. Fay, with whom she'd shared everything ever since. But now there was no Fay to ring. Two years had passed and she still couldn't get used to the idea.

She certainly wasn't ready to go home. She drove on past the village and down to the quay. A wrecking coast. Beyond the sea wall, mass on mass of ink-black jagged rocks reared up from the beach, impervious to the bombarding breakers. It still astounded her. Unchanging, violent, beautiful. She shuddered.

Turning her back on the sea, she made for the terrace of buildings that had been uncomfortably harnessed together to form the Stagworthy Quay Hotel. Nothing had changed – the entrance where she expected it to be, reception, as always, in the bar. She booked herself in for the night.

2 *Meghan*

Meghan wiped her hands down her apron as she went to open the door – a habitual gesture given that her palms were usually smeared with paint and black ink. She was a tall, big-boned woman who had suffered as a child because her arms and legs seemed to get in everybody's way, including her own. She'd become friends with her body since then. She was no beauty – too broad a brow, too long a nose, too wide a mouth – but she was all of a piece. She fitted together. Folks saw themselves when they looked at her, and she did her best to take that image and calm it down before she gave it back to them.

Her visitor would be Rita from across the road, eager for coffee and gossip. Rita, by contrast, was short and wiry. She reminded Meghan of a blackbird, eying the ground for worms, pouncing, yanking. They had no more in common than their appearance suggested. But their friendship was strong, built over years of seeing each other through hard times.

Rita had been the first person Meghan spoke to when she first arrived in the village, pregnant, penniless and on the promise of a non-existent job. The hotel where she would eventually work was being renovated. There would be a job – a room even – but not for a couple of months. Rita had taken her in. Meghan had cleaned and cooked and cared for Rita's baby and toddler while Rita established her new business, letting holiday cottages to tourists. In the evenings, Meghan designed posters and ran up curtains and cushion covers. Ever since, they'd bailed each other out whenever needed, and although their jarring edges still clashed, the friendship endured.

'Fancy seeing you,' Meghan said as she opened the door.

'I saw you had post?' Rita made the statement into a question and stepped forward expectantly.

Of course. Rita had spotted Barry the postman coming to her door. Meghan set the postcard from her daughter, Alex, on the table while she put the kettle on, so that Rita's blackbird eye could take in all there was to see of the stamp and the small, neat handwriting.

It was because of Alex – or, more accurately, the bump that was to become Alex – that Meghan had decided to stay in Stagworthy. A job, a roof, and a friend in Rita, who knew about babies – these were not to be sniffed at. But there had been more to it. Apart from those practicalities, the coastline got under her painter's skin. She would feel her pulse quickening, a nagging that compelled her to capture its moods. She carried a notebook in her overalls so that she could snatch a pencil and make rapid sketches when the urge took over.

Meghan glanced back to see Rita examining the postcard with forensic attention. 'Sure you don't need a magnifying glass for that?'

Rita laughed and continued to turn the card this way and that. Sometimes Meghan resented the way Rita assumed as much connection with Alex as she had herself. But then she'd remember how Rita had included Alex with her own two boys and made her feel she belonged when Meghan had been out at work.

She dropped a teabag into one pottery mug and spooned Nescafé into the other. 'Two postcards in a year. I shan't know myself.'

Rita perched on a stool at the table. 'She doesn't exactly put herself out, does she, our Alex? Why don't you email? You've got her address, haven't you?'

'I suppose. I've never got to grips with the whole email thing. Anyway, a card's better than nothing – at least I know she's alive.'

'And in Spain.' Rita turned the card over and examined the picture: prickly pears cavorting down a cliff into a sapphire sea with a yellow strand stretching beyond. 'She always was a little scamp. Costa Brava, even.'

'Seems so. Bit warmer than here.' Meghan handed Rita her mug and settled on the saggy sofa in the corner.

'I never could understand why she threw up a perfectly good job to go off like that.'

'She got bored of her perfectly good job.' This was a lie. Alex had loved the job in a bank in Bristol but had unfortunately loved the bank manager too, inevitably a married man. Meghan and Alex had decided that nobody had any need to know about the affair.

'You're so accepting. Don't you worry about her?'

'Of course. But it does no good.' Meghan waved a hand dismissively. 'She's her own person.'

'Hmm. I wonder what she's doing now – to earn a living, I mean.'

'Bookkeeping's a useful skill. Plenty of demand I'd say – especially in the expat community, lots of them in Spain. And people like you, doing holiday lets and so on.'

'It was always money she loved.'

Meghan winced, wishing that wasn't true.

'She always wanted her pocket money in pennies. Remember? Not a twenty pence piece or a fifty. So she could count them out and stack them in little piles.'

Meghan nodded. 'She's still got that cash box you gave her. Up on the shelf in her bedroom. 'How are your bookings going, by the way?'

'Pretty good. Easter's full. Only one free for half-term. Napier's place. It's always last to go – no view.'

'Have you heard anything about Mill End? Would you take that on if it came on the market?'

Rita shook her head vigorously. 'No way. Certainly wouldn't buy it. Too isolated. Needs renovating. Every bag of cement having to be dragged through those woods.'

'I thought the old fellow had it modernised a few years back.'

'I wouldn't exactly trust his standards. It was '85 before he had the electric put in. He thought that was modern!' Rita stirred her coffee and licked the spoon carefully before placing it on the table. 'Wouldn't want to manage it either. Imagine, off down that awful track every time the idiot tenant can't switch the oven on.'

'So, you haven't heard anything?' Meghan was about to say that someone appeared to be living in the cottage. She'd walked over that way twice in the last week. From the headland, she'd seen smoke rising from the chimney. But Rita went off on another tack.

'Nah, he's not been dead that long. You know how long these things take. Anyway, that's not what I came about.' Rita took a gulp of coffee. 'There was a stranger down on the quay.'

'I suppose the sunshine brings them out.'

'She didn't look like a tripper.'

'So what does a tripper look like?'

Rita shrugged. 'You know perfectly well what I mean.'

Meghan did know, but she liked to interrupt Rita's tendency to stereotype people on sight. 'Okay. What was she like then, this stranger?'

'Funny mixture. Old jeans, tatty old Barbour, but the sort of hair that looks elegantly messy. Ancient Land Rover. A bit lady-of-the-manor-goes-to-market. But not from round here. Any biscuits?'

Meghan fetched the tin and pushed it across the table. A movement caught her eye and she moved to the window to watch a jackdaw on the chimney across the street, Rita's chimney pot, as it happened, in which they'd built a nest. Jackdaws were to be the subject of her next painting and she never lost an opportunity to watch them and make sketches. Her observations were interrupted. 'Would this be her now, your stranger?'

Rita half stood, craning her neck. 'Yes, that's the one. See what I mean?'

'You sure she's not from round here?'

'Well the Freelander isn't. Why?'

'I dunno. It's just…as if I've seen her somewhere before. But not recently.' She shrugged. 'May be imagining it.'

'Wonder where she's off to?'

'Church probably. People like to look round. Maybe she's looking for her great-grandfather's grave or something.'

'Anyway,' Rita said before many more minutes had passed. 'I must go.' She patted Meghan on the arm on her way to the door. 'Harry's going to put a cowl on that chimney, by the way, so you won't have those pesky creatures to watch for long. They make such a mess.'

'You'll let them hatch their young, though?'

'You'll have to speak nicely to Harry. You and your damn birds!' She paused at the gate. 'Tell you what, come over for supper? If you can put up with chilli again. And bring a bottle of red if you want to sweet-talk Harry.'

Meghan smiled to herself. Rita would be off to see where the stranger had gone. She topped up her tea with hot water and sat in the window seat with Alex's card, but she kept looking up, watching the pair of jackdaws, waiting for the stranger to reappear.

The card had taken weeks to get there. She read and re-read the brief message, milking it for more information than it contained. She loved the description of the prickly pears "like a bunch of cartoon rabbits" but worried over "this place is too small, moving down coast for some city life". Too small for what? A decent job? A man? Was there a boyfriend? Which city and what dangers would that bring? Barcelona, maybe. Rita was right – she should try the email. But she didn't want to nag. Alex was so volatile.

Volatile and surprising.

Maths had always been Alex's best subject but the decision to go into banking had been shocking to Meghan. She hadn't seen it coming. There had been all those short courses after she left school – secretarial stuff, computer skills, some accounting software Alex had got excited about – 'It's the future, Mum!' Meghan hadn't taken any of it very seriously. But Alex had gone on to reject Meghan's way of life in all its uncertainty.

She set the postcard on the mantelpiece. It was foolish, but she still worried that Alex had spent her whole childhood feeling insecure.

Just then the head and shoulders of the unknown woman appeared, moving smoothly along the top of the garden wall as if on wheels. A feeling of anxiety simmered for a moment in Meghan's stomach. That face. Vaguely familiar. But no one she could place.

Later, as she painted painstaking feathers and intricate twigs, an image kept floating into the space above her right shoulder – that face, looking down at her. Neither benign nor threatening. Just looking. But annoying. Particularly annoying because it seemed to tell her she couldn't dismiss this person. Some kind of connection existed between them. She had no idea what it was but, like the face, it wouldn't go away. Eventually she glared into that corner of the room and shouted, 'Bugger off, will you?' Obligingly, it did.

3 Naomi

After a disturbed night at the Stagworthy Quay Hotel, Naomi emerged to a bright day. She'd had bacon and egg for breakfast and a brisk walk up to Stuckton would do her good. She turned away from the quay and started to climb. It was steeper than she remembered and, panting heavily, she had to stop several times to admire the view before she reached the top road. The blue arc of the sky was criss-crossed with birds – rooks and herring gulls, the rooks black and busy at low level, the gulls gliding effortlessly at high altitude, their bright, white bellies masquerading as airliners heading across the Atlantic. Close at hand, cabbage whites fluttered along the hedge like feathers the gulls had let fall.

Sleeping on the problem of Gordon's presence in the cottage had brought no solutions, only hauntings, and she felt her hopes unravelling at every step. The fierce whip of the Atlantic gale would not be hers to breathe. No salt on the tongue and in her hair. No standing under the icy avalanche of the waterfall. No drying off in the smell of wood smoke. But above all she was being cheated of the solitude – the space she needed to find out who the hell she really was.

A fit young man with a rucksack and bedroll powered past her. She expected a whiff of male sweat, or the mud-grass smell of damp tent, but it was the scent of fabric conditioner that drifted off his well-ironed shirt – less intrepid hiker, more Mummy's boy. Intrepid or not, he was out of sight by the time she reached the top of the hill. She'd forgotten how the church tower dominated the landscape, drawing travellers towards it. The village felt strange to her after so many years – a manicured look to hedges and verges, hard standing where a lawn once was, an ugly extension to a cottage she used to love. Eyes must be watching her. That's how it was in a village. A stranger in April. She would sit and think in the church, give herself time. Book in for another night, maybe.

As she turned in to the churchyard, she noticed a movement back down the street. A small person, scurrying. Yes, she was under observation. She veered away from the church porch, imagining the dark interior space with saints looking down their holy noses, an unspeakably serene Mary, the risk of a lurking priest. Dandelion suns blazed from an overgrown path leading her to the oldest part of the graveyard, a mossy area carpeted with celandine, woven with periwinkle. A forgotten corner, too cramped for the mower, which had cut swathes between the more recent graves. She sat on a tree stump and contemplated the headstone of one, Prudence Wilkins. How prudent had Prudence been in her life, she wondered. Had she lived to regret it? Or had she rebelled against her name? Then she noticed the dates: Prudence had died in the middle of the nineteenth century at the age of twelve. Not much chance to try being reckless.

But what about Gordon? At that moment she hated Wilson and Gordon in equal measure. She was damned if she'd give either of them, dead or alive, the satisfaction of a long-term fight. Should she get legal advice? But there was nothing lawyers liked more than a conflict and she couldn't afford it anyway.

Gordon, she now remembered, hated Mill End cottage. Always used to complain about everything – from the lack of electricity to the isolation. She'd heard him describe it to someone once as a primitive shack in a godforsaken valley with only the sea for entertainment. 'One Atlantic roller is much the same as the next – and the next, and the one after that,' he'd added. 'And the noise! Tedious non-stop roar. People complain about road noise, but traffic on the M4 is nothing compared with that racket.'

He'd been exaggerating of course, but only a little. Would he really stay there just to spite her? Sure, it had electricity these days, probably even a telephone. But not much else in the way of convenience. No heating, which meant carrying logs and coaxing them to burn. No reassuring traffic noise, no morning walk to fetch *The Times*, just the wind and the sea and the gulls. And looking out into a dark night – the last straw. He would be dying to get out of there. Back to his stuffy serviced flat in Pimlico.

Gordon seemed programmed to reappear at significant points in her life. She'd known him since she was four, and they hadn't always been enemies. As a child in the tall, thin house, she'd witnessed her mother's affair with "Uncle" Gordon without knowing what she was seeing. Then he had reappeared at her mother's funeral – remarkable that he'd turned up to pay his respects after all that time.

Naomi's father pressed her arm as they turned away from the grave, checking their progress. 'Who's that fellow over there under the tree?' He jerked his head backwards. 'Fiftyish chap with a ginger moustache. Don't recognise him, keeps staring.'

Naomi looked in the direction indicated.

'It's Uncle Gordon,' she heard herself say.

The words popped out of one part of her brain, while in the next instant another part was thinking, *Oh my God! Not Uncle Gordon*. She took a step back for fear her father could hear the clang of pennies dropping, connecting the two parts of her brain, two parts of her life. She was hurtling back in time and down the stairs of the tall, thin house before she was ready to reach the bottom, stretching her arms up to reach that porcelain knob before she was ready to push the door open. A magical, sad, frightening time she'd rather stayed forgotten.

'Uncle Gordon, eh?' her father was saying. 'You don't have an Uncle Gordon.'

'No, of course not. I meant Fay's Uncle Gordon. And anyway, it isn't him at all. Just looks a bit like him.'

She was proud of her quick thinking. Dad knew she and Fay had always shared their relatives as if they were sisters. Fay hadn't had an Uncle Gordon either, not as far as she knew.

Her father nodded and rubbed the end of his nose. 'So you don't know who he is?'

She shook her head and they continued, arm in arm to the gate. And there, lying in wait, was Ginger-Moustache. He must have made an effort to overtake them.

He stepped forward at their approach and held out his hand. 'Gordon Fanshaw. I wanted to offer my condolences. Knew Imogen just after the war. Wonderful woman. She was very kind to me.'

Dad took his hand and shook it as briefly as it is possible to shake someone's hand and extricate one's own.

'And this must be young Naomi. Well, well. How time flies.'

She inclined her head, feeling her neck hot into her throat, aware of her father watching her, one eyebrow raised.

'Imogen was kind to a lot of people,' he said, taking her arm again and steering them round Uncle Gordon and out through the gate.

Back at the house, she settled her father in his armchair with an upright one on either side, so that people could come and talk to him and move on easily. She spotted Uncle Gordon on the far side of the room and avoided him. Eventually, he ambushed her in the kitchen. He'd carried out a tray of dirty glasses as if trying to be helpful.

'Your younger sister here?' he asked as he set the tray down. Too obviously off-hand.

'My younger sister?'

'Yes, foolish. Name slips my mind.'

'I haven't got a younger sister.'

He stared round at her. 'I must be going daft. Brother, I mean.'

'I don't have a brother either.'

'Are you sure?'

'Of course I'm sure!'

'And you never did?'

'You'd think I might remember! What *is* this?'

She was just about to carry on about siblings not casually slipping her mind, but he looked suddenly so winded, as if he'd been punched in the stomach.

'I'm sorry. I'm so sorry,' he managed at last. Gone was the brisk and helpful guest. He wandered out of the kitchen like an old man.

It gave you pause for thought, didn't it? As you grew up, of course it had dawned on you – but slowly, because you weren't a very canny child – that he was your mother's lover. Which meant seeing *her* in a new light. Reassessing. Seeing how the relationship with your mother was carefully stitched together with "our special secrets", "our mystery outings" and all the events that were "just for you and me" or "best not talked about". In all the years, you'd never given Gordon a second thought. Now it occurred to you, as you watched Gordon's retreat, that maybe he wasn't the only one taking advantage. Maybe he got hurt. Maybe he felt betrayed.

Gordon's questions, his deflation, they made you curious and, as you circulated among the guests, your eyes kept flicking in Gordon's direction. Always with a glass in hand, on the edge of groups, keeping at a distance from your father. Then he vanished and you registered disappointment, not relief. No chance to find out why he had come.

Dad was done in. 'Had enough,' he said. 'Think I'll turn in early.'
Naomi went upstairs with him, fetched a hot water bottle, hung about while he was in the bathroom. After her father was comfortably tucked up, she lingered on the landing, toppled by memories, staring into the garden. As she thought to go down and lock up, a figure emerged from the shrubbery, hands coming away from adjusting his fly. Gordon. She went down to meet him.
'Thought I'd keep out of the old man's way.'
She nodded, waiting for him to take his leave.
He hesitated, shifted from one foot to the other, cleared his throat. 'I could help with the clearing up.'
'No need. The caterers are seeing to it.'
There was an almost pleading look in his eyes. To be fair, Uncle Gordon had been different from the other uncles. He didn't just bring her a bag of sweets. He had bothered to learn the dolls' names and address them politely. He would push her on the swing in the garden and read a story. Now Dad had gone to bed, she could allow herself to remember him fondly.
'Coffee?' she offered.
'That would be… If it's no trouble.'
Always the dutiful daughter and the competent hostess, she went to put the kettle on.

Except it hadn't been quite like that, thought Naomi, watching a wren flitting in and out of the ivy behind the headstone of Prudence Wilkins. Ever since clapping eyes on Gordon in the cemetery that day, there had been that seething in her gut. She'd been struggling to hold it together in the face of the memory that threatened her composure. While the kettle boiled, she'd crouched on a stool in the larder and allowed the long-buried childhood memory to surface. And now, in this unfamiliar graveyard, that lurking, betrayed child was back, refusing to be faced down by the likes of Prudence Wilkins, who must surely have endured greater hardships.

I'm making my way downstairs in the dark. I can only stretch to one step at a time, clutching the banister, nightie flip-flapping against my legs. Halfway down the last flight, Mum laughs. She must be on the telephone. And if she's laughing, it must be to her best friend, Joanie. Then she laughs again and it's the wrong sort of laugh. The lino in the hall is cold underfoot. I clutch the lounge doorknob. It's shiny-smooth with bobbly bits where the roses are painted.

It's hard to push the door against the pile of the new carpet. A man came for a day with a hammer and Mum kept taking him cups of tea. Then it went quiet, the man had gone and the lounge sounded like Mum had put her hands over my ears. Mum was dancing about, excited, happy, arranging the furniture. The floor was fawn all over and it was like walking on a bed. No wind blowing out of the bare boards and up my knickers.

As I open the door, it smells of night-time house where only the grown-ups live. Until then, even though it was dark, it still felt like day-time house, which is just for Mum and me. The smell is of cigarette smoke and Uncle Gordon's moustache and the blue glass bottle with the silver top that lives on Mum's dressing table. It's the taffeta dress smell. I hope there isn't a party.

When I push the door far enough, I can see a dress on the arm of the settee. It isn't the taffeta dress. It's Mum's new blue woollen dress with the French seams that made her say a lot of rude words at the sewing machine because they were so difficult. The fire is blazing and the pink shades of the lamps make the room all rosy.

Mum sees me then. There's a jerky movement as if she's pushing something away, but I can't see because of the settee. 'Naomi!' she says, and when she gets up, she's only wearing her petticoat. 'Did you have a nightmare?'

I nod, although it isn't true. 'I couldn't get back to sleep.'

Then I see Uncle Gordon. He's sitting next to her on the settee with a glass in his hand and his tie all skew-whiff. He waves his glass and says, 'Cheers, Naomi,' as if he's pleased to see me, but I know he isn't.

'I was just going to fetch my sewing basket,' says Mum. 'A button came off my dress. Come on, I'll tuck you up.'

You knew something then, didn't you? You didn't understand what you knew. But pieces fell into place like a mosaic: Mum's laugh, Gordon and his tie, bits of petticoat and the night-time smell. They lodged in your tummy along with all those special secret times. You carried them within you.

That was the trouble with the past. It crept up and sucked you in, down corridor after corridor of memory. Then it spat you out and you found yourself raw with emotions that didn't fit with being a middle-aged woman sitting in a graveyard with the damp from a tree stump penetrating your trousers. To hell with the past. Time for a warming elevenses. With a nod to Prudence Wilkins, Naomi picked her way back between the luminous dandelions.

That evening, after her mother's funeral, they'd got to know each other as adults, she and Gordon. They'd even become friends. So what had gone wrong? For a start, he'd introduced her to his brother, Wilson. Right on cue, as she left the churchyard, Wilson's voice interrupted her thoughts, complete with his wise-guru face. *Why does Gordon keep reappearing in your life? What is the lesson that he keeps bringing you? Why are you so reluctant to learn it?*

'Go away, Wilson,' she said out loud, causing a white-haired gentleman to turn from his hedge-shearing with startled eyebrows.

Back at the hotel and still chilled from sitting in the churchyard, Naomi ordered a Scotch with her coffee and took it into the snug. Newspapers were laid out for guests, but the headlines weren't engaging enough to pull her attention away from the past. Wilson and his homilies aside, why *did* Gordon keep turning up in her life? After the funeral, for instance.

'There is no doubt,' Uncle Gordon had said, selecting a log from the basket beside the hearth. 'She had a facet missing, your mother.' A shower of sparks erupted as he lobbed the wedge of oak into the fire.

Naomi considered this remark as she poured the coffee. Several facets missing would be nearer the mark, while also possessing other facets not looked for in a mother. As to Gordon, she must stop thinking of him as the trusted uncle. She was discovering things about him that caused her memories to shift like pieces of coloured glass in a kaleidoscope.

'What d'you mean? What facet?'

'Hard to describe. What *do* I mean?' Gordon pulled at his moustache. 'Not commitment, nothing to do with being faithful. Nobody ever expected that of her.'

But Dad had expected it. Hadn't he? And who were those nobodies who didn't expect it? The other uncles, she assumed.

'I suppose what I mean is, she lacked a sense of continuity. I always felt, when I walked out the door, as if I ceased to exist. For her, I mean.'

'Oh, yes,' Naomi said. 'I recognise that. She'd put me to bed and go downstairs and enter her other life.'

Gordon nodded, focusing on the fire.

'It wasn't that she bundled me away. There was always a bedtime story – and bath night – and a song sometimes. But if I woke up in the night and came down – well, sometimes she was so surprised to see me, as if she'd forgotten I was in bed upstairs. Forgotten she *had* me, even.'

'Ye-es.' Gordon stared round at her, a thinking stare, and looked back into the fire. Then he nodded. 'I remember that.'

They sipped their coffee, hands wrapped carefully around the mugs as if to contain the memories. It was uncomfortable to be analysing her mother like this, but it seemed necessary to Gordon. Why was he here? What would he say next? She held herself together, elbows in, fearful of being ambushed by the past. The coffee wasn't hitting the spot. It left a bitter aftertaste.

'She used you when she got bored with me,' Gordon was saying. 'Towards the end. If you had a nightmare, she'd tuck you up and read to you and then just go to bed. Ignore the fact that I was still down in the lounge – or the drawing room, as she liked to call it.'

He raised a questioning eyebrow and Naomi nodded, remembering. Safe ground.

Gordon sighed and shook his head. 'I'd stand on the stairs and listen to her voice. Then it would stop, she'd waltz off into her room, and I'd give up and let myself out.'

Naomi tried to make a "poor Gordon" face but her brain was fogged, a headache was gathering. She'd had enough of this conversation.

'I tried to recreate the good times.' Gordon pulled out his wallet, extracted a dog-eared photograph. 'And they *were* good times. You can see. Here.'

Naomi felt obliged to take the black and white snap and her hand flew to her mouth as she looked into her mother's face. Imogen leaning on a farm gate wearing a short-sleeved frock. Polka dots. She remembered that dress. Black dots on a pink background. But it was the way her mother was laughing: wide-mouthed; eyes alight; head thrown back. So totally relaxed.

'She looks so *happy*.' It was the only word, but her voice couldn't quite articulate it, cracking under the pain that welled up inside her. When was her mother ever like that with her? With her and Dad?

'Day out in the New Forest,' Gordon was saying. 'Brockenhurst, I think.'

Could be Buckingham fucking Palace for all she cared. Naomi returned the photo, saying nothing, taken aback by the depth of sadness she felt, the force of her fury.

'I kept trying to fix things up. Outings. Treats. She'd pretend to be delighted and then cancel with some ludicrous excuse. It would have been funny if I hadn't been so – what's the word?'

'Pissed off?'

'No. Broken-hearted, if I'm honest.'

Gordon gave the photo a fond smile and tucked it away. He had the same winded look she'd seen earlier when he'd enquired about her non-existent sister or brother. That was the conversation they ought to be having.

'It accounts for a lot,' Gordon was saying. 'That lack of continuity.'

Naomi rallied herself. 'So, what about what you said earlier? When you asked about my sister?'

'Oh. That. Yes.' Gordon put aside his mug. 'I think we need something stronger.'

Naomi nodded towards the corner cupboard. 'You might find something in there.'

She added another log to the fire while he clinked in the cupboard. If only she didn't feel so sorry for him.

'This looks half decent.' Gordon held out a bottle of single malt, poured generously into two cut-glass tumblers.

'So, Immo got pregnant. I guess you worked that much out. I was never so thrilled. Yes, you may well look amazed. Uncle Gordon a father! I was amazed myself, amazed that I was pleased. Which Immo certainly wasn't.'

Naomi nodded. 'One was enough for her. One too many, in fact.'

'Don't say that. She loved you – in her way. But another? No. She was appalled at the thought. I told her how much I wanted her to have my baby. She softened a little at that and I begged for the life of that child. My hope for posterity. We talked and talked, and I talked her into it. At least, I thought I had. Your father was due home on leave, so you see, that would be all right.'

Naomi frowned. 'All right?'

'He'd believe it was his.'

'Oh. I see.' Naomi gulped her whisky, swallowing how not "all right" that seemed. More like appalling. Something to think about later. 'Of course,' she added and wondered why she was being so polite.

'I thought we had a plan. Huh!'

'But – if that was "all right", as you put it, how could you possibly be a father? Be involved in any way?'

'I was an idiot. I imagined he'd go back to sea, and we'd carry on seeing each other and there would be Immo and me and you and the baby, my baby. And we'd all be together. Happy ever after!'

'Mum wasn't a happy-ever-after person.'

'She was not. And anyway, your father got a shore job and I got posted abroad. I sent her money. I wrote. But when I came on leave, there were new people in the house. No forwarding address. Nothing until the notice in *The Times* last month. No idea where she was.' Gordon drained his glass. 'Did I have a daughter? A son? No fucking idea, excuse my French.'

'There was no baby brother or sister. And no, I don't know how that happened.'

Gordon shook his head. 'No continuity. You see, she didn't *want* to be found. I no longer existed. Curtains for Gordon.' He refilled his glass. 'Like I said, the missing facet. Cheers, Immo!'

They sat there talking until the fire went dead and he agreed to kip on the sofa with a blanket. When she'd come down the next day, there'd been no sign of him. Just a note of thanks with his London address and phone number on top of the neatly folded blanket.

Naomi shuddered in the so-called snug. There were no hotel staff around, so she went behind the bar to help herself to more coffee, contemplated another shot of Johnnie Walker and decided against it.

So, her mother had a lover. People coped with far worse. So, what with the other uncles, her mother was a bit of a tart. No big deal either and not why she felt betrayed. That phrase Gordon had used – "a facet missing". That was it. Her mother's elusiveness: the promise of intimacy, the skidding away, never properly being seen by the person who's supposed to love you best.

She'd warmed to Gordon during that talk. He really had loved her mother, it seemed, never quite got over her. And was clearly hurt by her silence, and the fact that there had been no surviving child. Naomi did wonder how hard he had tried to trace her. Surely her parents couldn't have been that difficult to find. But, of course, that was back then, the sixties. Dad had been posted frequently – a service life on the move. Married quarters, as well as eccentric rentals when Mum refused to live among "those other wives". And no World Wide Web to help in the search. So she'd had every sympathy for Gordon. Without that sympathy, even when she made her little discovery, she wouldn't have thought to let him know. She would never have arranged a meeting. And it was that meeting which resulted in Gordon introducing her to his brother, Wilson.

4 *Meghan*

Meghan was restless. She stepped back from her easel. The painting – of rooks taking flight from the bare branches of a tree – had progressed, but she needed time to reflect without losing the focus and energy of the work. And certainly before relaxing at Rita's with the usual banter and glass of wine too many. She would take a walk to the one place that would give her that kind of space. As she left the house, she grabbed her sketchbook, slipping Alex's postcard between its pages as an afterthought.

She strode through the woods and, on the far side, passed through a tiny wicket-gate opening onto a steep pasture. Climbing some fifty yards up the bare hillside, she sat down in a spot where once there had been a tree. In memory of that tree, she stretched out her legs, imagining the roots in the ground beneath her, and looked up, picturing new leaves fingering the sky.

She had first discovered the place some ten or fifteen years ago. On that occasion, a rowan tree had been growing a few yards from the wicket-gate and she had clambered up to sit on its roots. It was an ancient tree, bent over by the wind and heavy with glowing berries. She had stayed there for some time and thanked the tree for the sense of safety and peace she felt beneath its canopy.

A few weeks later, feeling in need of both insight and comfort, she had visited the spot again. There had been a turbulence in the trees that morning, the rooks rising and falling in a dance with the thrashing branches, but when she stepped through the wicket-gate, the air was suddenly still. And the rowan tree had vanished. There was no stump to mark where it had been. No disruption of the turf or piles of earth where it might have been uprooted. No sign of a tree ever having grown there. Meghan was baffled and disturbed. Had she imagined the tree? Had she slipped into some time warp? Eventually she had settled in the place where she judged the rowan to have been growing to reflect on what had happened.

Over the years she had come to accept the experience of the vanishing tree as a mystery. The fact that the tree was no longer physically there didn't seem to matter. It was still a special place, and Meghan now set aside her sketchbook and breathed in the musky smell of grass and the peppery scent of bluebells drifting across from the wood. She knew about rowan trees. Her grandmother used to have one by the back door and called it the gateway tree and the tree of protection. One day when she was small and staying with Nan, Meghan had asked about the lady sitting under the rowan tree. That was when she first became aware of having what her grandmother called "the sight". Except aware wasn't the right word as she was only five years old. It was Nan who had become aware.

'What lady?' her nan had replied.
'The lady in the brown dress. She's trying the berries for earrings.'
'She's the rowan tree fairy,' Nan said. 'The guardian of the gateway.'
Meghan didn't know about guardians, but fairies were familiar, and she was happy with them, so she looked out for the fairy and saw her a few times more.
Some years later, she asked Nan what Mrs Protheroe from down the street was doing under the tree.
'That'll be the fairy, the guardian.'
'No. It's someone quite different. Looks just like Mrs Protheroe. In her blue mac.'
Nan looked at her hard then and said nothing. But later, when they heard Mrs Protheroe had dropped dead while frying liver and onions for her husband's tea, Nan sighed and shook her head.
'Ah, cariad,' she said. 'You have the sight. I'd thought when you were younger it would fade. I hoped it would.'
Nan sat Meghan down at the kitchen table with cocoa and the biscuit tin. She told her not to be afraid of seeing things other people didn't see, but not to try to do it. She told her just to notice when it happened, respect it, but say nothing to other people.
'But I can tell you about it, can't I? Ask you what to do?'
'Of course you can, bach, but I might not be much help. Different for everybody, it is. And you don't need to do anything. Just ask yourself what it might be telling you. It's a gift – to see into another world. Like having

another set of net curtains.' She'd pushed the biscuit tin towards Meghan. 'That's how I look at it,' she'd said. 'Another set of nets. And ones I don't have to wash.'

Meghan smiled to herself at the memory and picked up her sketchbook. The net curtains had never been relevant to her but she understood what Nan had meant. She had discovered there was a fine balance between "not trying" to see into another dimension and neglecting the gift. The experience of the vanishing rowan had felt like a wake-up call to honour that gift and give it space, which was one reason for coming to this place. It was also where she felt closest to her grandmother.

She flipped through scribbles of crows and rooks and her most recent sketches of Rita's jackdaws, but they all looked flat and dead on the page. She picked Alex's postcard up off the grass where it had fallen. The Mediterranean colours looked garish in contrast with the soft greens of the Devon hillside.

She was getting nowhere with an answer to her question. In fact, she wasn't even sure of the question any more. Was it about the painting or was it about Alex?

When she'd come here all those years ago as a young artist seeking direction, the question had been clear. She had wanted advice about her painting. Should she keep churning out acceptable seascapes? Her pictures weren't cosy or chocolate box — she doubted even Mabel Lucie Attwell could make this coastline child-friendly. She had, however, found ways of using the light and the weather to domesticate it enough for people to want to hang the pictures on their walls. The local gallery took everything she produced and her work sold well. But she had a growing urge to portray the rocks and cliffs as they spoke to her in all their raw savagery. There was, no doubt, a very different market out there for such work, which would lift her income — but that was a long-term prospect. What drove her was the urge to break out, an urge that tended to get in the way of producing the domesticated art.

She'd received a clear answer to her question on that day. It had come in the form of a rush of images of the rugged shoreline, and she'd run most of the way home to commit them to sketches. It had been a key turning point in what she began to call her artistic career, and almost as important as the first turning point, which had happened at school. That had been a life-changer without which Meghan might never have become a painter.

But today her mind wouldn't settle. She was distracted by the insistent mooing of cattle at the far end of the pasture, by a money spider and various bugs and beetles that landed on her arms and scuttled or flew away again. A startling green shield bug arrived on her knee and made an equally startling departure. So much teeming life. Creatures doing their own thing. Why turn them into art? What was the point? Sometimes what she did with paint seemed futile.

And yet art had always been Meghan's thing – in junior school she had excelled. But art as she knew it – an escape into another world of intriguing lines and magic colour – didn't feature at big school. It had a slot in the timetable, certainly, but working from imagination was not allowed. Every week pupils were obliged to reproduce the work of a well-known artist. Halfway through the period, Meghan would have produced a creditable Degas or Monet, which, in the early days, earned enthusiastic praise. Her protest was to overpaint it into brown oblivion during the second half of the lesson. The teacher quickly learned to ignore Meghan completely. The comment on her end of term report simply read, "Wastes her ability."

Disappointingly, this had not worried her parents, Bronwen and Lewis Owen. They'd been more concerned about the "Could try harder" remarks scattered among the more useful subjects, particularly mathematics.

Bronwen and Lewis were quiet-living people who'd always seemed astonished – and even a touch guilty – to find themselves comfortably off and even more surprised to have a daughter who towered over them by the time she was eleven years old. Her father was a man who liked things to be tidy – from his clipped moustache to the dotting of *i*'s and crossing of *t*'s. He must have sometimes wondered about the daughter who wouldn't fit into any of his compartments. The closest they got to acknowledging her difference was to sit her on a chair in family photographs.

Meghan flipped over the postcard from Spain. How much had she, Meghan, acknowledged her own daughter's difference? And not just acknowledged it, but valued it? No, she hadn't done very well on that score. She and Alex needed to talk about that.

Meghan herself had always felt like a misfit, a giantess once she'd grown past both her parents. She'd drooped into secondary school, sagging at the knees and shoulders in her effort to fit in at the level of her peers. The domestic science teacher, Mrs Pennyfeather, had been the one to notice her, to see her potential.

'Meghan Owen, come up and see me please,' she'd said halfway through the second term.

Meghan had gathered up the canary-yellow blouse she was cobbling together and slouched up to the teacher's desk expecting to be chastised for her spidery buttonholes.

Mrs Pennyfeather spoke quietly. 'Do you suffer from frequent headaches?'

Meghan's head jerked up. How the hell did Pennyfeather know that? She nodded.

'I'm not surprised. If you're not careful, you'll have a life of unnecessary pain, visits to chiropractors and the like. You're tall. Get used to it. Just think, you'll always be able to use the top shelf!'

The teacher had paused and spread the blouse on her desk, cocking an eye at the buttonholes, then looking straight up at Meghan. 'I know you're trying to hide. But what's the point? It doesn't work and you just end up looking peculiar. Reach for the sky, girl. And take flight. *Take flight.* That's my advice.' Mrs Pennyfeather had glanced out of the window as if she wished she'd taken flight herself. 'And, by the way,' she'd said. 'These buttonholes won't do. You'll have to unpick and start again.'

Meghan hadn't thought of Pennyfeather in years. But she'd sown the seed. Because of her she *had* taken flight. After a difficult conversation with the art teacher, she had changed her ways and obtained her support to get into art college in Swansea. Even more difficult conversations with her parents followed. No, not conversations. Confrontations. Arguments. A big row. She regretted parting on bad terms with them, but college was more important.

Somewhere she still had that blouse. Her mother had made her wear it once – only once. A hideous garment, but she'd kept it as a talisman, a reminder to take flight.

Meghan stretched and lay back on the coarse grass of the hillside. A gust of wind brought the sound of the church clock striking the hour, but only intermittent notes reached her, so she wasn't sure whether it was five or six o'clock. She sat up and shivered, retrieving her sketchbook. The jackdaws still refused to offer any insight into her painting dilemma. What did it need? Where was it going? And what about Alex? Annoyingly, the only so-called wisdom that came to her was the image of that woman, Rita's stranger. She had a surprised and enquiring expression on her face. Not very helpful.

As her grandmother often used to say, asking direct questions rarely worked. The answers would come in their own good time. Best to put it all aside and enjoy an uncomplicated evening with Rita and Harry.

5 *Naomi*

Naomi left the hotel bar and went to her room. All the preoccupation with the past had made her forget the need to make some admin calls. Most urgently, she must talk to her solicitor about delaying the completion date on the bungalow. She was obviously going to have to go back and live there until she reached some agreement with Gordon. But in her room, she was confronted by the cleaner. Well, not confronted exactly but – she was hoovering into the bay window, greeted her with a flick of her ponytail. The look wasn't hostile, but it made Naomi apologetic. She abandoned her admin plans. 'Just popping back for my car keys,' she said. It was her room but it felt like the cleaner's domain, as if she had to explain herself.

The change of plan was a good one. A drive would do her good – a circuit through the lanes, windows open, breeze blowing through her hair. On the way back she'd stop off at the interesting art gallery she'd spotted in Stagworthy. But if she'd thought to outdrive the memories, she was mistaken, for inevitably Gordon went with her.

Her father had wasted no time after her mother died. It had been a shock to discover the house was already on the market before the funeral and his focus was on packing up and moving to a bungalow. 'Makes no sense without her,' he told Naomi. She had to agree. The house wasn't that big but the style of it was grandiose and shrieked Imogen's personality – from the red range in the kitchen (neither of her parents had ever been cooks) to the brocade curtains and four-poster bed in their bedroom. Ever practical, Dad had already had an offer accepted on a bungalow conveniently situated on the bus route into town. The morning after the funeral, he pointed at her mother's desk and asked her to clear out the "personal stuff" before she went home.

The discovery of the badge had given her a strange thrill. It was inside her mother's leather writing case. Naomi remembered that case. Mum had thought it rather grand. 'I'm quite the lady, attending to my correspondence,' she used to say in her posh voice as she opened it up. Naomi was surprised to realise it wasn't leather at all. Only Rexine, which had cracked and flaked with age. She was disappointed on her mother's behalf.

A miniature envelope was tucked into the compartment intended for stamps. Inside, two visiting cards and a strange piece of felt. She turned the fabric round and round, making out the design – a green salamander nestled in a generous outburst of red and yellow flames. Khaki background. But it was what she read on the back that made the hair on her arms rise up. "From Gordon to Immo with Love".

It was like being a voyeur of her mother's secret love life. Mum had kept it for over thirty years, if the dates on the accompanying two visiting cards were anything to go by. Proof, maybe, that Gordon really had meant something to her.

The more she studied the badge and its message, the more emotional she felt. Gordon really had cared. He and her mother obviously shared an intimacy – a web of real relationship, not just sex on Saturdays. They must have talked about the badge – and it probably carried a hidden meaning, a coded message beyond what she was looking at. Tears pricked her eyes at the waste of it all. She was sad for her mother, sad for Gordon, and sad for her father, too.

The visiting cards made no sense. Two appointments, a week apart, at a dentist in Harley Street. Strange. One, Mum was always hard up. Two, she never had trouble with her teeth. She even used to boast about it. Baffling.

She tucked the badge carefully back into the envelope with the cards, closed the case and took it home with her. Just the sort of thing Dad didn't want to stumble across.

She also took a packet of Sobranie coloured cocktail cigarettes and the long cigarette holder her mother had occasionally used. They reminded her of the tableau that stuck in her mind: Gordon and Mum on the sofa in the lamp-lit lounge. It had become a stylised image influenced by book covers for *The Great Gatsby* and television intros to series like *Jeeves and Wooster* and Agatha Christie's *Poirot*, evoking a bygone era. A man in a dinner jacket leans in, moustache jutting, elbow jaunty, raising a cocktail glass, gazing at a woman with a sleek bob. She gazes back, her dress swings and she kicks up her heels in the Charleston. They are young and gay, caught forever in a bubble of pleasure. The scene in the lounge of the tall, thin house was not as elegant and streamlined. Gordon's elbow was not so jaunty, and when Mum stood up, she was not wearing a flapper dress, but her petticoat. It was all in the gaze that passed between Mum and Gordon and gave the scene its meaning, billowing across the room on the curls of cigarette smoke to be inhaled by Naomi's uncomprehending nose. It took years for that meaning, stored in her gut, to travel to the level of consciousness and even longer for it to be translated into words.

Back in Stagworthy, Naomi parked the Land Rover in the middle of the village and walked back up the narrow street to Gracie's Gallery, the art gallery-cum-gift shop. Nobody behind the counter. She cast her eye over the seascapes – all much of a muchness and designed for tourists, she suspected – and picked out a couple of postcards. Then she'd spotted a very different painting on a side wall. Recognisably this coastline. The black rock formations like mammoth fossilised encyclopaedias stacked against each other. Threatening. Alive.

It made her gasp and at the same moment a woman materialised – as if she'd conjured her. Naomi jumped halfway out of her skin and they both laughed. When Naomi looked at her properly, she was startled to recognise the cleaner from the morning. But now a sophisticated woman – the same grey eyes, chiselled features, but with hair swept up into a bun, deep red lipstick, gold earrings, big hoops.

The woman nodded toward the picture. 'What do you think?'

'Frightening,' Naomi said. 'But in a good way. Compared to these others – well, it's like another world.'

'I just knock those out for the visitors. This one will have to come down – they don't like me hanging my proper paintings in the season. Scare people away. That's what they say.'

'You mean…? You painted this? All these?'

'It's what I do.' She held out a hand. 'Meghan Owen, artist. How do you do?'

They talked some more, Naomi paid for the cards and she hurried back to the car. The paintings were haunting but not as haunting as her memories, and she felt a sudden need to dwell on that second meeting with Gordon. She drove to the small car park on the headland, which was deserted and gave her the peace she needed to tease out these different versions of Gordon.

When she'd told Gordon she had something to show him, he had wanted to meet in the evening, take her out to dinner. But that was out of the question.

'My husband doesn't let me out, the funeral was an exception.' She'd tried to make it sound like a joke. A brittle laugh only added to the information she'd had no intention of revealing, but Gordon made no comment. They'd agreed to meet for lunch in a pub near her work.

It was a warm day in late April and Gordon was informally dressed – open-necked shirt, sleeves rolled up, tawny forearms. He waved expansively at the sight of her and gave her a peck on each cheek. A different kind of Gordon.

'I owe you a slap-up lunch,' he said. 'And I want to hear all about you – we did nothing but talk about me last time. I realised afterwards I had no idea of *your* life.'

He was disappointed when she insisted on a sandwich but made up for that by ordering a bottle of Chablis to go with it. An ice bucket at the table. Naomi was stupidly impressed. It was the sort of extravagant gesture her mother would have loved.

'So, what have you been doing all these years?'

'Since I saw you last, playing with my dolls in the house in Devon? Nothing very exciting. Boarding school, university, marriage.'

'Bet you got a first at Oxford!'

Naomi shook her head. 'Two-one at Bristol. Modern Languages, which led me nowhere – except, crucially, out of Devon, away from Mum. I worked abroad for years.' And so she had. It seemed a lifetime ago. But once she had been that confident, independent person boarding boats and trains with her backpack.

'Now, that's interesting. What did you do? Which countries?'

'France, Germany, Italy a couple of times. Nothing grand, anything legal that came my way. Au pair, but not for long, can't stand kids, terrifying creatures. Receptionist, clerk. Then I worked for a German tour operator for a while, escorting bemused Brits and pushy Americans on package holidays. That was the closest I came to a proper job.' She gave a dismissive laugh.

'Sometimes it was fun, sometimes it was awful. And then I just moved on. Kept thinking I'd wake up one morning and know what I wanted to do with my life. Hasn't happened yet.'

Gordon raised an eyebrow and looked across at her. 'And the husband?'

Naomi shrugged. 'Met him on the cross-channel ferry. Dover/Ostend. He gave me a lift to Berlin. And before you ask, no children. Fortunately he didn't want any either. Turns out it's the only thing we have in common.'

He looked at her, head on one side, questioning. 'How did that happen?'

'Feeling wanted? Needing security? Thinking I was in love. Seeing Fay married – my best friend, Fay, remember her? – and thinking I ought to be doing that too. How do these things ever happen?'

'Dear, oh dear, Naomi. That doesn't sound ideal.'

'It isn't. Living in smart Wimbledon, but with a man I loathe and working as an estate agent. Which could be fun, but it's bottom end of the market and only part-time, so I get the tag-end clients. Funnily enough, the only job Tony would contemplate letting me do.' She gulped the delicious Chablis. Why on earth was she telling Gordon all this? She tried a lighter tone. 'If only I'd taken the train to Berlin! Now, that was a good job. I might still be there with the lovely Dieter. But that's another story.'

Gordon raised an eyebrow as if he'd like to hear more but changed his mind. 'Why are you staying?'

'Staying?'

He paused as the waiter delivered their plates. 'With the loathsome husband.'

'Who said I was? I'm biding my time – have to be careful.'

'Because he knocks you about?' Gordon leaned across the table and gently lifted the curtain of hair she'd carefully combed to cover her fading black eye. 'I couldn't help noticing. When you came in. It did make me wonder.'

'He does. Not often. But…well, it seems to be getting worse.'

'We can't have this. What—?'

'It's none of your business, I mean, I appreciate… What I mean is, you don't need to worry about me.'

'I can *make* it my business. And, yes actually, I do have to worry about you. Why? Because you are Immo's daughter, I've always cared about you, and it seems to me you're in trouble.'

Such unexpected warmth. Naomi felt tears pricking at her eyes and looked down at the table. There was his arm still stretched towards her. Those freckled and furry forearms. Big hands he used to make into lion claws to roar and chase her. She'd dive into the narrow tunnel of the runner beans, breathless and safe in the shifting green shade. And Gordon would paw the ground outside until summoned back to where Mum reclined in her deck chair under the apple tree. Happy days.

Naomi took a deep breath. She wasn't used to feeling cared for. 'I made a bad choice. Mum always said so. She couldn't stand Tony and she didn't hold back – you can imagine.' She cradled her glass and took a sip. 'Up to me to sort it out. Dad never said anything directly against Tony, he was more practical. He set up a special account. And on my wedding day he made me promise one thing, not to let Tony know about that account. Said it all.'

'Sound advice. At least Immo managed to marry a decent man. Always thought highly of your father.'

'Didn't stop you getting off with his wife.' Naomi felt herself blush. That sounded so crude. 'Sorry, that was unfair.'

'Let's say it didn't stop me *falling in love* with his wife. Anyway, don't change the subject. How can I help?'

Naomi took a gulp of the cool Chablis. 'Put your ear to the ground? Find me a proper job, maybe? I've got somewhere to stay. Fay will have me in Richmond until I find my feet. It might be quite soon. I have to pick my moment. He's going off to a conference in a few weeks' time, and I plan not to be there when he gets back.'

'Any time. I'll do my best. Ring me when you need me.'

'It's very good of you. Reassuring. Thank you, Gordon.'

He raised his glass and she met it with hers. 'To the future,' he said.

'Anyway, that is not why we are here.' Naomi burrowed in her handbag, pulled out the little envelope and extracted the badge. 'This is what I found.'

Gordon's face paled as he took it and a glaze of sweat appeared on his forehead. 'Good God! She kept that!' He mopped his brow with his napkin, taking a surreptitious swipe at his eyes. 'Sorry. Making a fool of myself. Bit of a shock, seeing this after all these years.' He turned it over, shook his head and smiled down at the message on the back.

'What is it exactly?'

'My old badge. No. 1 Commando.' He touched it briefly to his left arm.

'You were a commando?' She was aware of heads turning at the next table and dropped her voice. 'What did you do?'

He shrugged. 'Cross-channel raids, landings. That sort of thing. Lost a few good mates. Brave men. And before you run away with any ideas of "hero Gordon", I wasn't. I was just there. It was a bit of a joke between me and Immo.'

'Doesn't sound very funny.'

'Well, no. Maybe joke's the wrong word. But you know what she was like.'

Naomi clenched her napkin as the picture of Imogen laughing in the New Forest hovered briefly over the bread basket. No, actually she didn't really know what her mother had been like.

A few moments passed before Gordon looked up and handed the badge back to her.

She gently pushed his hand away. 'No, you keep it. If you'd like to.'

He nodded. 'Where did you find it? Anything with it?'

'Only these.' She held out the cards. 'In her writing case. All together in this envelope marked G.'

Gordon looked from one to the other and frowned.

'I don't understand it,' Naomi said. 'She never had any problems with her teeth.'

Gordon grunted. 'Huh! Nothing to do with teeth.' He closed his eyes and turned away.

She could see his jaw clenching and unclenching and a few moments passed before he gained control and turned back to her.

'Now I understand. Harley Street. It was a front. As you know, abortion was illegal back then. But there's always a way. If you've got money. A few select doctors lined their pockets by providing a much-needed service. A different kind of clinic hidden behind the shiny brass plates of one or two highly respectable dentists and doctors.' Gordon drained his glass.

'Common knowledge at the time. And what with the prestigious address, blind eyes were turned. Tells me all I need to know.'

The buzz of the restaurant faded into a dark blur. As if she and Gordon floated in a bubble of the past, a pocket of her mother's life that had been completely unknown to her. Gordon stared into his empty glass, jaw tight, moustache drooping over down-turned mouth. She dragged her nails across the weave of the tablecloth to bring herself back to the present. What could she possibly say?

'I'm so sorry.'

'Nothing to do with you. I might have known. Immo did what suited Immo. I gave her money and she used it. Eminently practical. I should have known better than to have held out foolish hopes all these years. Hell! This calls for another drink. Bottle's got a hole in it. Don't know about you, but I need a stiff one.'

Naomi shook her head. 'Coffee, please. I have to work.'

She walked slowly back to her office. So Mum had done the right thing by Dad. But her mother didn't deal in dilemmas. So, more accurately, she had simply done the right thing for herself. Never mind Dad. Never mind Gordon. And then she'd filed away the badge and the cards – not thrown them away – but kept them. A record of a phase in her life. Gordon done and dusted. You had to respect the woman. Except respect wasn't quite the right word.

Naomi jolted back into the present as a jeep swept into the headland carpark and walkers got out, busy with changing into their boots. She stared out to sea. What an extraordinary meeting with Gordon that had been. Fleetingly she wondered what it would have been like to have a real sister, but she found it too hard to imagine and it felt like a betrayal of Fay. The memory of how warm her friendship with Gordon had once been lifted her spirits. She was also hungry, having somehow missed lunch. It was already early evening. Back at the hotel, she ordered fish and chips and munched some crisps with a large glass of Chardonnay while she waited for her food to arrive.

It took a while before she realised that the girl behind the bar was both the cleaner from the morning and the artist, Meghan Owen, she'd met in the gallery that afternoon.

She was a shape-shifter, this one. But what did she really mean by that? Just that, every time she saw her, it was like the first time. Each time it seemed somehow significant, as if they were meant to meet. And then would come the recognition: that same woman again.

What was going on? She was just the barmaid, for crying out loud. Or she was now. That lazy way of moving, the flicker of bedroom-eyes at the pair of locals up at the bar. All that dark glossy hair loose this evening, halfway down her back. Looked idle, but in fact she was washing, wiping down, polishing all the time, while managing not to look busy. Confusing.

And that morning. Such a direct look, which was unexpected from the cleaner. Could you be statuesque with a vacuum cleaner and a ponytail? Well, this one could. And she'd had such presence in the gallery. Now here she was, just a few hours later, being the most convincing barmaid Naomi had ever witnessed. Except now she knew different.

Meghan had more or less invited Naomi round to her studio. She would definitely go. Enough of the past and why Gordon kept turning up in her life. Why had Meghan Owen turned up? What did she have to offer? These were more interesting questions. It would be interesting to see her on her own territory.

6 *Meghan*

Meghan turned on the computer, which lurked in a dark corner of her living room, and went to put the kettle on while it chuntered to life. Time to follow up Geoffrey, in the gallery in Barnstaple, who had more or less promised her a one-woman show.

While the kettle boiled, she scrubbed at a burnt-on saucepan from last night's reheated Bolognese and watered the herbs on the windowsill. That reminded her to feed the ailing tree fern in the living room, which took her past the washing machine. By the time she'd untangled the wet clothes, hung them on the airer and made her tea, she'd forgotten about the computer. That was the trouble with admin mornings – one thing led to a trail of other neglected tasks. On a painting morning, she would simply make tea and go straight to the easel without looking to right or left.

The screen blinked at her from its corner and, reluctantly, she pulled up a stool. Alex's name leapt out from her inbox. An actual email from Alex, who'd insisted she get the computer in the first place. *So we can keep in touch, Mum.* But Alex rarely communicated and Meghan was disappointed to find that, even when she did, the message did not reveal her daughter's whereabouts. What had inspired her to get in touch at last?

Hi Mum, she read.

I wish I could phone you but it's far too expensive.

Meghan sipped her tea. Still abroad, then. Could be anywhere, but she assumed still Spain.

And anyway I'm too much of a coward to hear your voice when you get my news.

I'm pregnant, Mum. There, I've said it. I'm feeling shit, to be honest. Where's that euphoria you talked about? Puking up every morning, not fun.

So, apart from her conventional career, Alex hadn't apparently changed that much. Outside of work it seemed she was just as impulsive, just as volatile and unpredictable as ever. Idiot child! How could she be such a fool? Meghan walked away to the window. A fierce salvo of rain rattled against the glass. A fool just like her mother, of course, and a terrified fool, possibly. Meghan longed to hug her daughter and tell her everything would be all right. So much to talk about – and somewhere underneath it all the thought that she would be a grandmother. How did she feel about that? At least for Alex there would be none of the disapproval, the rejection that Meghan herself had endured. She would never forget her own return home under similar circumstances.

Mid-morning, mid-week. The station hadn't been busy. She'd stepped into the train at the first open door, found an empty compartment, flung her bag into the overhead rack and dropped into the forward-facing window seat. All in one panic-stricken burst of energy.

So, she was on the train. She stretched out her legs and leaned back as if she didn't have a care in the world. But, when she stood to slide back the window vent, her knees were like squashed balloons, her hands shaking.

Still time to get off again. But where would she go? Mandy, her landlady, wouldn't be pleased to see her back – not after she'd subsidised her train fare. She'd probably be halfway to re-letting her room by now. The slamming of doors and windows and the shriek of a whistle said it was too late anyway. Posters and benches slid past the window. Like it or not, she was on her way.

On her way back home. Funny how people still used that word for the place where they grew up. Even when it wasn't really any kind of home any more. The last time she visited – and that word *visited* said it all – was for her father's funeral. She'd hoped to make some connection with Mam without his controlling presence. Big disappointment. Mam had hardly seemed to see her. Looked at her – but it was more like she was looking through her. Not into her – that would have been something – but just through and out the other side. Meghan had kept glancing behind to see what the interest was. Nothing more than a blank wall, or a coat on a hook, or a jug of wilting daffodils, papery and giving off the rank smell of stale water. But all of them more worthy of attention than she was.

Head in her hands, she gazed down at the floor, gritty and grey with curls of fluff and sweet papers visible under the opposite seat.

She was roused by the ticket inspector sliding back the door of the compartment. He stood there, almost rudely appraising her frayed jeans, straggly hair and her men's work boots, which had never seen polish. He was clearly surprised when she produced a valid ticket, and further embarrassed by the smile she treated him to when he handed it back.

Having her ticket checked meant she was officially on this train. She would arrive. She would tower over her mother and feel awkward all over again. Being away from home had allowed her to accept her dimensions. And then, just when Logan – and various modelling jobs – had helped her to make friends with her body in what Logan called "*all its glorious dimensions*", it wasn't her body any more. It was inhabited by another being and felt stranger to her than it ever had.

She should probably have let her mother know she was coming.

'Just phone her,' Mandy had said.

But then there would have been questions. And besides, her mother hated the phone. She was at her most distant and disapproving with what she called "that thing" in her hand.

Blimey. Cardiff already. She grabbed the bag containing all her pathetic worldly possessions and made her way towards the bus station and the last leg of her journey, a tall figure striding through the knots of Lowry-like people who had spilled onto the platform.

Her mother greeted her with suspicion. She looked almost triumphant when Meghan told her why she was there. As if the fulfilment of her prophecies was the more important issue.

Meghan's dead father was invoked in every exchange; exchanges that never developed into conversations.

The *shame of it* was a recurrent theme. 'He wouldn't want to see you back here in this condition, shaming the family.'

She also referred to Meghan *abandoning us* when she left home.

'You were quick enough to leave when it suited you. Never mind that it broke your father's heart, seeing you dressed like a tramp and no interest in the position he found for you as clerk in the bank.'

'I did well at art school, Mam. You two never did seem to understand that.'

'Art school!' was all her mother had to say to that.

Her mother didn't ask about the father of the child. The closest she came was to say, 'If only you could get married.'

'You don't think anyone would have me, then?'

Her mother shrugged. 'Why would they?'

'Luckily, it's not something I'd ever want to do.'

'No. That would be far too boring and conventional for you, I suppose.'

'It's just that I value my freedom.'

'Freedom! Huh! See how much freedom you get with a babby, my girl!'

Now her own daughter was pregnant. Meghan suppressed a smile. Alex wouldn't take kindly to having her freedom curtailed. Questions surfaced – how far gone was Alex? Who was the father? She turned back to the computer.

Now you're going to want to know who the father is. It isn't quite straightforward.

So, either she didn't know or he was married or… Endless possibilities. History repeating itself from one generation to another. At least, between her and Alex, the absent father, Logan, had always been talked about, even though there'd been precious little to say.

But Meghan's mother, Bronwen, had guarded her secret until the end of her life when she revealed that the father Meghan had known was not her biological father. Remembering how shocked she had been, Meghan looked up at a pair of rooks dive-bombing a predatory buzzard. 'You think you know someone and then you discover, you really don't,' she said to the glass, watching it cloud with her breath and then gradually clear again.

Her real father was apparently Norwegian, an identity that explained her rangy physique. Meghan preferred not to think about it and had no desire to visit Norway. Similarly, Alex had shown little curiosity about her Irish blood. Would that change now? And what new nationality was Alex bringing into the family? All she said was:

I'd rather wait until I see you to explain about that.

Meghan's heart lifted at *"until I see you"*.

She couldn't wait to see her daughter and hear her story.

Like her mother, Meghan had known the father of her child, and like her mother she hadn't told him she was pregnant. She often wondered whether Logan had guessed her condition and if it had prompted his sudden departure.

Logan had been Meghan's Thursday admirer. From Swansea she'd moved to Bristol with a boyfriend who eventually dumped her. By then she was working part-time in a gallery and as a barmaid, cleaner and artist's model – a jigsaw of jobs to make ends meet. On Tuesdays and Thursdays she posed for a Life class.

The fastidious Tuesday instructor would bring a laundered sheet to spread behind the screens where she changed. He would lock the studio door behind the last student and use a condom to groan into '*The magnificent architecture of your body.*' At first, she wasn't sure she'd heard right, but it was his weekly mantra, which made her choke with laughter and loathing. She went along with the situation, believing the job might depend upon it. But the encounters came to an end after a few weeks when Meghan couldn't stop giggling during intercourse.

Meanwhile she had become involved with the bearded older man who came to the Thursday session, always arriving late and sitting at the back. It amused her that he was often visibly turned on and made no attempt to hide it. He would take her back to his one-room flat above a pub on Blackboy Hill for fish and chips and sex. At that time she was living on cornflakes and tinned milk with beans on toast for a treat, so she went mainly for the fish and chips and because his paintings of her made her look beautiful in a dark and mysterious way. 'The beauty is in the shadows,' he would say. It was years before she understood what he meant. When the room next to his became vacant, she moved in. Not living together, just next door. Cheap and convenient.

He'd told her she reminded him of the Giant's Causeway in Ireland, which was across the water from where he came from in Donegal. It was the most unusual chat-up line she'd come across.

'Load of Irish baloney,' Mandy said. 'He comes from the north, from Derry. Just doesn't like to talk about the troubles. You do know, by the way, he has a family over there?'

Meghan didn't know, but as Logan hadn't told her, she felt there was no cause to feel guilty. The existence of a wife and children didn't worry her any more than his reticence about them. She was no more looking for commitment than he was.

One time when she was sitting for the class, she was positioned on the floor, with her arms wrapped round her knees and leaning sideways against a cupboard, draped in heavy brocade that hung in deep folds. Logan's painting of this difficult pose was dramatic, but she looked more like the side of a cliff than a human being. When Meghan got to Stagworthy Quay and saw the black rocks piled up in the cove, she'd laughed out loud. They were so like that portrait of Logan's.

'This is obviously where I'm meant to be,' she'd said to herself. Pity she couldn't send him a postcard. It amused her that she longed to share the joke with him, although it had never occurred to her to share the news of their baby. It said everything about their relationship.

So Alex was pregnant and coming home. At least she could be confident of a warm welcome. History might be repeating itself, but so much had changed in the course of two generations. She and Alex would talk everything through.

Meghan turned back to the email – and here was the crux of the matter.

Because of all that I need to get away from here asap and anyway I want to have the baby at home. I had to leave my job for reasons I'll explain later, so am a bit skint. So please lovely Mum could you put some more money in my account for fares etc. You know I will pay you back!!!

Meghan smiled. Alex had never in her life paid anything back, and they both knew it. In the early years she'd needed constant subsidising, but those days were long gone. It gave Meghan a frisson of pleasure that Alex was once again asking her for money. She topped up her tea and nursed the hot mug to her chest, tears wetting her cheeks. Alex was on her way home! Just wait until I tell Rita that.

7 *Alex*

Alex nursed her unhappy tummy as she sat on the edge of the bed, breathing carefully, willing the nausea to subside. The reek of fish from the street below didn't help. Was it the shouts of the vendors or the usual one-sided row René was having with his wife in the next room that woke her? It wasn't just her condition making her sick. She was sick of the fish market, of René, of her stuffy cluttered room, of her body that had managed to do her out of her freedom. And now it was that treacherous body she was left with.

She'd left her apartment, a good job with an accountancy firm and her lover. It was definitely the apartment she missed the most. The job was neither here nor there and she was surprised – and relieved – to find that the same applied to Salvador, the father of this baby. She missed her work colleague more. It confirmed that her decision to disappear with her secret was the right one. Her current job in the café next door was hard work but she only worked afternoons and it was only a temporary measure. She must leave before her condition was obvious. She'd moved a few miles down the coast but there was still a risk of bumping into Salvador and that must be avoided at all costs.

She'd emailed Mum for money but none had arrived in her account. A bitter blow to her pride, that had been, admitting to being pregnant. It wouldn't be like Mum to be angry. Maybe she hadn't even seen the email.

As her stomach abruptly lurched, she grabbed a roll of toilet paper and shot out of the door and across the landing to vomit in the shared toilet, which stank of drains and the spray of René's night-time piss.

After her waitressing shift Alex liked to walk down to the sea of a summer evening. She'd wait until the last sand-blasted toddler had been hauled off the beach by its pink-skinned parents; until the sun sent elongated shadows of palm trees across the promenade; until it posted itself, sometimes quietly, sometimes with fiery drama, into the dark slit of the far horizon; until the fishermen started arriving on the twilit foreshore, setting up their stools, their hampers and their rods in a well-established ritual.

This was the cue for the cats to arrive, appearing as if from cracks in the pavement, slinking along the low wall above the strand, creeping down the slipway, crouching in neat rows along the steps leading up to the pier. They came in every colour but were turned charcoal by the dusk, each one skeletal, lithe, focused on the hunched shapes of the fishermen and their lines.

She'd like to come back as a cat, could do with nine lives. Until a few months ago she'd done well with her one life. But now it felt at risk, her careful plans sabotaged. She sank down onto the low wall and watched a ginger tom with a bullet head jump silently onto the sand and vanish into the darkness.

She was glad not to be missing Salvador, but it was disturbing to find Keith filling her thoughts after two years of successfully banning him from her mind. When she first left England, she imagined him everywhere. Keith masqueraded as every city gent on his way to work in Lyon, as every British tourist with his family in Berlin, Hamburg or Heidelberg. In Spain the apparitions started to fade and by the time she settled in Barcelona her heart no longer missed a beat at the sight of a medium height male with curly dark hair. Which was fortunate as there were plenty of them about, Salvador for one. He had never reminded her of Keith. He was far too Spanish in his looks, his style and his whole way of being.

She was suddenly hungry and left the promenade to find her favourite dishes in the tapas bar round the corner. As she crossed the road, a camper van passed, an ancient VW, very retro, with flowers painted on the side. She paused and watched until it disappeared from sight, the GB plates giving her a pang of homesickness. She was done with travelling. But she would miss the warm welcome that came with Carmen's patatas bravas and abondigas. Her passion for those spicy meatballs was turning into a craving, a healthy enough, protein-rich craving. She wasn't too sure about the potatoes, but it was too soon to worry about gaining weight. A worse disaster would be to return to England with her head full of Keith.

Their affair had started not long after she joined the bank where he was manager. She was a lowly clerk, but was quick and able, and he found reasons to use her increasingly as his personal secretary. She thought they had been so discreet, but there came the day when the chief clerk, Miss Martin, asked her to stay late.

The younger girls laughed at Miss Martin behind her back for the way she answered the phone after midday. 'G' *Daft*ernoon,' she would begin in her flat northern accent and giggles would be smothered in the outer office. She would also use the phrase, with heavy sarcasm and the lift of a carefully pencilled eyebrow, to greet any of the girls who were more than a few minutes late in the morning. Three greetings of this kind warranted an interview with Miss Martin and a warning.

Alex was never late, so she was puzzled at being summoned for an interview.

'You will hate me for what I am about to say,' Miss Martin had said. 'But as your manager, I may be old-fashioned, but I feel I have a duty of care.'

Alex waited, refusing to admit she knew what was coming. She respected Miss Martin, who was no gossip and seemed to genuinely care for the young girls who worked under her, regardless of the giggles.

'Three things.' Miss Martin lined up her stapler, hole-punch and staple extractor in front of her. 'One, don't imagine you are the first.' She moved the stapler to its normal position.

'I don't know what…'

'You know quite well what I am talking about. Two, don't imagine you will be the last.' The hole-punch joined the stapler. 'And three, don't waste your precious life.' Miss Martin dropped the staple extractor into a drawer and slammed it shut. 'That is all I have to say. The rest is up to you.'

Alex had been shaking as she left the building, shaking with fury, which she later admitted was a cover for the fear that Miss Martin was right. Of course she believed she was the first and certainly the last. She'd harboured hopes that Keith would leave his wife and make a life with her. But the evidence had been there when she'd cared to look: seeing him out with his wife, she'd been eaten up with shock and jealousy at the way they had wrapped around each other as they left the restaurant; spying on him in the park had shown her the look of delight on his face as he pushed his daughter on the swing. Several times he cancelled arrangements to attend events at the children's school. But the crunch came when they had finally managed to arrange a longed-for night away, and he cancelled because his wife had flu. When Alex protested, Keith had simply said, 'Remember, my family will always come first.'

A few weeks after Miss Martin's warning, Alex had left the country. When she handed in her resignation, Miss Martin had smiled upon her with something like pride, and Keith had been unable to disguise his relief. So much for true love.

Carmen interrupted her musing, leaning across the bar for their usual chat. She quickly wiped out any tendency to harbour a soft spot for Keith. Carmen, as ever, was eager to have a rant about her husband (whom she adored), and they ended up declaring good riddance to all men, knowing full well that neither of them really meant it.

Alex paid for her meal and kissed Carmen goodnight, grateful for the slice of tortilla that Carmen folded into a napkin and pressed into her hand. Breakfast taken care of. No more hankering after Keith. 'Water under the bridge,' she said to herself as she walked back to her room, eager for an early night.

Next morning Alex was excited to spot the flower-spangled camper van with its GB plates in the supermarket car park. The money still hadn't come through from Mum and she really needed to get out of this town, out of Spain. It was worth a punt and easy enough to strike up a conversation as the pair loaded their shopping into the van. They introduced themselves – Alfie and Esther. From Devon, funnily enough. A chat over hot chocolate in a nearby café followed. She discovered they were heading to France next morning.

When Alex asked if they'd give her a lift, Alfie shrugged and started to say 'Why not?' but Esther cut in before he could finish the sentence.

'What's that about? Fleeing the country?'

She'd said it in that half-joking way that you knew was serious underneath.

'I want to get home and my money hasn't come through for the train fare. It should be any day now.'

An exchange of glances. Then Esther. 'So why the rush?'

'Well, the thing is, I'm pregnant. I just want to get home.' She gave a winning smile, mostly directed at Alfie.

Her explanation sounded lame but hadn't seemed to warrant the look exchanged between them – Esther's eyes skidding sideways, Alfie's gentle, protective even. What was that all about? She'd escaped to the toilet to give Alfie a chance to dispel Esther's suspicions. But she hadn't expected to overhear their discussion.

'She's faking it.'

Three words floated in through the overhead grille as Alex sat on the toilet. That unmistakeable East London accent. It had to be Esther. They were the only English people in the café anyway.

Alfie's deep voice, replying, didn't carry so well. He must have said something like 'Why would she do that?' Esther came right back. 'To get the sympathy vote. Make us more likely to take her.'

That was, of course, precisely why she'd told them of her condition. Esther was a shrewd one. As sharp as Alfie was trusting. But she resented the flash judgement. It was only half an hour since they'd met, for fuck's sake. Disappointing. She'd really begun to like the girl.

Alex flushed and washed her hands. She needed to tell them about Salvador, lay it on thick about the threat of being corralled into his family. That might do the trick.

Back at the table, Esther was leaning into Alfie, blonde hair swinging, her hand on his arm, and Alfie was grinning at whatever she was saying. Alex had taken them for father and daughter at first, but noticing the body language between them saved her from putting her foot into that particular trap. She judged Esther to be a lot younger than herself, early twenties, maybe, while Alfie was at least twice her age.

Couples like them made Alex envious: subtle messages exchanged with a single glance; a sense of being permanently connected. There had been nothing subtle about Salvador. He could be gentle and sensitive, for sure. But she'd found that, with him, gentle and sensitive were always a means to an end.

Alex started, 'The thing is, it's about my boyfriend, ex, I should say…'

Esther interrupted. 'Don't worry. No need to tell us more. It's no big deal. We'll drop you off wherever we first stop in France. Montpelier, perhaps.'

She said it dismissively, as if to say, don't tell us any more of your stories. There was something almost feral about Esther. The green eyes like a cat? That was a bit strong. But as if the East End showed through her tan.

'Thanks a lot. I'm well over the morning sickness, by the way. Such a relief.'

'Glad about that!' Esther's expression made it clear she was glad for herself rather than for Alex. When Alfie said they were heading for Sète, she glared at him.

Alex jumped in. 'Oh, I've always wanted to go to Sète!' She gave Alfie her best smile. 'It sounds a magical place.'

'Uhuh,' Esther said. 'Anyway, we're off early in the morning.'

'Cool. No problem.'

'You need to be ready by six. We'll pick you up in the car park, yes? And we won't hang around.'

8 *Meghan*

Meghan was having a painting day when the person she'd come to refer to as "that woman" turned up on her doorstep. Meghan was in the studio out the back, so it took her a while to answer the door.

'I'm so glad I met you,' her visitor said, stepping inside.

Naomi, that was her name, and she seemed to think their conversation in the gallery had been an invitation.

'I'm interrupting you at work,' Naomi said, evidently taking in Meghan's paint-spattered dungarees. She sounded pleased rather than apologetic, which got up Meghan's nose right away. That, and the flicker of a blue-grey aura made her wary. It wasn't the kind of energy she wanted in her creative space. On the other hand, she might be seriously interested in the pictures – a buyer. Couldn't afford to send her packing. Next thing she knew, the woman was in her studio. This was something Meghan rarely allowed to happen. What was it about Naomi that was both intriguing and off-putting?

Meghan pulled out the latest versions of the coast – the raw versions that Naomi had appeared to like in the gallery.

While the woman was surveying them, she quickly covered the canvas on the easel – of the rooks flying from the tree. It was the first of a series that she was not ready to talk about.

'Where d'you get your inspiration?' Naomi was asking now. 'What's your process?'

She had a hungry look, as if she really needed to know. As if she wanted to use that information, copy the "process" maybe.

Meghan shrugged. She couldn't tell her. And wouldn't, even if she could.

'Do you just see? And take photographs? Sketch?'

'It's not like that. I just wake up with it. Or it creeps up in the shower.' Meghan tried to sound casual, dismissive.

'What, fully formed?' Naomi was pulling canvases away from the wall, peering at the ones behind.

This was getting annoying. 'Occasionally. But usually a thread. Something to pull on.'

'Hmm.'

The woman seemed to be losing interest now. Not getting the answer she wanted. Not getting anything she could use for herself.

How could Meghan tell her that every time she painted a big raucous untidy crow, she was really painting her mother? Her neat mother with her petite frame and precise Welsh features and tiny hands and feet. Only the eyes resembling the bird's – hard and bright as jet. And the glossy black plumage – her mother's furled into a tight bun, wings securely clipped.

'Coffee?' asked Meghan, thinking to take it through into the living room, get the woman out of her creative space.

'Sure,' Naomi said as if she expected it, as if it was her due. A turn of phrase Meghan often heard from American tourists who carried the same sense of entitlement.

Meghan busied herself with mugs. She could make do with the Nescafé she kept in the studio. Naomi didn't seem like a buyer after all. She wasn't biting and Meghan couldn't understand why she was here. She poured boiling water onto the coffee, nearly spilling it at an exclamation from behind her.

'Umbrellas! What the devil?'

Meghan spun round and strode across the space between them. 'Where did you…? Oh, you've got in there. No. Sorry. That's my private store.' She took the canvas and tucked it back behind the curtain that Naomi had pulled aside. Blimey, this woman had a nerve.

She wasn't about to reveal how it had all started with the umbrellas. Portraits of Mother again – except she'd had no inkling of that at the time. Mother as a furled, neat umbrella; as a slightly open umbrella propelling itself like a sinister jellyfish; a twirling parasol; a comet shape; a series of unpleasant mannequins, like the dolls wearing Welsh national costume sold to tourists in every gift shop in Brecon. They'd all come from dreams. Paint your dreams, some teacher had said in an effort to get his students into a sense of Surrealism. Meghan hid the pictures in embarrassment and guilt, but she had never brought herself to destroy them.

'But it's so interesting,' Naomi was saying.

Meghan was regretting the offer of coffee, but she grabbed the tray and ushered her visitor out of the studio, kicking the door shut behind her.

There was one umbrella incident that was not a dream, but a vivid memory from when she was about ten years old. A blustery wet day and they'd just got off the bus – she, Mam and Dad – and were making their way to the George Hotel to meet Uncle Dai and Auntie Blodwen, who were celebrating their golden wedding. Dad striding ahead, Meghan annoying Mam by trying to step on every other paving stone, Mam fiddling with her umbrella, upset about the weather because she'd had her hair done specially. Whatever Mam did with that brolly meant that it closed on her and she couldn't find the catch. She shouted out for Dad, who turned round and started to guffaw at the sight of his wife in a witch's hat of an umbrella, clinging on to a lamppost. Meghan was already giggling, and by the time Dad had come to the rescue, she was bent double with laughter. But she remembered that guffaw and how unpleasant it had sounded, not just amused but mocking. She'd been embarrassed when Dad had told the story over lunch in spite of Mam being upset.

Naomi took her coffee black, which was fortunate as Meghan had no milk. Or rather, it was disappointing. In her present mood, Meghan would have enjoyed seeing the woman going without and puckering her lips.

'I hope I haven't been intrusive,' Naomi said when they were settled.

Meghan shrugged, wrong-footed once again.

'Obviously, I have. I get carried away.' Naomi brushed a stray lock of hair back behind her ear. 'But, I have to say, you're very defensive. I mean, for such a talented artist.'

'Defensive? What's that supposed to mean? Private is the word I would use. I don't usually let people into my studio.' Meghan cringed at how defensive and hostile she sounded.

Naomi just smiled in response. Insufferable woman, sitting there sipping her drink and looking superior.

'What brings you here, to this part of the world?' asked Meghan, uncomfortably aware that her tone implied "And when are you leaving?", and trying, unsuccessfully, to smile.

'It's possible I may be moving here. In fact, that is what I was expecting, but it turns out not to be that straightforward.'

Meghan's heart sank. Worst possible scenario. 'Sale fallen through? Happens all the time. So I guess you're house-hunting?'

Naomi shook her head. 'No. I'm not looking.' She gazed away, out of the window. 'Now it's my turn to be defensive. But it's too difficult to explain.'

'And none of my business.'

Naomi made a face and shook her head, possibly in agreement, but Meghan sensed she would like to make it her business and wished she'd never asked the question. If only the damn woman would leave.

Naomi placed her mug back on the tray. 'I really must be going. Mustn't take any more of your time.' She stood up and waited for Meghan to open the front door. 'Thank you. It was interesting.' She started down the path, then turned, and Meghan resisted the urge to slam the door for fear she was coming back in. 'You see, I only came because I had the very strong feeling we'd met before. But now I don't think so. You have no recollection, do you?'

Meghan shook her head, then remembered what she'd said to Rita a few days ago – that sense of familiarity when she first saw the woman. She shook her head again.

'No. I thought not. Never mind.' At the gate she turned, laughing. 'Must have been in another life.' And was gone.

Meghan stood staring at the space Naomi had left behind as if it might reveal some meaning. But she only saw Rita's neatly clipped privet hedge. 'Woman's an enigma,' she announced to the jackdaw landing on Rita's chimney pot.

She wandered back to the studio, hoping to pick up her painting where she'd left off, but was annoyed to find she'd lost the impetus.

Pulling back the curtain that screened the storage space, she looked long and hard at the canvas of umbrellas that Naomi had unearthed. She'd forgotten it existed, and yet it seemed bizarrely familiar, a foreshadowing almost of her present work. She shrugged and took the mugs to the kitchen to wash up.

9 *Naomi*

Naomi walked swiftly away from Meghan's gate. Blimey, what a prickly woman, this Welsh Meghan. Where was the calm and poised presence she'd met in the gallery? She was all awkward angles, elbows, knees. And the way she kicked that door shut when she brought the coffee in! You'd think she'd be glad of some interest in her damn paintings. She had talent, no doubt.

Naomi wasn't too clear why she sought Meghan out. A fascination with her shape-shifting ways? A potential friend in a place where she knew nobody? For she was always looking to replace Fay. She'd used the paintings as an excuse, of course. Wanting to get closer to the woman. Maybe Meghan sensed that. She did like the dark coastal scenes, that much was true. She might even have bought one. But she didn't want Meghan to think she was a pushover. Maybe she'd gone to the other extreme and come across as rude.

But she'd been ambushed by that thing on the easel, unfinished. A work in progress. Meghan had hastened to cover it but the image stayed with her. Surprising technique – and totally different from the loose style of the coastal scenes. Painstaking skeleton tree, every twig inked in precisely. And the birds. Clearly well observed in every stage of perching, take-off and flight. Sunlight on plumage, dangerous beaks, disconcerting eyes.

They haunted her, those witchy Welsh birds, bearing down on her like demons. She increased her pace, brushing strands of hair from her face as if they were soft feathers.

It was a blustery morning. She would blow the discomfort of the visit away up on the headland. This Meghan clearly wasn't a Fay substitute. She had to face it. Nobody would replace Fay.

Fay had been the very best thing about her childhood. But Fay's marriage had put a strain on the friendship. Fay had always wanted a husband and family, and her wish came true with Daniel, Tom and Kate. All went well at first. Naomi played auntie to the children and didn't notice when the demands of family outweighed Fay's need of Naomi. It always came as a shock when this imbalance was brought to her attention, occasions that lodged like grit in a shoe. Negative thoughts and memories weaselled into her brain.

Forget – forgive – for granted. Fay words fumbling, tumbling through her head, snaking between her ears, refusing to go away.

Fay forget. Not possible. She was part of her, like having an extra leg. Always there, except she's not. She ought to have got used to it by now – *adjusted*. But she still lost balance.

Fay forgive. She still can't. Made her feel guilty. Blaming the dead for dying. Hit and run. Hardly Fay's fault. Or was it? Was she careless? Stepping out from behind a parked van? Distracted by some dog or child or passing bird? No witnesses. No one would ever know. But Naomi couldn't forgive her for the outside chance that she wasn't paying attention, wasn't intent on staying alive for her. Fay had taken part of her, too. How dare she? The anger kept simmering.

And there's that other guilt. Why did it have to be Fay? Fay who was desperately missed as a wife and mother. Whereas, if it had been herself who was killed, who would have missed her? She couldn't think of a single soul. It really wasn't fair.

Fay for granted. That's the one she most avoided. Because it wasn't about Fay dead. It was about Fay for all of both their lives. "For granted" had its good bits: familiarity; comfort; always reliably available. But it made assumptions. That was fine when they were little girls, plugged into each other from the age of three or four. But it was dangerous to make assumptions as an adult. And Naomi certainly did. She'd assumed she'd always be first in the queue for Fay's attention, that she'd drop everything for her. Fay's other life – her devotion to her family, her close friendships with other people – took Naomi by surprise. Be honest. She resented them. When Fay wouldn't go Christmas shopping with her because of a nativity play; when she cut short a "put-Naomi-back-together" session and left her in tears just to be on the touchline at some football match of Tom's. She'd been hurt. Then there was the time when Fay dyed her hair without even telling her. It was like getting to know a whole new person. Fay no longer blonde to her mouse.

Those were all small incidents. But it was when she'd left Wilson that a marked distance had opened up between them. Not a big distance, but nothing had ever been quite the same after that.

Naomi watched a yacht, heavily reefed down, making its way across the bay, dipping into the white-crested waves. She could still feel the bleak disappointment of that first morning.

She'd phoned from the station and arrived with her rucksack, feeling both triumphant and terrified. After an evening with the family– Fay, Daniel, Tom, now a good-looking twenty-year-old, and Kate just seventeen – she went to bed early. Next morning, desperate to tell her leaving-Wilson story and soak up Fay's sympathy and support, Naomi made for the kitchen expecting Fay to join her for a chat. No Fay.

She took her tea back upstairs. Hearing strange noises from the attic, she continued up the next flight. Music or not music? Whales perhaps. The door was half open. A foot extended into view, another, an orange leg warmer. Fay's freckled arms reached for her toes until she had folded herself in half, her fuzzy ponytail the only thing to stick up in the air. Fancy Fay being able to do that.

'Come on in – there's a chair,' the ponytail said, bouncing up and disappearing.

Naomi stepped into the space. Gone was the table football she used to play with the kids. Instead a few rugs and cushions, a poster of a tree, a tape player and an incense burner. All very minimalist.

'Wonderful way to start the day.' Fay was cross-legged now, grinning up at her.

Naomi made a face and Fay snorted. 'For me, I mean. Changes how I approach absolutely everything.'

'Including me!' It slipped out and Naomi thought for an awful moment she was going to cry, so neglected and inadequate did she feel in face of this supple and enlightened Fay.

'Oh, Naomi! Not you. I'm sorry. It's just that it's my routine now – coming up here as soon as I wake up. I thought you'd sleep in and...'

Now she was making excuses. Naomi took a breath. 'I made tea.'

'Just hot water for me.'

'Oh,' Naomi said.

Fay got dressed after that and they chatted in the kitchen as they always had. Fay seemed as warm and supportive as ever.

'I'm just so glad you got out of the clutches of that creepy man!' This was the nearest Fay got to saying "I told you so".

'But you only met him once.'

'Oh, it wasn't so much meeting him as seeing the effect he had on you. The look in your eye when you came back from the so-called interview. Everything you said was, "Wilson this and Wilson that." It was almost as if he had put a spell on you. I can't believe it all lasted so long.'

Fay hadn't even asked how she'd broken away, but Naomi had told her anyway. From up here on the headland, she could see where it had happened, that breaking away – the roof of her cottage, the picket fence round the so-called garden and the path winding out of sight towards the waterfall. The river wasn't visible but she could picture it vividly. The place where she had at last found her courage, the courage to walk away from Wilson – 1985, it had been.

Naomi knew she couldn't do it. She could hardly breathe for the noise of the water. The plank was no more than a foot wide. There was no rail or rope. Gone was the gentle cascade where she'd watched salmon leaping the previous September. After a wet spring, the river was in full spate, fuller than she'd ever seen it, sliding over the lip of the fall only inches from the plank.

Wilson was on the far bank with the two young acolytes who were here for their taster weekend, camping in the meadow. Gordon was somewhere in the vicinity on her side of the river. Normally he didn't stay when a course was in progress, but he'd missed a train evidently. Said he'd stay well clear of the sessions, but there he was, curiosity getting the better of him, she supposed.

Wilson had shown her how firmly the board was set. She knew that. It had been embedded in the turf for decades, a century even, for all she knew. Because of the sheer drop, it had never occurred to her to use it as a short cut.

'Come on, Naomi! It's only a couple of strides. You can…' His voice was drowned out by the roar of water hurtling over the edge to thunder down into the boiling cauldron of boulders at the foot of the fall.

'I'm here to catch you, Naomi.'

She heard Gordon grunt and move away upstream; looked down at her feet, appraising the turbulent water and the narrow, weathered plank; lined up her feet to the plank, her knees shaking.

She'd met nearly every challenge Wilson had faced her with – becoming stronger every time, as he always claimed. Now, as she looked up towards him, a shaft of sunlight fell across Wilson. She saw not only the encouraging half-smile but the glee in his eyes. He knew she would do it. But would he be proud of her? She'd always thought so. Now, he turned to the two young women sitting cross-legged behind him, made some comment, and they gazed up at him with rapt attention.

In that moment it became clear. He would be proud of himself, rather than her. He would be demonstrating his prowess to those students. For the first time, she didn't want to succeed. She didn't want to be another exhibit in his virtual trophy cabinet.

Seconds stretched into minutes as they faced each other. Should she turn away and be branded a coward, a failure, but know that she had won? Or would she cross into his embrace, and keep on repeating that pattern, forever in his power? Or was she making all that up? Giving herself an excuse?

Another consideration entered her mind. There had been one occasion when she had refused the challenge. Had he consoled her? Had he sketched a different approach to the problem as he always did with others? No. He had sulked. He hadn't spoken to her for the rest of the day. He had been punishing, shutting the door of their room in her face, taking one of the "successful" women to bed with him. It wouldn't do to humiliate Wilson, especially in front of the students.

This wasn't an either/or decision. She could see a way forward. It was a way of testing her theory.

Stretching her arms out like wings, she stepped onto the plank. Focusing on a gorse bush on the hillside beyond Wilson's head, she was distracted for a moment by a burst of shrill cries. A buzzard was circling high overhead and two rooks from the nearby colony had launched to see off the predator, tiny black arrows hurtling towards the canopy of unhurried wings.

Wilson was standing with his fists clenched, willing her towards him. She returned her gaze to the gorse bush and walked steadily across the plank.

Did he embrace her as expected? He did, but not before he had raised his fists and galloped about in a victory dance. The two young women clapped, but without looking in her direction. She turned on her heel and, to her own surprise, ran back across the bridge and kept running, a plan forming in her mind.

As she left the river bank and the uproar of water receded, Gordon strolled into view, and she heard Wilson call out to him, 'I won! I did it. Told you!'

'I rather thought Naomi did it,' came Gordon's laconic reply.

So it was all about a bet. Driven by fury, she ran on, glad to witness the triumph of the rooks as the buzzard was driven higher and higher, eventually swooping away over the cliffs into the next valley.

At the cottage, she filled the kettle and set it to boil before racing upstairs. A couple of shirts, warm jumper, spare trousers and a handful of knickers. Back downstairs, she stuffed them into the bottom of her rucksack, which hung by the door. Into the bathroom to catch her breath and flush the toilet.

Wilson had arrived as she emerged. 'What got into you?' he'd asked and then laughed, unkindly she thought. 'Gave you the shits, did it?'

'Something like that. Tea, everyone?'

Here she was, decades later, looking down on the scene of her triumph, ironically because of Wilson himself. All she could think was, why hadn't she done it sooner? It had all been so easy. Sliding out of bed in the dawn, dressing silently in the kitchen, grabbing rucksack, handbag, boots, and climbing out of the window. After jogging along the track through the woods, she'd been lucky enough to encounter the estate manager on his way into town. So she was heading for the station and the London train long before Wilson would have noticed she was gone. She often went walking on the hills in the early morning and that's where he would have assumed she was. He'd have been hungover, staggering belatedly downstairs, desperate for coffee, irritated to find no kettle boiling, no milk, no sizzling bacon.

It might feel easy now, now it was all over. But her legs had been shaking as she climbed the hill, her heart racing until she gained the shelter of the trees, and the track bent away, out of sight of the cottage. Mike would never know how grateful she'd been to sink into the muddy front seat of his pick-up.

'Where are you off to, so bright and early?'

'Exeter. Sometimes a girl just has to shop.' She sounded unconvincing and could see from his raised eyebrow that he was not convinced. How much did he know about what went on at the cottage? Did the locals speculate? Who knew? Enough that he was giving her a lift. She would stay with Fay and work out what to do next.

Had it been melodramatic to escape in that way? Could she not simply have announced she was leaving? No. That would have been the melodramatic route. Nobody did melodrama better than Wilson.

Walking down Barnstaple High Street, she'd felt light-hearted, light-headed, like dancing. Meeting Evie on the train had been extraordinary. She'd been looking for a seat on her own when these arrestingly blue eyes had smiled up at her in welcome and she had automatically sat down opposite the woman. Her long white hair was tied loosely back and a warm tan exaggerated the blueness of her eyes. She wore a faded denim pinafore over a hand-knitted polo neck. Business-like boots. A tapestry bag slouched on the seat beside her.

An eruption of schoolgirls shattered the peace of the carriage. The woman smiled up at them and pulled her bag towards her to make more room. The lead girls looked from her to Naomi, nudged each other and moved on down the aisle.

'Shy creatures.' The woman spoke in Naomi's direction.

It wasn't the word Naomi would have used, but on reflection she was probably right.

'I'm Evie,' the woman said as the train pulled out of the station. As if they were embarking on a journey together.

She continued to throw out odd facts about herself and Naomi made inadequate responses. Evie was a jeweller, but not as in silver- or goldsmith. She made things from stained glass, but small things – no cathedral windows. She lived in a yurt on a farm belonging to her brother. Naomi had never heard of a yurt, so at least she had a question to ask. The response startled her. Would Naomi like to come and see? Naomi was intrigued – by Evie more than by the yurt – but just now she needed familiar Fay, not a new adventure. She'd declined and Evie had written her address on a page of her notebook in case she was ever in the area.

Ah, Evie. That was a whole story of its own. Naomi pulled her hair loose and let it stream in the wind off the Atlantic. Leaving Wilson had probably been the healthiest thing she'd done in her life, although leaving Tony had been vital, too. Why was it always about escaping *from* people and situations? Why hadn't she chosen opportunities to run *towards*? Well, of course, Mill End was supposed to be just such an opportunity – but look what had happened there. Fay had been the only person she ran towards. She flung herself onto the damp turf and focused on the clouds moving across a blue-grey sky.

The past hadn't finished with Naomi yet. That night sleep came quickly but briefly. At two o'clock in the morning it became elusive. A car engine started, roared up the hill and faded into the distance. Even opening the window to listen to the ocean didn't pull her out of the loop of images and memories that came flooding in. A gust of wind and raindrops made her shiver. She closed the window, trying to ignore how it rattled in its frame, and got back into bed.

On that day, nearly two years ago now, she'd been on her way out when the sound of the phone had stopped her at the door. It was Fay's birthday and they were meeting up in Salisbury, a good halfway point between Devon and Richmond where they'd often met. The arrangements were rarely cancelled and then only by Fay. To Naomi they were sacrosanct. Her aim today was to close the door behind her before Dad woke and made any demands. It was all planned: cappuccinos in their favourite coffee bar; a spot of shopping; pizza and prosecco at the really good Italian; a visit to the exhibition in the cathedral – 'Angels,' Fay had said, with a nod to Naomi's agnosticism. 'You can manage angels.'

But now the phone. A harsh jangle. She was tempted to ignore it, to run the few paces to her car and drive off on her perfect trip. But it would wake Dad. He'd panic at such an early call and have a bad start to his day. Come to think of it, 7am was early for someone to call. It couldn't be work, they knew she had the day off. Surely not Fay with a last-minute crisis? But Fay would have used her mobile. But then again neither of them had the mobile habit, not like Fay's kids, who used them all the time.

These thoughts filled the few seconds it took to turn back into the sitting room and pick up the handset.

'Hello?' a voice said.

'Yes. Oh. Daniel.'

So it must be Fay. Fay too chicken to call herself? Or too ill? Throwing up perhaps. The plug pulled on their special day by a tummy bug. No seeing Fay's face as she unwrapped her presents. No grasping the hand of the *Walking Madonna* on the way through the Close. No banter with Italian waiters. It would all have to be rearranged, the week after next, maybe.

Daniel was speaking again.

'Say that again. Slowly.'

Daniel's words didn't make sense.

'But I'm just on my way to meet her.'

Why was he telling her about a white van?

'This doesn't make any sense. I told you…'

Daniel was louder now. There was one word he kept throwing like a stone, bombarding her with it. Her ears bounced it back. *Fay is stone. Fay is stone.*

'Stop it, will you! Stop it! Stop it!'

She flung the handset away. Watched it ricochet across the sofa, rebound off the bookcase and spin its way to rest against the hearth.

Still shouting, she sank to the floor against the side of the sofa, rocking into the rhythm of *Stop it, stop it, I tell you!* The yelling subsided into a moan and she became aware of her father standing in the doorway, tying his dressing-gown cord.

He crossed the room, retrieved the handset and restored it to its cradle. Disappeared. Returned with a glass, which he set on the coffee table. He told her to get up and settled her with a cushion on the sofa. Handed her the glass.

'But I'm driving.'

'You're not going anywhere.'

The back of Dad's hand holding out the glass was a landscape of raised veins, liver marks and a tracery of fine wrinkles like crumpled tissue paper. A strong hand. A practical hand. It told her that her day was broken, and that behind her broken day something much worse was lurking, a time when disappointment would seem like a luxury. She took the glass and sipped the brandy.

Later, Dad handed her the phone. 'You must ring Daniel back.'

She shook her head. 'I never want to speak to him again.'

'You must hear the news properly. Now you're ready to hear it.'

She would never be ready to hear it.

'Think how he is feeling.' Dad pushed the phone into her hand. 'Anyway, you were damned rude. Need to apologise.'

Still she shook her head.

'You owe it to Fay,' he said.

So she learned that Fay had been killed by a hit-and-run driver. A white van, allegedly. She spoke to Kate, who called her Auntie Nay like when she was little. When she asked to speak to Daniel, she was told he was sleeping, he'd been sedated. Yes, Kate would pass on the apology but she was sure he understood. When Naomi offered to come, to be with them, there was a silence. Then Kate said they needed to be alone. 'Just us,' she said, and added, 'We'll let you know when the funeral is.' Naomi swallowed hard. Once she'd have been part of the "us". Now there was no Fay, there was no "us". Not for Naomi.

She must have stayed on the sofa all day. When she woke in her bed next morning, she half-remembered Dad pulling off her trousers and tucking her up as if she were a child again.

Beyond going to the loo, she had no idea what she was supposed to do next.

In the hall, her bag was still slumped where she'd dropped it. Beside it sat Fay's birthday goody bag. Three books wrapped in paper printed with red and yellow balloons – an Italian cookbook, the latest Kate Atkinson, and a copy of *The Great Gatsby*, which Fay had never read. She'd been looking forward to discussing those when they next met. She'd added a honeycomb from the beekeeper's down the road, and several bars of chilli chocolate from the local chilli farm.

She turned back in to her room.

Later, when her father came and led her into the kitchen, the bag was no longer there and her handbag was hanging on a coat-hook by the door.

In the kitchen, Dad sat her at the table and busied himself with a tin opener. When he handed her a mug of soup, Heinz tomato, she pushed it away. He pushed it back.

'Why?'

'Because you must have something to...'

'But why would you...?'

'Need to keep body and soul together.'

'But why are you bothering?'

He turned to the sink, running noisy water into the soup saucepan. 'Why am I bothering. You're my daughter, dammit. Because I...'

'You don't have to.'

'Of course I do. Good grief, child! I can't change anything, but I can look after you. What else can I do? It's my ham-fisted way of saying I love you, dammit.'

Naomi reached out for the mug of soup.

He stomped off into the sitting room. 'Music! We need music.'

A few moments later, the robust chords of Beethoven's fifth concerto filled the bungalow – the Emperor – Dad's go-to tonic for a grey day. Naomi started to laugh. The music was so obscenely wrong and so completely right. Dad stood staring at her. She couldn't stop laughing. He shrugged and smiled, gave her a clumsy sideways hug and took her empty mug to wash it up.

The very next day she had gone back to work. She'd done sensible things, maintained ordinary conversations, even laughed at jokes, in between going home and howling in her room because there was no Fay to phone and share it all with.

She made herself face the reality of Fay's death. Hit and run. Surely you must know if you hit someone hard enough to kill them. You would hear a thud. You might see something, a sliver of colour, a shadow, in your peripheral vision, on the edge of the wing mirror, something that came back to haunt you, that you couldn't quite dismiss. And if you didn't hear anything, wouldn't there be a vibration, a judder?

She supposed the size of the vehicle would make a difference. So the impact of a body would be more obvious in a small van or car. A big rig could be forgiven for not noticing. And a truck with a lot of builder's tools in the back, rattling about, might drown out the sound.

What was alarming about the possibility of not knowing was that she, Naomi, could have run someone over without knowing it. She was one hundred per cent sure she never had. But it opened the possibility. Could she be one hundred per cent sure?

So much for the rational stuff. The irrational, the emotional caught up with her at Fay's funeral. She didn't presume to sit with the family. That was evidently no longer appropriate. And sitting close to them, but not with them, would be too upsetting. So she sat well back, which turned out to be fortunate. She kept looking round, searching, expectant, scanning the rows, inspecting each person who entered the church.

Then the coffin was carried in. You got it then, didn't you? You realised your waiting had been in vain. The person you'd been expecting to join you had just arrived. Such an imposing box for such a slight person. Your Fay. Inside that box. You nearly screamed with the realisation and had to hold your mouth inside your scarf as you rushed from the church. You leant up against a yew tree in the churchyard and howled into its branches. *You didn't come! You didn't come! Fay, why didn't you come?* You yelled until you were hoarse. The passing traffic drowned you out, and only a squirrel paused to stare before sprinting away down the path. You gradually calmed down, the sobbing stopped and you blew your nose. You were determined to see the family, show them you were here. How could that have happened? You'd truly believed that Fay would come. You'd even put your bag on the seat beside you to save the space. Back in the church, the organ was giving inappropriately full throttle to *The day thou gavest, Lord, is ended* and nobody noticed you slide into a pew at the back.

Outside, Kate gave her a warming hug while Tom limited himself to a formal handshake. They were standing either side of Daniel, a trio against the world. No place for her there. Daniel's dark suit hung off him as if still on its hanger in the wardrobe and he stared at her with blank eyes. 'Don't come,' he said. 'I couldn't bear it.' Naomi nodded. 'Don't worry. Me neither.' And she had walked to the Tube and caught the train straight back to Devon.

*

It didn't seem like two years ago, Naomi reflected, sitting up in bed and now thoroughly irritated by the rattling windowpane. At least one good thing had come out of what she thought of as "the phone call day". Not from Fay's death, but from her father witnessing the news, from him being there for her and coming clean about their situation.

'I know it's hard for you,' Dad had said out of the blue. 'I know Fay was like a sister. But I can't help saying it's a great relief to me that you've stopped being so damned cheerful – the dutiful daughter, doing the right thing all the time. Made me feel like an old codger. And a nuisance – the price you had to pay for the convenience of living here.'

They'd laughed together then. She and her father. She hadn't felt so lonely. It was the beginning of getting to know each other and made his last illness so much easier for them both to cope with.

Naomi hugged her knees, reluctant to get out of bed. All those deaths. All different.

Fay's so public and yet not witnessed, unknown, trapped in a silence.

By contrast, Mum's had been public and noisy, a drama. Decades ago now. She'd had a stroke at the local supermarket checkout. She was known to be difficult and people thought she was having a tantrum. She'd just sent Dad to fetch a tin of baked beans and by the time he got back he couldn't reach her for the people gathered to watch. It was the cashier who recognised the signs and called the ambulance.

Dad's death, only last year, had been as quiet as Mum's was noisy. He had died of a series of minor strokes, drifting in and out of consciousness after the third one. Naomi played his favourite music and sat holding his hand, that same gnarled hand that had taken care of her when Fay died. It was the same music playing – Beethoven's Emperor Concerto – on his last day. When she gently squeezed his hand during the opening bars, he opened one eye and looked at her. As if he really saw her. As if he said thank you. It was his goodbye.

She finally left the warmth of the duvet to investigate the rattling windowpane and hunted around for something to fix it with. The beer mat on the table was too thick, so she folded a strip of newspaper over and over and jammed it into the sash.

When she'd eventually got round to clearing out her father's wardrobe, there, at the back, was Fay's birthday bag. She'd stood at the window, clutching it. Presents that would never be opened. Hugs that would never be shared. Discussions that would never take place. And Dad – he'd known he must get it out of her sight that day, but he obviously hadn't known what to do with it.

The tears had come at last. Noisy, gasping, torrential. Until she had dropped down onto his bed and fallen into a sweaty, snotty sleep.

Now, having once again laid her nearest and dearest to rest, maybe she could sink into sleep here in this strange hotel on the north Devon coast, lulled by the moaning wind.

10 *Meghan*

Meghan woke in the night, which she rarely did. Not a gradual shift into consciousness, but sudden, as if there had been a banging at the door or a clap of thunder overhead. She lay listening to familiar sounds – the creaking of her cottage in tune with the creaks of the trees alongside. No further knocking at a door; no storm: it was her own psyche jolting her into awareness.

It happened from time to time. The first occasion not long after she had arrived in this place. Some invisible force had drawn her out into the chill of a pearly dawn light, and up onto the headland. She'd been neglecting her yoga practice, but performing a salute to the sun seemed a natural thing to do. Her limbs protested at the wet grass and the cold wind, but it left her invigorated. It was on that day she had felt the first flickering of movement in her belly: the first communication established between her and the unborn Alex.

But now she checked the time and turned over. Dawn was a long way off and she had no intention of clambering around out there in the dark. An early walk, yes. First some more sleep and maybe an illuminating dream. But every time she found herself sliding down into sleep, she noticed it and was awake again. What had woken her? Her Welsh grandmother's voice was telling her, as she had told her often enough in life, that those who had the power must use it. That gentle lilt imposing such a serious duty. Her grandmother had the power, no doubt. And the sight, but that was another matter. Nan used her gift unobtrusively in her work as a midwife – healing, saving lives, being a trusted friend, marriage guidance counsellor, child psychiatrist and careers advisor all rolled into one, although she would not have acknowledged any of those skills. Meghan had always been reluctant to accept that this healing power had passed down to her. The fact that her mother had rejected it made it attractive when she was a rebellious teenager, but she'd quickly shied away from the responsibilities it entailed. The ambivalence had never left her.

Together with her grandmother's voice was the image of Naomi. That wide-open brow, and a pleading look in the grey-green eyes. Naomi wanted something from her and Meghan couldn't understand what. Not a painting, evidently. The image wouldn't go away, not even when she opened her eyes.

She had eventually overslept. The headland would now be busy with dog-walkers. The wood would be more private. So she made her way down a little-used track to her favourite clearing, a place where she came to meditate. She leaned back against the trunk of the oak where the rooks were nesting, where rational thought was disrupted by the racket that came from the rookery in the tree's crown.

She didn't understand these episodes. But she knew it was useless to ignore them. They would continue to nag at her consciousness and interrupt her life until she did something about whatever was going on. Sometimes the trees and the birds showed her a way forward. Sometimes a clue emerged through her painting. Occasionally she would resort to the cards.

As a child she would often go to stay with her grandmother. Sometimes she crept out of bed and sat at the top of the stairs, peering through the banisters to where Nan was laying out the cards on the low table beside the fire.

'I know you're there,' she would say. 'Come and see.'

She would kneel beside Nan's chair and watch the layout and the pictures, listening to her grandmother's intermittent humming, which seemed to be part of the process. If she asked a question, Nan simply replied, 'That would be telling.' She would be allowed to shuffle through the cards afterwards and choose her favourite for that day before she went back to bed.

The wood was full of fluttering and twittering and a squirrel appeared almost at her feet, regarding her with a bright eye before dancing off up the trunk of a nearby ash. Annoyingly, the rooks above her seemed to be clattering out the rhythm of "All You Need Is Love". Those three opening chords over and over again. Bother the Beatles. She'd never been a fan. It's only rooks, she told herself and tried to block it out.

Only when she was much older did Nan talk about the Tarot.

'These cards will be yours one day. Your mother has no truck with this sort of thing. Take your time getting to know them. There's no magic here. They just give you another way of looking at a situation. Another point of view. One thing, though. Never lay them out for a friend.'

Meghan had broken that rule once and regretted it. The Tower had appeared in the reading in the place of relationships. 'If I didn't know you and Ted were the most devoted couple I know, I'd say you were going to split up.' Talk about blundering in. Then she'd tried to laugh it off, saying they must be due to have a big argument. Her friend said nothing, but within a few short weeks the marriage was over and the friendship had cooled.

Since then she rarely used the cards and learned that listening was the best remedy, the sort of listening that included noticing what people were not saying.

Maybe it was time to consult the Tarot about Naomi. Reluctantly, she left the clearing. The rooks' refrain varied slightly but would not go away. All the way home, it invaded her head and her steps, reminding her that all she needed was love.

The knock at the door came soon after she got back. She hadn't had the chance to retreat into her studio and out of sight. Naomi stood there, blurting about her behaviour on her last visit. 'I was poking my nose in – where it didn't belong…' The apology was so unexpected that she invited her in. Naomi even apologised for not buying the picture she claimed to love. 'What with the accommodation… Wasn't expecting to have to pay.' An odd remark from someone staying in a hotel.

Even more oddly, as she opened the door, Meghan saw a small child clutching at the back of Naomi's jacket. Only for a moment. A breeze whipped through the hedge, a shadow fell, the light changed: no child. But it gave Meghan the shivers. She crossed the room and reached for her shawl – a wonderfully soft multi-coloured affair she'd knitted out of alpaca and mohair yarns when the wool shop in town sold off their leftovers. It was always to hand, draped over the computer chair where she could grab it on a chilly evening or at a moment like this.

A gasp came from behind her as she wrapped the shawl around herself. 'That chair…' Naomi said. 'Where did you get that chair?' She was staring and pointing at the upright chair with its chipped scarlet paint.

Meghan frowned. She really was a very strange woman, this Naomi. 'Some people were throwing it out. Happened to be just what I needed at the time. Never got round to repainting it and now I quite like it the way it is.'

'Was that Wilson? Wilson Fanshaw at Mill End?'

'Mill End, yes, don't think I ever knew his name. Years ago now.' How the hell did this woman know that?

'Of course,' Naomi was saying – a long, drawn-out exclamation as if a number of things were falling into place. And then… 'I think I need to sit down. No, not that chair.'

Naomi sank onto the window seat and she did look quite pale.

Meghan fetched a large tumbler of water.

'So kind,' Naomi said, taking the glass.

Meghan settled at the table. 'So what is it about a tatty old chair that sends you reeling?'

'That's a long story, too long a story. You won't ever paint it, will you?' Naomi was still sounding emotional.

Meghan shrugged. 'Probably not, but it is my chair.'

'Of course.' A more matter of fact tone. 'But at least now I know where I met you before. Remember? I said you were familiar?'

She nodded, curious. 'Really?' Then she had to wait as Naomi stared intently into the water, swirled it round with her finger and sucked her fingertip. Now she was impatient. Was Naomi playing games with her? 'Well, do go on.'

'It's a bit embarrassing really. You used to come and clean at the cottage, at Mill End.'

'Is it so embarrassing, to remember the cleaner?' Meghan kicked herself for going on the defensive when she saw Naomi's face.

'No, no. Not that. In fact I hardly recall seeing you inside. We used to go out, I guess, to let you have a clear run.'

'So?'

Naomi took a breath. 'It was you having sex with Gordon that I remember.'

It came like a smack in the face. Gordon. The man at the cottage. The ginger one. 'So I did. And you *saw* us? Oh. My. God.'

The shock of memory. Meghan's brain reeled back through the years. There was a heatwave that summer. She'd come away from two hours' hard labour with brooms and a dustpan and brush – no electricity in the place back then – and would leap into the deep pool by the waterfall to cool off.

She could feel that heat now: everything dry and brittle in the sun's burn; her hair stringy with sweat, skin prickling, itchy eyes; the rasp of brown grass underfoot. And then the bubble of water, deep, dark, brown. Irresistible. She would drop into the icy shock of it, knife to the bottom, gasp to the surface and lie back into the glory of the cold clawing at her scalp.

Then one day, Gordon. He'd happened by and teased her by gathering up her dress and knickers and making off with them along the bank to where the kingcups were the only succulent sign of life. She'd pursued him with predictable results. They'd both been voracious. She had no man in her life at that time and sex was something she missed. Gordon was a good lover. She'd been surprised, thinking of him as an old bloke, forty at least. She'd been more than happy to repeat the encounter until the weather broke or Gordon left, she couldn't remember which. It had never occurred to her that there might have been a witness to those long-forgotten couplings.

'More than once. By the stream,' Naomi was saying.

Meghan blinked. 'Yes. I'd be steaming after work and I'd strip off and jump in. Bliss. And one day Gordon came across me.' She paused and stared at Naomi. 'And to think, we were being watched. Jeez.'

'Did he…? He didn't…?'

'Oh, it wasn't rape or anything. I was more than willing! Randy as hell, both of us.'

'Yes.' Naomi sounded thoughtful. 'It did look like that. And it was hard for me, seeing it.'

'Didn't stop you coming back for more. More than once, you said.'

'It was chance, the second time too. But I'm ashamed to say I did stay to watch. You see, it set me imagining.' She paused, more examining of her water. 'Because, you see, Gordon used to be my mother's lover.'

Meghan felt her neck crick as she jerked upright and met Naomi's gaze. No end to the surprises this morning. How on earth to react to that one?

'Your mother's lover,' Meghan repeated, trying to make sense of it. Gordon must have been older than she'd thought, more like fifty. Not old at all, of course. But Naomi's *mother*. How was that possible?

Naomi gave a wry smile. 'I can see you trying to compute that one! He was a toy-boy, no doubt. Can only have been about twenty. And my mother must have been thirty-three or thirty-four at the time. But he was the best of the uncles. Was always good to me.'

Meghan nodded slowly and said nothing. So many questions. Who was this woman sitting across from her? She could no longer dismiss her as a slightly theatrical stranger who kept intruding into her space. Naomi was acquiring dimensions that couldn't be ignored. Fascinating dimensions, come to that. Meghan even saw Naomi's hair in a new light. Not carefully contrived to look casually windswept, but actually windswept – and no less attractive for that.

What must it have been like, growing up with a series of uncles? It could account for a lot. Including the little girl on the doorstep. Meghan grew hot and shrugged off her shawl.

They were staring at each other, only feet apart but staring across an ocean of years and memory, questions and answers rolling in on the waves. Questions surfaced, white crests on the tide, and were reabsorbed as the silence stretched and flowed around the two women.

How long that silence lasted neither could have said. Nor could they have said who broke it first. Was it for Naomi the shock of telling or for Meghan the shock of the unexpected that knocked them off balance? Who started to give way first? And did it matter? For suddenly they were both laughing. Hands over their mouths at first, as if it might be inappropriate, and then increasingly relaxed, leaning forward, and finally leaning back, wiping tears from their eyes.

It was difficult to know where to go from there, after such laughter. Hysterical? Cathartic? Naomi clearly had more stories to tell. Why was the chair so important? What was her connection with Gordon? Is that why she was here? Meghan herself had no more stories to tell. Gordon came to the pub a few times, but that was way back, early nineties probably. Neither of them referred to what had passed between them. She hadn't seen him in years.

Meghan ventured a question. 'So what is the significance of the chair?'

Naomi covered her face with her hands. Only briefly. So hopefully not in despair. Reluctant to remember maybe.

'It was part of a ritual. Good chair. Bad chair. I'd rather not go into detail, but…'

'Sounds heavy.'

Naomi nodded. 'Wilson called it our blue summer – skies of blue every day. And a new woman in his bed most nights. He'd go round singing "What a Wonderful World". Trying to imitate Satchmo. Gruesome. Really, it was. I called it my summer of the blues. But enough of that.'

'Is that why you're here? Because the old man's died?'

Naomi was staring out of the window. 'Probably only lasted a week or so, that heat. But it seemed to go on forever, the heat and, well, everything…'

Meghan feared she was going to go into the detail she'd avoided earlier. But Naomi looked back at her and refocused, as if running the question in her head.

'Oh, so you know why I'm here. I should have guessed. Everyone knows everything, don't they?'

'Not everything. But there's someone living there, for sure. And it isn't you.'

'Huh! No. And it should be me. That bastard, Wilson, left the cottage to me – but he gave Gordon the right to live there. God, what a nightmare. I came for peace and solitude and end up in an effing hotel.'

The hands went over her face again and stayed there for a while. Meghan said nothing, supressing the impulse to laugh at the cleverness of that will.

'He sounds a nasty piece of work. I always wondered what went on over there.'

'Nasty is right. Guru. Almost like a cult leader. He didn't imprison people or anything, but you did feel trapped.'

'So how did you get out of his clutches?'

Naomi looked away and made a face. 'I walked the plank. It's what he called this exercise he'd invented – the bridge across the waterfall – you know?'

Meghan did know and nodded, wanting to know, watching Naomi closely.

'I was scared of heights, the stream was roaring, I was terrified. All I had to do was walk across. Plus he had his fan club of adoring young women watching. No big deal.'

'Much!'

'Then I just had this kind of epiphany – if that's not too grand a word. Suddenly got it that it would be his victory, not mine. That it had always been like that, building people up for his glory. Okay, they might gain something too, but that wasn't why he did it.'

Naomi paused and Meghan noticed how her aura, which had brightened as she spoke of her epiphany, now settled, lighter than before.

'You may think I was slow on the uptake – imagining I needed him all those years!'

Meghan shook her head. 'All part of the manipulative process. People like that, they hook you in. You did well to see it when you did.'

'And, once I did, I was out of there. Crept out early and ran away. Not that he would have pursued me – but it *felt* as if he might. Does that sound crazy?'

'Not at all. You'd been stuck a long time and there was a lot at stake.'

Naomi nodded. 'Caught a train in Barnstaple the very next morning. That's when I met Evie. But that's another story. I don't know why I'm telling you all this. I haven't told a soul. I feel so – well, ashamed, if I'm honest.'

'I feel honoured.' Meghan stretched. She wondered who this Evie was, but chose not to ask the question. 'Silly, isn't it, what we feel ashamed of? You should feel proud. It was a real achievement.'

Naomi shrugged and gave a rueful smile, looking pleased, playing it down.

'Really. I mean it.'

'Thank you.' Naomi rubbed her hands over her face. 'And about the cottage, the will and so on, can I ask you not to tell? It'll be common knowledge soon enough, I dare say. But just for now?'

'Of course. Just as I'd prefer you to be discreet about me and Gordon.'

Naomi nodded. 'You know, ever since I saw you, I've been kind of drawn to you. I really don't know why.' She paused, looked into her empty mug and put it down. 'I must go. I expect you were hoping to paint and I've gone and got in the way yet again. I'll take myself off. And thank you.

I'm probably leaving today, or tomorrow perhaps. I'm not sure. Not really sure of anything at the moment.' She held out a hand. 'Thank you for everything.'

'Nothing to thank for.' Meghan ignored the hand and gave Naomi a half hug. It was awkward. Naomi didn't respond until it was too late and they drew apart with nervous laughter.

As Naomi left, a pair of jackdaws flew up from the hedge and settled on Rita's chimney stack, strutting and preening. Meghan stood in the window watching them long after Naomi had disappeared round the corner. What was it about the woman? What did she want? What could she, Meghan, possibly give her?

11 *Naomi*

Naomi had been bothered in the night by a persistent itch on the sole of her foot, the left foot. She'd wondered if that meant losing money in the same way an itch in the left palm was supposed to. She imagined pound notes fluttering out of her foot and over the end of the mattress and drifted into a dream where she was worried about money and seeking reassurance from a tall figure with ridiculously long black hair in a room full of chairs. In the background was a person who seemed to be laughing at her, a person who resembled Wilson, fading into her first husband, back into a shadowy Wilson.

Nightmares aside, she'd been here too long. She munched sadly on an over-poached egg, which she had hoped would redeem the Mother's Pride toast. She always looked forward to a cooked breakfast with eager anticipation, but it rarely lived up to her hopes. After four such minor let-downs it really was time to go. But she had a sense of waiting for something to happen. True, a lot had happened yesterday. That had been a real breakthrough with Meghan. But there was still a sense of holding back. Were they friends? Not really, not yet. But they might be, sometime in the future when – or if – she came to live in the cottage. And what about Mill End? No movement there. But the ongoing sense of unfinished business was less to do with Gordon and more to do with Meghan.

In questing mode, she drove up to the lighthouse. No answer from the grey ocean stretching to America. No clue from the clouds shaped like wise old men. Why men? Wise beings? No, dammit, they had beards, looked like men, and men could be wise – sometimes. Some men.

Those thoughts reminded her of Wilson, the dream and the chairs. Chairs. It had been such a shock, suddenly coming face to face with that chair. Chairs had always been a thing with Wilson. Soon after she met him, he'd set up a kind of puzzle in the woodland behind his house. He hadn't prepared her, just told her to walk round his garden.

Lush walkways open up in all directions, overhung by vines and creepers. But whichever one she takes, she finds herself ambushed by wicker chairs gleaming like teeth in the green shade.

A pair facing each other, expecting an intense tête à tête.

Three grouped for an informal chat.

A row facing outwards as if to view a procession.

She keeps on walking past them, but they sap her strength as if each sterile dazzle of white paint defies her to ignore it.

What is she afraid of? That, if she sits down, other people will materialise to occupy the nearby chairs – calling her to account, asking to explain herself?

One of Wilson's games. Obviously. Where is he? Watching her discomfort, no doubt. He says they must build trust if they are to work together. Most of the time she does trust him. But today she feels abandoned.

When he comes, she asks what the chairs mean.

'They mean whatever you see in them,' he says.

'What was the point? Why...?'

'Just to see how you'd react.' He sounds detached, clinical. As if she is just an interesting experiment.

Naomi perched herself on a rock near the entrance to the lighthouse. *The chairs mean whatever you see in them.* Yes, it was the same story with the red chair. An ordinary kitchen chair. One of a set of four. Wilson had made a special trip to the hardware shop and came back with a small pot of red gloss. 'That won't be enough,' she'd said. But he only wanted one chair painted. Painting that chair had been thrilling. The first scarlet brushful transferring onto the crosspiece of the chair back gave her goosebumps. She worked steadily, careful to leave no runs, drips or visible brushstrokes. When Wilson praised her for doing a good job, she'd glowed along with the chair, proud to have transformed a workaday item. If only she'd known then what the chair would be used for.

She hadn't known at the time that there was a vast array of programmes like Wilson's on offer in the eighties. He'd jumped on the bandwagon of the human potential movement, where management was being given a new look, team-building was the name of the game and everyone wanted a slice of self-development. Here were no wafty hippies preaching love, not war. In their place came dozens of ordinary folk, many of them housewives and mothers, who wanted more out of life, alongside a brigade of purposeful, shoulder-padded career women who wanted their voice heard in the boardroom. Wilson was eager to help all-comers achieve their goals.

On the small courses he staged at Mill End, tasks were set for members to complete. Sometimes they were simple – to do with climbing a hill or swimming, sometimes more complex like treasure hunts with obscure clues or challenges to scour the woods and beach for certain objects. There was always someone, often more than one person, who "failed" a task. The "F" word was not used, of course, but implied. These people were seen as withholding their potential, keeping it inside. They were labelled Buds – as opposed to the Bloomers who were letting their potential blossom. The Buds were told to sit in the red chair – which Wilson introduced, with some ceremony, as the Learning Chair – and explain to the group why they had not completed the task, what they would do differently on another occasion and so on. The group were then invited to remind that person of their good qualities.

However much the label, Learning Chair, was emphasised, it became known as the Naughty Chair. Naomi had always cringed to see perfectly normal, capable people beating themselves up because they hated cold water or creepy-crawlies or couldn't solve cryptic clues. She had sat in the chair herself and defended her right not to climb a tree if she would rather sit on its roots. She had referred to the rule that said no one should be forced into any activity. But deep down she had felt a failure, a coward, too afraid to take a risk or expose herself to ridicule.

She shuddered at the memory of how Wilson had treated her after that little performance: not speaking, and taking one of the Bloomers to his bed instead of her. But at least that was better than the threesomes he sometimes inflicted upon her, presenting them as "a special treat". Twenty years on, those memories still hurt.

Then there had been that girl, Sally. Oh, Sally. She could picture her still – a blue-eyed blonde with neat features, high cheekbones. Just so pretty. It was the only word. Sally had "failed" a couple of tasks and went to town on the red chair, listing all her faults. Anyone who couldn't see her would have thought she was fat, ugly, clumsy, useless. The outcry of positives from the group was overwhelming, but Sally had sat there in tears, unable to "hear" anything good about herself.

Then it came to the other use of the red chair. On the last evening, all participants were invited to sit in it and assess their experience – what they had enjoyed or valued, what they had learned, what they were taking away, and so on. On the first occasion, as they set up the room, Wilson had put the red chair out in front of the group. Naomi swapped it for a "neutral" blue chair and they had argued.

'Any chair is neutral,' he said.

'So why paint one red?'

'People must learn that their worth lies within them. It is not attached to a chair.'

'But the associations...' Naomi had countered.

'You miss the point.' Wilson sighed deeply and there was an impatient edge to his voice.

He had, of course, prevailed. But when Sally's turn came to occupy the Learning Chair, she started shaking as soon as she sat down.

'The chair is simply a piece of wood,' Wilson had said. 'Your job is to love and value yourself from the inside.'

Indignant, Naomi had fetched another chair and helped Sally into it. This caused murmurs of approval from the rest of the group, which Wilson had later interpreted as murmurs of disapproval.

The occasion marked the point at which the trust between them was broken, as Wilson put it. Or, as Naomi saw it, he could no longer manipulate her. Very soon after that she had escaped.

What happened to Sally? She had attempted suicide not long after the course. Her parents had contacted Wilson, who had seen fit to let Naomi know in an ambiguous note.

'I told them that no blame can be attributed in such circumstances. Least of all to the parents or the therapist. It is nobody's fault. So you can rest assured that your clumsy intervention was not what tipped her over the edge.'

She'd never been able to stop feeling guilty about Sally. Not because of what Wilson implied, but more deeply. What could she have done to support Sally? To persuade her she was in the wrong place? To get her out of there? Futile thoughts. Unhealthy. She hoped Sally had found the therapy she needed. Meanwhile she, Naomi, must focus on her own needs.

Being here and being in limbo had stirred up too much of the past. She would go home. She was lucky she still had a place to go to – not quite sold, still habitable. She would treat this whole Gordon business like a traffic jam that would eventually clear. Meanwhile the memories needed washing away. It was not enough to gaze at the ocean like this; she needed to immerse herself. She remembered a secluded cove not far away and followed her nose to find it. Parking in the lane, she made her way down a winding path lined with foxgloves just coming into bloom, the soft thumbs of their buds barely showing colour.

The beach was a mix of stones and sand with a few sizeable boulders and smooth reefs running into the water. She stripped to her underwear, black and matching for once, so perfectly presentable, especially as they were big knickers, not the sort that float away after a few strokes. Once she would have run down to the water but the stones were painful. When did her feet become so tender and what was this complaint from her hips? She edged into the water, steadying herself on a rocky ledge, until the chill of it hit her crotch and crept up her tummy. Deep enough to swim. She plunged forward and struck out furiously until the lung-catching, breath-snatching iciness ebbed away. She turned back towards the beach, treading water, getting used to feeling buoyant and free. Then she rolled onto her back, gazing at clouds against a pale blue sky as the water crept through her hair and clawed her scalp in a delicious weightless massage.

She swam across the little bay and back, out beyond its boundary cliffs to get a sense of perspective and then, suddenly tired, she made for the beach again. Tender feet, creaking hips and loss of stamina. Time she got into better shape. Getting dressed was a further struggle. It was too chilly to dry off in the breeze and her woollen jacket was useless as a towel. Eventually jeans and shirt were persuaded over wet skin. Thank goodness for no witnesses. Her shoes squelched as she climbed the path and her hair, despite being wrung out, dripped relentlessly down her back. But she felt invigorated and triumphant. Even the darkening sky and build-up of clouds did nothing to spoil that delight.

She was also hungry and stopped in Stagworthy to buy a pasty at the bakery before dropping in to Gracie's Gallery. No sign of Meghan.

Back at the quay, she leaned on the sea wall to eat. By now her whole body seemed to be encased in a cool, silver slick – like a mermaid skin, she thought, enjoying the sensation, at the same time as savouring the hot pasty. There was clearly no hope of solitude and healing at Mill End, not in the short term. She would return home, make a plan and write a conciliatory letter to Gordon, suggesting compromises.

She brushed crumbs of pastry off her jacket and watched a gull swoop to hoover them up. By now the cool slick was causing her to shiver. A shower was called for, but she was still reluctant to wash away the salt and shreds of seaweed caught on her skin and in her hair. However, one look in the bedroom mirror told her she was less Mysterious Mermaid and more Sea Scarecrow, not a look that did her any favours.

Clean clothes and dry hair brought civilisation a little closer, and the thought of her own bed in the boring but familiar bungalow was suddenly attractive. One more night, and she'd be on the road at crack of dawn. Decision made, she re-entered the gloomy bar, which was beginning to feel a bit too familiar. Gavin, the landlord, looked down on her from his considerable height and gave her a quizzical smile as if wondering what could possibly be keeping her. The room was indeed available for one more night. She took it and asked for a cafetière. At least Gavin produced decent coffee.

She settled in a corner table with a view of the bar, ready for some anonymous people-watching. Meghan wasn't on duty, so she couldn't buy her a drink. Forget Meghan. She was becoming an obsession. A walk along the cliff path would blow that away. What she needed was some sea air, followed by a few glasses of Merlot, the cottage pie and an early night. She could call on Meghan in the morning, just to say goodbye. Then she would set off back to the bungalow she'd be calling home for a while longer.

Her attention was grabbed by a man at the bar – early sixties probably, medium height, well-worn tweed jacket, bald except for a band of unnaturally tawny hair that stretched across the top of his head from ear to ear. Bushy, energetic eyebrows and expressive hands were part of the conversation, and his eyes brightened and widened as he listened. He laughed easily, throwing his head back to show the glint of a gold tooth.

His nearest companion was altogether more contained. His weathered head emerged from a black polo neck like the polished top of a well-loved cane. Her father used to have just such a walking stick.

The third man in the group was the dominant talker, taking up more space than the other two put together, being not only taller but bulky with it. One hand was thrust into the trouser pocket of a mismatched suit, the other held a pint, which he used for emphasis. His face was jowly, topped with heavy-rimmed glasses, and straggly grey hair was pulled back into an unexpected ponytail. Why unexpected? Why shouldn't he have a ponytail?

Just as her coffee arrived, the door was flung open and Gordon made a noisy entrance. He went straight to the bar, making a show of taking off his coat and shaking off the rain.

'Helluva shower, just as I was nearly here.'

The group at the bar shifted positions to make room for him with exclamations of surprise.

'Good lord, if it isn't Fanshaw!' 'Gordon! It's been a year or two.' And 'Drinks on Fanshaw, I think.'

Gordon kicked out at one of the dogs. 'About time, eh?' He prodded ponytail in the ribs. 'Good God, Eddie, there's a bit more of you than there used to be.'

Gordon was clearly enjoying being the centre of attention and was busy buying a round. Naomi wondered if she could slip out before he noticed her. But it would look furtive if he turned and saw her. She didn't want to take that risk. In any case, maybe it would be a good idea to meet him in a public place among others and have a normal conversation.

The well-polished gentleman at the bar was now facing her and she noticed that he often looked in her direction. After a while he detached himself from the group and came over.

'May I?'

She nodded, curious.

'Colin Morrison.' He took the chair next to hers and leaned in, uncomfortably close. 'I've noticed you over the last day or two. Not wanting to intrude, but thought you might be in need of a bit of local knowledge?'

Naomi shook her head. 'That's very kind, but I'm off again tomorrow.'

'This may be a shot in the dark but my professional nose tells me – and my nose is pretty reliable – that you're property-hunting. Am I right?'

Naomi resisted the urge to swipe the end of his professional nose. How dare he make assumptions? 'It seems your nose is letting you down. No, not house-hunting.' She felt gleeful and also mean. He was almost right but she was determined to guard her privacy.

The group at the bar had once again reshuffled. She saw that now Gordon noticed her for the first time.

'Not looking to move here, then?' Colin was fumbling in his inside pocket.

He was obviously looking for his card. She was at a loss, not wanting to lie. Local estate agent? The last person she wanted to know her business.

'Naomi! What a surprise! I thought you were long gone.'

Colin started as Gordon came up behind him. He looked uncomfortable.

'Chatting up a likely prospect, Colin? Have you no shame?'

'I had no idea you two knew each other.'

'Why should you?' Gordon laughed. 'We go back a long way, don't we, Naomi? Has he told you who he is?'

Colin at last produced a card. 'I was just getting to that.' He held it out.

Naomi made no attempt to take it. 'Let me guess. Local estate agent?'

Colin beamed. 'Morrison Morrison. You've probably seen our boards.'

'I don't think so. But then, you don't notice, do you? When you're *not looking?*'

Gordon set his glass on the table and pulled out a chair. 'Have you even offered the lady a drink?'

Which was worse, being targeted by the local estate agent or being labelled "the lady" by Gordon? 'I'm happy with my coffee, thank you, Gordon.'

As Gordon settled himself, Colin made to stand up.

'Sit yourself down, Colin.' Gordon turned to Naomi. 'He's not really that bad, you know. Funnily enough, it was Colin's father who sold Wilson the cottage in the first place. You hadn't joined the firm then, had you, Colin?'

Why did Gordon have to mention Mill End? How much did Colin know? She looked from one to the other. Colin was staring fixedly into his pint, and she couldn't catch Gordon's eye. What was Gordon up to?

Gordon gulped his whisky. 'You see, Colin, the bizarre thing is, Naomi here, is my landlady.'

Colin looked up abruptly and she felt him appraising her with new eyes.

'For God's sake, Gordon! Do you have to tell everyone my business?'

'*Our* business. And Colin would have truffled it out anyway. He's a real terrier.' Gordon replaced his tumbler carefully on its mat. 'It's fine, Naomi. We're among friends. Colin, you've met. The big guy at the bar – that's Eddie Edwards, our esteemed GP – and Aubrey, he runs some kind of wine business. You can trust 'em all at least as far as you can throw them.'

'Even so,' Naomi said, pleased to know who those people were but still not happy for them to know her business.

'Anyway,' Gordon continued. 'I came over to ask you, are you planning to sit it out until I leave? Do you climb the hill every evening to see if my chimney is showing smoke? Hmm?' That needling tone. He must know it got under her skin. 'Does it remind you of those times we had with my beloved brother? Does it by any chance put you off the whole venture?'

What was Gordon up to? What was he thinking of? She wasn't going to stand for that sort of conversation, especially not in front of Colin-the-Nose-Morrison. She pushed back her chair and stood, gathering her coat and bag in one furious gesture.

She glared at Gordon. 'I thought I was quite pleased to see you, but I've changed my mind. Time for a walk.'

12 *Alex*

Sète was everything Alex had hoped it would be. Yes, of course Alfie had insisted she come that far with them. Her dazzling smile had not been lost on him. Esther had relented and they had all rubbed along pretty well. The main reason Alfie and Esther were there was to catch up with Gaston, an old friend of Alfie's. They'd apparently worked together in a local vineyard in their twenties and had always kept in touch. The three of them had met up with Gaston on their first morning, and he and Alfie had rabbited on about various nostalgic escapades, while Esther and Alex rolled their eyes and soaked up the sun.

That evening they were to dine with Gaston's family at the harbour front restaurant where his son, Davide, was working. Davide had saved them a table under an awning on the edge of the pavement, but there was no sign of Gaston when they arrived, so Esther walked on down the quay to take photographs. She'd spotted piles of fishing gear – nets and ropes and buoys that she said were photogenic. Alex looked all around her, taking in the scene and enjoying the fact that it was just her and Alfie. But she'd lost Alfie. He was watching the quay on the far side of the canal, but he seemed much further away than that.

'L'Orque Bleu,' she said, following his gaze.

He smiled.

'Looks like one of those traditional French hotels with a concierge with her hair all piled up, smoking Gauloises. And it would have a huge brass bed.' She paused to consider Alfie in the huge bed but got nowhere. 'I fancy coming out on that balcony in the morning to have coffee in my *peignoir*.'

'Good guess. Concierge spot on. Straight out of a Colette novel. And the bed. Plumbing was something else – huge pipes and a lot of knocking and hissing. Then scalding water and lots of steam. Huh!' He shook his head and laughed. 'I came here with my late wife. But we had wine on the balcony and went round the corner to that little *tabac* for coffee and croissants for breakfast.'

It was the first she'd heard of the late wife, which wasn't surprising as she hardly knew the guy. What was surprising was that he mentioned her at all. Judging from the look in his eyes, he must have been mad about her. So that was the real reason they'd come here. Alex didn't know what to say but he filled the silence.

'Sorry about that. The past just grabs you by the throat sometimes. Happy memories, though. Don't want to be maudlin.' He lifted his glass. 'Ah, here comes Esther. Best not to mention all that to her.' He nodded in the direction of the hotel with its blue shutters and pretty iron balcony. 'She knows all about Meg, but – well, she doesn't need to be aware of the ghosts.'

Alex nodded and waved at Esther, surprised at the use of that word. He had hidden depths, this Alfie, but no ghosts appeared to overshadow the evening. The food was delicious, wine and conversation flowed in a mix of French and English, and Alex found herself mesmerised by Davide's waiting skills. He was single-handedly managing at least twenty tables – greeting, bringing drinks, taking orders, delivering food and clearing plates. He never seemed to hurry, always had time for a friendly conversation and advice about the menu, and no one seemed to be kept waiting for service.

'It's like magic,' Alex said. 'Just couldn't happen back home.'

'Too right,' Alfie said. 'Mind you, Esther's pretty ace at running a bar single-handed.'

Alex frowned.

'It's how we met,' Esther said. 'Me serving a pint and cottage pie to the surly bloke in the corner. Admit it, Alfie. You could be *soo* grumpy. And yeah, I was okay at that, gave me a kick to juggle it all. But nothing like Davide! It was only a little pub. You're right, Alex. There'd be chaos if you left this many tables to one waiter in England.'

It was on their last day in Sète that Alex finally got through to Esther. They'd been to market that morning, and Alex had discovered her money had come through and presented Alfie with a wad of cash towards the petrol. Esther thawed noticeably – Alex was at last living up to her story.

Gaston and family had been invited to the van for a farewell meal that evening. She and Esther were standing side by side in the cramped space, preparing the food. Alex was chopping onions, Esther slicing huge, richly red tomatoes, when Alex felt the baby move for the first time. She gasped and Esther looked up.

'Hey! It moved! My baby moved.' Alex grabbed for Esther's hand. 'Feel here.'

But Esther was gone with some backward-flung remark about fetching eggs. Alex stared after her, shrugged and sat down to cradle her stomach. That very definite but gentle prod had flipped her world upside down. That presence, which she'd been doing her best to ignore, had asserted itself. Itself? Herself? Himself? Certainly no longer an "it". She sent the presence a silent question and the response was decidedly feminine. She hoped it wasn't wishful thinking.

After a while Esther returned with no sign of eggs. She stared almost accusingly at Alex. 'To think, I thought you made all that up. I thought you were faking it.'

'Did you think I was stashing drugs in my t-shirt or something?'

'Something like that. Shit! If only you knew. The irony of it!'

'Irony?'

Esther nodded. 'We'd never have taken you if I'd realised you were really pregnant. But that's another story.' She crossed to the stove and lit the gas, suddenly brisk. 'Let's get going with this sauce.'

Once the sauce was bubbling lazily on the stove, Esther made a pot of tea and passed Alex a cup. They sat outside on the grass in the shade of the awning.

'Sorry I over-reacted,' Esther said. 'It's just, I've absolutely never wanted to be pregnant – it's like a phobia. Don't know why, won't say more.' She sipped her tea. 'So, what does your mum think about it? All I know is, she sends you money when you need it.'

'I honestly don't know. She doesn't do email properly. But I guess she can't be too mad as she's sent the money. Anyway, it's what she did. She had me on her own. Not even her own mother for support.'

'Not so easy back then.'

'I guess the money makes me seem like a spoilt brat. She's not rolling in it. But she's better off than when I was a kid. We were skint back then.

Mum had several jobs and I was left a lot with our neighbour and her boys. I spent a lot of time with them.'

'What does she do, your mum?'

'Anything to pay the rent, cleaning, barmaid at the hotel down the road, serving in the shop. But really she's a painter. She's always kept a roof over our heads, but apart from that she's very single-minded. Has strong opinions. Time for painting was sacrosanct. That's why I got left to my own devices a lot. She'd be there, but not there. Out the back in a sort of shed where she painted, and I was never allowed through that door.'

'So she and Alfie would have something to talk about.'

'I guess. But she doesn't paint people. Trees a lot. The sea – and there's plenty of that. It's a bit wild, the coast where we are.'

'Hmm. Sounds a bit like the moor. I miss the moor. I'll be glad to get back.' Esther gazed away into the distance.

In the silence that followed, Alex wondered how a born-and-bred Londoner had tipped up on Dartmoor and become so attached to it. Where was she really from?

Alex tried to sound casual. 'So what was *your* mother like?'

Esther narrowed her eyes. She often did that. As if she was deciding what story to tell, what Alex was ready to hear. 'My mother? That question always makes me think of that silly schoolboy joke – when is a door not a door?'

Alex frowned. 'So, when is a door not a door?'

'When it's ajar. Groan.'

Alex also groaned. 'Of course. But what's that got to do with your mother?'

'Just – when is a mother not a mother? When she's *my* mother. It's a long story. She was never a mother in the real sense of the word. I don't talk about it. I went to a children's home, then my lovely foster mother, Auntie Em. Now, she really was a mother. Saved my bacon.'

'Oh blimey, Esther. That's a terrible story.'

'I used to think so. But no, actually it's not. I had someone who really cared about me. Lots of kids don't get that.'

Alex was quiet, twiddling a stem of grass around her finger, pulling it tight, letting it go and watching the blood flow back under the white skin.

'I can't get over all that. How much you've coped with. I sometimes complain about Mum, but now, listening to your story, I just think I was amazingly lucky. An idyllic childhood – out playing in the woods most of the time. And you're so…well, normal is what I want to say, but that sounds awful.'

Esther laughed. 'It's why I don't tell many people. I do a good job of normal. But what's that anyway? I have my shit days – ask Alfie!'

Alex nodded, not knowing what else to say.

She wanted to say that her mother was always there at the important times, always listened when things went wrong at school, rarely interfered but left Alex feeling she could cope. But it all sounded too cosy, too comfortable compared with being in a children's home.

Esther poured more tea. 'So how did your mum cope on her own with you?'

'She found her way down to Devon. Got taken in by the folk in the village. Quite a community.'

'Hmm.' Esther sounded as if she didn't believe in such a community.

'Well, I guess I was lucky.' Alex was tiring of this conversation. Esther seemed so edgy, and no wonder.

'Maybe,' Esther said, chewing the side of her thumb. 'But I bet your mother knew who your father was. Mine hadn't a clue. Or if she did, she never let on.'

'Yes, she did know. But she never told him about me and she never knew where he went to. So we have something in common.' Not that it's a competition, thought Alex.

'By the way,' Esther said after a while. 'There's a topic to keep well away from while you're with us. Never get into anything about euthanasia, assisted suicide, whatever you might fancy calling it.'

Alex started to protest at this picture of herself as a tactless loudmouth, but Esther ploughed on. 'Alfie helped his wife to die – when she couldn't face going on and becoming totally dependent. I'll not say more. He'd hate you to know. But just in case. I thought it best. Sometimes these things come up.'

'Wow, that's big.' It seemed an inadequate response. She wanted to ask more, but Esther's face told her that questions would not be answered. 'Well, just for the record, I think that's brave and amazing. Say no more.'

Esther smiled. 'Thanks,' was all she said.

13 *Naomi*

Naomi stomped out of the bar, the voices behind her abruptly eclipsed by the thud of the door and replaced by the roar of the wind down the narrow street. She turned away from the sight of the bay. Yesterday the thunder of surf on the shore had been exhilarating. Today all she saw was the jagged outline of the rock formation – giant tomes leaning against each other, satanic ledgers describing the end of creation toppling gradually and inexorably to crush the world as she knew it.

Instead she turned north towards the coast path. *The world as she knew it.* As she had tried to shape it, along with her own personality, using all those carefully learned disciplines and practices. What good were they to her now? Her calming mantra was powerless against the onslaught of the breakers pounding the cliffs. Breathe! Breathe! *I'm staying centred in the midst of conditions.* The hell she was! Who was she kidding?

It had only taken one encounter with Gordon for her poised persona to slip out of sight.

As she turned the corner onto the footpath the wind blew all sight from her eyes. She slithered, grabbed at a fence post, recovered herself. The path was slick with rain. Damn these unsuitable boots. The cliff dropped steeply away and she could hear the boom of waves in caves far below. Don't look down.

The encounter with Gordon had been so *public*. People would remember.

She'd always kept her Gordon experience apart and private. There was "Uncle Gordon" when he visited Mum on summer afternoons. He would never ignore her and she loved him for that. Mum resigned herself to this but would never join in. So it was just the two of them playing "Hide-and-Seek" or "I Spy" or "What's the Time, Mr Wolf?" until Mum got bored and reclaimed Uncle Gordon as if he were a toy Naomi had borrowed.

Then there was "Gordon-after-Mum-died". That had been totally private and had a special quality. An unspoilt quality, she wanted to say, but that gave it too much significance.

Even "Gordon-with-Meghan" had been a private thing, although less so now she'd told Meghan.

The way Gordon had behaved when Wilson was around was definitely private, as in family-private. She could not bear anyone to know how he had humiliated her and how Wilson had not prevented it.

And now these people in the pub were aware that there was a long-standing connection between her and Gordon, a link that was twisted with tension and conflict and frayed at both ends. It surprised her how bad this made her feel.

She was losing it. Mantras, meditation had all gone out the window in the excitement of setting out on this trip, in the disappointment of arriving. And forget the Relaxing Breath in that freezing hotel room. It was all very well in a candlelit room with music that tried to recreate that special Evie atmosphere, or the CD of birds in the rain forest that Fay had given her. Out here the wind brought nothing but the shriek of gulls, also known as the cries of dead sailors, drowned on the wrecking coast, not to mention the thought of sharks feeding off their bodies.

The north-westerly gale caught her again at the top of the rise, knocking her sideways onto a rocky outcrop, grazing her cheek on its rough surface. She pulled herself onward, braced now against the force of the storm, pushing forward as if against a strong tide until the path dropped to a lower level where the wind had less impact. Now came the rain, needles that stung her face and penetrated her inadequate jacket. She should turn back at this point if she wasn't intending to go to Mill End or beyond. There was the path, curling into the shelter of the valley. Before long she would have sight of the cottage. Her cottage. And yet not her cottage. The place that was to have been her sanctuary, which was now a dilemma, an embarrassment.

But she could still go there. She knew Gordon wasn't in. He was back at the bar, holding forth. He'd be there for hours. She had the right. The key was in her pocket, in the unlikely event he had locked the place. She could light the fire, make tea. Wait for the storm to pass.

Something held her back. Trespass wasn't the word. But she wasn't ready. Ready for what? When she had first arrived, she had been sure of who she was, confident, looking ahead into a new future. Now, all that positivity had disintegrated. She only had bravado left. She couldn't enter the cottage on bravado. It wouldn't stand for it. She started to retrace her steps, clutching at every rock to help her on her hazardous way.

Surprise was what she felt more than anything when she fell. No slip or stumble. Just no control, roly-polying down rough grass, catching brambles, stones sharp. Clutching turf, where's the edge? Then came the boulder. A hard stop, solid matter. Relief came before the pain of the impact hit her. Her body was still, bones heavy, and she caught her breath in the earthy smell of roots and bruised bracken. The world shrank into black soil.

When she came to, the sky was already darkening as she pieced together where she was, what had happened. She scrabbled onto her knees, but the pain in one ankle overtook the pain in her ribs and she sank back down.

She was cradled now by roots and woody plant stems and had no desire to move. It was as if she had moved back in, back into her body. A sense of everything settling into place. Just as long as she didn't try to move. She could stay here peacefully, fall asleep to the sound of the sea.

Mother Earth carry me, child I will always be.

One of the songs from her time with Evie. Most of those songs she'd found embarrassing. She'd sung along and danced, or whatever was required, but always she'd had the fear that if someone from her "regular life" were to see her, they would think she was weird, flaky, untrustworthy. But the Mother Earth song was different. She'd always found it comforting.

Mother Earth carry me, back to the sea.

The words brought with them the rich colours of the yurt – the sapphire tapestry by the door, the azure and indigo stripes of her bedcover, Evie's violet-blue eyes and the soporific aroma of incense. She longed to sink into sleep. But now she was shivering. Even though the wind had stopped howling and the boom of breakers below had ceased. How long had she been here? What time was it? Panic took over from the peace she'd been feeling and jolted some survival instinct into action. She could die out here overnight. That would serve Gordon right. As if that mattered. Must work something out. Maybe she could worm her way back up the slope on her tummy, dragging the ankle. Truth was, she was fearful of leaving the safety of the boulder that had stopped her fall. She levered herself into a sitting position, leant back on the rock and tried calling out. Her voice was more feeble than the most distant gulls' cries. Again she tried to get onto hands and knees but the pain was too much. She sank back, exhausted, and relaxed into the vibrant dyes and embroideries of the yurt and the comfort of Evie's eyes gazing down at her.

14 *Meghan*

Meghan dumped the shopping and slumped beside it, fielding tomatoes as they escaped the bag and rolled across the table.

Rita had caught up with her in the greengrocer's in Stagworthy that afternoon as she gathered peppers, courgettes and a flawless purple aubergine.

'Ratatouille, is it?'

Meghan fingered the aubergine. 'Always think these are too beautiful to eat.'

Rita grunted. 'I saw that woman was round at yours again.'

'Ah, Naomi.'

'Oh, Naomi, is it now?'

'Well, it's her name, is all.' Meghan grabbed a bunch of carrots, brushing the feathery leaves against her cheek.

'My! Look at the price of those!' Rita deliberately turned to the tray of old carrots, selected several carrots and dropped them into her bag.

'Tasty, though,' Meghan said.

Rita shrugged as if taste was the least of her considerations. 'So, not "that woman" any more.'

'She actually came to apologise. Realised she'd been a bit out of order the other day.'

'That's something, I suppose.'

'We ended up having a good laugh, as it happens.'

'Whatever was funny?'

Her narrative skidded to a halt under Rita's beady-eyed look. She was not about to spill the beans of her sexual encounters with Gordon.

'I'm not sure.' She picked out a handful of mushrooms. 'You know how it is, sometimes you end up laughing about nothing…'

In the early days of their friendship, Rita would always twitch her lips at what she called Meghan's promiscuity, although that had to be the exaggeration of all time. Stagworthy in the eighties – or ever, come to that – presented precious little opportunity to be promiscuous. Apart from the occasional one-night stand with a hotel guest, Gordon had been that opportunity.

'Oh,' she said, dropping the mushrooms into a paper bag. 'I know what started it. She recognised my old chair. You know, the red one? I got it from Mill End when they threw it out and she remembered it. It was funny, her getting so wound up over a chair.'

Rita rolled her eyes. 'Sounds hilarious.'

They moved on down the shop.

'So she knows them – the folks at Mill End?'

'Seems she was there that summer when all sorts went on.'

'That might be interesting. Get her to tell you all about what exactly did go on. I always wondered.'

'Long time ago now. Anyway she's off home. Tomorrow, I think she said.'

Before Rita could pursue the question of why Naomi was visiting, Meghan moved to the till to pay and chat to her friend, Jo, who ran the shop.

Having tamed the escaping tomatoes, she unpacked the rest of the vegetables, made them into a pattern and realised she had no desire to cook them. She pushed back from the table, assessing her gloomy mood.

So Rita was, for some unknown reason, taking the hump. That always cast a shadow until they were back on good terms. Surely she wasn't jealous of Naomi? Peeved at missing out on the encounter, more likely. But it did seem that Naomi caused ripples. For Meghan it was an anti-climax to have shared that crazy laughter and to know Naomi was leaving – there would be no chance to follow it up. Two good reasons for feeling at sixes and sevens. Then again, she had heard nothing from Alex since she transferred money into her daughter's account. Not exactly a worry, but nagging all the time at the back of her mind. And her painting was going absolutely nowhere. No wonder she felt low.

She could do nothing about Naomi or Alex, and Rita would get over it. But the painting was in her control. It was demanding attention.

After half an hour or so she had to admit that the painting was not in her control. She stood back from the easel and turned abruptly away from it.

'Bloody useless.' She made herself face the canvas again.

Half a dozen rooks were taking off from the bare branches of a tree – a cacophony of black feathers lifting through a tracery of twigs. It was accurate. She'd studied the damn birds long enough. But it was dead. There was movement, yes. But it wasn't alive. Anything she did now would only make it worse.

There was only one thing for it. Marmite toast. Cut it thin, wave it around to cool it off, lashings of cold butter, a good smear of the brown stuff. She took her treat out to the bench under the apple tree, catching the warmth of intermittent sun, munching, savouring the perfect mix of flavours and textures.

Why paint? Why bother with so much complexity when something so simple was there for the asking?

A flutter and scuffling caught her attention. A rook had landed on top of the fence and was eying her sideways. Birds from the nearby rookery often landed in the garden and strutted about in the grass, ignoring her. This one was giving her his (or her?) full attention. What was that about? Protesting at the thought she might abandon his portrait? Or greedy for toast? 'Don't even think of it,' she told the bird, taking a large bite. Did corvids even like Marmite? Interesting question. She lobbed a corner in the bird's direction and after a moment it dropped down onto the grass and took it in its beak. Instantly dropped it and fiercely stabbed its beak into the earth, wiping it back and forth on the grass.

Meghan laughed out loud. 'Fancy not liking Marmite! But then, lots of people don't.'

The rook was on the fence again, one foot lifted, giving her the eye. Its head feathers were snug as a hoodie round the pale face of its beak and eye, their iridescence glinting in the sun. So handsome. So purposeful. It paraded along the fence, turned and came back to survey her once more.

She met its gaze. A powerful eye, all encompassing, reducing her to a pinpoint at the same time as making her the focus of its universe. Although she didn't move, its magnetic force seemed to draw her closer and closer so that the trees, the daisied grass and the nettles along the fence faded into a blur. For a moment reality – or time and place and consciousness, or whatever reality consists of – flipped inside out and she was sharing the perspective of the awe-inspiring bird on the fence.

Just for a second.

Then the garden came back into focus, the rook took flight and Meghan brushed toast crumbs from her jumper.

She eyed her canvas on her way back inside. She knew what it needed. That eye. But which bird? She would let it mull and all would become clear. But the rook seemed to be giving her a bigger message. In her experience the birds didn't make visits like that for nothing. So she fetched the Tarot cards. Not her grandmother's traditional pack but the new set of round cards she'd stumbled across in a charity shop in Barnstaple a few years back – a feminist Tarot. She still remembered how strangely the elderly saleswoman had looked at her as she paid.

Meghan didn't call herself a feminist, mainly because labels of that sort tended to invite people to take up a hostile position or to attach to the label a collection of values that she didn't necessarily share. A minefield. Nor had it occurred to her that the traditional Tarot could be seen as oppressive. Not until she found the round cards and the booklet that accompanied them. It pointed out how the traditional Tarot supported a patriarchal system, encouraging judgemental attitudes and suppression of feminine values. By contrast, the feminist system celebrated creativity and sexuality as positive energy.

She decided on a full layout and placed the cards face down on the table. The question? What was Naomi doing in her life? As she turned them over, she was astonished at the amount of fiery energy and light in the cards. They seemed to light up the room. Surprise followed surprise – from the gloriously yellow and over-arching Sun to the upside-down figure of the Hanged One re-inventing herself. It could not have been a more transformational reading.

Most cards were from the suit of Wands – for fire and creativity. They danced across the table in scenes of women working, healing and dancing together. One card in the challenging suit of Air showed women leaping over a cliff, which Meghan supposed represented a new beginning.

Everywhere – in the angle of the cards – Meghan saw hesitation, a holding back, ambivalence, which fitted with what she'd observed of Naomi. Similarly, the presence of just two Major Arcana cards indicated a pause, a waiting period. Fascinating.

And what of her own position with regard to the reading? 'A new era.' The words slipped out. What? Naomi might be creating ripples in her life, but a new era? That was going a bit far. Alex and her baby would bring in a new era, for sure. But nothing to do with Naomi. She studied the layout again and noticed a confrontation between two of the women, which she had so far managed to ignore. Was that supposed to be her and Naomi? She could well imagine such a scene and, not being one to give in easily, it made her smile. 'Bring it on,' she muttered.

Outside, a bevy of rooks was making a racket, rising and falling across the valley and back again, having some sort of stand-off. She felt infected by their restlessness and reminded of the work to be done on her painting.

Laying out the cards had proved – as ever – unsettling, but gave her a buzz of excitement. Her life was satisfactory – she was at last earning enough to give herself space to paint what she wanted on at least one day in the week. But a disruption to the routine wouldn't go amiss. Alex's arrival would certainly provide that in the short term, but after a while Alex would settle to her own independent life.

She shook herself, drank a glass of water and gathered up the cards. Meanwhile, there was Rita. Some damage limitation was required. She grabbed a nearly full bottle of Merlot and set off across the road.

Rita faced her, hands on hips in the doorway. 'So that's what you weren't telling me! Your friend Naomi inheriting Mill End! But not being able to move in!'

Meghan presented the bottle of wine, wondering if she'd be allowed in. 'Peace offering?'

Rita relented and fetched glasses. It turned out that she'd called in at the pub with a fresh batch of leaflets advertising her holiday cottages.

'That man Gordon was banging on – pretty well-oiled he was – so it's common knowledge now. That Naomi was looking pretty peeved.'

'Sorry, Rita. Yes, she did tell me. But she asked me not to spread it.'

Rita snorted. 'I think I'm a bit more discreet than that Gordon.'

'Oh, Rita! Of course you are. Forgive?'

Before Rita could reply, they both heard a muffled thump and crash from the next room.

'What the dickens?' Rita shot off and was back in seconds. 'It's one of your damn birds. Can't catch it, it's up on the ceiling. It'll make such a mess. Go on! You try.'

Meghan dived across the hall. 'First rule, shut the damn door,' she called back to Rita, closing the door softly and adding 'idiot woman' under her breath.

The bird eyed her from its perch on top of a wall cabinet. As she waited, it fluttered down onto the table and from there onto the windowsill, where it deposited a modest pile of poo and looked round expectantly.

As she approached, it started strutting and posturing, its wings like defensive elbows as if anticipating and warding off any attempt to catch it.

Of all people, Meghan reckoned she had given more than the usual attention to the meaning of the words "black" and "feather". But she now saw that she hadn't begun to peel away the layers of complexity behind them. Someone could do a PhD on the plumage of the jackdaw. Maybe they already had. But how on earth could she get anywhere near rendering the wonder of it in paint?

The feathers! The black gloss of them, the way they caught the light, the way they were both delicate and muscular. She longed to gather the bird in her hands, just to know how it would feel. But that would achieve nothing. She moved to the other end of the windowsill. The bird folded its wings, still looking expectant. The casement opened easily and it hopped towards the opening. The bird gave her one last look, which seemed to say, What took you so long? Then it positively strolled onto the outside window ledge and took off into the garden.

Meghan scrabbled in her pockets for a tissue and removed the pile of poo, which had already left a pale stain on Rita's paintwork. She fastened the window and checked the room for breakages and more mess. There was nothing. The jackdaw had been the most intelligent and courteous of visitors. But that wasn't what Rita would want to hear.

'All done and dusted,' she announced in the kitchen, where Rita was well into her second glass of wine.

'Beastly birds! They give me the heebie-jeebies, hanging about like thugs in their hoodies.' She shuddered. 'That cowl will be going on first thing tomorrow, come what may, Harry Jenkins. Nuisance is one thing. Breaking and entering, that's too much.'

'Clever, though. It knew just what I needed to do…'

'Fiddlesticks! Or maybe they really do have cunning criminal minds. That cowl would have gone on last week if it hadn't been for you.'

Meghan held up her hands. 'Sorry, Rita. I'm grateful. I've got some great sketches – and there's no harm done.'

Rita grunted. 'Anyway, where were we before we were so rudely interrupted? That Naomi, that's where we were.' Her tone put Naomi almost on a par with the jackdaw when it came to intruders.

Meghan tried being conciliatory. 'That woman does get to me in a funny sort of way.'

'I know what you mean, actually,' Rita said. 'I keep finding she's on my mind. Odd really. And she's certainly ruffled your feathers.'

'Anyway, she's off tomorrow. And if and when she does move into the cottage, there's no reason we'll see much of her at all.' Meghan didn't for a moment believe that, not after the message of the Tarot, but it was what Rita wanted to hear.

'I'll drink to that. Then we can settle back into life as we like it. Now, have I told you about Mike and his new girlfriend? Wait a sec.'

As Rita stretched into the back of a cupboard, Meghan steeled herself to hear the latest on Rita's younger son.

'Here, would you believe? A bag of crisps that's escaped Harry's foraging.'

15 *Naomi*

She was enchanted, held her breath. The amber fox in Evie's wall-hanging had come to life. It had nosed its way out of the appliquéd bracken and was stepping towards her. It nudged her sharply in the ribs and the pain snapped her out of her dream. Naomi's mind clicked slowly into the context of where she was, like tumblers falling into place in a combination lock. No, she wasn't being befriended by a curious fox, merely being woken by an over-enthusiastic dog. How long had she been here? The light was fading, but it was a dull day. The cold nose and wet tongue stopped nudging her and she could hear the animal brushing through undergrowth. A dog. Where there was a dog, there was usually an owner. She managed a croak and tried again but failed to turn up the volume. Useless. She pushed herself upright. Everything ached – sharp pain in the ribs; right leg numb, turning to piercing pins and needles. Agony around the left ankle. The dog was back, but only briefly. A Labrador. Teasing. Or maybe not. A heavy tread vibrated through the ground, the sound of a skid and a scramble. 'Shit,' said a male voice.

Then, 'Ah, I see you now. Well done, Rubes, good girl.' The dog being made a fuss of before attention turned to her. Questions. Answers. 'I won't attempt to move you. Be as quick as I can.' He unzipped his coat and laid it on top of her, told the dog to stay. She wasn't sure whether the coat was for her benefit or the dog's.

The dog whined softly as the man was swallowed by the gloom, then settled with its nose on its paws. She ignored it, afraid that it would knock into the painful end of her leg, and pulled the coat tighter around herself. She hadn't recognised the man as any of those who'd been in the bar earlier.

The light was fading as she heard a noisy party approaching, a tall figure in the lead. Various exchanges floated on the wind.

'We're almost at the spot, just round the next bend.'

'Some bloody silly visitor, no doubt.'

'Shut up, Gordon.'

Damn, she could do without him.

Shapes materialised. That tall figure in the lead must be Gavin. Hefty arms hauled her upright. She found her voice then, bellowing at the pain in the dangling ankle.

'Some caterwauling!' Gordon again.

'Sorry,' she heard herself say.

'You yell all you like, lady,' came another voice.

'Support the foot,' someone else said, followed by 'Good girl, Ruby.' Must be her rescuer.

Somehow they got her up to the path and onto a length of fabric that had been laid out on the ground.

'Introducing the Stagworthy Quay patented stretcher,' Gavin told her. 'Constructed some years ago under similar circumstances. You see, you are not the first, my dear.'

They started unsteadily along the path, which was of uneven width. One minute she was lying precariously on a flat bed consisting of a hammock slung on curtain poles, afraid of being bounced off the edge. The next she was at the bottom of a canvas valley with the poles almost meeting above her head. That felt safer, enclosed, cocooned.

Gordon's voice again: 'If you wanted to end it all, you should have gone another fifty yards. Sheer drop here.'

'For Chrissakes, Gordon, shut up.'

'Just trying to lighten the mood. Wonder how long the ambulance will take. They won't like it that we've moved the patient.'

'By the time they arrive she could have died of hypothermia.'

'Now who's being cheerful?'

And so they processed towards the harsh light and exposure of the bar.

16 *Meghan*

Back at home, Meghan reflected on Rita's phrase "ruffled your feathers". It was especially apt, given her current obsession with painting birds. Rita was intent on smoothing ruffled feathers or protecting them from being ruffled – protecting the status quo. But Meghan was only too willing to have her feathers ruffled. In fact the phrase itself had given her an idea. She rushed into her studio and pulled out several of the umbrella pictures Naomi had unearthed. She lined them up along the wall and added a selection of paintings and sketches of crows, rooks and jackdaws. The shapes and colours were arresting in their similarities and contrasts. Almost a coherent progression. An exhibition. Possibly? Could it be?

Her thoughts were interrupted by the telephone.

Gavin's voice came down the line, tense and abrupt. 'Can you get down here pronto? There's been an accident on the coast path. Need everyone to help me with the stretcher. Nobody left behind to serve. Can you fill in behind the bar?'

'I'm on my way.'

She hung up and gave a last lingering look at the display of pictures before striding out of the door and leaping onto her bike, pausing only at Rita's door to pass on the news. It would not do to leave her out of the loop twice in one day. The gale was funnelling down the street outside the hotel, and she chained her bike to a ring once used for horses – a precaution against the wind rather than thieves.

Inside she found Colin's wife, fumbling with the Jameson's optic to make Irish coffee for some tourists.

'Blimey, Doreen, they'll be singing about goblins before we know it!'

'You'd better take over. Colin and everyone rushed out the door. And I haven't got a clue.' Doreen's hand shook, nearly spilling the liquid she had measured out. 'Not being a drinker,' she added in that flat voice of hers.

'Thanks. Here, pour that lot into a cup for yourself. Must be a triple at least, but you look as if you could do with it. Strictly medicinal. Any idea who the casualty is?'

Doreen shrugged. 'Some woman. It was a stranger came in with the news. His dog found the body.'

'Body? Not as in dead?'

'Probably not. No, I think he said unconscious.' Doreen sounded almost disappointed.

'Was Eddie one of the party?'

'No, he was in here earlier, but he'd gone home. Not answering his phone.'

'Never a doctor when you need one. Let's hope the ambulance isn't long.'

Doreen sipped her coffee and coughed. 'That's a bit…'

'Do you good. Like I said, medicinal.'

Meghan had her work cut out clearing tables, washing glasses and cleaning up behind the bar. Doreen was preoccupied with her 40%-proof medicinal coffee, so Meghan roped in the tourists to line up some tables in the alcove to make a bed for the stretcher. She was back behind the bar when a hullabaloo announced the arrival of the stretcher party. Shouts of: 'Hold it right back, can't you?' 'Hold the damn thing level!' 'Right a bit your end!' 'Mind the patient, dammit!' and 'For Chrissakes, Gordon!' interrupted each other as the men rattled and scuffled their way inside.

She made her way over as the men settled the makeshift stretcher and stepped away. A jolt of recognition went through her, a surge of panic. That profile, it was Naomi. She bent forward and stroked her hand, felt her forehead. Very much alive. Eyes flickered open and closed again. Meghan let go of the breath she'd been holding.

'Naomi? Can you hear me? You're going to be okay. In fact, I can hear the ambulance now. You're going to be okay, my friend.'

Yes. That was true. It was the first she knew it, but Naomi was indeed her friend.

The paramedics interrupted an argument, led by Gordon, about whether brandy should be administered to the patient.

Gordon resolved it by administering a large measure to himself and drew Meghan aside. 'It's all my fault. I upset her. This afternoon. She stormed off.'

Meghan was surprised to see tears in his eyes. 'Rubbish. That makes no sense at all. She's going to be absolutely fine.' She gestured to the activity around Naomi and put a hand on his arm. 'They'll sort her out in no time, you old softie.'

'Don't you want to know who it was got rescued?' Meghan leaned on Rita's gate, munching on a slice of toast and honey. 'Hey, Rita!' she added as Rita closed her kitchen window and disappeared from view.

What had she done now? Meghan approached the front door and wondered whether to knock or to open it and call out. But at that moment Rita burst through it.

'You closed the window on me!'

'Closed it because I was going out. And I already heard – that Naomi woman, wasn't it? Giving more trouble to more people. I bumped into Colin when I fetched the papers.'

With a rattle of keys, Rita unlocked her Mini and climbed in looking decidedly po-faced. 'Colin told me you were up to all hours fixing her up to use Patrick's annexe. That was beyond the call of duty.'

Meghan took a breath. 'Well it was clear she couldn't come back to the hotel, up those stairs and so on. Someone had to do something.'

'And it had to be you.'

'I just happened to be there and...'

Rita slammed the car door and wound down the window. 'Or was it the chance of getting to see Patrick? Now, *that* I could understand.'

'Oh, Rita, that finished ages ago. Anyway, I told you, it never was a thing.'

'Whatever a "thing" might be.' Rita shook her head, relenting slightly.

'I was just being practical – Patrick's got the ideal set-up. It was worth asking. Problem solved.'

'Well, good for you. But I must be off. They've got a blocked toilet at number six and I'm going to stop by Melvyn's and persuade him to come with me.'

Meghan grinned. 'Good luck with bypassing Mrs M!' Melvyn was the local plumber, who would be only too willing to oblige, but whose wife guarded Sunday as the day when her husband got jobs done at home.

Rita pulled away. 'I'll call in when I get back.'

Meghan decided it was late enough to ring Patrick and see if his new lodger had indeed returned from the hospital and was in residence. It was nice to be back in touch with him. Just as a friend. They'd had a fling during the time Meghan had cleaned for Patrick. His wife had died the year before, and they had helped each other through a difficult time. No more, no less. Rita had wanted her safely married to Patrick, and couldn't understand that marrying anyone was the last thing Meghan wanted to do.

17 *Naomi*

At nine o'clock there was a knock at the door. Naomi pulled the zip on her dressing gown a little closer to her chin, picked up the book, which was splayed on the covers, and said, 'Come in,' her voice croaking annoyingly because she hadn't yet used it that morning.

The door swung open a few inches; there was a pause, a gentle kick, and a man she dimly remembered was called Patrick appeared in jeans and a crisp white shirt, carrying a tray.

'Morning! Morning! You're probably starving but I didn't want to interrupt earlier in case you were still asleep.' He set the tray on the table in the window and turned to her.

'How was it, the night? How's it feeling? Hungry?'

'I slept amazingly. Ankle feels fine. And I have to confess, yes, I'm hungry.'

Patrick was rearranging her bedside table. 'Trays in bed are hopeless,' he said.

Naomi couldn't believe her luck that this man, Patrick, had evidently invited her to use his quirky little annexe. It was a lot more convenient than the hotel and she tried not to worry about money, which hadn't been mentioned. In fact, nothing much had been said at all. She had simply arrived in the dark, been introduced to Patrick Sullivan in the lobby and transferred swiftly to the bed, still swimming in the effects of morphine.

Naomi set her book aside and watched as Patrick pulled the table forward and transferred items from the tray. Sunlight reflected off his glasses and caught the crinkly strands of hair that refused to succumb to an otherwise neat cut.

'There. Can you reach it all? I'll pour the coffee. Milk?'

Naomi dragged her attention to the practicalities. 'No. No milk, thanks. I never take it.'

She heard her voice crack and felt tears pricking her eyes at the sight of a boiled egg in a blue-striped eggcup and slices of toast on a willow pattern plate.

'Hey! What's up?'

'Oh, Patrick! Nothing. It's just… You're being so incredibly kind. I couldn't imagine… I feel so helpless…'

'Well, that's just it. You *are* helpless!'

'Just thank you.'

'I tell you, I won't be doing this forever. Just until you can get about in the kitchen – if you can call it that. As soon as they say you can manage, I'll get you supplies in.' He backed off towards the door and gave her a cheery wave. 'Right-o. I must be getting on. Don't worry, bound to be a bit emotional with all those drugs.'

And he was gone. Naomi knew it wasn't the drugs. Partly it was being helpless. She hated not being in control. It made her cross and that made her cry. But mostly it was being so thoughtfully cared for. She sliced the top off the egg and found the white firm and the yolk just the right amount of runny. She really could cope with the dishy Patrick doing this forever. Stop it, she told herself. The last thing you want at this stage in your life is a relationship with another man to create mayhem down the line. And anyway, you might not be old enough to be his mother, but, even so, he must be at least ten years younger.

If only he hadn't had his sleeves rolled back. She kept seeing his hairy forearm as he poured the coffee. Why did she find that so sexy? Don't go there. She spread butter and dipped into the home-made marmalade, eating greedily. The coffee was the best she'd tasted for a long time. And she was pretty sure that wasn't the forearm effect. Stick with the coffee. Much safer.

When Naomi woke, Meghan was standing in the doorway. It took her a moment or two of wondering where she was and how Meghan came to be there.

'Sorry to wake you. Patrick seemed to think you'd be up to receiving the odd visitor.'

'Blimey, I went out like a light. What's the time?'

'Coffee time. Fancy some? I'll bring it in.'

Meghan disappeared. Naomi found her watch. She'd slept for well over an hour – and deeply, as she saw there was no sign of the breakfast things.

Meghan returned with a cafetière and mugs. 'So, did I do all right? Setting you up here?'

'I was wondering. You did this? How, what, where? I remember Gavin meeting the hospital transport and leading the way in the hotel van. He even poked his nose in the ambulance to say hi, but when I asked him what was happening, he just said not to worry and it would all be clear in the morning. Somebody tucked me up and that was the last I knew until this morning.'

'How are you managing with the crutches?'

'I got to the bathroom with the Zimmer, only a few hops. And there was my bag and my stuff – like magic. Then this dishy man brought me a wonderful breakfast.'

Meghan grinned and raised an eyebrow. 'Faculties still working, then. Not just a dish. Patrick's a thoroughly nice guy.'

'But how come I'm here? It's not a guest house, is it?' Why were these people doing this for her?

'Well, it was clear they couldn't cope with you at the hotel – not with all this.' Meghan waved at Naomi's plaster cast. 'I knew this place was empty. Not a guest house. Patrick had his mother here until she died – and no, not in that bed. She had to go to the hospice in the end, poor love. So I just phoned Patrick. My neighbour, Rita, might have had you in her dining room – and I could have popped in and out.'

'But Rita absolutely loathes me.'

'How do you work that one out?'

'You should see the looks she gives me from her kitchen window.'

Meghan gave a half laugh. 'That's just Rita. Don't go getting paranoid. You'll get used to her. But, Rita aside, well, let's just say I thought you'd prefer a bit more privacy.'

Naomi was grateful she'd been spared the opportunity to get used to Rita. 'I – I don't know what to say. That you've taken so much trouble. And you hardly know me. I just can't begin to…'

'Forget it.' Meghan gazed across at her as she slowly pressed the plunger into the coffee. 'It's what we do. We're a community and we look after each other.'

Such a penetrating look. Naomi felt she was being carefully appraised. The intense moment – had she imagined it? – passed as Meghan handed her a mug. Emma Bridgewater. Colourful spots. Nice.

'Tell you what, I'll tell you a story,' Meghan said. 'Liz was my best mate at art college. One night she burst into my room in tears, waving a half-bottle of vodka and saying, "There are no giants." Giants, as in our code of special men who stood head and shoulders above the rest, who would meet our every need and make us happy ever after. Our little fantasy! Anyway, Liz thought she'd found one in Graphic Design, but he'd just dumped her.

'So, we got royally pissed and coined the phrase *There are no giants*, which we would hiss at each other in a stage whisper when either of us met the other in the company of a bloke.'

Naomi nodded, wondering where this story was going. 'With you so far.'

'The thing is, we were looking in the wrong place. Barking up the wrong beanstalk, if you like.'

'Certainly a fairy tale – the giants, I mean.'

'Exactly. It's the ordinary small people that matter. You know, when you're having a bad day, and then there's a stranger who smiles. Or you share a joke with the checkout person at the supermarket; they're the ones that make a difference. Know what I mean?' Meghan looked out of the window. 'It could be a tree, even. Or a bird.'

Naomi grunted. 'Hmm. Couldn't agree more about the giants. But not sure about the rest. I mean, lurching from one random scrap of kindness to the next?' She shook her head. 'I just see myself falling into the cracks in between.'

'Ah, but there's good stuff in the cracks.'

'Or shit, in my case.'

'Yes, shit too.'

'Sorry to be so negative. Everything's so uncertain. Hate not being in control. No amount of jollying along is going to change that. I mean, how many friendly strangers am I likely to come across?'

'I thought you already met one at breakfast.'

Naomi managed a smile. 'So I did.'

'There are, of course, rituals to carry you over the cracks. Mind you, I'm a fine one to talk. I know perfectly well what helps, but I don't do it. Occasional yoga, maybe.'

Naomi grunted again and said nothing. She knew plenty of rituals, but there were currently none in her life beyond the brewing of coffee and the opening of a bottle of wine. She didn't think that was what Meghan had in mind.

'Just lately,' Meghan was saying. 'My default is sitting under a tree.'

Naomi grinned. 'I might manage that. Trouble is, my friend Evie had a lot of blooming rituals. Sometimes I used to think they were a substitute for life. But then again she did use them to help other people – including me. I think they *became* her life.'

'I suppose that's just another way to be.' Meghan shook her head. 'Who knows? Sorry if I was banging on. I was just trying to describe how it works in the village full of ordinary people.'

'Ah! I see where you're going. You get rescued if you fall into a crack.'

Meghan laughed. 'I actually hadn't thought of that. But you said it. Exactly.'

Naomi recalled the voices of the night before during her progress on the stretcher. People looking after her. Kind strangers. She had to wipe her eyes and Meghan fetched some kitchen paper.

'Looking after me. When I don't even belong... I'm so grateful, and I do see what you mean. Not like me to get emotional.' She blew her nose and gulped some coffee.

Then she continued in more practical vein. 'But one thing is worrying me – and that's how much it's going to cost, living in the lap of luxury like this. I mean, it could be some time – this is just a temporary cast, until the swelling goes down and they can operate.'

'Ah. Well, one thing it will cost you is that you'll become part of our little community. Up to you, of course. Don't look so alarmed. You won't be required to do the church flowers. As to Patrick, it's up to him but he's a generous soul. And you do have the advantage of being a friend of mine.'

Naomi glowed. Meghan said that so easily, as if their friendship was long-established. Tears threatened again. 'People are being so kind.' She took a breath. 'Tell me about Patrick. How long's he been here?'

'About ten years permanently, but he came for weekends yonks before, when he still had a practice in London. Hampstead, I believe, somewhere rich, anyway.'

'Practice?'

'Oh, he's an osteopath. Thought you knew, but why would you? Still sees people – he's got a consulting room on the other side of the house.'

'So not in here. I'm not…?'

'No, he built this for a studio for his wife. She was a painter – the abstracts in the hall. But she died and then his mother moved in when she got frail. He hasn't had a fun time.'

'That's sad. So he had a wife.'

'Still misses her, I guess. No one since. Lots of people – people who didn't know her – think he's gay. But he certainly isn't.'

Naomi had wondered that herself and was glad she hadn't said so. 'You sound very sure.'

'I used to clean for him. We came to an arrangement. Suited us both for a few months. We were very discreet. Then, when he was nursing his mother, I used to come up here to see her. But by then neither of us felt inclined. It wouldn't have felt right, anyway, in the circumstances.'

Naomi nodded. So much to take in. About Patrick. About Meghan. 'And what about the man who found me? With the dog. That wasn't Patrick, was it?'

'No – just a visitor – giving his dog a walk before heading back to the Midlands apparently. He didn't hang around.' Meghan glanced at her watch, took the rubber band off her wrist and gathered her hair into a ponytail. 'So, now tell me,' she continued. 'What happened? How did you fall? They say you stormed out. What was that about? It set me wondering what was in your mind.'

'*They* say, do they?' Naomi covered her face with her hands at the thought of being talked about. Bloody Gordon! 'I had a spat with Gordon. He was intent on telling the whole world our business. I just hate that! Had to get away.'

'But where were you going?'

'Just out. Into the weather. Did I have to have a reason? I just…' She trailed off. Meghan was watching her again, eyes narrowed. Her witchy look. 'Oh! You didn't think I *meant* to fall? That's not what they're saying, is it?'

'One or two people were speculating. I didn't think it very likely, but then I wasn't there. I don't know you very well, but you don't strike me as someone who'd do something so uncertain and uncomfortable.'

Naomi laughed out loud. 'Too right. No. I'd had enough by then – I was heading back and thinking I'd have a nice hot bath.'

'Even so, falling always means something. In my experience.'

'Slippery path, unsuitable boots?'

Meghan nodded. 'Of course, but above and beyond. Just something you might want to think about.' She crossed the room and paused at the window. 'I knew something was going to happen this week. The rooks have been going crazy.'

Naomi started a question but Meghan continued.

'The ones in my head as well as the real ones. I never told you, of course. Remember you dug out those umbrella pictures? When you were being nosy and intrusive? Well it did me a favour. I had an idea and I think it might be quite exciting.'

'You were furious. And I did feel bad. But what do umbrellas have to do with rooks?'

'Can't say any more. Never works to talk about it. But trust me, there's a connection. I just wanted to let you know. A thank you, I suppose, for doing something that made me mad at the time. Sometimes I can be too quick to judge.' She smiled across at Naomi. 'Anyway, I need to get on. Due at the hotel. Patrick's going to take you to the fracture clinic tomorrow, by the way. Best take your overnight bag. They might keep you in for surgery.'

Meghan was suddenly brisk and suddenly gone.

Naomi was still staring at the door when she reappeared. 'Forgot to say, Gordon wasn't one of those imagining you might have jumped. Said you were far too obstinate, and determined to give him a hard time. The thing was, he said it with real affection.' She grinned. 'You're a dark horse.' And she was gone again.

'Dark horse, yourself,' Naomi said, as the front door slammed. She smiled down at her hands. A hum of excitement went through her. Like when she'd stood at the edge of the wood and had run down the hill to the ocean. Was that really only four days ago? Here she was, laid up far from home, unable to walk, let alone run. But she felt so… Yes, that was it. She felt happy.

18 *Naomi*

Needs washing, thought Naomi as she dragged a brush through her hair and coiled it into its usual bird's nest. She heard the front door and supposed it was Meghan dropping in as she often did on her way to whatever work she was doing. Naomi had told her to use the Land Rover to stop the battery going flat and the arrangement suited them both.

Her door burst open with hardly a knock. 'I've got Gordon waiting outside,' Meghan said.

'Here? Now? That's a bit sudden.'

'He said not to give you time to think about it.'

'Blimey, Meghan! And you colluded. Obviously.'

'Hold your horses. You can say no. But he also said, he comes in peace.' Meghan held out a scrap of paper, torn from a diary, with the word *PEACE* scrawled across it. 'Go on, Naomi, why not? You know you've got to talk. Now's as good a time as any.'

'Looks like I've got no choice. And it's wet. Can't even go outside.'

'Shall I make you coffee?'

'Certainly not! He can make his own. Here, pull that chair out – no, a bit further away. Are you coming back for him?'

'Said he'd walk. The rain's beginning to clear.'

Naomi settled into her chair with the cast supported on a footstool. 'Let him in, then.'

Meghan vanished, to be replaced by the turbulence of Gordon, shaking rain off his jacket and greeting her effusively. Naomi gestured at the empty chair before he could get close enough for an embrace.

'At last, Naomi! At last. I've been wanting to see you, but everyone said you needed space.' He looked around the room, bent to peer into the kitchen area. 'Seems you have plenty of it here. You've struck it lucky. All very jammy.'

'People have been very good.'

'Especially Patrick?'

Naomi swallowed her irritation. 'Well, yes. Patrick, obviously. Anyway, you are right. We do need to talk.'

She watched the nervous puff of his chest relax. Taking it on board, she hoped, that teasing her about Patrick was hardly coming in peace.

'I always seem to rub you up the wrong way. It's not my intention...'

'It used to be your intention. When Wilson was around. Before Wilson, we were pretty good friends, I thought. Remember? After my mother's funeral?'

'Ah, Immo. Yes. You were very understanding, I seem to remember. And then I went and introduced you to my damn brother. I really believed he was running a straightforward outfit and that it would get you away. You needed to get away from that husband...'

'Yes. Out of the frying pan and all that. But Wilson had his points. He wasn't as bad as Tony.'

'More subtle, maybe. But still a bastard of the first water. And you were taken in. That's what really got to me. That you fell for him. Not just for his methods – all that infernal navel-gazing – but for his charm.' He leant back in his chair. 'Huh! Reminds me of when we were kids and he'd suggest we swap sweets. I always ended up with the green fruit gums while he nabbed my best gobstopper. Fell for it every time. That was his trick – good-looking, clever, the golden younger child who could do no wrong, and me, the carroty big brother. But that was the thing – you fell for that charm. You – Immo's daughter – and you fell for him like any bimbo...'

'Thanks a bunch, Gordon. I thought you came in peace.'

'I do. I do. Don't you see? I was so disappointed in you. I was afraid you were turning out just like the worst side of your mother – serial lovers and so on.' He stood up and walked to the window, staring out at the rain. 'Plus, of course, I was bloody jealous. Of Wilson. I fancied you myself – like mad. Of course I did. But I didn't even think of it. Well, obviously I did. For a nanosecond. It was unthinkable. Incest of the first order.'

Naomi sat staring at his profile until he finally looked round at her.

'I seem to have rendered you speechless. That's a first.'

'I just don't know what to say. I thought you hated me. Never understood why.'

Gordon spread his hands and slowly shook his head.

Naomi shifted her leg into a more comfortable position. 'So why didn't you support me? You were always undermining...'

'Didn't dare get anywhere close – for the reason given.' He sank back into the chair. 'Plus I was always a bit scared of my damn brother, how he might retaliate. All I could do was stir it up. Try to break it up, get you away from him. I don't think I helped.'

'You didn't.'

He sank forward, head in hands. 'What can I do?'

'Right now you could make a pot of strong coffee. It's all round the corner in the kitchen, by the kettle.'

She watched him walk away. A little unsteady. But upright. He hadn't fallen into that old-man gait, weight shifting from side to side. It was odd to have him waiting on her. What a fool she'd been over Wilson. She already knew that, but here it was coming back at her from Gordon's viewpoint, bringing another wave of self-loathing. Waste of time. Don't go there. She could hear him filling the kettle, opening and closing cupboards to find what he wanted. Out of her window, small white clouds like shreds of Kleenex were scudding high above the trees, leaving a paler grey sky in their wake. Everything was dripping and she wished she was out there scooping raindrops onto her face, into her hair.

'How long do you reckon you'll be here?' Gordon was saying from the kitchen.

'Weeks! I was at the fracture clinic yesterday and it's still too swollen to operate. That will probably happen next week, if I keep the damn thing elevated most of the time.'

Gordon set down the coffee pot. 'You are having a rough time.' He pottered back to fetch mugs and sat down opposite her. 'Poor old girl. First me in the cottage and now this.'

He meant well but his expression of remorse mixed with concern made her want to scream. Instead she said, 'At least you could open the window!' It came out more forcefully than she'd intended.

Gordon looked startled, fumbled with the catch and threw up the sash. A swirl of damp air reached her and she could breathe again.

Usually she liked the pause, the anticipation while the coffee brewed. It was part of the ritual. But today she was too jumpy, impatient for the fix of caffeine.

Gordon seemed equally unsettled and fell back on discussing the weather.

'There's so much more of it down here. No hiding place.' He peered up at the sky. 'But seems to be clearing. I won't get too wet on the way back.'

Naomi took the mug he passed her and peered into it. 'Do you still wish you had a daughter? Do you remember – talking about that? But maybe it was just that particular daughter? Did you ever…?'

She surprised herself, starting the conversation in that way, and Gordon looked equally surprised.

'Yes. Funnily enough, I do. I tried a few relationships. Never worked for long. So I became the quintessential confirmed bachelor. Always good to make up numbers at dinner parties. But all the time wishing there might be someone to remember me when I'm gone.'

'Bit late now, I guess.'

Gordon laughed. 'Certainly is! I'm an old man. Don't know how that happened. I keep myself fit, exercises, walking the park and so on. But I'm not exactly eligible.'

'Me neither. So you can forget making remarks about Patrick.'

'Furthest from my thoughts. But one thing I was thinking – you've had a pretty raw deal with men. I wondered if you'd ever come across a decent one? One that might redeem us…? Or am I being too nosy?'

Naomi gazed out of the window at the scudding clouds. 'Oh yes. There was one. Dieter.'

'Dieter from Berlin?'

'How do you know that?'

'You mentioned him in passing – years ago when we had that lunch. It did something to your eyes, so I often wondered.'

'It was extraordinary. The first time we looked at each other, it was as if…' Could she really say this to Gordon? 'It sounds fanciful, but it was as if we looked into each other's souls.'

'Oh yes. Not fanciful. That's how it was with Immo.'

'Of course! I should have guessed.'

'So what happened? Why…?'

Naomi sighed. She heard Meghan's voice from their earlier conversation. *There are no giants.* Might Dieter have been a giant? Probably best not to know. 'Long story short, he was gay. He was only beginning to work that out when we met. I think he hoped I'd "turn" him! As if. I didn't have that power unfortunately. And both being madly in love wasn't enough. When I left Berlin we wrote long letters – until I married Tony, that is. He wasn't standing for that. And Dieter couldn't bear it either.'

Gordon shook his head. 'What bloody bad luck. Talk about drawing the short straw.'

'I can't believe I told you that. I never talk about Dieter. Apart from Fay, I never told a soul.' She held out her mug for a top up of coffee. 'Anyway, what we should really be talking about is the cottage, the will.'

'You probably guessed I don't want to stay there.'

'I remember you hating the place.'

He laughed. 'True. I suppose I appreciate it more now. It's amazing – if you like that sort of thing. Which I don't. Wilson knew that, of course. No morning paper, no club down the road. No transport. No bloody civilisation!'

'So?'

'So – I thought I'd stay for the summer – or at least until you're in a fit state to move in. Help you do that, if I may, and then take myself back off to the Smoke and the normal conveniences. How does that strike you?'

'Perfect. Where's the snag?'

Gordon laughed. 'Yes, there is one. I'd like to be invited down from time to time – when the weather is clement. And I'll bring a hamper of real food with me to fatten you up. Could you cope with that?'

'It's a deal.'

19 *Meghan*

Why does everything have to happen at once? Meghan muttered as she pulled on her clothes in the dark. Her creative drive had reached a peak just as Naomi was in need of company at Patrick's, just as Alex's homecoming was imminent and just as the squalor of her house had reached an all-time low.

For the last week she'd been working early and late to make her ideas about the umbrella and bird pictures into a coherent subject for an exhibition before she lost the thread. After a long evening working up a sketch onto canvas, she would wake before dawn with her head full of images that must be captured before she dared turn on a bright light. She would sketch furiously by the dim lamp in her studio as the sky gradually brightened. After two hours she would be exhausted and took her breakfast outside to share with her friend, Rocky the rook. Not an original nickname but she liked to think he recognised it when she said hello.

She'd spoken to the gallery owner in Barnstaple about the project but Geoffrey was clearly baffled and far more concerned about whether she was making good progress on the paintings for her one-woman show in November. 'Need to fill the space,' he said. 'Christmas market. Good solid stuff that will appeal as presents for the nearest and dearest.' He'd think about the other project later but would need a series of photographs in order to get his head round it. What she needed was a digital camera, one with a screen for viewing the pictures, and she certainly couldn't afford that. Might Naomi have such a thing? She'd never seen Naomi taking photos but it was worth a shot.

She added her breakfast mug to the dishes piled in the sink and promised herself an afternoon cleaning the house. Meanwhile there were six rooms to be turned round at the Quay and the whole downstairs to be cleaned. There was just time to call in on Naomi before she was due at the hotel. Naomi would have coffee on the go and she needed a strong one to keep her awake.

Naomi was still in her dressing gown, filing her nails, and greeted Meghan with, 'You're bright and early. Well, early anyway.'

'What, no coffee?' Meghan said.

'I thought you were giving it up. The other day you said you drank too much of it when you were with me. It was making you jumpy.'

'This morning I need it.'

Naomi hurried into the kitchen. 'I'm on the case. You look done in.'

Meghan confirmed this by managing to fall asleep while the coffee brewed.

Naomi handed her a mug. 'What's going on?'

Meghan heard the concern but it clashed with a sudden wave of resentment. The luxury of a dressing gown at nine in the morning, of clean rooms, of sitting in a chair doing nothing. While here she was, run ragged and bursting with creativity. She had to make a living but here was Naomi, owner of two properties she wasn't occupying.

'Not enough hours in the day. Need to paint.'

Naomi narrowed her eyes. 'Sounds like an understatement. Is this the new project? The one I'm not to ask about?'

She nodded. 'It could be good. I know it. Really good. I work late, I get up early and then I have to stop to clean other people's houses while mine is a slum.'

'Not helped by the sight of me sitting round like the idle rich.'

That did it. She tried to laugh but struggled not to burst into tears. 'You're not wrong. But hardly your fault.'

'If only I could help, but I'm bloody helpless at the moment. I would, I'd clean your house like a shot.'

Meghan nodded. She tried to imagine Naomi scrubbing her kitchen. It wasn't as difficult as she had expected. Then she remembered the camera. Naomi didn't have such a thing, but Patrick did. She would ask him.

'I could fix up to make a visit to Geoffrey, see if I can convince him.' She rounded on Naomi, struck by a sudden idea. 'I suppose you wouldn't come with me? If we took the wheelchair? A bit of moral support?'

'I will if you promise me one thing.'

'I suppose so.'

'You go to bed early tonight. Two things, actually. You take yourself to the woods in the morning.'

'Really? You really would come? That would be wonderful. It's a promise.'

Meghan left for the hotel puzzled as to why she felt so much better. She was still short of time to paint, she still had a filthy house and she still had to spend the morning cleaning and changing beds. Nothing had changed. And yet everything had changed.

Geoffrey was a tall man with a slight stoop and a rapidly receding sandy hairline. He ushered them into his gallery and busied himself rearranging a chaise longue and a footstool while Meghan and Naomi inspected the current display of pictures.

Naomi got Meghan to park the wheelchair in front of a semi-abstract moorland scene. 'That I like.'

'Good taste,' Geoffrey said from behind just as Meghan felt a stab of irrational jealousy that Naomi admired the painting more than her own work.

'It has the same sense of being in two worlds at once that Meghan achieves with her seascapes.'

Geoffrey looked at Naomi over the top of his glasses and angled the chaise longue to give her a view of the painting. Meghan breathed again. Naomi seemed to be making quite an impression.

She and Geoffrey settled at his vast mahogany desk in the far corner of the room to pore over the pictures on the little camera screen.

'Love the new seascapes. They will definitely sell. But we need plenty of them. Different sizes, too. Something for everyone.'

He scribbled some numbers and dimensions on the back of an envelope and handed it to her. 'So, what about this new stuff?'

He frowned into the camera screen, shook his head several times and was clearly going to be hard to convince.

'It's seriously weird as a concept,' he said eventually. 'More of an installation. Doesn't fit my image at all. Sorry to disappoint my favourite artist, but too much of a risk, I'd say.'

She was about to say she quite understood and something about Geoffrey's reputation, when a voice came from the back of the room. 'You wouldn't regret it.' Naomi putting her oar in. This could be embarrassing. 'It's powerful stuff when you see it in the flesh. None of my business, of course.'

Geoffrey started. He'd clearly forgotten Naomi was there. 'And there speaks a woman of discernment,' he said.

'It was actually Naomi who triggered the whole thing,' Meghan said. 'She unearthed the umbrellas and saw their potential.'

Geoffrey snorted. 'The potential of umbrellas. Hmm.'

There was silence while he picked up the camera and scrolled through the photographs a second time. Meghan reckoned Naomi might have lost her reputation as a woman of discernment.

Geoffrey tipped back his chair. 'There *is* the arts festival. Next summer. I wonder. Could sell the idea to them, maybe?' He combed his fingers through non-existent hair. 'They want "different" – allegedly. Cutting-edge. God knows what that means. But it might be worth a stab. Can't do any harm.'

As they drove away, Meghan said, 'You turned out to be a bit of an asset.'

Naomi laughed. 'As an outing, it certainly beats going to the fracture clinic.'

20 *Naomi*

"Next of kin", it said on the form. It had never occurred to Naomi before. She didn't have any kin. And, since Fay was no longer there, not even a friend to put in place of kin. Unless you counted Evie – a woman who might or might not still be living in a yurt in the corner of a field about a hundred miles away. Address? Whatever was the name of the farm? She drew a blank there. She would be one of those people who have their funerals arranged by the local authority, just a slot at the crematorium, nobody in attendance.

Patrick – that would be mortifying. She'd already been obliged to use his annexe as her temporary residence. She even considered naming Gordon. At least she knew his full name and address. But it would look pathetic. She'd tell him it was a joke but he'd see through that. But he wouldn't know, would he? Or only when she was either dead or too ill to care. But then again, she supposed you were meant to tell people when you named them as next of kin. A warning. A courtesy. Supposing they refused?

What about Meghan? She'd said they were friends, hadn't she? But she didn't even know Meghan's surname. She must know it, tried to visualise the signature on her paintings, but it wouldn't come. Couldn't remember the name of her cottage either. C/o the Stagworthy Quay Hotel would reach her, but that made her look as transitory as Naomi herself appeared. Meghan, artist, Stagworthy village. That would reach her. That was what she wrote.

It was strange that these two people, Meghan and Patrick, whom she hadn't met a week ago, had now become her closest companions. When Patrick had driven her to the fracture clinic for the second time, they'd admitted her for surgery, and here she was in yet another unfamiliar situation, fortified by a good luck text from Meghan.

She was now in a bay of six beds and it was noisy. Partly from the understandable cries of pain when patients with multiple fractures were attended to; partly from the unfathomable distress of her neighbour who suffered from dementia and who struggled constantly to pull off her nightdress, only to shiver and cry uncontrollably when she succeeded. Kate, an elderly lady at the far end, was distraught at having missed her eightieth birthday celebration and further upset at having mislaid her glasses, so she was unable to read the cards sent in by her family. Next to her was Lou, who coughed almost continuously, but forfeited any sympathy due to the cough by behaving like a diva and hijacking staff en route to other patients.

What must it be like to be a nurse? The never-ending work of toileting, cleaning, medicating, feeding and placating. As far as she could tell, she and her fellow patients shared their nursing team with at least two other bays of five or six beds. Never enough hands, but never a cross or impatient word.

Naomi watched and listened, overawed by what she witnessed: especially the hard-pressed staff nurse who knelt beside Kate; told her it was fine to cry, that we're all human; read her a poem sent by a grand-daughter. It was an act of love. It meant Kate calmed down and slept peacefully that night. But she could just as easily have been left to cry herself to sleep.

Her bed gave a view of the staff exit. Seeing the nurses in their outdoor wear with bags and umbrellas was a reminder that they all had other lives, many stressful. Naomi knew of at least one disabled child and a confused mother waiting at home. She wondered how they coped and whether maybe, off-duty, they were as bad-tempered and impatient as she would be in their place. It was hard to imagine.

There were jolly nurses, noisy nurses, brisk nurses and quiet nurses. But they all used gentle humour to good effect – whether it was to ask 'Shall I put some more laxative in your water?' or to warn of the next manoeuvre, as in 'Hello, Mary! How are you for rolling? We're going to roll you, darling' or 'Are you ready for this, Mary? I'm going to tip you up into a headstand.' And what skill behind those apparently throwaway remarks. It was overwhelming.

It contrasted with the lack of tact shown by the young doctor who'd prepped Naomi for surgery. She still shuddered at the question she'd been asked. The doctor was actually leaving the cubicle, when she paused at the curtain. 'Oh, one last question. Do you want to be resuscitated?'

Did she want to be resuscitated? Well, of course she did! Naomi had answered with indignation, before pausing for thought.

The doctor was already moving away, closing the curtains.

'Hang on a minute. Come back,' Naomi said. 'I mean, what a question to ask as you go out the door! There's more to it, isn't there? I mean, I don't want to be kept alive as a vegetable.'

She'd imagined people gathered around her bed debating whether the life-support should be turned off. What people? The same rag-tag bag of non-next-of-kin. Gordon making a crude joke and nobody to shut him up.

The doctor made a head movement, which could have been a shake or a nod. Did she perfect that in front of the mirror while cleaning her teeth?

'I mean, there must be degrees…' Naomi tailed away. Degrees of what? It was a minefield.

The doctor broke in, an upbeat tone now. 'No worries. Your answer is fine.'

A brisk swish of the curtain and she was gone, all boxes ticked on her form.

My answer might have been "fine", thought Naomi, but your question was not.

It was 2.30am. Her bladder had woken her. The overhead strip-lights had finally gone off at five minutes to midnight. What with several catheters to see to, Joan's ravings, Kate's grief, Lou's cough and a late admission, it had taken that long to get everyone settled. Now it seemed they were all unconscious, deeply sedated, and she was the only one awake.

She was struck by the stillness. No sound of voices, muffled or otherwise. No purposeful footsteps. No heads passing the end of the bay. No figure bent over a screen at the nurses' station. She could hear the flutter of Joan's breathing in the bed next to hers.

Where were the staff? She pressed her buzzer. No sound. That was turned off at night, but she could see the ghost of the light pulsing in the corridor.

From the window she had a view of the back yard of the hospital – a flat-roofscape dominated by the soaring incinerator tower. All those severed limbs, organs, bodies even. It could have been the stage set for a horror movie. Two-tone grey, concrete and asphalt. Harsh geometric lines cast by security lights. Triangular shadows tapering into dark corners. Cats slinking along the margins, dodging between smokestacks.

Occasional headlights at the top of the picture reminded her that there was a world out there, people driving home, a road which might one day lead back to normal.

But just now it seemed unlikely she would ever escape. She shivered, not with cold but with fear.

They had been abandoned. Left to their fate. The whole ward. The pressure in her bladder was building. A voice tried to reach her throat.

It was too much like the times in the tall, thin house when she was left alone after she'd fallen asleep. But she always knew back then that her mother would come back. She tried not to remember those times, but those eerie silos reminded her of looking down from her bedroom window, high up on the fourth floor, and feeling giddy. She didn't like being up on the top floor because the house rocked in a strong wind. She could feel it swaying. She'd been told this made it safe. But it didn't feel safe. The images crowded in on her.

She is four years old and has woken up feeling peculiar. She sits up in bed and calls out, 'Mamma, Mamma.' No sound. She tries again, very loud this time. If the door is closed two floors down, Mum may not hear. If she is in bed, one floor below, this might wake her up. The peculiar feeling gets suddenly worse and moves from her tummy up into her chest. And then, equally suddenly, it is jumping out of her mouth. A foul-tasting stream arrives on the sheet. It's on her nightie and in her hair. She should get to the bathroom, she knows that. Because she knows she's going to be sick again. One step at a time, one after another, taking her wobbly tummy down the stairs. Keep going. There are ten. Then the turn and another ten. She knows that. There's the squeaky bottom step and she runs for the toilet. Mum will be mad if she ruins the carpet. Just in time.

She stays sitting on the edge of the bath until her tummy feels more like normal. Then she climbs on the stool to wash her face and wipes her hair and her nightie with the towel that hangs on the back of the door.

By that time, she knows Mum is out. It's all dark downstairs and Mum isn't in her bed. Her own bed is disgusting so she climbs into Mum's.

That isn't such a good idea as it seems. When Mum comes back, she's mad that there are now two sets of sheets to change. She puts Naomi in the bath and washes her hair in water that is one minute too hot and the next too cold. Mum is trying not to be cross, and she says things like, 'Poor darling,' but the way she combs her hair feels like a punishment. She goes back to bed with wet hair and next morning the nasty smell is still lingering in the bathroom from the dirty sheets, which Mum dumped in the bath.

But it wasn't the nasty smell that stayed with Naomi. It was the desolation. The whole memory was swathed in the grey of damp dishcloths, the grey of the clinker in the boiler when it went out, the grey of loneliness and absence. The very air in that house used to turn grey whenever she found herself alone in it. The colours only came back when her mother came home.

Naomi shuddered. It was the grey of the view from this hospital window. But at least she was only dealing with a full bladder, not an upset stomach. Maybe the staff had walked out. She'd overheard the muttering of discontent, the totally understandable protests at their ludicrous pay rise. They'd reached the end of their tether. Or they'd been taken by the forces of darkness out there.

Bleak didn't begin to describe it. And the bladder wasn't helping. It had progressed from urgent and uncomfortable to painful. The cot sides were up on her bed, preventing her from getting out. She couldn't even pee on the floor and save the sheet.

Patrick and Meghan and her bed with the view of the garden seemed to belong in another, totally inaccessible world. That was the fantasy, an illusion of friendship and happiness. This was reality.

Twenty minutes had passed. She strained her ears but could only hear a faint hum coming from the wall lights.

It might have been better to have gone over the cliff – swallowed by the clean, cold sea and no trouble to anyone. Those people in the hotel had taken such trouble. They had cared for her in a rough and ready way, but they'd been, what was the word? Respectful. She'd kept her dignity intact. Patrick had been wonderful and Meghan, in arranging for her to occupy his annexe, had understood her need for space. But now, here, she'd been abandoned in what was about to be a pool of urine.

But then again, she thought, if we are abandoned, does it matter if I'm urine-soaked or not? And even less if we're to be eliminated by alien forces. She knew, in some part of her that clung to life and a belief in those caring, giving nurses, that this was fantasy stuff. But one glance out of the window and it didn't seem fanciful at all.

Thirty minutes now since she pressed her buzzer. She focused on the ceiling, counting the ceiling tiles. The pain was getting worse. She'd have to let go. What did it matter, anyway?

As she had that thought, a faint sound reached her ears. A door banging? Further sounds. Footsteps. Voices. A nurse was suddenly at her bedside. She'd hardly said, 'I'm desperate,' before the commode appeared, the nurse as solicitous and quick as ever.

'I'm sorry you had to wait. Was it long?'

'Half an hour. I nearly…'

'We had a crisis down the other end.'

That's when she discovered how many patients there were, how many staff. Ridiculous ratio.

Next morning when a nurse brought her a bowl of water to wash in, she burst into tears.

'Oh, my love, what is it?'

Naomi shook her head.

'You've always been so cheerful.' The nurse put an arm round her shoulders. 'You let it all out. Sometimes it all just gets to you, doesn't it?'

Naomi nodded. 'That's it. It all just came over me.'

Next day came the journey home – or was it the day after? For time passed both quickly and slowly in a way that blurred and almost erased its normal significance. On the one hand, Naomi became anxious at the delay in discharging her. On the other, she thought it really didn't matter where she was. She was used to the routine and the nurses. She cared about what would happen to Mary, who would sometimes smile and wave across at her. She was content. Later she realised that might have been to do with the level of morphine she was being given.

But time did move on. Here she was, cocooned on cushions in the back of Patrick's Volvo, talking occasionally to the back of his head. It made her giddy to watch buildings, lorries and then hillsides sliding by. She looked away. Enough, when they passed under trees, to see the rich green of their foliage framed by the sunroof, which was tilted to allow a pleasant breath of air to circulate. From time to time, when her eyes closed, she was still on the ward with the familiar shapes of the hospital friends she had left behind, heard their voices, wondered how they were getting on. With open eyes her gaze fell naturally between the two front seats, another safe rectangle containing Patrick and the steering wheel. He sat in an upright position, hands relaxed on the wheel, one hand occasionally beating time to some tune in his head, sunlight flickering on the gold rims of his driving glasses. It was a hot day but, even with shorts, Patrick wore his usual crisp white shirt. He drove smoothly and was not one to turn his head to talk to a back-seat passenger. It was a calming view, disturbed only by a tanned and muscular thigh appearing above the armrest whenever he changed gear.

Now she stood in the hallway, resting after the walk from the car. The door to her suite straight ahead, door to the garden on her right flanked by windows, door to the main house on her left, framed by pictures, abstract blocks of colour. She hadn't noticed before that it was octagonal. It accounted for the shape of her room, which had some unexpected angles.

'Anyone could have made this square.'

Patrick's laugh came from behind her as he shut the door. A laugh the colour of Marmite.

'The nearest I could get to round. I wanted to make your room round – so restful – but too costly, too much wasted space. Little Hobbit cupboards you couldn't get into.'

He stood in front of her. 'Okay? Steady?' He looked her up and down and smiled. 'You know, it's a shame, but it's impossible to hug a person on crutches. I might knock you over.'

Their eyes met and their gaze seemed to merge, as if she was seeing past Patrick's public persona into a more intimate space, a soul space almost. Almost like her memory of Dieter. Almost. And only for a second. Don't think about Dieter. She never did allow herself to think about him. All the unhappy memories claimed her, but she kept Dieter in a separate place. A glow crept up her neck into her face. She hoped it didn't show. 'I consider myself hugged.' The words came out sharply, as if hugging was the last thing she wanted.

Patrick turned away and opened the door to her room.

She swung forward and stopped. 'I didn't mean… Anyway, it wouldn't be fair. I couldn't hug you back.' She felt another wave of heat wash over her.

21 *Meghan*

Meghan was sitting with Naomi in Patrick's garden, enjoying the mellow evening sun with a glass of rosé. It was the opportunity she'd been waiting for to get to know Naomi a little better, to understand the child-wraith that sometimes clung to Naomi's skirts.

'I could get used to this, you know,' Naomi said. 'It's really not so bad being waited on hand and foot.'

Meghan nodded. 'It's all very well for some!' She sipped her drink. 'Anyway, I've been thinking – I wonder what it was like for you – after what you said the other day – growing up with all those uncles?'

'Huh! What to say?' She'd been half expecting Meghan to ask that question, but it was a difficult one to answer. 'Some of them were all right. But it was the *fact* of it that was hard as I got older and realised.' She paused and sipped her wine. 'I mean, I spent a huge amount of time with my friend Fay. But Fay's mother never wanted Fay to come to my house. She obviously knew what went on, they were neighbours, didn't want Fay to see it, come under the influence.'

'I suppose it happens to quite a lot of kids, though. Uncles, I mean.'

'But to kids who don't have a father in the picture. I had a perfectly good father. It was just that he was at sea a lot. I would feel guilty if I liked one of the uncles. It felt disloyal.'

Meghan held her glass up to the light. 'Did you ever wonder – whether you were his?'

'Sure. But not for long. I was the spitting image of him. Funnily enough, they got on fine when he was home, him and Mum. She loved him, I think. But when he wasn't there – well, I guess Mum conveniently forgot about him. Like she forgot about me quite a lot of the time.'

'Forgot?'

'She'd look really surprised sometimes when I came home from Fay's, as if my existence had quite slipped her mind. And she'd go out at night, of course.'

Naomi had already told Meghan and Patrick the story of her night of abandonment in the hospital, but she'd told it, not as a joke exactly, but to entertain, hadn't mentioned the memory it had evoked. Now she found herself telling Meghan the true version, her terror and the story of waking up alone in the tall, thin house and being so sick when she was only four years old.

As she finished, she tried to wave away the tears that started. 'Happy tears,' she said. 'It was double scary I guess, what with that memory coming back. I can't believe I made it back here, all this, with you.' She waved her glass to take in the garden, roses, trees and Meghan.

'I'm glad you did.' Meghan paused and Naomi followed her gaze to the rook winging its way purposefully towards the tall trees on the edge of the wood. My friend who watches black birds.

Meghan broke the silence that followed. 'Do you have any happy memories of your mother?'

The question took her by surprise. She peered into her glass for inspiration. 'We used to go shopping,' she said at last. '"Nobody needs to know when we go shopping," Mum would say. By that she meant the neighbours in the road at the front of the house. The ones at the back didn't matter, I suppose. Anyway, that made us conspirators. It would be an adventure and we'd be in it together. She would drain the glass of the funny-smelling water she always had if ever we went out – gin, it must have been. And she'd hook her jaunty basket over one arm.'

We go out the back way through the shed where the cobwebs and big, spotty spiders live and out of the door made of planks with gaps in between. The back lane smells of stinging nettles and cat wee-wee. Poor Mrs Hammond is usually in her garden, wrapped in her flowery overall among the pea sticks and the tall artichokes. We stop to talk to her, however hard I try to pull Mum along. Mrs Hammond has a fat, wet lower lip, which never closes her mouth. I can't hear what she says and I don't want to. It's very boring.

Next is Mr Wall, who always pops out from behind his garage door, smelling of oily rags and the cars he mends. 'Who have we here?' he says, lowering his face to mine. I twist behind Mum as my mouth refuses to open. How to say my name? Why? He knows perfectly well who I am.

Then briskly across the road, Mum's irritation with me sounding in the clip clop of her heels. That means we miss out Mr Freak's sweetshop on the corner. No lemon sherbet today.

Past Braunton's, the wool shop, where Mum sometimes buys a zip or a reel of Sylko. Next door is the chemist. We don't need any headache pills this time. On to Mr Cook. He is safe, not seeing any need to torture a child with greetings. His shop smells of tea and currants. He weighs out sugar into a blue bag and Mrs Cook just smiles with her soft eyes and gentle freckles. I love Mrs Cook. Later she would become "poor Mrs Cook" and her voice would disappear and come back as gentle as her freckles. Then it was just Mr Cook and I was sad.

Outside of Cook's we cross the road. There's nothing coming but Mum takes my hand and looks both ways. She grips my hand so tightly I nearly say ouch. But halfway across the road I look into the purple-green oily swirl in a puddle and I know something I didn't know before: it's me taking Mum's hand, getting Mum across the road.

We make our way to the other half of the village where the hairdresser is and the baker and the shop that sells newspapers.

Oh, good, we're going to Mrs Price up by the oak tree. I like the way her hair is plaited so thinly and wound round and round over each ear. She is so tiny and so quick with the big knife, slicing off the cauliflower leaves. Her tabby cat sits on the counter next to two purple beetroots that are steaming on an enamel plate. I can never get the cat to look at me.

After that we escape back to the tall, thin house.

Mum's different when we get home. She finishes what's left in the bottle of smelly water and lights the fire. She says I'm her good girl and makes a treat for tea – a Mars bar sliced up on bread and butter. We sit by the fire and eat it. After that, instead of Mum getting on the telephone like she normally does, we play snakes and ladders and tiddly winks until bedtime. It's magic. She says I can have four whole stories and she lets me undress in front of the fire.

'There's your happy memory.' Naomi refilled her glass and waved the bottle at Meghan, who shook her head. 'If only Mum had always been like that.'

'She must have loved you.'

'Loved me? If only. How do you work that one out?'

'Don't look so startled! She obviously didn't have much clue about being a mother, but there are mothers and mothers. There's no right way.'

'She never felt like a mother. Not once I noticed how other people were with their kids. How easy they were – whether they were happy or cross or whatever – just *easy*.'

'Hmm, yes, I know what you mean. Lots of people probably thought I was a terrible mother. Were we easy together? I'm not sure. But Alex survived. Yours probably had a touch of agoraphobia. She couldn't have gone shopping without you. So it must have been a strong bond. You were her safe place. She trusted you. So she loved you.'

'You really think so?'

'I know so.'

'I'm still not sure that follows. If only.' Naomi sighed. 'And what about *your* mother? Tell me about her.'

Meghan was eying her uncertainly. Was she being too intrusive? She waited.

'I had a very conventional, small-town upbringing. Mam worked part-time as receptionist at the doctor's, but mostly she was a housewife. Clean house, meals on the table, washing on the line Monday morning, never behind with the ironing. But I worked out later it was more for the benefit of the neighbours than for Dad and me. Because when I went home pregnant, she wouldn't let me stay. I mean, what would the neighbours say?'

'That must have been devastating.'

'Sort of was. I'd wound myself up to go, borrowed the train fare – and then that.' Meghan paused, gazing at the sky, but no rooks offered themselves. 'The odd thing was, she was kind of really nice to me as well. Almost as if she wished she could do it differently. We spent a strange few weeks, hedging around each other. Mam made a fuss of me – favourite meals, trimming my hair just like she used to. But when push came to shove, she still said she had "no choice". I had to leave before my "condition" showed.'

Meghan rolled her eyes. '"My condition"! That was Alex she was talking about. My baby. And she never even asked who the father was.'

Meghan fell silent, staring at the grass, and Naomi waited.

'And yet, on the doorstep when I was leaving, Mam said, "Let me know, won't you? How you get on," and there was a crack in her voice. I wondered afterwards what would have happened if I'd just said, "Mammy, please!" But I was too proud.'

'I can see that,' Naomi said. 'And it would never have been on your terms.'

'You're right. *So* right.' Meghan paused. 'You know, all that talk she had about the shame of it, all Mam's protesting, I always sensed it was the ghost of my dead father who was being protected. Even the words Mam used were his words. Once or twice I caught her watching me over her knitting. A softer expression, but it would just vanish.'

Meghan looked so sad. Naomi wanted to jump up and hug her, but the plaster cast kept her firmly seated. 'No wonder you're keen to give Alex a good welcome.' It was all she could think to say.

'Alex didn't get the upbringing she wanted. She wanted *stuff*, and a conventional mother with a clean house and a regular income – security, in other words. And she got me! I'll never forget when she got her first job. She'd done really well, getting qualified – I thought she was having a wild old time in London, but actually she was studying and taking exams – which meant she got taken on by the Barnstaple branch of Barclays. Alex was almost too embarrassed to tell me.'

'But you must have been proud of her,' Naomi said.

'I suppose I was.' As she said it, Meghan's stomach lurched. Had she ever let Alex know that? She put the thought aside to come back to later. 'But the worst of it was, Alex was right to be embarrassed. I found it difficult to cope with. Hell, this was exactly the future my father planned for me! Which I scorned. Plus, there was Rita taking secret satisfaction from Alex turning her back on my hand-to-mouth existence.'

'But you didn't get in her way, didn't try and stop her,' Naomi said.

'No, never. It's her life. I suppose that was one step on from my parents.'

'And you're still close.'

Meghan nodded. 'I've finished turning out her room, by the way. Coat of paint going on tomorrow. But Mam, well, it turned out she was a bit more complicated than I realised. But that's another story.' Meghan looked at her watch and got to her feet.

'Tell, tell! You can't stop there.'

'I'm due at the hotel. It'll have to keep. Shall I wheel you back inside? Or do you want to wait for Patrick?'

'Ask him to come and help me finish the wine? And come by tomorrow, won't you?'

22 Alex

The first major stop on the journey north through France was at Carcassonne. What a place! When Alfie had described a mediaeval fortress town, Alex had to admit to finding the prospect yawnworthy. Alfie was into his history, and Alex would zone out while Esther lapped up everything he had to say. It was an expensive place, apparently, so they'd be staying outside the walls, well away from the shops and cafés. So, another tedious, history-laden trek, Alex guessed. But the first sight of the town in the distance changed all that. It looked just like the cover illustration on her childhood book of fairy tales.

The three of them approached the old town at dusk and encountered a candlelit procession coming over the bridge. It was some kind of religious ceremony and the combination of voluminous robes, masks and headdresses, swinging lanterns and hypnotic chanting was enough to transport them back several centuries. Alex felt she had stepped right into the pages of those fairy tales with the princess in the tower and the knights on their fine horses. The effect lasted for their early morning walk on the ramparts – Alex expected a gentle stroll but fortified herself for the hike by imagining herself in long skirts and a wimple, riding a palfrey (whatever that was) and inclining her head graciously to passers-by. Alfie explained that wimples weren't the fashion of the period but she ignored that and continued over-acting until Esther got thoroughly exasperated and told her to stop simpering.

'You're on toilet duty when we get back to the van,' she said, shaking her head. 'That'll bring Lady Wimple back down to earth.'

But Alfie and Esther seemed to have caught the magic of the place too. They walked on ahead and she could see them canoodling in every other parapet and not bothering with the spectacular views or the ancient stones. Alfie was such an old romantic and Esther didn't stay grumpy for long. She felt a rush of gratitude that they had brought her here and was even moved to treat them all to breakfast in the old town. They had eventually set off on the next leg of their journey in a good humour, toilet duties complete. Alfie and Esther were headed for a longer stay on the Canal du Midi with friends of Alfie's who ran a boutique hotel. It was high season, so they were to help out with the chores. Alex would stay for a while as an extra pair of hands if needed, and they would then part company while she continued her journey home by train.

Alex lay on her bunk listening to fat raindrops bombarding the roof of the van. They started slowly and built to a steady drumming like the heels of a toddler having a tantrum, which suited her mood to perfection.

Perfection. She'd had enough of perfection. Why did they all have to take it so seriously? After all, she hadn't spoilt anything. She'd thought it was quite a laugh, but none of them had even cracked a smile. Not even Esther. In fact, especially not her. Did Esther think she'd done it deliberately? Okay, she could understand Marcel and Johannes not being amused. They were both so ludicrously fussy –OCD she would call it, except Esther told her that was not an acceptable term - about every aspect of their hospitality and they seemed to attract guests who expected that level of attention to detail – every towel precisely folded, the soap at the exact perfect angle to the shampoo and so on.

They'd been here at the Château du Pommier for three weeks. Marcel and Johannes had greeted the arrival of the flower-power van with a great deal of mirth and enthusiasm. Esther was introduced and welcomed with equal enthusiasm, which faded a little when it came to explaining the presence of Alex. Surely they didn't imagine Alfie was running a ménage à trois? The two men were charming friends, but turned out to be exacting employers, and Alfie and Esther seemed delighted to earn their keep by becoming their slaves. When Alex protested at the volume of work, Alfie pointed out that they were all getting free board and lodging, including three delicious meals a day. Esther was happy to be kitchen dogsbody and Alfie worked the garden. Alex had been less happy with the role of chambermaid. But so far she reckoned she'd done a good job, scrubbing and dusting, folding and polishing – and gritting her teeth when Marcel moved a chair two centimetres to the left after she'd hoovered.

One day, when Esther came upstairs to help with making up beds, she had asked about Salvador. Alex was surprised as Esther had showed no interest before.

'He was good-looking, good company, but to be honest I'm shocked how little I miss him.'

'You can't have cared about him that much.'

Alex dumped a pile of fresh bedding on the side table. 'He was really only after one thing.'

'Maybe he thought that was all you wanted.'

Alex laughed. 'Maybe it *was* all I wanted. But only to begin with. Then it wore thin.'

'The thing about me and Alfie is, we were friends first. It's made such a difference.'

Alex nodded. 'It shows. I envy you that.' She picked up a pillow. 'But the main thing was his mother. She was something else – all fake tan and bling – but she thought the sun shone out of Salvador's arse.'

Esther didn't react.

'You know, eldest son, first grandchild, ready to eat me alive, suck me into the family. Much as I liked his sisters, I couldn't cope with that.'

'Hmm, so you could have had a ready-made family?'

'I've already got a family. Mum, anyway.'

Esther shook out a sheet and fitted the first corner. 'And you wouldn't have had to work, I guess?'

'Wouldn't have been *allowed* to work. I love my work, can't wait to get back to it. I'll get something in a bank or something when I get home.'

'So that's what you do? Work with money?' Esther paused and held out a hand. 'Chuck those pillows over. You get the duvet. I mean, isn't that weird? That sort of work? Not having anything to show for it, anything you've done, produced?'

Alex stared. 'What do you mean? I've got all those numbers. Figures. Answers.'

'But nothing sort of real. Like here – lovely rooms, happy punters.'

Alex tried to explain but Esther, shrugging pillows into their cases, didn't get it. She stayed long enough to position the decorative cushions exactly on the bed and went back to her kitchen chores.

*

Alex felt side-lined. She couldn't make Esther out. The girl blew hot and cold, sometimes laughing at something Alex said, sometimes prickly as hell. Certainly, the intimacy they'd shared in Sète was gone. Alfie and Esther had a room in the house, which was fair enough – they had some privacy at last. She respected that need and had not complained about being stuck out in the van. Admittedly, she had use of the shower room, but they seemed to think it was a privilege for Alex to have the van to herself. Some privilege. Especially as it was parked at the back of the chateau where the peacocks hung out at night. She was frequently woken by their bloodcurdling screams. The first time, she'd been convinced a murder was taking place and had shivered in terror in her bunk until other more bird-like noises gave the peacocks away. The whole household found that hilarious, but the collective sense of humour hadn't been triggered by her latest escapade.

The day had been chilly; she'd been tired after cleaning three rooms, three bathrooms. And that bath had been so enticing. Deep and gleaming, taps reflecting the clouds from the skylight above, delicious bath oil and fluffy towels at the ready. There were no guests expected. So why not? It would take her no time to restore it to order when she was finished. So she'd filled the bath and sunk into the sweet-smelling depths, feeling her whole body relax in bliss. And then she had fallen asleep.

Sod's law had it that a passing traveller booked in unexpectedly and it was Marcel who showed him to the room, Marcel who sniffed the air and discovered her. The abrupt click as the bathroom door closed had woken her. She'd heard Marcel ushering the visitor downstairs, explaining 'a slight irregularity' and promising afternoon tea and cake, after which the room would be ready.

She was damply dressed with the extractor fan going full blast when Marcel returned, white with anger. Apologies were useless. She had caused a blemish on their unsullied reputation and so on. He stood over her while she scrubbed and dried the immaculate bathtub and polished the taps and mirrors into pristine condition.

Downstairs she encountered Alfie and Esther with Johannes, lined up as if to pass judgement. Only Alfie put in a good word for her.

'Okay,' he said. 'It was cheeky, a cheeky mistake. And unlucky. After all, nobody would have known if that visitor hadn't turned up.'

Alex gave him a grateful smile. Johannes grunted. Marcel said she wasn't to be trusted and Alfie wandered out onto the veranda. Alex tried to catch Esther's eye to see if she showed any spark of amusement. Esther was a bit OCD herself – in the galley of the van for instance. But it was a tiny space with no room for mess, so Alex could understand that. She'd been grateful when Esther had helped her out with the rooms from time to time, but they'd hardly spoken since the awkward conversation about her work. Now Esther was watching Alfie's retreat, miffed no doubt that he'd defended Alex. That girl could be jealous of a mosquito.

Alex had escaped to the van and here she was, furious and powerless. It was time to leave. She was tempted to pack up and vanish without any goodbyes. But that would be childish and ungrateful. Alfie and Esther had done so much for her. And in any case, she'd be soaked to the skin in minutes if she left in this weather.

At first she'd marvelled at the culture of the Château du Pommier – particularly Johannes' delicious Swiss-French cuisine and the music that greeted guests at breakfast and dinner. Chopin and Puccini, Beethoven and Mozart, Alfie told her. But just now she was suddenly homesick for Mum's sausage hotpot and Mum singing along to Bob Dylan and Elvis, with ABBA blasting out from Rita's kitchen window opposite. Ironic that Mum earned most of her money from cleaning. Where would she be on the scale of perfection? Perfectly clean, yes. Perfectly fancy, absolutely not.

It was time to move on. The rain had stopped and the vegetation was steaming as she walked through the garden to join the others for dinner. She announced her decision to leave over dessert and it was as if they had all expected it. No one batted an eyelid. Not even the offer of a lift to the station. Damn the lot of them.

But next morning, as she walked under the avenue of plane trees towards the main road, there was a creaking behind her and Alfie drew alongside in the Château's ancient 2CV.

'I guessed you'd leave early,' he said. 'Couldn't leave you to walk all that way.'

'Nobody seemed to care a fuck.'

'They're very particular...' Alfie hesitated as if he would say more but stopped.

'What?'

'Maybe you should know this. I don't think it's intentional, but there are times when you can come across as a tad arrogant. People don't like it.'

'Gee, thanks. A character assassination as a leaving present.'

'That's not how I meant it – and you know it. I just thought you should know. So you can do something about it.'

'Cool.' She flashed him a smile.

'And that's another thing. That smile. You know the one. Emergencies only, I'd say.'

'Can't think what you mean.'

Alfie grinned and they drove on in silence. Maybe he had a point. That smile got her what she wanted. It also got her into trouble. Sometimes what she wanted and trouble were one and the same thing. Which is what had happened with Keith.

At the station he handed her a plastic box. 'Johannes made you a picnic. When Marcel wasn't looking. Now I need to get back before Esther thinks we've eloped. She did send you her best, by the way, says she'll miss you. Good luck.'

She leant in and kissed him on the cheek. 'Thanks, Alfie. You're the best.'

On the train, Alex munched Johannes' baguette sandwich with its slippery roast vegetables and thought of Marmite toast, the ferry crossing and how best to cadge a lift from Plymouth. Chatting up a middle-aged couple was probably the best bet and should get her at least as far as Exeter. Careful use of the smile when the wife wasn't looking might even achieve a diversion to the train station.

23 Meghan

As Meghan cycled through the village and down to the quay, she wondered about telling Naomi her mother's story. Was it fair, or was it a kind of betrayal to take it outside of the family? She'd told Alex, of course. She had a right to know who her grandfather was. But what was it to Naomi? Could she be trusted to react appropriately? It had been a bombshell in Meghan's life at the time, but she was long past wanting a bombshell reaction now.

All through a not very busy evening behind the bar, the shreds of memory came back to her, floating off the foaming top of a pint, ambushing her as she turned to load glasses for washing.

Meghan had gone home to nurse her mother as she was dying of an aggressive stomach cancer. Bronwen had made it downstairs to sit by the fire as she did most afternoons.

'There is something I need to tell you,' she said as Meghan shovelled more coal on the fire.

'Your father wasn't your father, although he never knew it.'

Meghan rocked back on her heels. 'Daddy wasn't...?'

'He never suspected. Nobody did. I mean, who would ever have guessed meek little Bronwen would do such a thing?' Mam smiled into the flames, yellow tongues licking out from the dark heart of the coal.

'I was already engaged to Lewis. He was studying hard for exams. I was working in the local hotel, waitressing, chambermaiding, saving up so we could move out of the valleys. We were both set on that.'

She was smiling into the fire again and Meghan was doing mental cartwheels to imagine this version of her mother.

'I knew what I was doing. I loved your father – my fiancé, I mean – he was steady. I knew he'd make a good husband. But there was no spark. I wanted to find out what spark would be like before it was too late. And here was my chance. I was amazed this handsome man even noticed me. It might never happen again.'

It was probably the longest speech her mother had addressed to her, except when listing her shortcomings.

'I noticed him as soon as he checked in at reception. Tall, dark and handsome wasn't in it. Foreign, but with good English and perfect manners. Norway, he was from. Or was it Denmark? No, Norway. I was waiting at dinner and he took a fancy to me. Asked me to his room.'

Meghan waited. Mam seemed sunk in memories. Would she say more?

'I hoped the spark might somehow get kindled with your father – well, not your father but you know what I mean. But it never did. No more babies either. I'd have liked another. After the first miscarriage, I knew I wouldn't have any more. It was like a judgement.'

'But are you glad? That you took the chance?'

'I wouldn't have you if I hadn't.'

'And you didn't regret that?' Meghan had to ask. It would explain a lot.

'I never regretted it. Maybe I've not been too good at letting you know that.' Bronwen stretched out a frail hand and gave Meghan's arm a brief squeeze. 'Anyway, who would be looking after me now?'

Meghan took in "I never regretted it" and stored it for later. 'That wasn't what I meant, anyway. I meant, were you glad about finding the spark?'

'Cheeky child! What sort of question is that to be asking your mother?' But she smiled so broadly into the fire that her dimples showed for a moment in her thin cheeks. 'Why don't we have a glass of that sherry? I'm glad to have got that off my chest. You had a right to know.'

Memories of her mother kept on coming to Meghan beyond closing time, during bottling-up, her most-hated bar job, and then afterwards as she pushed her bike back up the hill. She was struck by the mood of celebration that took hold of her mother when the story had been told, her face illuminated by the firelight.

Meghan had brought two crystal glasses of the sickly Bristol Cream sherry her mother liked. Bronwen held her glass to the light and they chinked.

'To absent fathers,' Meghan said.

Bronwen sipped her drink, neatly ignoring the reference to Alex's father. 'Yes, Norwegian, he was. Bjorn something. A funny name. I have it written down.'

Meghan let it pass. This was Mam's story.

'Just a name. It's not much to go on. If you wanted to look.'

'Why would I want to do that?'

Her mother looked relieved.

'But I'm glad you told me, Mammy.' She paused and decided to take the plunge. 'I understand – I mean it makes sense of that time when I—'

'I'll be going back to bed now, if you don't mind.' Bronwen stretched out her arms, ready to be half lifted from the chair.

The confessional was over. After only a glimpse of how her mother might have been, Meghan was left to have "If-only" and "What-if" conversations between herself and the fire until the embers went grey and cold.

Bronwen didn't make it downstairs again after that and died in her sleep a few days later.

As to what to share with Naomi, the answer was to tell her the bare bones. No need to share the intimate side.

'So, back to my mam,' Meghan said next morning as she helped Naomi with her washing-up.

'You did promise.' Naomi positioned herself on her Zimmer with a tea towel.

'I kept in touch over the years, but we weren't close. I took Alex when she was about five. I thought she ought to know her grandmother. But then I found Mam had told the neighbours that "my husband" worked abroad. So that was that. Didn't stop her asking me to come and nurse her when she was dying. Actually, to be fair, that was down to the district nurse. But Mam took it for granted.'

Naomi was polishing a plate. 'They do. Same with my dad. I guess that generation expected it.'

'That was when she told me Dad wasn't my father.'

The plate arrived with a clatter on the table. 'That must have been a shock,' Naomi said, steadying the plate.

'Mam was working in a hotel – saving up for a deposit on a house for when she and Dad got married. He – my biological father, that is – was a travelling salesman. Norwegian. She took a fancy to him and he to her. She was such a goody two shoes nobody suspected a thing, least of all Dad, her poor fiancé.'

Naomi leaned forward to take a clutch of cutlery to dry. 'Intriguing. It sounds quite out of character.'

'Certainly was. I knew all about meek Bronwen. She'd been something of a paragon by all accounts – hard-working, chapel-going, choir-singing and angel-faced. You only had to see the photographs! That clear brow, baby blue eyes and her hair – which was wavy – always carefully under control and the top button of her blouse always neatly fastened. You get the picture. The last person to be suspected.'

'But your father…?'

'I've wondered since then – whether he wondered as I grew up. Did he really have no inkling? I was such a misfit. It might account for his negative attitude to me.'

'That is so sad. And, you know, it makes so much sense of how your mother was when you went home pregnant.'

'I know. Must have brought it all back.'

'She was probably dying to tell you and didn't dare.'

'The conversations we could have had!' Meghan emptied the washing-up bowl. 'Leave the rest to drain. You must be tired, standing on one leg all that time. I'll make you a coffee as a reward.'

As the kettle boiled and she watched the bubbles rise, she smiled to herself. Naomi was proving to be a better friend than she'd given her credit for. 'This is new! The glass kettle. Love it! I'd watch it all the time. Like the first automatic washing machine – watching the clothes go round. Did you do that?'

'I did. Daft, we are.'

Meghan nodded and lifted the kettle. 'And wanting to get inside the fridge to see if the light went off.'

'That would be you, all right! Always wanting to know what's on the inside, behind the closed door.'

'Am I that bad?' Meghan set down the coffee. 'Well, I may as well live up to my reputation. There's one door I'd like to knock on. How is it with

Patrick?' Yes, the question definitely got a reaction from Naomi. Nothing as obvious as a blush, but a frisson, an eye flicker.

'He's a very good friend. Has an uncanny knack of knowing when to leave me to my own devices and when to drop in.'

Meghan nodded.

'And he's going to help me with my exercises, the physio stuff.'

'Ah.'

'Oh, stop it, will you! There is absolutely nothing…'

'But you do fancy him, don't you?'

Naomi covered her face with her hands. 'Does it show? How do you know? Except I mean, how could I not?'

'I just knew it.' Meghan tried not to smile too broadly.

'Is it ridiculous? A woman of my age? I suppose—'

'Ridiculous yourself! Of course it's not. One, you don't look anything like your age, and two, it's how you feel that counts. People get it together in their eighties and nineties these days, and good luck to them.'

'He must be ten years younger than me at least. And in any case, he hasn't given any sign.'

A flush crept into Naomi's cheeks. So Patrick probably had given a sign. Something subtle and Naomi was keeping it to herself. 'So what, if he's half your age? Give it time.'

'I *am*. It's you that's jumping the gun.'

'Sorry. I'll never mention it again.'

'Until next time.' Naomi tucked a strand of hair behind her ear. 'One problem is – I have too much time – I overthink things. You know how it is. I need a project. So if you have any ideas in that direction? A bit limited obviously, but I can be quite handy with a needle, for example.'

'I'll have a think. Meanwhile, I do have a few diversions lined up. Rita, for instance. I've been fending her off, but she's very keen to visit.'

'Your friend, Rita? Really? No problem. Any time.'

'Ah, then that could be pretty soon if you're up for it. She's picking me up from here in about half an hour. Dying to see the place.'

'Well, I didn't imagine it was me she was dying to see. But no mention of Patrick please, no innuendos.'

'Definitely not. Your secret is *not* safe with Rita, fond though I am of her. And you're wrong. She's very curious about you.' Meghan crossed to the window. 'It will be a distraction. Rita's in a great fizz because the farmer up the road is setting up a glamping business – diversifying, he calls it. Getting yurts, if I've got that right. Just glorified tents, I imagine…'

'More than that. More a way of life. My friend Evie lived in a yurt, they're amazing.'

'What, as in permanently?'

'Yes, she built it in her brother's field. I stayed there for a while. After I left the Wilson set-up. Yurts are really adaptable, cosy with a wood-burner…'

'What, inside the tent?'

'Oh yes. There's a smoke hole, all quite safe. And…'

'Sounds interesting. But best stay off the subject. Rita's not exactly going to appreciate your enthusiasm! She thinks it would be competition for her cottages – which I doubt. But once Rita gets an idea in her head…'

Before Naomi could reply, Meghan was distracted by a pair of rooks swooping onto the table outside. They strutted about, one flew off and the other began pecking at something in the groove of the wooden surface.

'Your birds,' Naomi said. 'When did that all start?'

'Now you're asking. I mean, rooks, been there forever. Jackdaws, seeing them nesting, mating season. But when did I start noticing them? I really couldn't say.'

'Perhaps they are your power animal. Evie was always on about power animals. Maybe they have a message.'

'Never been there. "Power animals", that's a big area. Not me. As to a message, there are messages all the time, some of them quite rude, no doubt. I probably miss most of them. Best not to take it too seriously. Just notice. Because they are special creatures.' Meghan was still watching the bird on the table. 'And that project of mine that I mentioned, it's coming on. And not a whisper to Rita. I never tell her about my projects until they're done.'

'I feel privileged.'

'You are. There! Talk of the devil. I think I hear her car.'

It was amusing to watch Rita investigating both Naomi and the annexe while pretending to take an interest in Naomi's progress. Her eyes flicked into every corner and she was obviously dying to explore the kitchen. Eventually curiosity overcame her and she leapt to her feet.

'Make myself useful,' she said, gathering the coffee things onto the tray and taking it out to the sink.

When she came back, she commented on the shape of the room. 'Very peculiar, neither one thing nor the other.'

'The nearest he could get to round, apparently.'

'Round indeed! Wait 'til I tell Harry that! He'll go on about getting things to fit. Have to get it purpose-made. But I suppose Patrick's loaded, so it's no problem.'

'I wouldn't know about that.' Naomi shrugged and looked out over the garden.

'What's the rest of the house like?'

'I wouldn't know about that either, haven't been in it.'

Meghan didn't dare meet Naomi's eye. Rita made a few more comments about the curtains and carpet before deciding it was time to leave.

'You've certainly landed on your feet,' was her parting shot to Naomi. 'Well, one foot, anyway,' she added as if she realised she'd sounded harsh and was trying to soften it.

All the way home she gave exaggerated imitations of Naomi's accent – *I wouldn't know about that* – which Meghan let pass. It was true that Rita had brought out the haughty side of Naomi, so much so that Meghan had begun to feel quite sorry for her old friend. Meghan was less patient when Rita started lecturing Meghan for letting Naomi steal Patrick from her.

'She's sitting there queening it and you're letting her get away with it.'

'As I keep telling you, I want no claim on Patrick. And I wish you'd stop talking about him as if he was up for sale. All a load of rubbish!'

'She's clearly smitten.'

'How you work that out, I do not know.'

'Elementary, my dear Watson. She's using anti-ageing wrinkle cream. Why else would she bother?' Rita reversed into her parking space with a flourish.

'I'll save my breath,' Meghan said.

24 *Naomi*

Naomi was reading when Claudia arrived. She'd found a full set of Virginia Woolf novels on the shelves behind her bed and was having another go at *To the Lighthouse*. But she wasn't in the mood and kept staring out at the misty rain drifting across the garden.

So she was pleased by the brief knock at her door and delighted when Patrick appeared. But he hardly had time to say, 'You have a visitor,' and something about Meghan, when he was swept aside. He withdrew with a most uncharacteristic wink.

The stranger entered the room as if stepping on stage. 'Helloo, Naomi!' she hooted. 'I'm Claudia. Meghan will have told you *all* about me, I'm sure.'

She ignored Naomi's proffered hand and swept about the room, a slender but imposing figure in a long velvet skirt and ankle boots. A silk shirt in purple and green floated as she moved and a purple scarf was wound around her silver hair, which hung to one side in a long tress. How theatrical. Had she forgotten her lines? Was she waiting for a cue?

When her visitor eventually turned to face her, Naomi put her book aside and gestured to the other chair. 'Meghan has told me absolutely nothing. I wasn't expecting you. Please enlighten me.'

'Oh, my dear! You must think me so *rude*!' Claudia clasped her face in both hands as if in shock.

She was like a Modigliani painting. Oval face, long nose, arched brows over huge dark eyes. In fact, the whole of her was elongated as if someone had taken the fabric of her body by the head and the feet and gently stretched it. Naomi checked these foolish thoughts to listen to what Claudia was saying. Evidently she was responsible for costumes in the local amateur dramatic society.

'Meghan said you were desperate for a project – and a needlewoman! Just what we need!'

'Ah, now I begin to understand.' Naomi was wary. "Desperate" was an overstatement, and she could kill Meghan for not warning her.

'Oh dear, how remiss of me! I haven't even asked about your leg. That's an *amazing* boot you have!'

'Ankle,' Naomi said. 'Ah yes, the Boot with a capital B. The relief of it after the cast. I'm still not allowed to put weight on it, but the joy is that I can take it off at night, which is bliss.'

'I can well imagine. But you're still not very mobile, then. No wonder you need a project.'

'But I'm really not up to making costumes.'

'Oh, no, no, no, no, no! You get me wrong. It's all about *embellishing, adorning*. Some appliqué here, embroidery there.' Claudia dived into a capacious tapestry bag that had been hidden in her skirts and pulled out several lengths of fabric, plain satin in pastel and jewel colours. 'These are skirt panels. Think Cinderella's ballgown. But adaptable! To fit – d'you see – a *number* of Cinderellas, ugly sisters, sleeping beauties. Cinderellas who may not look half-starved, Beauties who may be *lacking* in the beauty department. We can't choose who we get.' Claudia gave a throaty chuckle. 'The fat, the skinny, the ugly. The panels can be made to measure and the embellishments can be attached as required. Clever, is it not?'

Naomi nodded, a little dazed by the amount of fabric and Claudia's equally extravagant way of speaking.

'Here are some designs.' Claudia scrabbled in the bag and produced a notebook. 'Just a few scribbles I jotted down. *Ideas*, only. I'm sure you're *full* of your *own* ideas. You can ignore these.' She leapt up, opening a page, and handed Naomi the notebook, then sat back expectantly.

Naomi examined the sketch, noting that the detail went well beyond a casual scribble. Two pages in and she was aware of Claudia leaning forward and watching her intently. The message was clear: ignoring Claudia's designs was not an option.

'What do you think? What do you *think*?' Claudia was saying.

'They're wonderful. But can I do them justice?'

This appeared to be the right response. Claudia threw up her hands and clasped her face once more, this time beaming with pleasure. 'Oh, I know we're going to be such a *team*! Wunderbar!'

Claudia produced silk thread and cotton yarns and they discussed the forthcoming production of *Puss in Boots*. No, she wouldn't be taking part – *I don't like to steal the limelight*. Naomi smiled inwardly and was not surprised at Patrick's comment later in the day that Claudia was terrible on stage. *Overacts and then some*.

'No, my role is *guardian* of the wardrobe. My forte. We have hundreds of costumes, literally *hundreds*.'

'Where on earth do you keep them all? Has someone got a free barn?'

Claudia looked shocked. 'Indeed not! They are all in my attic rooms, properly temperature controlled.'

'So you really are the guardian.'

'Yes. Someone has to be in control. But anyway, this costume is not for the pantomime. It's for the pageant at the carnival. Next month. So you see, a *bit* of a deadline. Which is where you come in! Oh, and by the way, would you consider filling the role of Prompt for the pantomime?'

'January, did you say? Well, it's rather far ahead. I really can't say where I might be by then.'

'So it's a maybe! Probably. Wunderbar! But meanwhile…' Claudia left a pause for effect. 'There's *Carnival*. Big village event, in case you didn't know. Appliqué hearts for the Queen who made the tarts, such fun! And the *Alice in Wonderland* float has asked me to come up with something for the White Queen. "Off with their heads!" and so on. We can get on with those straight away. Perfect!' She leapt up, took another turn around the room, wandered into the kitchen and appraised the garden and terrace. 'What a grand little love-nest you have here!'

'Love-nest? What *are* you talking about?'

'Oh, come on, Naomi darling! Settled in here with the lovely Patrick right next door? Don't tell me you don't *absolutely* adore each other!'

'Rubbish!' Naomi hoped the heat she was feeling in her neck and face didn't show too much. 'I'm a pensioner with a bus pass, for heaven's sake.'

Claudia cackled. 'Aren't we all! No one would think it to look at you. And a mere *babe*, anyway. *Carpe diem* is what I say. And I speak as one older and wiser, being seventy-one.'

'Never!'

Claudia simpered and stroked her cheek. 'My skin. I've always been most fortunate with my skin. But what I'm saying is, don't *waste* the opportunity being offered!'

Naomi was about to tell the lovely Claudia to mind her own business when the door opened on a brief knock and Patrick appeared.

He nodded to Claudia and spoke to Naomi. 'I'm off to shop – have you got a list?'

As Naomi pointed to the kitchen, Claudia cut across them. 'I was just saying what a *perfect* love-nest this is! And don't tell me you haven't fallen for this perfectly stunning woman.'

Patrick didn't miss a beat. He fetched the shopping list from the fridge door and waved it at Naomi. 'Got it,' he said before rounding on Claudia, one eyebrow raised. 'As for you, Claudia darling, you're incorrigible. You really can't help it, can you? Just take your moth-eaten bag of tricks and depart – with an apology for weaving ridiculous innuendos out of thin air and your fertile imagination.'

He waved at Naomi and vanished. Claudia did indeed gather up her bag and make for the door, but with no sign of an apology.

Instead she gave another of her throaty chuckles. 'Methinks the gentleman doth protest too much! I wish you well, my dear, and will call by next week to see how you're getting on.' At the door she turned. 'With the sewing, that is.'

And she too was gone, leaving Naomi in a ferment of fury and confusion. Claudia was taking advantage of her, Meghan had left her in the dark and, although Patrick was clearly on her side, she couldn't deny feeling a quiver of disappointment at being reduced to a "ridiculous innuendo". Just wait until she got hold of Meghan! But Meghan did not appear and was not answering the phone. Naomi grabbed her crutches and made her way to the garden, where she collapsed onto a damp chair and stared at the sky.

It was early evening before Patrick reappeared with her shopping and a bottle of wine. That morning he'd been wearing a baggy cotton sweater but he'd changed into a crisp white shirt with the sleeves rolled up that showed off his tan.

'Sorry about Claudia,' he said. 'Hope she wasn't too annoying.'

'Annoying? Excruciating! Embarrassing! Intrusive! You name it.'

'Oh dear. Definitely calls for some of this particularly good Rioja.' He poured them each a glass and settled in the chair opposite her. 'She's impossible, that woman.'

'And what if she goes gossiping around the place that we're having an affair?'

'She won't. Claudia is a lot of things, but not a gossip. *Rather common*, you know! I think of her as a catalyst.'

Catalyst of what? Naomi briefly wondered and let it go. 'She looks so extraordinary. Like a Modigliani, however you pronounce him.'

'Oh yes, she likes to cultivate that image. As if she were his muse. In some kind of time warp. No, she's eccentric, good-hearted and totally impossible.' Then he raised his glass. 'But of course, impossible she may be, but she is also right.'

Naomi's glass juddered as she raised it to her lips. 'Right?'

'You see, I *have* fallen for this stunning woman right here in front of me. But I didn't want to make any move that would cause a difficulty in this situation. You see what I mean?'

Naomi was shaking. She managed to put her glass down without spilling it but didn't have the same success with her tears. Inexplicable tears. She shrugged and waved her hands about and took the immaculate handkerchief that Patrick handed her, but they would not stop.

Patrick waited. Eventually he said, 'It's what I was afraid of. I've upset the applecart. I should have just told you to ignore Claudia. Don't worry, I'll keep my distance. You can stay and nothing will change.'

Naomi shook her head vigorously, so that strands of hair escaped and fell about her face. 'Except everything has changed,' she said and paused. It took her a few moments to look up at him. 'You see, she *is* right. I feel the same. And I didn't want to let you know for the very same reasons – and some other reasons as well, to be honest.'

Patrick's smile spread from his mouth to his eyes, hesitantly at first as if he dared not risk it, until his whole face was beaming. He stepped across the space between them, took her face in his hands and kissed her gently on the lips.

'I can't tell you how happy that makes me.'

Naomi smiled up at him. 'Me too. But it's not that simple.'

'I know. Go on.'

'It's not what I was looking for. An affair. A relationship. Any kind of commitment.'

'Me neither. The last thing on my mind. Until I brought you breakfast on that first morning.'

'Oh yes! That boiled egg!' Naomi's eyes pricked with tears at the memory. 'I guess that's really when…'

'Love at first sight, then. Mutual.'

'Yes, and it wasn't just the egg.' She took his hand. 'This is what I wanted to do then, and I've wanted to do it ever since.' She stroked his forearm and kissed the back of his hand where a further sprinkling of fine hairs grew from along the knuckles. 'I don't know how an arm can be soo sexy.'

They kissed again until Naomi, not trusting what she might do next, pushed him gently away.

'But love is so complicated. Patrick, you need to know, I'm not good at love.'

'But it does come in many forms.' He sat back down and sipped his wine. 'Let me just say this. I've been thinking it out all afternoon. I'm perfectly content with how I live and work at the moment. And though—'

'So, you mean, I'd upset your applecart?'

Stopped in his tracks, Patrick gulped. 'That's a bit harsh, but I suppose, yes. In theory, I'd like to be with you every moment of every day, every night, but if I'm honest, I'm not sure it would work.'

'It wouldn't.' Naomi sipped her wine, noting the fleeting look of surprise in Patrick's expression. 'As far as applecarts go, what you're describing – a 24/7 relationship – would completely scupper mine.'

Patrick gazed out of the window, apparently lost for words. 'So we agree,' was all he said.

She nodded. 'That's good, isn't it?'

'We've become friends and I value that hugely.'

'Me too. And, anyway, it doesn't have to be either/or, does it?'

Patrick shook his head and topped up their wine. 'Of course it doesn't.'

She eyed him sideways as she took her glass. 'So much new territory to explore. So much we don't know about each other. Exciting, but scary. Like, I don't even know the colour of your kitchen units or whether you wear pyjamas or not.'

Patrick laughed and visibly relaxed. 'I thought you said you didn't know anything about love.'

'Correction! I said I was no *good* at it. Plenty of opportunity – from marriage to so-called casual affairs, but I never seem to learn.'

He shrugged. 'Stories to tell. Bound to be – at our age.'

'But not now. And it need not be that complicated.' The least complicated thing in Naomi's field of vision at that moment was her bed, just beyond Patrick's chair, which she had painstakingly made up with fresh sheets that morning. It had worn her out, hobbling from one corner to the next, but now it seemed worth the effort.

'One day at a time, is how I see it. No need to rush into anything.'

Naomi was experiencing a strong urge to rush into quite a lot, but she nodded. 'Are we mad?'

'Quite probably we are. But somehow we can make it work. Let's drink to that.'

25 Naomi

Naomi was in the garden when Meghan called in on the morning after Claudia's visit.

'At last!' Naomi greeted her. 'Have I got a bone to pick with you!'

Meghan made a grovelling gesture as she crossed the lawn. 'I've already had a ticking-off from Patrick for letting Claudia loose on you.'

'That monstrous woman! I couldn't—'

'But now I see you, I'm not sorry.' Meghan sat down, head on one side, appraising her friend. 'Let me guess. She was indiscreet, you were both indignant, and then one thing led to another.'

'How dare you suggest what I think you're suggesting!'

'I only have to look at you. All "aglow", as they say, after a rattling good night of it.'

'Meghan!' Naomi started out indignant and tailed away. 'You are so right.'

Meghan hugged her. 'I just knew it. Even when I heard Patrick's voice – he was ticking me off, but his voice – well, he didn't sound too displeased. Kind of jaunty.'

Naomi grinned. 'We had such a talk – decided to take things really slowly – and then did exactly the opposite.'

'That is such good news. And where's the sense in taking things slowly?'

'At my age. Not that sixty is old these days.' Naomi grinned. '*Carpe diem*, as Claudia would say. In the end it all happened so quickly that I forgot to worry about my saggy bits.'

Meghan clapped her hands. 'Why would you?'

Naomi laughed, clutching herself around the waist. 'Didn't seem to be a problem. The worst of it will be Claudia finding out she's right!'

'Claudia's okay. Really she is, when you get past the façade. She'll be happy for you.'

'Maybe.' She shrugged. 'I thought I'd hit the jackpot ending up in this place, but to find it comes with a live-in lover… Well!'

Meghan looked towards the house. 'Not bad, I'll say that. I've always liked the place. You won't want to leave. Or, will you—'

'No plans to move next door, if that's what you're thinking. I'll still move to the cottage. Suppose I moved next door and it didn't last?' She shook her head, laughing. That seemed so unlikely, but it could, of course, happen. 'That wouldn't suit Patrick, anyway. In fact, much more likely to last if we don't live together. No, the cottage is my base, my anchor. I don't want to be at a loose end any more.' She stretched her arms above her head, into the warmth of the sun. 'Meanwhile, this beats all the dreary places I've lived in over the last few years.'

Meghan nodded and smiled across at her, lifting her face to the sun. 'Oh, yes, that reminds me. Rita was going on about that glamping site again. It reminded me – I keep meaning to ask you about your friend who lived in a yurt. Evie, was it? Did you say you met on a train?'

Naomi stared at the grass, wondering where to begin.

'Sure, yes. On the train when I left Wilson, yes. But I didn't take her up on her offer to visit for some time. Evie was quite unassuming in contrast to her yurt. That was sumptuous, as I must have said. I couldn't think what I was coming to. There it sat, blending with a dull corner of an ordinary field – but inside! It was just a glow of vibrant colours and textures – rugs and hangings, brass jugs, polished wooden platters and this overwhelming smell of incense and spice. She told me she'd got half the stuff out of skips. There was an especially beautiful hanging – animals worked in browns and amber – I loved it – and that came from a skip. The things people throw out you wouldn't believe.'

'I would believe, actually. I've done a bit of scavenging in my time, and it drives Alex mad. You can imagine.'

Naomi nodded, reluctant to be diverted now she had got started. 'Anyway, there I was being welcomed into this Aladdin's cave. Evie lit a Primus stove and made dandelion coffee, which was absolutely disgusting. But the home-made hummus and home-baked bread made up for it. But baking bread in a tent?'

'I was wondering the same.'

'It was her brother's farm and he lived alone. So every so often she'd go up and bake, fill his freezer. Do a bit of cleaning. Counted it as her rental.'

'So why did she cotton on to you, why did she invite you? Was she in the habit of picking people up on trains?'

'I know. It was a bit weird. But it came at the right time and I went with that. She told me she sensed I was in need of a rest, to recuperate from whatever I'd left. I mean, I hadn't even told her I'd left anything, so that was a bit spooky.'

'It was probably written all over you,' Meghan said.

Naomi laughed. 'Likely it was. And Evie definitely had a sixth sense. Of course, what I didn't know about her then was that she was a healer. She ran healing circles, evenings, weekends. But she didn't mention that then. Just offered me her caravan. It was just up behind the yurt, used mainly for storage.'

'A better bet than the yurt?'

'Hmm. Yes and no. It was a very old, old-fashioned two-berth job. At first it seemed compact and cosy, but it wasn't long before that turned into cramped and smelly, but I had nowhere else to live at the time, so I moved in.' Naomi grinned, remembering the smell of rotting vegetation mixed with paraffin. 'I took one guy back to the van – bad idea! But where else was I to go? We'd been out a few times and I was hopeful, but the muddy field and the smell put him right off, plus he was convinced that anyone living in a yurt must be sectionable, which made him nervous. So that was the end of that! Just as well, really. Obviously wouldn't have lasted.' She sighed and shifted the boot on its footstool. 'It was an odd time. My peripatetic year, I call it. If you really want to hear about that, I think it needs some coffee. Would you? I've even got some chocolate digestives.'

'I do.' Meghan leapt up. 'Coffee on its way.'

Even now, it still hurts, doesn't it, when you think of how that came about, the moving between Fay and Evie. Fay and her family had moved to leafy Twickenham and the first blow was that there was no room in the new house known as Naomi's room. Of course there wasn't. Why would there be? But that didn't stop you feeling hurt when Fay put you on a sofa bed in a tiny room, which seemed to be part storeroom, part office.

It became clear to you that Fay's easy-going husband wasn't as keen on your lengthy stays as Fay maintained. He had a way of narrowing his eyes when he came home to find the two of you in the kitchen with a bottle of wine. And Fay – she had other friends, new interests. The children were now teenagers, so no bedtime stories. They didn't exactly ignore you, but sometimes you felt invisible.

'A peripatetic existence, you said.' Meghan set down the tray and opened the packet of biscuits. 'How did that happen?'

Naomi explained the shift in her friendship with Fay, and Daniel's veiled hostility. 'So, when Daniel started narrowing his eyes, that's when I first came to find Evie. Then when the compact and cosy caravan became too cramped and smelly, I'd still go to Fay, just for a long weekend.'

'Reckon this is brewed.' Meghan poured the coffee.

'There was another thing. My father lived just down the road from Evie – in a bungalow he'd found on the edge of town. Not far from the house where I grew up. View of the river, roses in the garden, bus stop at the end of the road. I needed a permanent address – for jobs and so on. We got on, me and him, not close. But he was happy to see me from time to time.'

'Jobs,' Meghan said. 'Yes, I was wondering how you were supporting yourself.'

'I did a shedload of stuff. Even got a proper job teaching at a girls' boarding school. They made me head of modern languages eventually. It allowed me to save. But the school trips finally did me in. All those kids on the loose in a foreign city and I was supposed to be responsible!'

Meghan nodded in sympathy. 'And then what?'

'I worked cruise ships for a couple of years. Plus, there was always estate agency work – you knew about that? Yes, useful stopgap depending on the housing market. My London experience stood me in good stead. Meanwhile dating such a hotch-potch of the male species. Trying on different ways of loving and being loved, I suppose. Except love rarely entered into it, or was one-sided. Mostly lust or loneliness or thinking I could fix a bloke. Huh! Or curious about what made a guy tick – only to find out it was football or steak pie. But then, I didn't even know what made me tick.'

'But you do now?'

'I think I'm beginning to. Evie had the answer, of course. She'd say, *Let go, just let go!* I didn't understand. Now I think I know what she meant, but I still can't do it. Anyway, back to the Evie-to-Fay-to-Dad time. This is the difficult bit.' Naomi paused and sipped the hot coffee. 'I went back and forth for several months. Working whenever I could and going to Fay when I was out of a job until I'd think, Fay's had enough of me. Or it was a case of having enough of the smelly caravan, or if Dad told me that story one more time I would scream.'

'So you were always escaping something? Not looking forward to anything positive.'

'Oh, I did always look forward to seeing Fay. But it was usually disappointing. And then this happened when I was staying at Fay's. I overheard Daniel as I came downstairs. "She takes you for granted," he was saying. I just froze. He couldn't mean me? Surely? He was washing up, running the tap, clattering the cutlery, so I didn't hear it all. Only "The moment things go pear-shaped…" and Fay was shushing him. He even said I was a good sort, but that wasn't the point.' Naomi grabbed a biscuit and spoke with her mouth full. 'And then Fay said, "But, darling, she hasn't got anyone else." I stopped going to Fay's after that.'

'Oh, Naomi, that was tough.'

'Fay and I had our first row the next morning – first and last. I packed my bag and went down to the kitchen to wait for her to get back from the school run. Meant to just say an ordinary civil goodbye. But her kitchen got to me. Ridiculous really. Whether it was accident or design, the layout was just like her mother's kitchen used to be – the sanctuary I never wanted to leave as a child. Not just the dresser, the table and so on but the feel of it – that heart-of-the-home, cosy atmosphere.' She paused, fiddled with her hair, looked out the window. 'I was *jealous*, would you believe.'

Meghan nodded, said nothing.

'And the longer I stood there, the more resentful I got. She was hardly through the door before I accused her of caring more about her yoga than about me. I told her she was letting Daniel turn her away from me, that she'd better be careful or she'd end up with no friends. Crazy! Of course, Daniel wasn't like that. It was my ex, Tony, who'd behaved like that. I knew that. Fay knew that.' She sighed heavily. 'But by then I was on a roll. And I said an equally ridiculous and unforgivable thing. Seems I wanted that kitchen so badly that I persuaded myself that it could or should have been mine.'

Meghan's grunt had several question marks attached.

Naomi nodded. 'You may well grunt. Wait till you hear this one. I accused her of stealing Daniel from me.'

Meghan's eyebrows shot up.

'Ludicrous,' Naomi continued. 'We met at a dance. The New Year hop at the local tennis club. Fay and I had arranged to meet at the bar and I got there a bit early. Got chatting to this very fanciable guy, and he seemed to take a shine to me. After ten minutes I was smitten, thinking my evening was made. Then Fay arrived. Blonde, petite, sexy Fay in a strappy black dress, bouncing in with a funny story about why the cat had made her late. He was mesmerised. Eyes locked. Love at first sight, the whole bit. When he offered to get her a drink, she went with him. End of story, they never looked back.' She shrugged and took a gulp of her drink. 'So, he was never mine to steal. Obviously! But all that garbage came pouring out in Fay's kitchen. Afterwards I couldn't believe I'd even thought it. And it was certainly better left unsaid.'

Naomi put her head in her hands and spoke to the earth. 'My big mouth. Fay was still holding the car keys. She waved them and said she'd take me to the station. Very calm as if she was a bomb disposal expert working on a particularly volatile device. We drove in silence.'

'I hope that wasn't the last time you saw her?'

'Fortunately, not. But listen. I wrote to her and had a very careful letter back. As it happened, she was planning to tell me something when she got back from the school run that morning.'

Naomi took a deep breath.

'She had a breast lump. She'd just got the date for surgery and she was going to ask me to come and hold the fort while she was in hospital and convalescing at home. But she'd thought better of that, of course. It was caught in time, and she got the all clear. But she didn't know that then. My chance to be there for her for a change and I blew it. Never forgave myself for that.'

'Oh crumbs, what terrible timing! Poor Fay. Poor you.'

'I never stayed with her again, but we still saw each other. Met up for the day. Salisbury was a good halfway point. We were still mates, but something shifted after that. It was never quite the same again. And, then, when the caravan fell apart, I moved in permanently with Dad.'

Meghan gazed across the garden. Breaking the silence, she said, 'You know, it's a funny thing, but your story of Evie turns out to be all about Fay.'

'Huh! Yes I suppose it is. Everything seems to lead back to Fay.' She held out her mug. 'Can you squeeze any more out of that pot?'

She stared into her drink. 'D'you really want to know about Evie? Okay, then. As I said, she was a healer, held these circles with local women. Evie was usually serene. As you'd expect from someone who lived according to the principle of being at peace with the earth and who meditated twice a day.'

'Ooh! You say that with a bit of an edge! Did you even like her?'

'Oh, I did. I really did. She was genuine, she knew who she was, she didn't pretend. But I guess she made me feel a bit inadequate, superficial.'

'So, what about the circles?'

'They invited me to join in but I wouldn't. There was one I liked to listen to. Chanting, with steady drumming in the background. I would fall asleep to the chanting and slept more deeply than at any other time.'

'Sounds good.'

Naomi nodded. 'One evening when the group had been convened for an hour or so, there came a knock at my door. They offered to put me in the centre of the circle for the chanting. How could I refuse? It was amazing. It was as if I could *feel* their voices almost tangibly. They vibrated into my body. And they chanted the song I most loved.' She sang:

The river is flowing
Flowing and growing.
The river is flowing
Back to the sea.

Naomi paused with a flush of embarrassment, but Meghan joined in and they sang together:

Mother earth carry me
Child I will always be
Mother earth carry me
Back to the sea.

'Come to think of it,' Naomi said. 'That song is what kept me sane when I fell off the cliff path. It was a turning point. I left Evie's not long after.'

'Any particular reason?'

'Lots of things. The caravan. Dad. I suppose I hoped Evie might become a friend. But she didn't do friends, not personal friends, that is. Just impersonal ones.' She laughed. 'Odd idea, sounds weird, but what I mean is, she related best to people in groups. She was brilliant at that, when the focus was on the common cause, activity, whatever, and not on the one-to-one.'

Meghan nodded. 'I've known people like that. Have you seen her since?'

Naomi shook her head. 'I went back once, but the yurt was gone. They told me in the shop that she'd moved into the farmhouse with her brother. I've never had the courage to go and see.'

26 *Naomi*

The curtains lifted gently in the air from the open window, sending ripples of pale sunlight round the room. Naomi stretched and stared at the shadow patterns on the ceiling. Such a deep sense of well-being. The past week had been like a honeymoon. Well, it *was* a honeymoon. Seeing and being seen. Trusting and being trusted. She'd known nothing like it since Dieter. Without the angst and with the sex. The sex was truly amazing. Age turned out not to matter at all. Their bodies just found each other. Thank goodness they hadn't had to negotiate the plaster cast – the timing had been just right.

It must be an hour since Patrick got up, leaving her to luxuriate. He'd reappeared in his clinical white jacket bringing her a mug of coffee. 'Appointments right through today,' he'd said. 'So I won't be around for lunch. But you are summoned for afternoon tea at four.'

Summoned. The word echoed back at her. Not asked. Not invited. But summoned. He'd made it sound mock formal and jokey, of course. But even so. It was a reminder that honeymoons come to an end.

After a promising start, by four o'clock, the day had turned dank and chilly, and Patrick had lit the wood-burner in his snug. 'I know it's July but it feels more like November,' he said, adding a log and turning to kiss her.

Scones and jam and cream were laid out on a coffee table along with a tea strainer for the Earl Grey leaves. Too-good-to-be-true never looked better.

'Time to tell each other about our past lives,' Patrick said as he poured the tea. 'Don't you think?'

It took Naomi by surprise but it made sense. 'So that's what this is about.'

'So much we don't know – things that have shaped who we both are. You go first. My story is short and not very interesting.'

'I doubt that, but we'll see.' She took the mug he handed her. Fine porcelain, and a relief not to be juggling cups and saucers. 'I guess that's how it is – when you meet people later in life. Lots of water under lots of bridges. Don't know where to start.'

'This Wilson chap? Who seems to have been a bit of a nutter.'

'That's a bit of a simplification.' Naomi was surprised to feel so indignant at this description of Wilson. However much she hated the man, she wanted to be fair, and to keep the monopoly on insulting him. Patrick didn't have the right. 'Actually, I'm not going to let you get away with a remark like that when you never even met him.'

'I was just being flippant.'

'Flippant doesn't suit you.'

'Call it jealousy. I suppose I'm nervous about what I might hear.'

Naomi grinned. 'So you should be. That makes more sense. So, from the beginning.'

She took her time, moving from the good, through the weird and on to the bad times as she outlined her involvement with Wilson. She described how she escaped, but left out any reference to Wilson's more unsavoury practices. There were things Patrick didn't need to know.

When she'd finished Patrick set his plate on the table. 'So it was a case of out of the frying pan into the fire when you linked up with him.'

'That's exactly what my friend Fay said. As I told her then, that's not really fair. Wilson encouraged me no end. He showed me who I was, who I could be.'

'And that was worth all the pain? You don't wish…?'

'It was a revelation that there was such a thing as getting to know yourself. There was a lot of it about back then. Self-development, the Human Potential movement. It was the beginning of a journey for me, I suppose. Of course, there are things I should have handled differently. I wish I hadn't got so entangled.' Looking up, she caught a look in Patrick's eyes, a shadow that darkened them. 'And I certainly should have left sooner. But overall, no, I have no regrets.' She stretched her hands out to the fire. 'And anyway, think about it. If it hadn't been for Wilson, I'd never have come to this neck of the woods. I wouldn't be here with you now. So how could I regret it?'

Patrick beamed across at her. 'So, if Wilson was or wasn't the fire – a crucible perhaps – you'd better tell me about the frying pan. More tea?'

'Huh, Tony. He only ever wanted me as a possession. A possession he could shape to his requirements.' She took a mouthful of scone and held out her mug. 'It was abundantly clear, even on our wedding day. I didn't see it, of course, but my father did. He warned me.'

Patrick nodded, filled his own cup and sat back, giving her all his attention.

'"Watch out" is what Dad said. Just those two words.'

She could hear them now, so serious, so intense. 'They took his goodbye peck on the cheek to a whole new level, I can tell you.'

She took a sip of tea. 'If he'd said, "Take care", or "Safe journey", or even "Be careful", it wouldn't have been that significant. Those phrases are so commonplace – you know what I mean? –the clichés of saying goodbye, I suppose – well-wishing, mind-how-you-go. But "Watch out" sounded more like a command. And that from Dad, who wasn't one for making a song and dance.'

She paused, reluctant to embark on the sorry tale of her marriage, but Patrick prompted her to go on.

'Even Mum chipped in. She had one of those rare moments of remembering she was my mother. She was touching up her make-up. She turned round from the mirror. I can see her now, lipstick poised, and she looked right at me. Which was unusual in itself. "Your father may well have a point," she said. That might not sound much but I knew she didn't like Tony and her remark – and the fact that she bothered to chip in – massively underlined Dad's warning. Then she carried on titivating and complaining about the poor light.'

'And this was on your wedding day, you say?'

'Yes, we were in the hotel lobby at the time – me with Dad and Mum in a sort of uneasy limbo, waiting for Tony to join us on the steps for the "going away" photographs. So we'd only been married a few hours. I was wearing a striped dress under a narrow navy coat with a matching cap. Thought I looked the bee's knees. Mum had fixed the cap at a jaunty angle and she'd tucked my hair behind my ears. I'd protested about the hair, but Mum insisted, said that otherwise I looked like a hamster. So that was that. And I was actually quite pleased with the look. Mum always had a knack.'

Naomi paused again and drew breath.

'Anyway, the first thing Tony did in the cab to the airport was pull off the cap. I thought he was going to kiss me, romantic idiot that I was. But no. He started tugging my hair forward, pulling on the clips that held it back. It hurt. I remember saying "*Stop*" and "*Ouch*" loud enough that the driver half-turned his head.

'"Bad hairstyle," says Tony. "You should never show your ears. They're too big. Remember?" I protested but not a lot. I'd never considered my ears before. True, I inherited them from Dad and he'd been teased about his from time to time. But his stuck out and mine did not, so mine were less noticeable – or so I thought.' Naomi found herself touching her ears, pulling a few loose strands of hair over them. 'You see? Self-conscious about them even now! I tried a hamster joke but Tony ignored me. He just stared out of the window. Not a word until we reached the airport. Big sulk.'

'So how was the honeymoon?'

'Funnily enough, we had a wonderful week. It was like going back to when we first met and travelled all over Europe. The fun Tony, he was a charmer, we had a high old time. And in Venice, I managed like this.' She clamped her hands on either side of her face. 'Kept a few locks in place with sunglasses. What a farce!'

They were both quiet, staring into the glow of the fire.

Patrick broke the silence. 'So when did the fun Tony evaporate?'

'Oh, not long after we got back. There was a heatwave and I was agonising one morning about whether to wear shorts to a neighbour's barbecue. I was peering into the wardrobe, muttering about hating my thighs. As you do. And then came this voice – "But they're better than your calves by a long chalk." He was right behind me. "Pity about your legs," he said. And he meant it, he was *serious*!'

'The man's pathetic. Nothing whatsoever wrong with your excellent legs.'

'Not my best feature, admittedly. This time I inherited from Mum.' She laughed and re-crossed her legs, stupidly glad that she was wearing jeans. 'And her legs never got in *her* way. If I'd ever thought about it, I'd have preferred Dad's slender ankle and finely turned calf. But I never did think about it – not until Tony drew attention to the unfortunate state of my pins. At the time I just laughed it off and wore a long skirt to the barbecue.'

'I guess that was just the beginning.'

She nodded. 'There were the parties where I was kept on a short lead, and moved on if I talked too long or smiled too much with any particular man. "Don't want you going the way of your mother," Tony would say as if it were a joke. I'm not sure how he knew about that side of Mum, but he'd picked it up somehow. Maybe I'd mentioned one too many uncles. Maybe he'd picked something up at the wedding reception. Mum behaved impeccably, but people love to gossip and he might have overheard something. It was a weapon he could use.'

'Bastard.' Patrick spoke with a force that startled her. 'When did you decide enough was enough?'

'It took me a while. Because, all in all, it was a reasonable life. From what I heard of other people's marriages, I was well off. Plenty of money, plenty of sex and security in return for toeing Tony's line. I managed to develop a whole new set of values. Detached house in Wimbledon, shiny car, shopping at Waitrose, having whatever clothes I fancied. Superficial wasn't in it. You wouldn't have liked me one little bit.'

'Oh, I think I would. Give me credit. I might just have seen past all that.'

'Fay used to tease me for being the perfect suburban housewife and I learned to keep Fay and Tony in separate compartments of my life. Fay kept my old self alive. She used to say it took at least an hour for her to surface. She'd open the kitchen cupboard and say, "Is Old Naomi in here – alongside the baked beans and bottle of plonk?" Or she'd poke about under the debris of trikes and wellies that cluttered the hall or in amongst the children's toys and say, "Still can't find her," and in the end we'd fall about laughing and there I was, old Naomi back at last. She was such a good friend. Never gave up on me.'

'You must miss her horribly.'

Naomi nodded. 'Every day. We shared everything. And when things came to a head and I finally left Tony, she took me in.'

She wasn't about to give Patrick the sordid details of how things came to a head. There were some things best left unsaid. She didn't want him to picture her humiliation.

You were blonde in those days, of course. Because gentlemen preferred blondes and Tony certainly liked to think of himself as a gentleman. The tyranny of those roots. It was sluttish to let them show, or to have chipped nail varnish, or no nail varnish at all, come to that.

Then there was the business of your legs being written off. Lucky it was no longer the era of the miniskirt. You hid all the photos of you and Fay in your Mary Quant lookalikes – yards of unremarkable legs getting away with it. But even though they never appeared in public, your legs had to be smooth, hairless and tanned. And none of those creams which produced a tiger effect and which she and Fay had once giggled over, waving their orange hands as they tried in vain to wash it all off. No, it had to be a salon job. Tony insisted.

You had to admit that the security Tony offered was beginning to feel like high security. Vigilance was a habit you'd learned as a child with Imogen for a mother, so it had been no big deal to begin with. Your other childhood escape, *Let's Pretend*, had also worked well, but both strategies were wearing a bit thin.

For instance, you struggled with putting on weight back then and there was no pretending about those extra pounds. Comfort eating, of course. But Tony liked his women slim. Being able to pinch an inch was another slutty offence in a hierarchy of misdemeanours that would incur a slap. In those days, your favourite unwinding treat was a hot bath with a secret Mars bar, the latest edition of *Cosmopolitan* and old favourites Slade or the Stones belting out from the cassette player in the living room.

But that was your undoing. It was your day off and Tony came home sick and caught you at it. The first you knew was the abrupt silence. Hazel O'Connor choked off in the middle of "Writing on the Wall". He stood in the bathroom doorway looking as if he'd caught you in bed with your lover.

You leapt up, of course, full of wifely concern for the flu symptoms that had brought him home. Before you had time to grab a towel, he'd taken several non-too-playful swipes at your too-fat, too-red buttocks as they emerged from the steam, and you could tell how things were going to go. There would be hell to pay, dragged out over days. More than a slap. You were having to admit that by then.

'Go to bed,' you said. 'I'll bring you a honey and lemon, a hot water bottle.'

You grabbed your housecoat – the fluffy pink one with the matching mules he gave you for Christmas – and headed for the kitchen. But he grabbed your wrist, rattled the Mars wrapper in your face and dragged you into the living room. He flicked open the tape deck, brandishing the offending cassette. Then he made a great play of snagging the shiny brown film with his door key, twisting and pulling it until it fell in scrolls and spirals to the floor. And just to be sure you wouldn't find a suitable pencil and wind it carefully back, he flicked out the tiny penknife on his key ring and sliced neatly through one of the loops.

'I always knew it would come in handy one day,' he said.

It wasn't clear which was the worst transgression. The fattening chocolate bar? The subversive songs? Or the magazine that dared to talk to thinking women about sex? And which was worse – reading about your own sexuality or aspiring to be a thinking woman? Or was that all far too subtle for Tony? Who knows, but it was certainly the turning point for you. The writing on the wall was very clear.

'You're miles away,' Patrick said.

'Years away. Memories coming back to haunt me. Things I don't want to talk about. Enough is enough. I've been yakking away about me for hours. It's your turn now.'

The tea had gone cold, the scones were partly demolished and the fire was low.

'I guess it is.' There was a shake in his voice. 'I'll just clear this lot. Put a few logs in the stove, would you? Can you manage?'

He returned with two gin and tonics, an unusual choice for Patrick. 'I reckoned the sun was over the yardarm.'

She watched as he bent to adjust the vents on the stove and orange flames leapt up behind the glass. 'Your turn,' she said.

'So, about Laurie.' He paused and took a deep breath. 'Laurie was the love of my life. Simple as that. She was a neighbour, daughter of friends of my parents. We were fifteen when we met and I never wanted anyone else.'

There was a greyness in his voice that Naomi had never heard before.

'The thing about Laurie was that she never really left home. Even when we were married – we lived close to her parents and she saw her mother every single day. One sadness was that she couldn't have children. I always thought that might have helped her grow up. But no. Down to some medical condition that I never understood and she wouldn't explain.'

Naomi raised an eyebrow and Patrick nodded.

'I know. I came to doubt that there was any such medical condition. But I never challenged her. It would have seemed like a betrayal. The love of my life – but I couldn't trust her?' Ice cubes chinked as he swirled the drink in his glass. 'But I suppose, by having that thought and saying nothing, I was being dishonest. Betraying her in another way.'

'That's being a bit harsh on yourself, I'd say. And not your fault if she wouldn't talk about it.'

'She couldn't bear any kind of conflict. In fact, she was only ever completely happy when she was painting. That was her "for real" activity. Even though she never thought her pictures were any good. The rest of the time it was like she was playing at keeping house, acting the role of hostess, wife, even. Or she'd be round at her mother's telling her every last detail of what she'd done in the last twenty-four hours.'

As this picture of a marriage unfolded, Naomi tried to keep her eyebrows under control. The role-playing was familiar. She'd done it herself with Tony. But in the context of a loving relationship? Tony wasn't, had never been, the love of her life. This was not what she'd been expecting.

'But I still loved her. There was something magical about her. Delicate, and needed protecting – or so I thought. Frail, yet strong. Magnetic. I was probably under some kind of enchantment.' He gave a short laugh and gulped his gin.

Naomi nodded, said nothing.

'When her mother died – that's when we got this place. I thought a change of scene might help. I thought I was in with a chance – to be the important person in her life. She used to say I was the love of *her* life, too. But when her mother was no longer there, she stopped saying it. Maybe she realised that Mother was the only real love of her life.' He paused and peered into his glass. 'I think we need the other half.'

He took her glass which was still half full and disappeared into the kitchen. Patrick, who rarely drank spirits. The story was very different from the one she'd heard from Meghan, where Laurie came across as an arrogant snob who thought her pictures too good to be exhibited in the local gallery. 'Fur coat and no knickers,' was apparently how Gracie of Gracie's Gallery had described her. 'A tad unfair,' Meghan had added, 'as Gracie had never seen any of her paintings. And pretty rich coming from Gracie, anyway. She might own the gallery but she doesn't know the first thing about art.'

Patrick returned with the drinks and sat down heavily. 'No, this place backfired. She came down when we moved in. But the coast didn't inspire her, as I'd hoped it might. It terrified her. She hated the countryside. Cattle scared her, birds were annoying. She was even scared of the locals. Couldn't understand what they were saying. I mean, that's ridiculous – the accent isn't that broad! But she was convinced they were laughing at her.' He paused, twisting his glass in his hands. 'You know what she said to me? It was a wild evening not long after we moved in here. We were going to bed and she looked out at the trees lashing about in the garden and she said, "Mummy's never been here. She won't know where to find me."'

'I see what you mean about never growing up.'

'Not to mention the fact that her mother was dead. I couldn't think what to say. I drew the curtains to shut out the trees and just folded her up in my arms and rocked her to sleep.'

She heard the tenderness in his voice. 'Best thing you could have done.'

'Mostly when I tried to comfort her, she wouldn't let me near. She seemed to have grown an extra skin, a carapace which I couldn't get through. Held herself back from me. I realised Laurie had always done that.'

A tear ran down Patrick's cheek and he brushed it away. Naomi stretched a hand across the table and he brushed her fingertips with his. 'I'm sorry. I've never told anyone this before. Never admitted it. Not properly. Not even to myself.'

Naomi nodded and waited while he took a gulp of gin.

'Anyway, it seemed I needed another strategy. We'd sold our place in London and I'd built up a practice down here by then and I didn't want to move. Couldn't afford to. So I built the studio – your annexe – for her to have to herself. No need to go outside – she could paint all day and every day. Hoped it would persuade her to stay. But that didn't work either. Oh, she was ecstatic at first. Spent all her time in there, hardly ever with me. But it didn't last. She kept on going through the motions a few times – it was almost as if she hoped it might work. But it never did. After a week or so she'd make some excuse and go back to London to her cantankerous old father. There was no need, he had a live-in housekeeper. But Laurie moved back into her childhood bedroom.'

'And did she still come here at all?'

He shook his head. 'Not for the last year of her life. I went up there a few times. Nothing was said. We were still married. It was an odd limbo.' He set down his glass and stared into the fire. 'She was in London when she died. Collapsed suddenly on the stairs. It turned out there was indeed a medical condition, but not one anybody knew about. Sudden Death Syndrome, they called it. I was numb for months. But it felt as if I'd lost her long ago. I had years of grieving to catch up on.'

'I can imagine. And what a shock that must have been.'

'It was. Didn't seem true. Even after the funeral. But what I do know, in case you're wondering, is that I don't regret any of it.' He leant back and stretched. 'And that's it, really. You see, you've led a much more colourful life than I have.'

'But what's colourful, and what does that matter? To have loved. That's more important, isn't it? Okay, it was far from perfect, but Laurie was the love of your life.'

Patrick gave a tiny shrug and spread his hands on his knees. 'She was. And I can't answer your question. Except maybe you, we, learn from it all.' He got to his feet. 'And now, I can't talk about it any more. I'm totally knackered – need to go to bed.'

'Can I at least give you a hug?'

'Of course.'

She stepped into his open arms. 'You'll be okay?'

'I will. And in future, remind me, I should never drink gin. See you for breakfast at your place. But not too early.'

27 Naomi

Naomi wriggled into the seat as she adjusted the driving position, which had been accommodating Meghan's long legs for the last few months.

Freedom at last. She could go where she wanted, take as long as she liked, beholden to no one. She drove cautiously at first, reversing in the drive, edging out of the gateway and creeping towards the village at twenty miles an hour. But the ankle was strong and had no problem with the clutch pedal. She even had a full tank of fuel, which was thoughtful and generous of Meghan.

Stagworthy Point was her first stop. She found a sheltered spot out of the inevitable wind and sat on the spiky grass among rabbit droppings, gazing out over the limitless ocean and breathing in the warm smell of gorse. The view and the hillside cradled her. It felt both safe and full of endless possibilities. She rested in the hollow until a pair of spaniels interrupted her musing, and she hobbled, struggling with pins and needles, back to the car.

Next she set off towards Barnstaple – the open road, a turn of speed would be exhilarating. But it wasn't that kind of road and she hadn't bargained for the volume of traffic. It was August and the holidaymakers were out in force, trying the patience of white van drivers and destroying the calm she had absorbed on the headland. She could go anywhere she liked. But where *was* this anywhere? Woolacombe maybe, with its wide sands? The north coast? Down to Exeter even? Nothing appealed. She turned off on a minor road and considered exploring the winding lanes until she got lost and had to get the map out. Eventually she parked near a footpath and set off through some woodland, but, when she saw the route would take her through a farmyard busy with barking dogs, tractors and livestock, she turned back.

She leant on the steering wheel with a sense of disappointment. She had looked forward to this day, to the freedom, to escaping. Had she been cooped up so long that she'd lost her sense of adventure? It was certainly good to be independent – but as to escaping? There was nothing she would rather do than return to Stagworthy and drop into the gallery for a chat with Meghan. She set off to do just that.

As she came into the village, parked cars and cyclists slowed her speed to well below the limit. This was fortunate, as halfway down the main street a woman stepped off the pavement without looking, directly in front of the Land Rover. Naomi slammed on the brakes and rocked to a standstill inches away from a collision. In a flurry of rainbow-coloured scarves, the woman stepped back, dropping her bag and clutching her head as if she had indeed been hit. Passers-by came to her assistance and she carefully repositioned the silver crocheted skull cap that had slipped over one eye. Claudia. Naomi joined her on the pavement.

'You could have *killed* me, dear one! How clever of you not to.'

Claudia was shaken but unscathed, and not nearly as shaken as Naomi, who found she could hardly stand.

'My dear, you look like death. You'd better come and have some soup.'

By this time, horns were sounding from the queue of traffic that had built up behind the Land Rover. Claudia climbed into the passenger seat.

'Right at the end here. No! Sorry, I mean left. Always get them muddled up.'

Naomi turned and turned again into the narrowest of alleyways.

'There. That's me. The skinny house with the yellow door. You can pull up on the pavement at the end. Nobody minds.'

Naomi had her doubts about who might mind, especially as a notice said "Garage in constant use", but she felt too shaky to argue. Suppose she had knocked Claudia over? On her first outing? Nobody would believe it was Claudia's fault. It didn't bear thinking about.

The yellow door opened onto an indigo hall, which, in spite of a lime green dado rail, was so dark that Naomi was surprised to find herself at the top of a flight of stairs, as Claudia led her down to the basement kitchen. Here she was settled into a squashy leather sofa with a blanket of crocheted squares thrown around her shoulders. Two Siamese cats, elegant in cream fur with chocolate markings, were entwined on a chair opposite. One of them stretched its claws and momentarily opened an eye of pure periwinkle blue. The claws relaxed as the eye closed.

'Shock,' Claudia said. 'Sweet tea or brandy?' Without waiting for an answer, she dived into the back of a cupboard and brandished a sherry bottle.

Naomi watched with interest, relieved that there was to be no sweet tea. The room was full of jewel colours – cushions and throws, and shelves of china and glass where each piece looked as if it would give its owner a pleasant surprise on *Antiques Roadshow*.

'Home-made plum brandy. Just the ticket.' Claudia pulled the cork and poured a rich brown liquid into a sapphire-coloured shot glass. 'Get that down you. I might just have a teeny one. After all, I did have a shock, too. Whatever was I thinking of?' She lifted a cover on the range and slid a pan onto the hotplate. 'Carrot and coriander. The ultimate comfort food.'

'So, what *were* you thinking of?' Naomi said. 'You must have been miles away.'

Claudia sighed with her usual dramatic exaggeration and stared through the French windows to the garden. A burly black cat stared back at her from the edge of the lawn.

'My Dearly Beloved.'

Naomi frowned. 'He looks a bit fierce.'

'Oh, him. No, no, *no*! He terrorises my two darlings if he gets half a chance.' She strode to the window and rapped sharply on the glass. 'Be gone, damned spot,' she shouted and the cat stalked off into the shrubbery. 'That's what I call him. Damned Spot.'

'So, not your dearly beloved.'

'No. I was referring to my dearly beloved Cyril, my late husband…'

'Oh, I'm so sorry…'

'Forty-seven wonderful years we were married. It is the anniversary of his death. Found him in the library, collapsed among his beloved books. Never made it to bed. I guess that's where I was when I stepped off the pavement. Oops! Soup's boiling, mustn't let it burn.'

As Claudia swooped over the saucepan with a wooden spatula, Naomi saw tears roll down her cheeks.

'Ten years ago that was, and it still gets to me. The shock of finding him. It's in here.' She clutched her heart. 'These things, they do lodge in the body, don't they? One's cells remember. And distract one and cause one to step out in front of cars.'

She ladled the richly orange soup into dark red bowls, a pleasing colour combination.

'But this time I was lucky. A car driven by a dear, clever friend with quick reactions. I'm quite amazed to be alive! I didn't know you were driving again.'

'It's my first day.'

'Oh! But is it safe?'

'Well, it was, wasn't it? You just said yourself…'

'Oh! Yes, I suppose so.'

They ate in silence for a while. The soup was delicious and went well with chunks of warm olive bread for which Claudia felt obliged to apologise. 'Sorry, not home-made but from that darling farm shop just down the road. I treat myself on special occasions.' Naomi was trying to fathom how Claudia's mind worked and wondering whether to enquire further about the dearly beloved Cyril.

Claudia pre-empted her. 'He was a dry old stick. Only interested in his books really. Archaeology. But not the messy kind. No romantic digs on the Nile where I could have pretended to be *dear* Agatha and written murder mysteries. No. Only in print. Mostly with a magnifying glass. Very well thought of up at Oxford. Professor, you know. Lovely house on the Woodstock Road. But he absolutely *adored* me, of course.' Her voice dropped. 'When he noticed I was there. He was devoted to his work. And we women, we are sometimes quite invisible to men, don't you think?'

Naomi nodded. 'They see what they want to see, if they see us at all. Certain men, that is.'

Claudia poured herself another shot of plum brandy. Naomi refused, reflecting on the tiny house, the cats and the way Claudia dressed. For the first time she saw the colours as the colours of loneliness.

'More soup?' Claudia's voice was bright now with a brittle edge.

The offer was interrupted by a heavy knock on the front door.

'That'll be Ed wanting to use his garage. Once in a blue moon. And only because you're parked across it.'

Naomi leapt up, eager to escape and followed Claudia up to the hall. She embraced her, thanked her for the soup and walked to her car apologising to Ed, an easy-going plumber who did indeed need access to his garage on a daily basis. Where else could he keep his van?

He gave a slow smile. 'She only does it to annoy,' he said. 'It means I get to knock on her door. She's a strange one, but she's a good sort, really. Do anything for anybody.'

28 *Meghan*

Meghan was poised with the brush inches from the picture when the telephone bell jangled and she startled. Half an inch nearer and she could have smudged the whole thing. Why did it have to be so loud? And who the hell was ringing her at this time? Her hand shook as she replaced the brush and went to answer it, as much to silence the racket as to find out who was there.

She had woken with such certainty about how to complete the painting. She'd thrown on clothes, galloped downstairs and grabbed an apple on the way to her studio. She'd stood before the easel, staring at the canvas. Yes, her idea would work. After a few bites, the apple was no longer of interest. She'd lobbed it out the door and watched as it came to rest against a fence post where Rocky, the rook, would easily spot it. A visit from him would be auspicious, and only a few days ago he'd pounced on an apple core with relish. No Rocky.

She took a breath as she picked up the phone. The caller probably didn't deserve the fury she felt at the interruption. Crackling on the line. Then a voice. 'Mum!' Alex. Something about Exeter and a lift. Meghan couldn't get a word in. So Alex was in this country. It became clear she wanted to be picked up from the M5 junction at Exeter.

Meghan's practical side kicked in. 'But you could be in Barnstaple on the train by the time I'm halfway there. Once I've fixed up a car. Rita…'

A lot of sighing, more crackling and 'I'll see what I can do.'

'Let me know…' But the phone went dead before Meghan finished her sentence.

She glared at the thing as she docked it. Already at odds with Alex before they'd even said hello. Uncertainty. Interruption. Had Alex forgotten her mother didn't own a car? Meghan made tea and took it out to lean on the fence. The half-eaten apple had gone, so maybe Rocky had come and claimed it. Gone was the inspired, purposeful mood of the morning. And where was the fizz of excitement she'd expected to feel at the prospect of seeing her daughter? She tipped the remains of her tea into the grass and raced upstairs to make up Alex's bed at high speed. By the time the phone rang for a second time, she had exchanged her filthy smock for a clean shirt.

Once behind the wheel of the Land Rover, her mood picked up. What did a painting matter when Alex was on a train speeding towards her? Strangely, when she had collected the Land Rover, Naomi had been the one to provide the excitement at Alex's homecoming that Meghan had been missing. She'd even invited Naomi to come too, but Naomi had handed her the keys, put up her hands and taken a step back. Naomi was right, of course. What had she been thinking? It had to be just the two of them – after two years! Would she have changed? How would she have changed? Pregnant, too. Why wasn't she excited?

She needn't have worried. There was Alex, barrelling down the platform on Barnstaple station, arms out, copper-blonde hair catching the sunlight as it always had. Her girl. And there she was, standing like a tree, transfixed, to receive her. Nothing like hugging the one person in the world she truly belonged to by blood, sweat and tears. The smell of her, the miracle of her: the tiny baby grown into this strong, warm woman, familiar and yet mysterious. *The two of us.*

But it wasn't just the two of them: the swell of Alex's belly was enfolded between them. Why so unexpected? A jolt of recognition: her child had been able to do this. There was shock in there, jealousy even – someone else claiming the role of mother – but most of all, astonishment, wonder. Another mystery.

Meghan was lost in the embrace. Amid the rumble of suitcases, whistles and slamming doors, she clung to her daughter and a memory came rocketing in – of how she'd wished for another human being to hug her in this way when she was pregnant with Alex so that the baby would feel protected all round. It was called a family. This baby would have one. She and Alex would be that family.

When Alex pulled away, she wiped a tear from her mother's cheek. 'Don't believe you, Mum!'

'Me neither!'

'The old lady in the car said it would be like this...'

'What old lady? What car?'

'She said, "Your mother will cry, she's bound to cry." I didn't believe her. Not my mum, I told her. But she was right!'

'So just who are you talking about?'

Alex took Meghan's hand and placed it on the side of the bulge with a questioning look. 'The couple who gave me a lift. How d'you think I got from the ferry terminal?'

Meghan could feel a firm protuberance, which moved. An elbow, a foot maybe.

'Feel her?'

Meghan nodded. 'Her? She? Do you know?'

'Not in the medical sense. Just optimistic.' Alex's tone changed. 'Hey, can we get something to eat? I'm starving.'

'I've been longing for someone to do that,' Alex said, pulling out a chair at a corner table in the station café. 'Feel it move. But the people I was travelling with – she was a bit weird, beyond squeamish, would hardly even look at me.' Alex peered at the menu. 'Pasty and chips. Just the ticket. Anyway, it's nice you were the first.'

Meghan thought so too, and still felt overwhelmed as she went up to the counter to put in their order. Alex was so much herself, and yet, also, somehow different.

As she sat down, she said, 'Until we hugged just now, I'd forgotten how much I wanted someone to do that to me when I was pregnant with you – to enclose me and my bump. So you were protected from both sides. Know what I mean? Keeping out the draughts.'

'Nice idea. And it didn't have to be a man?'

'Well, no. I guess not. My mother passed up the opportunity. And I didn't have close friends. Rita wasn't the sort. So I suppose I thought of it being a man. Not that there was one. Not one I'd have trusted.'

Their food arrived and Meghan watched as Alex squirted ketchup over everything. That hadn't changed.

'This one's father wouldn't have done as any kind of protector. But his family would have kept out the draughts, big time.' Alex waved a chip in the air for emphasis. 'His mother, his lovely sisters. Really got on well with them. Not that we did much apart from shopping. But they'd have kept me out too, totally taken over. That was my fear. They'd have seen Salvador's baby as their property.'

Meghan wondered what that would be like. She could only be grateful that Alex had opted out of an all-consuming Spanish family and chosen to come home.

Alex was quiet as they drove through town. Meghan stole looks at her profile. She was tanned, and leaner than she used to be. She looked more – what was the word? Alive, vibrant was all she could come up with. As if the pallid bank clerk who had set off on her travels two years ago had been her ghost.

As if reading her thoughts, Alex said, 'I'm not going back into banking. There must be more interesting places to work. Even in Barnstaple.' She laughed. 'Any ideas?'

'Time enough to think about that. See how the baby changes things.'

'Baby? No reason why it should get in the way. Surely? I'll get childcare and get on with my life.'

Meghan smiled to herself. How many times had she heard something similar? 'Maybe you will. But you can't guarantee your life won't change. That *you* won't change.' She slowed for traffic lights. 'Anyway, when are you due? Do you even know?'

'I haven't had any checks, if that's what you mean. That would have been madness – pregnant English girl – the doctor might have been Salvador's mother's second cousin for all I knew. Not a risk I could afford to take.'

'So you risk your health instead...'

'Rubbish. And you don't really believe that, Mum. Know your body and all that? I knew I was okay. And, anyway, I came home, didn't I?'

Yes, she had come home.

In bed that night, Meghan found she was listening for Alex's breathing just like when she was little. She could hear nothing. Alex's door was firmly shut. It was wonderful to have her there, and it was alarming too.

Picturing her own aura, Meghan saw a yellow canvas, citrus yellow, pocked with tiny black marks – brackets, question marks, full stops, exclamation marks. This was a first. Why so much punctuation? It reminded her of an exercise at art college. Each student took a section of wall. They were to slather it with thick paint and then hurl missiles at it in the hope that they would stick and create a supposed artwork. Something to do with Surrealism. Paperclips, feathers, cigarette butts, ring-pulls, buttons and beer cans flew through the air. She doubted they had learned anything. It certainly wasn't helping with Alex.

In the course of the evening, Alex had related anecdotes about where she had been and the people she'd met. Meghan had been particularly interested in the story of the couple in the camper van but Alex just kept on about how Alfie had flirted with her. It didn't add up with what she'd already said – that he and Esther were devoted to each other. As to the couple who'd given her a lift – she'd manipulated them shamelessly and was proud of it, which made Meghan uncomfortable. But as Alex said, a girl on her own has to look out for herself. Plus the couple had been really happy to have her. No doubt they were. Alex would have been her best charming self. The entertainment for their journey. All in all, she couldn't help but be proud of her daughter.

Alex, too, lay awake. Coming home was a mixed bag. Mum brilliant, so much easier than she'd expected. But the cottage was so much smaller than she remembered. Messier, too. They'd already fallen out over the state of the kitchen. Mum had told her, quite sharply, that if she didn't like it, she knew what to do. So she faced a morning of scrubbing before Mum carted her off to the doctor. If only Esther was here. She'd be appalled by the kitchen and in her element putting it to rights.

Her own bedroom had shrunk. Much as she loved its quirky shape, it was ridiculous to even think of adding a cot. The solution was obvious. Surprising that Mum hadn't already suggested swapping rooms.

She shifted position, trying to get comfortable. The mattress was only marginally better than the one in the camper van. Must be ancient, the same one she had as a child. She missed the way she and Esther had sometimes chatted if Alfie was late coming to bed and it was just the two of them. Esther said things in the dark that she would never say in daylight. Things about her grandmother who she'd been really close to, or the mother she'd never known. Funny, she really missed Esther.

So, Mum had a new friend it seemed. The owner of the Land Rover. Alex had already been disappointed that the insurance didn't allow her to drive it. She'd popped over to see Rita and, from the look on Rita's face at the mention of the newcomer, Alex had gathered that Rita was less than delighted with "that Naomi's" arrival in their midst.

She'd found Rita up a stepladder painting the dining room ceiling buttercup yellow. She'd dismissed Alex's travels with a remark about the wanderer returning, climbed down and parked her paint roller. She was so excited, Rita said as she put the kettle on, and told some story about her son Mike at last having a girlfriend and how they'd met. Alex wasn't interested. She was busy measuring up the room as a possible bedsit for herself and the baby. She and Rita had always got on well. It would be ideal. Rita made her usual instant coffee. Alex had forgotten how disgusting it was. But the bigger disappointment was that Rita was painting the room because Mike was moving in with his girlfriend. Alex cursed and said how lovely that would be.

Rita had been her usual, direct self. 'So. The baby. Intentional or mistake?'

'What do you think?'

'Don't imagine it was part of your business plan.'

But then Rita had blown it by saying it would knock her business plan for six. Just as bad as Mum. Rita had always had a soft spot for her and she'd expected to find an ally in her, someone who would help in making arrangements for the baby. She fell asleep thinking that Rita's welcome home had been an anti-climax. At no point had she said that she couldn't wait to get her hands on a baby.

29 Naomi

When Naomi knocked at Meghan's door a few days after Alex's homecoming, it was opened by a young woman with copper-coloured hair.

Naomi took a step back. 'You must be Alex.'

'Mum's out.' Alex ignored the hand Naomi held out. 'She won't be long. You can wait if you want.'

She moved away from the door, leaving Naomi to shut it. 'I'm Naomi, by the way,' she said to Alex's back. By the time she reached the living room, Alex was sitting at the table munching toast and slurping coffee. She didn't look up.

Naomi sat on the window seat. The aroma of coffee filled the silence.

'How did the visit to the doctor's go?' Naomi said, after some minutes had passed.

Alex shrugged and swallowed. 'It was okay. I'm all booked in at the hospital. Midwives and so on.'

'Is that what you wanted – you're not keen on a home birth?'

'Can you imagine?' Alex rolled her eyes towards the kitchen area. 'No thank you. I'm more concerned with fixing the childcare afterwards.'

Naomi said nothing.

Minutes passed. Alex was watching her.

Then she said, 'Rita's got her business, so she can only promise half a day. Fair enough. But Mum.' Alex slammed her mug on the table. 'Mum's only offered one day. One measly day.'

Naomi nodded.

'You don't seem surprised.'

'Your mother's got her work. Exhibition in December and an even bigger…'

'But it's just painting. She does it here. She could have the baby as well.'

'I don't think it works like that. But that's between you and her. None of my business.'

Silence.

'You don't fancy doing some childcare, do you? A couple of days a week perhaps?'

Naomi turned away to the window. 'I do not.'

'One day?'

Naomi looked down the road and shook her head. 'Negative.'

Alex scraped back her chair and took her mug to the kitchen. She refilled it from the coffee pot and went upstairs.

Naomi left the house, closing the front door quietly behind her.

Meghan was keen to introduce Alex and Naomi, and phoned Naomi to arrange it.

'We've already met. I called round the other morning.'

Naomi's tone of voice made Meghan uneasy. It did not suggest that meeting Alex had been the pleasure she'd hoped for. 'Funny, Alex never mentioned it.'

'Not surprised. She invited me in. But that was about it. Oh, apart from checking out my potential as a childminder.'

'She didn't!'

'I put her straight. And I did mention your exhibition, by the way. Have you got around to telling her about that? How your career has taken off? I mean, she needs to know.'

Once again, Meghan cringed at Naomi's tone. She obviously thought Alex was a little madam. 'Give me time. She's hardly been back and there's been a lot to talk about, and the doctor and so on.' Meghan didn't need Naomi to point out that Alex had shown zero interest in what her mother had been up to during her two-year absence. 'After all, she's pregnant. That's big and it does funny things to you. Plus she's not a morning person.'

Meghan heard a stifled grunt before Naomi enquired how the painting was going. She hadn't touched it since Alex got home and couldn't bring herself to say so. 'I tell you what, why don't we give it a second go, and I bring Alex over to meet you properly?'

The second meeting got off to a better start. Alex even apologised for her lack of hospitality on the previous occasion. She asked all the right questions about her ankle and enthused about the annexe. Meghan relaxed.

Alex sat back and looked around the room. 'Mum said something about the cottage over in the valley. That you plan to go and live there?'

Naomi explained the situation briefly and confirmed that she would move in when her ankle was stronger and when Gordon moved back to London for the winter.

'Cool. When do you reckon that will be?'

Naomi laughed. 'I can see exactly where you're coming from. The cogs in your head are visible a mile off.'

Meghan looked on as Alex failed to see that Naomi was teasing her and started on the defensive.

But Naomi brushed her protest aside. 'It had occurred to me, too, that this place could be a staging post for you. But that's a discussion for you and your mother. No point in having it before your baby has arrived, nor before Meghan has helped you through the early stages, nor before the two of you have exhausted all the delights of a three-generation household.' Naomi grinned and Meghan could see she was enjoying this. 'Even then, take nothing for granted. After all, this place isn't in my gift. It's entirely down to Patrick. He may have other ideas.'

Alex gulped a few times during this speech. When Naomi was finished, she simply nodded. Naomi certainly had the knack of taking the wind out of her sails. Meghan felt almost sorry for her daughter.

On the way home Alex was indignant. 'Wow, she didn't half have a go at me. I mean, I hadn't even mentioned taking her poxy annexe.'

'But you had thought it?'

'Well yes, but why does she have to mind-read? Make out I'm some scheming madam? Like, I might just go and tell Patrick I was moving in? I mean, I do actually know her precious Patrick. And I do actually know how to behave.'

Meghan made no comment.

'And what was that she said? "Not in her gift"! Looking down her snooty nose! How pretentious is that?'

Meghan held up a hand. 'Hold your horses. See it another way. That Naomi's aware of your dilemma, that we'll be a bit crammed in at home.

Wanted us to know she's given it some thought, and wants to help? Think about it, at least.'

Alex responded by asking to be dropped off in the village. 'Time I called in on Claudia.'

30 *Naomi*

The trombone droned, the trumpets were strident and the strutting feet irritating beyond belief. Naomi stood back against the wall until the brass band passed. Marching and playing at the same time was a remarkable skill. No doubt about that. But, in her opinion, not a skill that should be encouraged. Best left to the Grenadier Guards.

This was the Stagworthy Carnival procession – every bit as important to the village as any Trooping the Colour-type ceremony, and the culmination of a year's planning and a week of exhausting activity. The homecoming of Meghan's daughter had combined with Carnival to rob Naomi of Meghan's company for days. Claudia was flitting from place to place, making last-minute alterations to costumes. Added to which, Patrick had gone down with a filthy summer cold, which he was nursing at home with quantities of expensive honey and fresh lemons. He might sometimes be too good to be true, but he wasn't immune to man flu.

She breathed away the cacophony of the band and rejoined the crowd making its way to the square. There, a few yards in front of her, was Meghan arm in arm with Alex and Rita. They were bouncing along, almost dancing, looking about them, leaning in and laughing. Naomi slowed in order not to catch up with them. The prospect of linking with either Rita or Alex was uncomfortable. Her first two encounters with Alex had not been encouraging. Rita certainly didn't like her. She simply didn't belong. They wouldn't want her. Claudia was always happy to see her, but there was no sign of Claudia and she wasn't exactly easy to miss. She'd been kidding herself that being greeted by a few pub regulars, shopkeepers and Keith, the postie, meant she was part of the place. The truth was she was on the edge. Yes, she'd been invited to join Colin and his unctuous wife for a cream tea, but Doreen's condescending manner had simply reinforced the feeling of not belonging.

Let it go, came Evie's voice in her head. But she couldn't. She wanted to be at the centre of things, not just wandering on the periphery. *I thought you came here for the solitude.* Evie again. Damn Evie. Naomi retaliated that there was a difference between solitude and loneliness. But of course Evie knew all about that. Naomi mixed them up all the time, afraid that solitude would bring loneliness with it. She'd never given solitude a chance. To hell with this conversation. It was going nowhere. She stopped to buy an ice cream to shut Evie out and found herself watching a group of school kids twirling bamboo parasols. A twist of jealousy. Once upon a time she'd had one just like that. Except she hadn't had it, had she? Once upon a time in the tall, thin house.

Uncle Gordon's holding it out to her. A brown thing like an enormous chrysalis. He's brought it specially for her from some abroad place where he's just been. She takes it, fingers the wooden slats, which are smooth, with not very shiny paint. She doesn't know what to do, so Uncle Gordon takes it back, unbuttons the strap that holds the slats together and shows her how to ease her hand inside them, find the clasp and push it slowly to the top of the shaft. Magic! 'Umbrella!' she shouts. 'Parasol,' he says.

Mum is watching from her deck chair under the tree where Naomi had helped set out glasses on the table and Mum had brought a jug of fruit and tinkling ice floating in amber liquid. That was earlier, when it was all blue sky. Only two glasses, but she will get to eat a piece of apple, which will taste nasty, but she will pretend to like it and make them laugh before making a face and spitting it into the shrubbery. A cloud edges over the sun and Mum crosses her legs and jiggles her foot up and down.

Naomi lifts up her present and twirls the handle. She looks up into a canopy of pink-painted petals, losing herself in cherry blossom. Now there is sunlight on this dark day, birdsong and the shifting shadows of lacy leaves. The air smells of roses, the velvety depths of the red rose on the edge of the lawn.

The tinkle of ice in a glass interrupts, her mother laughs and lifts the parasol out of her hand, twirling and dancing as Uncle Gordon swoops her away across the grass with clever, twisty steps.

She's left staring at a cloudy sky and, although the parasol is returned to her, she drops it on the ground. Later, she props it up in a corner of her bedroom where it gathers dust.

The rattle of another passing float brought Naomi back to Carnival and the urgent need to lick her dripping cornet. Her legs and back were aching. It was the furthest she'd walked since the accident. Patrick had insisted she did circuits of the garden to build up her strength but she'd often cheated, and anyway, walking on grass was very different from tarmac. She just had to sit down soon. But not here, where she'd probably get run over.

Now came the Queen of Hearts making her tarts, and Naomi was ridiculously proud to see her red satin appliquéd hearts scattered over the costumes. Here was the *Alice in Wonderland* float, followed by *The A-Team* with a B A Baracus lookalike (not) draped in bling, kids on tractors with balloons, *The Wizard of Oz* with the yellow brick road almost obscured by pink hydrangeas, and children everywhere with tiger faces. The cheer leaders marched and danced with enthusiasm in their spectacular black and gold dresses, brandishing even more spectacular huge golden pom-poms. Claudia had said fitting the dresses had been a nightmare.

The *Top Gear* float rumbled past, strikingly black among the predominant reds and yellows of other entries. It revived memories of the bitter disputes about their filming stunt at Stagworthy Quay, which had still been simmering when Naomi arrived in the village. Fans had loved the occasion and labelled the objectors as spoilsports. Meghan had fulminated about "those Neanderthals" being allowed anywhere near their beautiful coast, about their disrespect for the environment, the inanity of the stunt and how she wished their unmentionable leader had been inside the camper van when it hurtled over the cliff face. Naomi felt very naïve. When she'd last seen an episode of *Top Gear* she'd thought it amusing and had fallen for the Stig. It had been something she and her father could watch together and she'd simply viewed it as entertainment. How very superficial. Meghan had jumped in to put her right and persuade her that things had got out of hand when "those louts" got away with taking four-wheel drives into wild places and destroying wildlife habitat.

Be that as it may, the carnival float was clever and well-supported and was collecting a shedload of money for charity. She didn't have the energy to be for it or against it. The driver of a quad bike that was following close behind gave her a happy smile and waved a flowery forearm. She thought at first he was wearing a skin-tight floral shirt. Skin-tight yes, his arms were covered in a tattoo of roses from shoulder to wrist. An unlikely and amusing addition to the *Top Gear* team.

The Square at last and the aroma of garlic and spices and roasting meat made her realise how inadequate the ice cream had been. Too thin, too sweet. She was ravenous. Before she had time to join a queue for jerk chicken and fries, she was grabbed around the waist.

'There you are! Been looking everywhere for you!' Meghan hugged her and stood back. 'You look done in!'

Naomi nodded. 'It's the longest I've walked...'

'Here, over here.' Meghan led her to a low wall bordering someone's garden. 'I'll fetch us some food.'

'Where are Rita and Alex?'

'Gone home. Thank God. Driving me mad, doing the *Top Gear* fan club thing. Partly to wind me up – which it did, of course. Don't get me started. We're supposed to be having fun.' She laughed and disappeared into the crowd.

Naomi settled onto the wall, finding a smooth hollow still warm from the sun, and absorbing the warmth of Meghan's hug. So she did have a friend in this place. A friend who might be a little tipsy, but what the hell did that matter? She was ashamed – she'd been like a child in the playground. But now she'd been picked for Meghan's team.

Meghan brought back beakers of cider and wraps generously filled with juicy, spicy chicken oozing with garlic, chilli and ginger. 'Watch out for the cider, it's wicked.'

'This is probably the best meal I've ever eaten,' Naomi said and felt tears overflow down her cheeks.

Meghan grinned. 'It's surely not that hot?'

Naomi shook her head and glugged more cider. 'It's just... I don't know...'

'Carnival.' Meghan put an arm across Naomi's shoulders and held her close until her wrap started to drip and needed attention.

Gavin from the hotel came and chatted for a while.

'So, it's the skeleton staff tonight, then?' Meghan said as he moved on.

Gavin looked back over his shoulder. 'Oh yes! She's in her element.' They both roared with laughter.

Meghan turned to explain. 'It's tradition for Gavin's mother to hold the fort on Carnival night. Skeleton staff – except she's no skeleton. You wouldn't know she had one – as round as she is tall. And it was her who made the joke, in case you're wondering.'

'I've never seen her around.'

'You wouldn't. She lives in Exeter. Consultant at the hospital. I forget what in. Her name is Rose Mary – absolutely *not* Rosemary. Woe betide you if you get that wrong! Quite fierce and very funny. Gavin adores her.'

Naomi nodded. 'That's nice.' She finished the last of her wrap. 'That was delish. No sign of Claudia. I thought she'd be here.'

'I heard her son had turned up. Which is a rare and special occasion. She'll be cooking him a feast. In fact, that's probably where Alex is. She's got a soft spot for Will. They had a fling years back and stayed friends.'

'Didn't know she had a son.' So Claudia had a son. Odd she'd never mentioned him.

'Long story. Get her to tell you sometime. But one thing I did forget to tell you – Claudia volunteered for childcare. Two days a week, no less!'

'Claudia? But she's always so busy! Why on earth?'

'Easy-peasy. So whenever Will visits, he gets to see Alex. Talk about throwing them together.'

'Do you like that idea?'

Meghan shrugged. 'Not up to me, anyway. Oh, look!' She pointed across the square to where Colin and Doreen were staggering through a slow jive. 'There's a rare piece of footage. Wish I had one of those phones that take pictures.'

The festivities were set to continue into the night. They watched and wandered, and watched some more until, a cider or two later, Naomi could go no longer. Meghan steered her back to the refuge of the wall.

'I don't think either of us is driving anywhere tonight.'

'But how...? Oh dear, and the car's so far away.'

'I reckon I can fix us a lift. No worries, my friend. Then I can cycle over in the morning and fetch the car.'

Meghan vanished, leaving Naomi on the wall, tearful again at being looked after. She was vague about how she got home. It involved a quad bike, alarming speed around every bend, being crouched together with Meghan and the wind in her hair. She recognised the roses on the driver's arms and warmed to her friend for compromising her principles and appealing to a member of the *Top Gear* float to get them home.

31 *Meghan*

Meghan flung herself down in the place of the rowan tree and lay back, gazing up at the unremarkable high grey cloud cover. After just a few weeks of sharing her space with Alex, she had an urgent need to reflect on their relationship. She was relying on the oracle of the rowan tree, the wisdom of her grandmother and the energy of the earth to give her insight.

She was having to get to know her daughter almost as if she were a lodger. The intimacy of their reunion had somehow evaporated and there were two things that disturbed Meghan – Alex's failure to engage with the arrival of her baby, being only interested in who would provide childcare while she worked, and the fact that Alex was behaving like a teenager. Meghan remembered the teenage Alex well, but this twenty-five-year-old teenager was subtly different. The tantrums were thankfully missing, but she'd lost her sense of humour and had higher expectations. Maybe it was just a reaction to months of keeping her secret and coping with being pregnant in a foreign country. Maybe it would pass.

Meghan sat up and hugged her knees. Over to the west, low cloud was rolling in behind a row of tall trees on the skyline, sycamore probably. They marked the boundary to a steep meadow where sheep were grazing. Huge sheep. More the size of cows, but the wrong shape. How come they looked so big at this distance? Then a gull soared across the valley and landed beside one of the ewes. More like an albatross. It was just as well she didn't paint pastoral landscapes – everything would be wildly out of proportion.

She smiled and shook her head over the bizarre trivia the oracle was throwing at her and waited for something more meaningful to surface.

So far with Alex she'd held her ground – for instance by refusing to swap bedrooms. But it made her feel guilty and selfish. She envied Naomi's approach to Alex – very direct and not afraid to challenge her attitude.

Supposedly, Naomi didn't care what Alex thought of her. But Meghan, of course, did care.

The clouds behind the sycamores had now turned to a threatening charcoal, while over to the east the cloud cover was thinning to give a hint of brightness. Anything could happen. As she glanced back at the sycamores, a patch of blue appeared on the left and edged its way along, filling the spaces between one trunk and the next. Then, quite suddenly, it disappeared, only to reappear, a smaller puff than the first time, but more determined. As if someone behind the hill were working a bellows. Meghan snorted. One of the enormous sheep perhaps. She watched, fascinated, as the process continued and the slick of Wedgwood blue spread along the tree line.

Enough to make a sailor a pair of trousers. This in the voice of her Welsh grandmother, which was immediately contradicted by her neighbour, who claimed the trousers were for a Dutchman. This argument used to crop up regularly during her childhood and Meghan had secretly supported Mrs Prout. She came from Portsmouth and was thought to know more than most about naval trousers. 'Those bell bottoms take a lot of fabric,' she would say, gesturing at the tiny patch of blue sky that had prompted the discussion. 'What with the seven creases, one for each of the seven seas. But a Dutchman is different – powder-blue and just baggy. You could run up a pair of them in half an hour.'

Meghan had seen those Dutchmen on the tiles in the dairy shop. They were probably sailors anyway but that would have spoiled the argument, so she said nothing. By this time the patch of blue would have long vanished.

The blue sky behind the sycamores, however, was persisting and growing in contrast to the still inky cloud bank behind it. All very interesting, but she hadn't come to study the weather and wasn't doing very well in consulting the oracle. She lay back on the grass and tried to focus on Alex, but was interrupted by a salvo of heavy rain drops, which made dark splodges all over her lime green shirt. The black clouds were evidently winning – hopefully not a metaphor for her and Alex.

Meghan was soaked through by the time she reached home.

'You mad cow!' Alex greeted her. 'Whatever were you doing, out in this?'

'Well, it wasn't…'

But before she had time to explain, Alex had fetched a towel for her hair and told her to go and change.

'Before you catch your death. I'll put the kettle on.'

Meghan felt quite overwhelmed at this unexpected attention and was moved to describe the giant sheep and the albatross, but Alex looked at her as if she needed locking up. Fair enough.

It was in the night that it came to her. She was revisited by the oversize sheep and the albatross. They troubled her. After all, she was an artist. She knew about perspective, and as a person she reckoned she kept most things in proportion. But as to a message, she didn't have to look far – the metaphors were everywhere.

Alex's look of disbelief also came back to her. It didn't just say she was bonkers. It was the same look she'd given her when Meghan had promised only one day of childcare. It said, is this all I have to expect from my mother?

She'd lost her sense of proportion. Why? Because Alex and her painting were in direct conflict. She was blowing things up because she feared Alex could win, would win. And Alex? Maybe she was shocked to realise that the painting would probably win.

Naomi, or indeed Rita, could have told her all this months ago, but it had taken a strange weather pattern to draw it to her attention.

'Those are something else, Mum,' Alex said, emerging from Meghan's studio where she'd been viewing the canvases for her November exhibition. 'I mean, I don't entirely love them. I'm not sure I understand them all, but they are so fucking powerful. Now I get why you've been so obsessive.'

'Have I? Do you really?'

'I also noticed the date of the opening night, the private view. My due date, Sod's Law.'

'Don't I know it! Geoffrey did his nut when I said I might not be there.'

'Might not be there? But surely…?' Alex's face was a picture in itself.

'You don't really imagine – if you went into labour – that I'd swan off in my finery to sip champagne and talk about effing pictures?'

'Well, yes. I guess that's what…'

Meghan took Alex by the shoulders. 'You know, don't you? That when it comes to it, if you need me, I'll be there every hour of every day for as long as it takes.'

She was shocked to see tears well into her daughter's eyes.

'Of course you don't know. Because I haven't said it.'

'You certainly haven't. In fact you've been telling me the exact opposite.'

Meghan sighed and sank onto the window seat. 'You know why that is? It's because I'm scared that you and your needs and your baby will swallow up my life and stop me painting. Which is extreme and ridiculous.'

'Funny you should use those words, "swallowed up".' Alex's voice faltered. 'I'm scared too – of being swallowed up by the baby. That's why I don't want to know about nappies and stuff.'

Meghan started to speak but Alex held up a hand.

'But not just that. That you won't be there to save me, nobody will be there. I just can't cope with thinking about it.'

Meghan leapt up and drew Alex into her arms. 'If you need saving, I'm going to be there to do it. Make no mistake. Remember what we said when you first came home? We're going to be a family.'

Alex was first to draw away. 'Coffee?'

Meghan nodded. 'Definitely. Mind you, in case this is getting all too *Sound of Music* for words, as far as the everyday goes, I still stick by not committing to more than one day of childcare.'

Alex snorted and filled the kettle. 'I thought it was too good to be true.'

'It's just, a distinction needs to be made. Between the everyday and the extreme case. So, for routine purposes, one day a week. But as far as the *in extremis* goes – the birth obviously and any time that baby is sick – or you are – that's different, and that's when the twenty-four seven kicks in.'

They were interrupted by the phone. Alex answered, looked surprised, annoyed, amazed in turn, teasing Meghan with her exaggerated expressions. Eventually she passed over the handset. 'It's Naomi, wanting to know when you're next meeting Geoffrey at the gallery.'

When she rang off, Meghan was still puzzled. 'I'm seeing Geoffrey in a couple of weeks. Fine. But she said something about shopping. Said you would explain.'

'Huh! Did she now? She wants to shop but says she's not quite up to it. Carnival was too much for her.'

Meghan nodded. 'That's true. It knocked her out.'

'Anyway, she says she can't cope with traffic *and* people *and* shops, so she wants muggins here to push her round in the wheelchair. Sounds a right fun little jaunt.' Alex rolled her eyes. 'But I can hardly say no. Just don't leave me at her mercy for too long. And she'd better buy us all lunch.'

Meghan chuckled inwardly. Clever of Naomi. Killing two birds with one stone. A way to make the peace, get to know Alex, as well as getting to go shopping. Naomi in charge but Alex in control. And she'd no doubt show her some seductive little babygrows and buy her nappies as a thank you.

32 Naomi

It was Naomi's birthday – the one she had expected to celebrate on her own in the cottage by the sea, indulging in smoked salmon and a good single malt. But here she was, the centre of attention at a pub party in the Stagworthy Quay Hotel.

Patrick had taken her out the evening before to a candlelit dinner in a special place with a jazz band and had given her a tiny lapis lazuli ring as a mark of his commitment. 'It's about wisdom and truth,' he said. So understated – it fitted both their relationship and her little finger perfectly and she had never felt so happy.

It came as a surprise that Patrick had also organised this celebration on the actual day. He wasn't a pub person. When Naomi took to dropping into the bar for an hour on a Saturday evening, he preferred to stay at home and cook them dinner. It suited them both. She enjoyed the space to chat to Meghan and get to know the locals. And now Patrick had acknowledged what that meant to her and had put a substantial sum behind the bar for free drinks all round.

A party. She wasn't good at parties. And she knew exactly why. There had been a party once in the tall, thin house. In the morning, the sun had been shining in her bedroom, but it was still night-time in the lounge. Like another country. The tall curtains still drawn and towering above her; Mum's suede shoes with the peep toes all crooked under the coffee table; little castles of grey ash in the pink porcelain ashtray shaped like a leaf.

Glasses crowded on every little table and shelf. Some had bits of lemon in them that didn't taste of lemon, but stung her tongue as if sliced from razor blades. Others smelled like Uncle Gordon's moustache when he crouched down that time and asked her the name of her doll. It was Heather, not a doll. That made him laugh, and it made her cross, but he was only trying to be friendly. Of course she knew that they were dolls, but really they were Heather and June and Daphne and Sally. Then Mum had come down in her housecoat and drawn the curtains and said there was a party. So she'd decided she didn't like parties.

But this party would be different. Naomi took a deep breath as Patrick ushered her through the door. She was touched by the welcome she received – a *ting-ting* on the last orders bell from Gavin, Meghan coming to embrace her and show off the silky red party dress from Oxfam she had promised to wear and Gordon shambling over to kiss her warmly on both cheeks. Over their table a birthday balloon danced and curtseyed in the draught from the door.

The day had started with Buck's Fizz for breakfast and had included a picnic, a walk and a swim, followed by smoked salmon blinis with Veuve Clicquot before they set off for the pub.

Now, several birthday toasts and a few sausage rolls and chicken drumsticks later, Naomi was feeling very mellow as she watched the scene. She had lost count of the bottles of prosecco that had been consumed. Patrick's friends, Claire and Philip, who had joined them earlier, had certainly ordered at least one. So had Eddie Edwards, the local GP – him of the wide girth and skinny ponytail. She secretly preferred prosecco to Veuve Clicquot. It was lighter and slipped down so easily. More than once, Patrick had mentioned that Naomi's glass seemed to have a hole in it, but she hadn't taken the hint. Not on her birthday.

It was a dark day outside – more like November than August, Meghan had commented – and the lamps had been lit on all the small tables, casting a warm light. People were now circulating around the room and she was sitting alone for the first time, looking around her and enjoying the moment. Patrick was talking to some people she didn't know at the far end of the bar. At the table across from her, Gordon and Alex were allegedly playing chess but mostly chatting. According to Meghan, Alex had met Gordon in the bar and they'd hit it off straightaway. Gordon was now animated, Alex attentive, her copper hair curling over her shoulders. Gordon's expression reminded Naomi of the day, years ago, when he had bought her lunch and talked about how much he would have loved to have a daughter. Dear Gordon. She sipped her drink as she watched them, feeling a rush of affection for her old friend. She'd so love to make him happy, ease his loneliness. She half-closed her eyes, seeing the scene in soft focus:

Gordon sitting back, stroking his ginger moustache; Alex laughing and flicking her hair aside. Ginger moustache, auburn hair. Those colours, each echoing the other. A rush of insight brought the memory of Gordon and Meghan in the sunlight by the river. Of course. A sense of joy and power flowed through Naomi on a tide of prosecco. 'I can do this!' she said to herself. 'I can do this for Gordon.'

Naomi drained her glass, crossed a little unsteadily to their table and perched on the end.

They were talking about Alex's unborn baby.

'I was wondering,' Gordon said. 'Whether the sprog would want to go looking for her Spanish father.'

'*I* never have,' Alex said. 'Gone looking for my Irish father, that is. But who knows?'

'Well, if you were looking for a father, you wouldn't have far to look here,' Naomi said, interrupting. 'Look at the two of you. The colouring and so on.' She paused and lifted a strand of Alex's hair with her forefinger. 'Gordon's always wanted a daughter, haven't you, Gordon? And I do happen to know for a fact that it's possible,' another pause, '*very* possible, that Gordon is your father, Alex.'

There followed a long moment. First silence, as Gordon looked up at her with such a mix of bewilderment and concentration that he could not have noticed the expression of horror that flitted across Alex's face. The moment contained the scraping of chairs, bursts of laughter, Colin waving from the door as he left with his dog. The moment stretched to allow Naomi to suddenly doubt her loving impulse, to allow a cavern of fear to open inside her belly.

Then Alex called Meghan's name. Meghan was clearing a table and nodded as she disappeared with the dishes. Naomi had time to admire her friend's skill in carrying so many items and still keeping her party frock clean. Then Meghan was beside her, swimming in and out of focus, and all smiles about enjoying the party.

'Something to ask you, Mum.' Alex's voice was quiet and even. 'Naomi here reckons that Gordon's my father. Mum?'

Meghan's hand landed across Naomi's face.

Meghan leant over and spoke urgently to Alex. Naomi heard, 'Nothing has changed,' and 'We'll talk at home,' before Meghan straightened up and looked across at Gordon, shaking her head. She shook off his restraining hand and returned to clearing tables. She didn't even look at Naomi.

Then Patrick was there. 'Did I see that right? What…?'

Naomi couldn't meet his eye. She clutched her stinging face and carved her way through the stares and curiosity of friends and strangers to the ladies. Jo from the greengrocers was wide-eyed; the owner of the café made a questioning face and put her hand to her heart. A few were laughing, but most were frowning. Others, thankfully, appeared not to have noticed.

Rita must have tailed her, pushing past to the basin where she turned on Naomi. 'Well, that was something! I never thought I'd see Meghan hit anyone, but you drove her to it. Can't keep your nose out, can you? Always poking it in, upsetting people.' She groped in her bag for a lipstick. 'Everyone knows Meghan was already pregnant when she came here.' She leaned into the mirror to apply the lipstick. 'As to Gordon, God knows where you got that idea.'

Naomi watched her. No amount of lipstick would make that mouth look generous, and the blue eye shadow did nothing for Rita's piggy eyes. The urge to tell her to mind her own damn business was strong, but she'd said enough for one evening. Besides, she was preoccupied with two words that Rita had uttered: *"already pregnant"*. Then there was *"everyone knows"*. No, Rita. Not everyone did know. She, Naomi, didn't know.

Rita blotted her lips on a used tissue, turned on her heel and made for the door. 'Don't even show yourself down our end of the village.'

Before Naomi could bolt for the empty cubicle, Claudia emerged from the other one. She must have heard everything Rita said. Claudia swept Naomi into her arms and wrapped her in the purple folds of her velvet kaftan, holding her silently for several moments longer than was comfortable. Then she held her at arm's length and gazed into her eyes. 'I don't know what you've said or done, dear one, but I do know that Meghan can sometimes be very Welsh. And I'm allowed to say that because I come from the Principality myself. Trust me, it will all blow over. And I'm right with you until it does.'

She stroked Naomi's inflamed cheek. 'Nasty red patch. Give it a splash of water.'

She patted Naomi's face dry with the end of her silk scarf. 'Now, let's go find that lovely man of yours. He'll be wanting to take you home.'

*

Patrick stared at the windscreen, ignition keys still in his hand. 'Let me get this straight. You actually said that to Alex? In front of Gordon? In a public place?'

Naomi nodded.

'And you hadn't checked it out with Meghan first? Meghan who's your best mate?'

Naomi shook her head.

He drove home without another word. In the hallway he paused, looking round at her for the first time. 'Oh, your poor face.' He made a move as if to stroke her cheek, but it was hesitant. 'I don't know…' His voice was thin and tailed away.

Could he not bring himself to touch her? She stepped towards her door. 'I can't… I don't know either. Actually I do know. I just want to be alone.'

He nodded and it was a relief when he turned away to his own front door. She couldn't cope with his hesitation.

Naomi sat staring at the wall for what seemed like hours. It was hours. She was trying to find the words to say to Meghan.

At 3am Meghan beat her to it. 'Don't even think of grovelling to me,' the text message read. 'Alex mad at me, my sex life public, Rita crowing.'

Naomi was still holding the phone, staring at the screen when it beeped again. 'PS drew Tarot card for you. Hecate at the x-roads, i.e. stop messing in other people's business and sort out your own life.'

Naomi kicked off her shoes, peeled off her dress and rolled into bed. Then she sat up abruptly. She twisted the little lapis ring off her finger and laid it sadly on her bedside table. So much for wisdom and truth.

33 Meghan

Meghan woke early on the morning after the party and set off to the woods.

'You never warned me about that,' she said to the rooks as she climbed past the rookery trees.

She had mixed feelings about the previous evening. On the one hand, it had felt good to slap Naomi. As if she had always wanted to. But that was only when she first met her. Last night it had been a clean expression of her feelings. But on the other hand, she felt shame at having hit another person. Her lean palm on her friend's soft cheek had been harsh. It didn't fit the image she had of herself as a calm and rational woman. The impulse was clean and clear. It should have stopped short of moving into action. On top of all that, she was not only angry with Naomi for interfering, and for not talking to her first, she was also hurt. And she was damned if she felt like apologising.

She strode about among the trees, muttering to herself, occasionally leaning against a trunk and gazing up through the branches until hunger drove her home. She was surprised to find Alex already outside, nursing a mug of coffee.

'You know something, Mum? I was really proud of you, the way you lashed into that Naomi. What was she thinking of?'

'Exactly what I've been asking myself.'

'But having it off with Gordon? I mean, Gordon of all people! He's so old!'

Meghan took a deep breath. 'But he wasn't then. We were young. This is years ago we're talking about. Obviously.'

'So how come?'

'Long story and really none of your business.' Meghan sighed. 'But if you must know, Naomi was staying with Gordon and his brother at

Mill End. I cleaned for them. Heatwave. Cool river. Skinny-dipping. And Gordon caught me.'

'Still makes my skin crawl.'

'So be it. It was fun. Fun and funny and totally innocent. Had no idea at the time that anybody had seen us.'

'But you've only just met the dreaded Naomi. Was it the first thing you told her?'

'Oh, don't be ridiculous. As if. Naomi already knew, she happened to see us. Now, do shut up about her. I'm feeling as bruised as she probably is.'

Alex got slowly to her feet and put her arm round Meghan. 'How about I make us some scrambled egg?'

34 Naomi

Naomi slept all morning, then lunched on coffee with aspirin and toast, and slumped in her dressing gown to look out over a windswept garden. All she could see was Patrick turning away, not angry any more, a forlorn figure. She wouldn't see him today, she knew that. He had a meeting of his professional practice group and was giving a lift to two other members. Not something he would cancel. She pictured him in a crisp shirt, driving and chatting, being wise and supportive with a group of people he respected. What a fool she'd been. Just as her fears about Patrick had evaporated; just as he seemed to see her for the person she was. The modest ring, the pub party, both clear evidence of that. Just as she had begun to believe she was good enough and he wasn't too good to be true, she'd gone and blown it, destroying her friendship with Meghan into the bargain.

In the late afternoon there was a gentle knock on the door. She hoped and feared it was Patrick. Could he be back so early? She hadn't yet worked out what she could say to him. Was there anything to say?

The visitor was Claudia. 'Hello, dear one. I brought you some soup. The one you liked so much. I'll decant this into a saucepan – keep the Tupperware for next time.'

'That's kind.'

'Pish, tish.' Claudia stroked Naomi's hair and retreated. 'I'll be back tomorrow.'

A very low-key Claudia. No grand entrance. A quiet exit.

When the phone rang, Naomi glared at it. Who else was eager to tell her where she belonged? She was ashamed of the thin 'Hello' she produced.

Gordon's gravelly voice came down the line.

'Is that the local Family Planning Agency? No? I guess you're in no joking mood. You had a damn nerve there, Naomi. It took me a while, but I have to admire your courage. What on earth got into you?'

'A lot too much alcohol got into me. And the sight of you and Alex so happy. And the thought that I'd like to make my old friend Gordon even happier. That's what got into me.'

'Christ Almighty, woman! Even happier? Embarrassed, confused, a tiny bit flattered. Then embarrassed some more when I caught up with the look on Alex's face. Happy? No! I mean how did you think it was even possible? I was shocked that Meghan had apparently spilled those particular beans.'

'Not Meghan. I was there, Gordon. Remember? Did you think you were invisible down by the river? And you and Alex have the same ginger colouring. So I put two and two together and…'

'And made one thousand and four!'

'And you always wanted a daughter.'

'But not one who looked so horrified that I might be her father. Didn't see her for dust.'

'If it's any consolation, everyone's avoiding me. I'm sorry, Gordon. I really am. All I can say is that I meant well, and I've always thought that was the most damning thing you can say about anyone.'

'I think there's a little more to it than that. And a lot more to you. We better have lunch some time. No hard feelings, but I don't feel quite up to that yet. Bumped into Colin-fancy-Morrison at the paper shop and he was muttering, "Preposterous, quite preposterous," as if I'm some Lothario. Jealous, no doubt. But I'm keeping a low profile. As it happens, I have to go up to the Smoke tomorrow. Back next week. It will all have blown over by then.'

She woke early the next morning. Still no sign of Patrick. She couldn't sit there waiting indefinitely. In fact, it might be best to pack up and leave. Would that be running away? No, she told herself. It would be removing herself from a place where she was not wanted and didn't belong. The snag was, in the scheme of car-sharing that she and Meghan had worked out, Meghan currently had the Land Rover. But that was a minor detail. Packing up would take time and she'd better get started. Fetch suitcase, tip drawers onto bed. The suitcase was nothing like big enough to take the clothes she'd acquired since being there.

As she fished a roll of bin bags from the kitchen she thought she heard an engine and waited for a knock, but none came. When she went to the front door to look, her Land Rover was sitting on the drive, keys swinging in the ignition. So Meghan had returned it without coming in. Probably had a lift back with Rita. It seemed like a heavy hint that leaving would be a good thing to do.

Not long after that, she heard a knock at the door.

She was disappointed to find Claudia on her doorstep again, with more soup. A spiced tomato this time. 'Comfort food for the invalid,' she said.

'But I'm not...'

'Of course you are. Nobody talking to you and everybody talking *about* you. Enough to make anyone sick.'

Thank you, Claudia. She'd guessed, of course, that she was the talk of the village but it was another thing to have it confirmed.

'I speak like it is. It's best to be clear.'

Naomi recalled the conversation about the dearly beloved Cyril. Claudia knew what it was to be lonely.

'Hey, what's this I see before me?' Claudia made a gesture worthy of Macbeth, indicating the suitcase.

'I'm leaving. I think it's for the best. I can't face anybody and they clearly can't face me. Just when I'd started to feel I belonged.'

'Nonsense!' Claudia spun round to face her. 'Of course you belong. I was having plans to get you back on the horse.'

'Horse?'

'You know, after a fall you must get back on. We'll go to the pub together. This evening maybe?'

Naomi was suddenly overwhelmed by the generosity of this woman who had remarked more than once that she disliked pubs in general and the bar at the Stagworthy Quay Hotel in particular.

She embraced Claudia, breathing in the flavours of stale patchouli, fried onions and some kind of spice. 'That is so sweet of you. So thoughtful. But I absolutely couldn't face it. Especially when I know you'd be hating it too.'

'Not exactly a fun night out, I know. But that's not the point. Even if you won't do that, you certainly shouldn't be thinking of leaving. Give it time. It'll all blow over.'

Naomi eyed the suitcase. She thought of the bleak bungalow she'd be going back to. The annoying neighbours who were constantly polishing their cars and pruning their roses while clearly annoyed that she refused to do the same. It wasn't tempting.

'Promise me you'll sleep on it at the very least? I'll not leave until you promise.'

Naomi nodded and Claudia heaved the suitcase off the bed and onto the floor before departing.

She was soon back. 'Look what I found outside the door!' Claudia handed Naomi a bunch of flowers with a note tucked among the petals, then retreated to the kitchen to fetch a vase.

It wasn't a florist's bouquet. It wasn't even made up of the best cut flowers in the garden. He must have gone down to the orchard and picked from the wild flowers and grasses – a mix of pinks and reds and blues of campion and cornflower and others she didn't know by name.

The note was brief.

You seemed like a stranger, someone I couldn't trust.
But I still want to trust your motivation. Am I right to believe in that?
P xx

Tears slid down Naomi's face.

Claudia came back into the room. 'I knew it! He was cross and stomped off and now he's come to his senses and realises he was hasty.' She took the flowers and dropped them into the jug she had found. 'Am I right? I can't bear you two beautiful people to fall out over some tiff in the pub. Too, too sordid. And a terrible waste!'

'It wasn't a tiff. I was massively out of order. You know, of course you do. You're just being tactful for once.' Naomi fingered the note. 'But it looks like I get a second chance.'

When Claudia left, Naomi thumbed through the CD rack and filled the silence with her favourite Beatles' numbers.

Could Patrick trust her motivation? What did he mean by that? Just a polite way of saying she meant well. But that was too simple. If she was honest, there was more to it than that – the fairy godmother bit. When the CD finished, she was none the wiser. Still a lonely old woman abandoned by all her friends. Except Claudia. She hadn't really counted her as a friend before, but she had certainly behaved like one, a friend in need.

Should she ring at Patrick's door? She couldn't bring herself to press the bell, so she wandered out to the drive, climbed into the Land Rover and fingered the ignition. But her mind went blank about where she would go. She just sat there gazing at the hedge.

Which was how Patrick found her. His voice over her shoulder through the open window. Warm, reassuring. 'What are you doing? Are you going out or coming back?'

She wanted to turn and hug him. Instead she shrugged. 'Making nowhere plans for nobody,' she said. That much at least was true.

'That good, eh?' He checked his watch. 'I tell you what – I've got a somewhere plan for both of us. There's a lot of talking to do but let's not rush into that. Let's have something to eat first. Somewhere I bet you've never been before. Shall we? A spot of lunch.'

He climbed in beside her. Hadn't even stopped to lock the house. Wasn't insisting on driving.

'Bit of a magical mystery tour,' he said, giving her a sideways grin.

'Oh, stop it.'

She drove to his directions, heading north on winding roads. When she glanced across at Patrick, he was smiling and humming softly to himself. Was this really happening? It felt surreal but those thoughts gave way to the need to focus on negotiating a steep, rutted lane into a deep valley. The sight of a whitewashed farmhouse nestled among beech trees made her wonder if she'd entered an enchanted land. Two other cars were parked in the farmyard. No sign of farm activity – all well-swept cobbles and tubs of geraniums. They were ushered into what must have been the old dairy – slate floor, slate shelving, cool after the heat outside. Two other couples were sitting at a table for four.

'It's pot luck,' Patrick said. 'No menu. Just the dish of the day. House wine. Very simple. Very delicious. Fingers crossed.'

Very not-Patrick. She watched as he chatted easily with the owner and his wife, who had opened the little restaurant a year ago and had been amazed at its success. He seemed somehow lighter, more relaxed than she had seen him before. Was it just her anxious perception or was there really a difference in his manner?

She was surprised to find she was hungry. After a mouth-watering sea bass and a meltingly delicious tarte tatin with clotted cream, she steeled herself to broach the subject that must have been on both their minds. She meant to say, 'About my motivation…' but what came out instead was, 'You're different. What's happened?'

'*You* is what's happened. You and your mistake. Which was crass and unconsidered and clumsy – let's not pretend.'

Naomi nodded and took a deep breath. 'But the motivation?'

'Ah yes! The motivation. So tell me. Was it to be trusted?'

'I saw them – Gordon and Alex – chatting so happily. I thought I could make them even happier. That was the good motivation. But then you get the dodgy bit – I'd be the benevolent fairy godmother. All that ego. Everyone would think I was wonderful. How wrong can you get something?'

'No such thing as altruism, there's always the underside, so forget that last bit. You wanted them to be happy. I'll take that.' Patrick shifted in his chair and took a sip of water.

At any other time Naomi would have interrupted to question how he could dismiss altruism so lightly. She even opened her mouth to speak but was glad he waved her aside. 'But you asked why I was different – and I am. You see, you came crashing off the pedestal I'd put you on. I can't tell you the relief. Once I'd got over the shock, that is. I'd been trying so hard. Trying to get everything right. I always try too hard. Hey, why are you laughing?'

'There was me thinking you were too good to be true and I'd never live up to you.'

'No! Really?' He took her hand across the table. 'Oh, Naomi! We've been doing it to each other.'

'Bloody hell, Patrick. I don't think I've ever been on a pedestal before.' That wasn't quite true. Wilson had put her on a pedestal in the beginning. But when she came tumbling off it, he punished her and the pattern of their relationship was set – with more punishment than pedestal.

'I prefer you off it. I'll try not to put you back on.'

'Remember there will always be that bit of me that will be crass and thoughtless and will get pissed.' She withdrew her hand to take a sip of water. 'I'm being good today, but I'm not making any promises.'

'Me neither. Because I shouldn't have been surprised about the too-good-to-be-true bit. I always try too hard. A habit I acquired with my mother and again with my late wife – she required it. They both did.'

Naomi ignored the reference to his wife. 'Mothers, eh! I could probably pin my behaving badly on mine, but I'm not going there. I'd rather think about us.' She paused, looking across the table at him, trying not to smile too broadly. 'Hey, did I say how much I loved those flowers? I didn't, did I? You knew exactly what I'd like and took the trouble to find them.'

He nodded. 'I had to resist the temptation to get lilies.'

'Exactly! Lilies would have been awful. Beautiful. But awful.'

Back at home, Patrick followed her inside. She'd forgotten how she'd left the room.

'What's with the suitcase?'

'I was going to leave. Remove myself from where I'm not wanted. Claudia persuaded me not to. She made me promise to sleep on it. And then she found your flowers. And I thought I might have a second chance.'

'Claudia! I didn't realise you were such good friends.'

'Nor did I. She's been brilliant, kept coming with soup and just letting me be.'

'She knows a thing or two about being lonely. Such a talented woman. Underneath all the posing. Did you know she's a graphic designer and a very well-known illustrator? Children's books mostly, of course. Works for several top publishers.'

'I had no idea. You mean she still does?'

'Oh yes, relies on it for an income. After her totally useless husband left her with debts. The beloved Cyril didn't like her career – her little hobby he called it – insisted she use a pen name. Didn't want his grand academic name to be associated with her "scribbles".'

Naomi thought of how Claudia had been on the day she had stepped off the pavement. Maybe the grief was more for the wasted years than for the husband. She was about to say as much, but Patrick interrupted.

'Why are we standing here talking about Claudia?' He took the corner of the rumpled duvet, shook it out and turned it back. 'Ah!' He picked up the lapis ring on her bedside table. 'I noticed you weren't wearing it.'

'Truth? Wisdom? It didn't seem terribly me. And I didn't think I'd ever see you again. So I took it off.'

'At least you didn't throw it away.' He held it out and she took it and slipped it on.

'Maybe it will give me some wisdom. I can but hope.'

He opened his arms. 'Come here.'

It was the third day before Meghan appeared, striding into the room and not sitting down.

'I have one question. Why on earth didn't you ask me first?'

Naomi sighed. 'The question I've asked myself over and over. One, it was an impulse. Two, I was pissed. It came to me in a blinding flash, seeing Gordon and Alex there, getting on so well – and the colouring. I wanted to make Gordon happy. He's lonely and he always wanted a daughter.'

'Well, he can't have mine!'

'And I thought of you and him and the timing. It all seemed to fall into place. It was so obvious.'

'But you knew about Logan! I told you. In Bristol before I came here. I was pregnant when I arrived.'

'So people have been delighting in telling me. Rita for one. But *you* never told me. Yes, you spoke about Logan. But you never said he was Alex's father. Was I supposed to guess?'

Meghan groaned. 'I thought I'd told you, assumed you knew.' She looked up at Naomi – a half-frown, half-smile as if she wanted to forgive her, was weighing it up. Then she was off again. 'But I told you about going home – my mam turning me out!'

'So?'

'Me going home from Bristol when Logan vamoosed.'

'How was I to know that? I assumed going home from here. But even so – I'm not excusing myself. Just that I'm not psychic.'

Meghan made that same face and shrugged. 'But even so. I felt invaded.' And with that she left.

Ten minutes later a text arrived. 'Forgot to apologise for hitting you. Not something I usually do.'

Naomi texted back. 'Hit people? Or apologise?'

A reply came immediately. 'Both xx'.

Naomi smiled and took a deep breath. Maybe she did still have a friend.

35 Naomi

It was Gordon who had suggested she have a trial period in the cottage. They'd been sitting in the bar at the Stagworthy Quay, her first visit since the disastrous birthday party. Patrick had insisted that she turn up on her regular night. A few days had passed since Claudia had suggested "getting back on the horse", and Patrick succeeded where Claudia had failed.

'Just buy a drink. Sit at your regular table. See what happens.'

'But people won't talk to me,' she'd said. 'I'll be ignored. It will be humiliating.' She'd only agreed to go on condition that Patrick would rescue her after a short time.

In the event, Gordon had joined her immediately. 'Revisiting the scene of the crime?'

Naomi made a face. 'Something like that. At least I haven't been barred.'

'Water under the bridge.' He raised his glass to her. 'Onwards and upwards. People have short memories. Ah, here comes Colin.'

By the time Patrick arrived there were no spare chairs at the table.

Gordon had then explained he had to go to London and it was a good opportunity for her to have a trial run.

'London again?' Naomi asked. 'It was only last week…'

'That was just a flying visit. I'll be staying a little longer this time. Stuff to get sorted out.'

He wouldn't elaborate on what "stuff" that was and had been surprisingly solicitous about her comfort in the cottage.

'There are bound to be things you want to get,' he'd said. 'Things you're used to, can't do without.' He'd raised his glass of Scotch, which looked paler than usual. 'My needs are simple – as long as I've got a bottle of the old Grouse, but the place is still pretty basic and there's no point in you depriving yourself.'

'You're on,' Naomi had said. It had seemed an excellent idea – she could make a list of things to get before she moved in more permanently in the autumn.

Last thing before she went to bed on that first night, she opened the big old door and peered up into the night sky. There, hovering above the cottage roof, was the Plough. Pretty much the only constellation she knew, it seemed to be protecting her. She smiled up at it and breathed in the starlit air before turning the heavy iron key in the lock.

She'd been surprised not to find Gordon's big mackintosh on the back of the door. No wellies either. He'd hardly be wearing them in London. No stacks of old newspapers with half-finished crosswords either. He'd taken a lot of care and she was grateful.

Next day, clear blue skies drew her outside and she spent the morning walking her domain. Golden light caught the dew-spangled spiders' webs that hung from every bramble. She revisited the river and the waterfall, scrambled down onto the beach and poked about in rock pools that reflected the sky. Later, she climbed the steep path up the hillside through the bracken until her ankle complained it could go no further. She collected a few late blackberries, and several mushrooms to cook for supper.

Once she'd gathered kindling and logs and laid the fire ready for the evening, the sun was still out and the cottage dim, so she took a blanket up onto the headland and lay on her back, gazing up at the azure sky. Azure. Basildon Bond. The only writing paper her mother ever used. Hadn't thought of that in years. Didn't want to think of it now. She must have fallen asleep remembering blue-black ink, *Quink*, in an odd-shaped bottle and Mum saying it had to be blue-black, anything else would be common. When she woke there was a chill in the air and puffs of seersucker cloud were drifting across the blue. She sat up and stretched, saw clouds gathering out at sea, building on the far horizon.

Back in the cottage kitchen, she sizzled the mushrooms in butter and garlic, boiled water for pasta and rejoiced. A whole day in her own company and not once had she looked toward the footpath for a visitor or waited for the phone to ring. Maybe she could crack this solitude thing after all.

Gordon had also left the kitchen sink and cooker unexpectedly clean and tidy. Not that she'd expected a mess, just not this degree of spick and span. It was a bit disturbing, as if it was trying to tell her something. Did Gordon think she was that fussy?

By the time she had finished supper, the weather had radically changed. Wind howled round the stone walls and rain lashed against the window as she washed up. There would be no Plough watching over her tonight. At least, not one that was visible to her. She pulled curtains wherever there were any and curled up by the fire, reading and not reading, staring at the flames and the fireflies burning the soot on the fireback. She coughed at the occasional puff of smoke. Maybe she'd put in a wood-burner. Much as she loved the open fire, a stove would be more efficient.

She glanced around the room. Another comfortable armchair for visitors would be nice. And one of Meghan's paintings instead of the rather boring local prints. The dying embers of the fire fell in on each other, giving out the last of their heat. Yes, she'd definitely get a quote for a wood-burner. And a toaster. A nostalgic toasting fork was all very well at teatime but no good at breakfast.

In bed, as she listened to the whine of the gale and the creak of the roof timbers, she reminded herself that the cottage had stood for centuries, solid against the elements. The walls would not collapse. The roof would not fall in.

She rolled on the waves of the storm, falling into deep wells of sleep. She would wake wrapped around with what felt like two hours of dream to find that only fifteen minutes had passed. And then she was gone again, rocked into oblivion.

At two in the morning she was pulled from oblivion by a splash of icy water landing on her nose. By the time she'd dragged the bed to one side and fetched the washing-up bowl to place under the drip, she was wide awake, so she pulled back the curtains to watch the storm. The brambles below the window were shuddering like a witch's brew coming to the boil, but there were no trees to measure the force of the wind, only balls of spume floating up from the ocean and landing in snow-like drifts on the headland. When she opened the window to hear the pounding waves, a gust of rain spattered her feet. She shut it again quickly and dived back into bed, hoping for the best.

When she woke she didn't know where she was. There had been times in the past when she'd found that experience disconcerting, even frightening.

But today it gave her a precious space, a no-man's-land where she might be anything, take flight, escape from her normal self. The moment only lasted seconds before the furniture and the floorboards rearranged themselves into shapes and colours she recognised. But it was exhilarating. As she dressed she wondered at how her movements echoed. The acoustic up here was so hollow, so empty. A few rugs would help, and of course her clothes. She stopped in the middle of zipping her jeans. Empty. Clothes. She almost ran into Gordon's room, which she had so far only peeped into out of respect for his privacy. What about Gordon's clothes? Empty wardrobe. Empty drawers. Here was the message she had failed to pick up. Gordon did not plan to return.

'Gordon's ill. I'm sure of it. I have to go to London,' she told Meghan on the phone.

'Aren't you rather jumping to conclusions? I mean, just because he's moved out...'

'I just know. There have been signs. For instance, it wasn't whisky he was drinking the other day. I've been so slow. And if you take me to the station, you can have the Land Rover while I'm away.'

'I must say, I've never seen Gordon without his Scotch. What does Patrick think?'

'I haven't told him yet.'

'Haven't told Patrick? Whaat? He'll want to take you to the station...'

Now that it was pointed out to her, Naomi was surprised she'd chosen to ring Meghan first, but it had seemed the obvious choice. 'He'd give me a lift, of course, but it makes no sense for my car to sit here.'

'Stop being so damned practical! The point is, he'll be hurt, not to be asked, surely? To be by-passed...and I can still fetch the Land Rover.'

Naomi grunted.

'Naomi, drive it up to his place and see what happens next. I'll be on standby to take you.' Meghan paused. 'But be prepared for him not to like it. Any of it. It's going to take him a while to get used to Naomi in practical I'm-living-my-life mode.'

'Oh surely not! Anyway, it's what we always agreed, me and him.'

'You're not listening to me, Naomi – agreeing and then discovering – two different things...'

Naomi pooh-poohed her. Patrick wasn't like that. She dialled his number.

He listened, concerned for Gordon, but more concerned that she was jumping to conclusions and would have a wasted journey.

'Why don't you phone him?'

'Never had the number and he's ex-directory – of course! As to a mobile, he always refused.'

'So you're going to London? Just like that.' A pause, which lengthened into a silence. 'Don't want me to come too?'

'No, really. I can manage. No need to disrupt your life as well. And Meghan's going to take me to the station.'

Silence.

'You still there?'

'Oh, yes, I'm here. So you've got it all organised. You will let me know, won't you, when you're coming back?'

'Oh, Patrick! Don't be like that. It's just – I'm worried. Of course I'll…'

'I'm not being like anything. But I won't hold you up. Hope you have a good journey.'

'Oh, bugger.' Naomi replaced the handset and covered her face in her hands.

She made coffee, burnt the toast and the roof of her mouth, and then settled for a banana, before furiously filling an overnight bag.

As she drove through the woods she barely noticed the rich smell of wet leaves after the storm. She was too preoccupied with the conversation in her head. Why did people have to be so over-sensitive? She slammed the first gate shut, so that it rebounded on her, hit her chin and made her bite her tongue. Not badly. But even so.

Gordon needed her. And she needed to get there quickly, to do it her way, on her own. Having Patrick there would just complicate things – like where they would stay and the need to eat a proper meal. She'd be happy to kip on Gordon's sofa and grab a sandwich. She'd known Meghan would understand all that and trust her instinct about Gordon. Hmm. She had, hadn't she? But Meghan had been on another tack. Afraid Naomi was messing things up with Patrick.

Oh, bugger. She knew it. Relationships get complicated. However not-like-marriage they'd tried to make it.

Meghan had pretty much predicted that phone call and obviously wouldn't think Patrick was being over-sensitive. Naomi didn't want to hurt him, of course she didn't. He was a dear man. A good man. She loved him. Didn't he deserve some consideration, too?

But the point was they'd agreed to lead their separate lives – and he'd fallen at the first hurdle.

But then again, supposing he'd done the same thing to her? Like Fay used to do when her family took over her life and she'd forget to share bits of news? That used to hurt.

'Oh, bugger, yes, I'd be hurt,' she said out loud as she closed the final gate. 'I'd want to be the first one to know.'

Which is what Meghan was saying all along. How could she have been so mad at him? She was going to have to grovel. No. Wrong word. She needed to be truly sorry. And loving. How was she going to get to that place of being sorry and loving in the space of driving that last half mile?

Patrick came to the door before she had time to get out of the car. 'There's a surprise,' he said.

One look at him as he stood there with the sunlight catching that kink of hair that always stood up at the back of his head and all her doubt and anxiety fell away. This was Patrick.

'Don't tell me you came to say goodbye?' A hint of a smile.

'More than that.' She stood awkwardly, still holding the door of the car. 'Oh, Patrick, look at you! How could I not…?' She shook her head so hard that a comb fell out and bounced at her feet. 'Sorry doesn't really cut it. But I am. Sorry I mean. What was I thinking of? I'm just not used…'

Patrick cut her off. He stepped forward, picked up the comb and put both arms around her. 'I'm so glad you came,' he said into her hair.

'I didn't mean…' she started.

'You're a tricky conundrum, woman. I'll say that. Keep thinking I know you and I bloody don't.' He let her go and fiddled with the comb, trying to fix it in her hair. 'I was hurt. I admit it. I always want to be your knight in shining armour. I get it that you don't want one of those, I really do. Even so…'

'Patrick, just as an exception to that rule, will you get your armour on right now and drive me to the station?' She repositioned the comb and closed the Land Rover door. 'Otherwise I'm going to miss the train.'

As they drove away, she texted Meghan: 'You win. He's taking me. Land Rover yours. Thanks for putting me right. Bloody relationships. Love him to bits.'

Mr Gibson, the porter at Gordon's apartment building, looked Naomi up and down over his gold-rimmed glasses and examined her driving licence carefully. With some ceremony he consulted a card index and produced a list of names.

'You are right there, at the top of Major Fanshaw's list. Not that there are many. I'm very pleased to meet you, Mrs Osborne. I'll fetch the keys.'

'So, Mr Fanshaw isn't here?'

'Oh, no.' Mr Gibson paused. He looked like a man governed by the proper protocols who was running through them in his mind. 'I think it best if Mrs Bolton explains the situation. She is the housekeeper and she will call by quite soon.'

Gordon's flat was small and grand and dark. In the sitting room, Naomi tussled with heavy curtains until she realised they parted on the press of a button. Tall windows, too heavy to open, with a view of the busy street a few floors below. Just one bedroom, smelling stale, a small kitchen, a bathroom with shower over the bath, and that was it. Coming back into the sitting room, she noticed the sofa had been converted into a bed and was made up with clean sheets. She looked for a letter or a note of instructions but there was nothing. Only the absence of Gordon confirmed that her instincts had been right.

The kitchen had no outside window but it was well lit, and a teapot and tea caddy were set out, ready to use. Before the kettle had boiled there was a ring of the front door bell, followed by the rattle of keys and a cheerful voice: 'It's only me, it's Mrs B!'

Mrs B for Bolton, a small round, grey-haired woman not bound by protocols, bounced into the kitchen at the prospect of tea. She found biscuits in a cupboard while discovering that Naomi knew nothing of Gordon's condition and had acted on instinct.

'You must know him well.'

'Just for a very long time. He's been like an uncle to me. I'm fond of him. And he hasn't let me know anything.'

'He speaks fondly of you. You were the only one he wanted in his flat. Oh, yes, old Gibson will have given the impression that there's a list. But there isn't.'

Naomi took a long drink of tea, disliking the taste but feeling the need of its heat and strength.

'He's one of the best, is Gordon,' Mrs B went on. 'A one-off, a true gentleman, and generous when he can ill afford to be. Unlike others who shall be nameless, who are mean and rude without good cause. You see, this is the smallest apartment in the building.'

Naomi had already noticed that the whole flat had probably been carved out of one big room. The cornices were abruptly cut off, the big windows in the sitting room were not symmetrically placed, and some doorways had ended up right against the wall. Gordon lived in a mean slice of the building, but the building itself suggested affluence, which had allowed Gordon to feel respectable.

Naomi nodded her understanding. 'So where is he?'

'I'll give it to you straight. It's pancreatic cancer and he hasn't got long. Here are all the details, hospital, ward, etc. He's on palliative care, they'll let you in any time.'

'How long?'

He's been in and out. This time, nearly a week. I visited him only yesterday and he asked if you'd been in touch. The sooner you go… I think – I don't want to dramatise – but I have the feeling that he can't be at peace until he's seen you.'

'Really?'

Mrs B nodded and left. Naomi sat staring into space. 'How long's he known?' she said, addressing the imposing curtains. 'Bet he's known all along, right from the time I first came across him in the cottage. "Fit as a flea," he said then. Kidding himself? Teasing me? Who knows? But oh, God, Gordon! I just can't believe it. That it should come to this. And what you've been going through, all alone, with just Mrs B for company.'

*

Naomi looked through the glass door towards the bed that the nurse assured her contained Gordon. All she could see was a grey, skull-like head on the pillow and a skeletal arm resting on the sheet. He appeared to be sleeping.

'Just say his name, or take his hand,' the nurse said. 'You'll know what to do.'

Naomi took the chair by the bed and stretched her hand to touch his fingers, which immediately closed around hers. Eyes flickered open.

'You took your time.' Croaky but unmistakeably Gordon.

'Why didn't you tell me?'

'Didn't want a fuss. But then didn't want to be alone. Bugger of a fine line. But you took the hint.'

'Lots of hints. But it was the wellies that did it. And the clean kitchen.'

He squeezed her fingers until they hurt, gave a deep sigh and seemed to fall asleep.

The nurse returned. 'He'll be tired after talking to you. You can stay if you want, but you look exhausted. Go and rest. Come back tomorrow, won't you? Any time.'

The next day Gordon was half sitting up. He'd had a shave, looked less grey.

He started to talk before she'd sat down. 'I wanted to tell you – it's difficult even now. Need to tell you how much you mean to me. Always loved you. Like a daughter, I suppose. As a friend. As an enemy, too.'

As he paused for breath, Naomi started to speak but he held up a hand to stop her.

'Always admired how you were scared and clumsy but you never gave up, and however much you seemed to hate yourself, you never stopped trying to find something likeable in yourself. I'm ashamed of how I undermined you. Dammit, you were such a bloody easy target. But all the time I was bullying you, I was loving you at the same time. That's the sort of bloody useless sort of person I was.'

He paused again and gestured towards the glass of water on his bedside table. 'Now I've worn myself out.'

Naomi passed the glass and steadied it while he drank. 'I love you, too, Gordon. You've always been my best uncle, and even when you tortured me, along with your damn brother, I couldn't forget how different, what a good friend, you could be.'

'Let's leave my brother out of it. Leave Immo out of it, too. It wasn't just because you're her daughter. You're special, and I've loved watching you become the woman you are.'

He slumped back on the pillows and seemed to fall asleep. Naomi stood up to leave, but his eyes flew open.

'You're supposed to have a dying wish, aren't you? So, take note. Gordon's Bar – you remember that old dive? I bumped into you at Embankment and took you there.'

How could she forget it? Death-trap stairs down into a series of dark and dirty rooms opening off one another. Crammed with rickety chairs and tables, thick with cigarette smoke and non-designer cobwebs. But so much more than a public health hazard. It had been like entering an enchanted wood.

Gordon seemed to have forgotten about his namesake bar. 'More important than dying wish – that is that you – look at me, dammit! That you believe what I said yesterday.'

'What you said? Yesterday?'

'Well, I'm darn well not saying it all again. Embarrassing us both to NAAFI breaks. In summary, believe that the world is a better place with you in it. Even when you're on your high horse being a silly cow, which has been known.' His head flopped back onto the pillow. 'Better place, Naomi.'

She took his hand and squeezed it. 'And Gordon's Bar?'

'Ah, yes. Ashes. Want them scattered there. Bit of fun. You and Meghan go and get rat-arsed on white port and eat a Scotch egg.' He smiled as if at a fond memory.

She remembered the Scotch eggs, home-made and delicious and brought up from the country by the cook every day.

Gordon laughed. 'Not all the ashes. Even Gordon's might notice that. A matchbox maybe. You'll do that?'

'Of course, that's perfect.'

'Had it now.' He released his hand from hers. 'Need a sleep.'

On cue, the nurse came through the door and helped him to lie down. She followed Naomi to the door. 'He'll sleep now. You're welcome to stay, but the thing is, he specially told me this morning, he didn't want you to hang about. It's up to you.'

'That figures. It's him all over.' Naomi nodded at the nurse. 'I'll come back tomorrow.' She turned at the door just as Gordon opened one eye and closed it again.

Gordon's funeral was every bit as soulless as Naomi feared it would be. She had hoped to inject some humanity into a short eulogy, but when it came to it, she found she knew hardly anything of Gordon's life. Mrs B pressed an envelope into her hand when they met at the crematorium. When she peeked inside, she saw the photo of her mother laughing in the New Forest, alongside Gordon's commando badge. It was tempting to stand up and describe the passionate affair she had witnessed as a child, and which had made Gordon so happy. But he would not have wanted that. She would stick to her meagre script.

'I have known Gordon most of my life in one way or another,' she began. 'But I find I know little of his life. All I can say is that he was a kind and caring man who liked to give the opposite impression. He was a dear friend and I loved him.'

Mr Gibson had instructions for the wake at Gordon's club, where sausage rolls and beef sandwiches were on offer and where a few cronies gathered to quaff the free Scotch. They gave the Devon contingent some sideways looks but were careful to avoid eye contact. Naomi grieved at the impression this gave of Gordon's club membership.

'I knew even less of him than I thought I did,' she said to Meghan on the train home.

'I guess we can never really know anyone, especially if they don't want us to know.'

Patrick put an arm round Naomi. 'Seems to me you knew him better than anyone.'

Naomi fingered the envelope in her pocket, her happy mother, the secret badge, Gordon's beloved Immo, everything that might have been.

'That's what makes me so sad,' she said.

36 Naomi

It was a warm day in late October. Naomi and Meghan were sprawled on the grass in Meghan's garden, sipping home-made lemonade.

Enough time had passed since Gordon's death to allow Naomi to plan the move to the cottage and her house-warming party. It would be strange that he wouldn't be there. She'd chosen November 5th – a suitably subversive date and a good excuse for the drama of a bonfire. Luckily it fell on a Friday, which meant it wouldn't clash with local celebrations.

'Love the idea that the whole headland will be warmed,' Meghan said. 'Just get on to Eric – you know Eric? The estate manager at the Manor? He'll be glad to cart down a load of material for the fire.'

Meghan had been less positive about Naomi's catering plan, which was to cook up two big pots of chilli and serve it round the wood-burner in the cottage. She wouldn't send out invitations but was reckoning on about a dozen people, those she was close to.

'You don't imagine there's going to be a bonfire and only twelve people will come?' Meghan said.

'Of course not. But they won't come in the cottage. They won't need feeding.'

Meghan had gone quiet at that and Naomi reflected on bonfire events when she'd been happy to buy a hot dog or a baked potato. But this was different. She couldn't see how to manage it, any more than she could manage fireworks. She'd had to rule them out as too complicated and risky. Anyway there would be a big display in the village the next day. She hoped the bonfire watchers would not have unrealistic expectations, but was left feeling uneasy, afraid the whole thing would fall flat. It was a relief when Meghan changed the subject.

'Love it when we get this weather in October, the light is just wonderful.' Meghan leaned on one elbow. 'Look, over there, on the hillside. All golden.'

'Maybe that's your next challenge. Light! After all the dark birds and stuff. I mean, you don't really do light in your painting.'

'Don't do light? I could be deeply offended by that remark. Of course I do light! You wouldn't actually be able to see the birds if I didn't.'

'Obviously, yes, I get that. I'm not totally stupid…'

'But I do see what you mean.' Meghan paused, staring up at the sky in all its blueness. 'I just think I would find it altogether too daunting.'

'Rubbish. I'd just love to see you try. I reckon…'

What Naomi reckoned was eclipsed by the sharp click of the front gate, the slam of the front door and the sudden eruption of Alex into the garden, apparently weak with laughter. She flopped down next to Meghan.

'Listen to this! The latest from *darling* Claudia.' Alex gulped lemonade from Meghan's glass. 'Will has evidently applied for a job in Stagworthy. So she's putting two and two together and making her usual five, right? So here's the scene – if he gets the job, that is – he'll be wielding pruning shears, a shovel and a chainsaw if he's lucky. He'll be living in that shed they call the Old Barn near the entrance and existing on a pittance. And Claudia thinks it would be perfect accommodation for me and a baby! I doubt Will has been consulted but if Claudia really imagines I'm shacking up with a woodcutter in the forest, then it won't be long before I turn into a wicked witch on the lookout for Hansel and Gretel.'

Naomi noticed how the story became more of a rant as it went on and sensed distress behind the laughter. If Claudia really wanted Alex as a daughter-in-law, then she was shooting herself in the foot.

'Claudia did tell me Will had taken on some training,' Meghan was saying. 'She was a bit vague, but something to do with trees. She didn't really suggest you move in with Will? Surely not.'

'Not in so many actual words. But her meaning was perfectly clear.'

Meghan nodded. 'I can imagine. Needs taking with more than a pinch of salt. I mean, where's Will in all of this?'

Alex shrugged and lay back on the grass, massaging her belly. 'By the way,' she said. 'I've decided. It's Nina. And nothing to do with Will or Claudia either.'

'That's a fine name,' Meghan said. 'I love it. Phew, what a relief. I was afraid you'd choose something weird, like Gertrude, and I'd have to live with it. No, I like Nina a lot.'

Alex giggled. 'Gertrude was just winding you up. I still like Agnes. But she just isn't an Agnes.'

'Will she have a middle name?' Naomi asked.

'Meghan, of course.'

Meghan's eyebrows shot up. 'You're teasing.'

'No, really. Definitely Meghan.'

For a moment it looked as if Meghan might cry. 'You don't have to.'

'If I had to, then I wouldn't,' Alex said and made Meghan laugh instead.

How much easier the two of them were together these days. They had the odd spat, and Alex never gave up on referring to her impossibly tiny bedroom, but it was good-humoured. Naomi, too, felt easily included ever since the shopping trip to Barnstaple. The drive there had been tense and, once Meghan had gone to meet Geoffrey at the gallery, Naomi and Alex faced each other over the mechanics of the wheelchair.

'It's kind of you to do this for me,' Naomi had said.

Alex retorted sharply. 'Not kind. Mum would have killed me if I'd refused.'

They'd proceeded to the shops, purchases were made and Naomi presented Alex with a bag full of first-size baby clothes and nappies.

'Cool,' Alex said limply. 'That's very kind.' She was almost visibly squirming.

But lunch at a pizza place loosened things up. Meghan was excited that Geoffrey was going to put her work forward for the summer arts festival. Alex allowed herself a glass of wine to celebrate. She even thanked Naomi, with no apparent effort, for buying lunch. 'That was kind of you,' she said.

'Not kind,' Naomi replied. 'You'd probably have killed me if I hadn't.'

For a moment Alex had looked shocked before she made the connection and laughed. Then they were all laughing and an invisible iceberg seemed to have melted away.

Now Naomi reached across the grass to refill her glass with lemonade. 'Reminds me, I'm due to meet Claudia any minute now at the farm shop.'

Alex looked alarmed. 'Don't tell her what I said, will you?'

'Of course not. But before I go, how about this for another perspective on Claudia's story? Instead of woodcutter in shack we have "Tree surgeon and landscape gardener required. Accommodation provided in historic heritage property on the famous Stagworthy estate". I just wonder if that would change your mind?'

Alex grunted.

'Nice try, Naomi,' Meghan said. 'You weren't an estate agent for nothing. But it actually doesn't change a thing.'

Naomi wasn't so sure. She'd seen a flicker of interest in Alex's eye at the title of tree surgeon, which definitely carried better earning potential than woodcutter. Who knew where all that was headed.

As Naomi arrived at the farm shop, Claudia greeted her from the back of the café with whoops and waves. She'd stopped being embarrassed by these displays – everyone was used to Claudia and nobody took much notice. Today she was wearing shades of green and turquoise, and presiding over a teapot and a plate of Eccles cakes.

She leapt up as Naomi approached and pecked her on both cheeks. '*There* you are, dear one. Sit thee down. I *do* hope you'll partake. I do *love* an Eccles cake.'

Naomi opened her mouth to speak but Claudia poured a cup of the palest of tea and continued, 'You'll know why I wanted to see you.' She replaced the teapot and smiled across at Naomi. 'It's all sorted.'

'Sorted? What's sorted?'

'Your house-warming, dear one!'

Naomi felt the heat rise into her neck. 'But what is there to sort?'

'Right. So. Will has got together with a couple of mates and they've got hold of one of the big barbecues they use at Carnival – for hot dogs. Nothing fancy. Just onions and those squirty sauces – *so* vulgar and *quite* delicious.'

'But...'

Claudia held up a hand. 'And we're all going to brew up vats of soup. Paper cups. Paper plates. All very simple.'

'All? We? Who?'

'Well, me, Meghan, Jo. Who do you imagine? Did Meghan say nothing?'

'No,' Naomi said more fiercely than she intended. 'She just implied that my idea – *my* idea for *my* house-warming – chilli round the fire for close friends – was inadequate.'

'But that's a lovely idea. Oh, darling, now you're offended. I didn't mean to crash in. Oh dear, I've got a handkerchief somewhere.'

Naomi was furious to be in tears, furious with Meghan for being right, furious with Claudia for taking over.

'You see, Meghan said you had no idea how many people would turn up.'

'It's only a bonfire.'

'No, it's not. It's *your* bonfire. People want it to work out for you.'

Naomi wiped her eyes on the square of jade silk Claudia produced.

'And when it came to it, Meghan was *sure* you'd want to feed the five thousand and you'd feel bad that you couldn't do that. So we thought we'd *bail* you out, so to speak.'

'Why do you all feel obliged to bail me out?'

'Well, it was an opportunity, to be honest. Our house-warming present to you, if you like. Oh, dear one, please don't be offended. Will's all fired up and he's getting Alex involved. She's a funny old stick, so prickly at the moment.'

Naomi saw an opportunity to change the subject while she got used to the idea of the extended hospitality on her bonfire evening.

'I'm not offended, really. Just a bit overwhelmed.' She sipped the watery tea. 'I hear Will is applying for a job locally?'

Claudia's eyes brightened. 'So that girl does notice things I tell her.'

'Things about Will, maybe?'

'Oh, do you *think* so? It would be so...'

'I don't think you should hold out any hopes whatsoever. They're friends, Claudia. Let it be.'

Claudia nodded. 'You're right. I must. I overdo it.'

Naomi took a deep breath. There was a subject she'd wanted to bring up with Claudia for some time but had never found the opportunity. 'Talking of Will, this may not be the time and place, but I've been meaning to ask you forever. To tell me the story. Meghan tells me there is one and you should be the one to tell it.'

A shadow passed over Claudia's face, dimming the light in her eyes.

Naomi pressed on. 'I don't want to intrude. But when I first met Will it was such a surprise.'

It had been in the hotel bar when this dark-skinned version of Claudia had walked through the door. He was taller and heavier but the features he shared with his mother were unmistakeable. Who would have guessed Claudia's son would be of mixed race?

'Now, of course, I don't think about it,' Naomi continued. 'But I think you don't want to talk about it. Forget it. I'm sorry.'

Claudia rallied. 'Of course I'll tell you. It's just that, even after all these years, it still hurts. More tea, I think.'

Naomi went to order more tea, leaving Claudia munching compulsively at an Eccles cake. When she returned, Claudia had recovered her equilibrium.

'Of course you should know. You are my *friend*. I suppose I thought you knew, but that Meghan – she can be a wise soul. So *much* in the telling.' She brushed crumbs of flaky pastry from her sea green scarf. 'So, I told you about my Dearly Beloved, my professor?'

Naomi nodded. 'It was the anniversary of his death. The day I nearly ran you over. You were very sad.'

Claudia raised one eyebrow and gave a twisty little grin. 'Sad that he hadn't died some years sooner, to be honest.' She tucked the long tress of her hair behind her left ear and continued. 'He was indeed dearly beloved in the beginning. But on our wedding night he announced – and I quote – he would not be burdening me with any intimate physical attention. *Burdening* me!' Claudia clutched her cheeks. 'So it was twin beds from the very start.'

Here Claudia took delivery of the fresh pot of tea and poured herself a cup. 'I have to tell you, I was a strange mixture in those days. Oxford *overwhelmed* me – sheltered upbringing, girls' boarding school. I was a very shy and conscientious student. But I was not a virgin. I wasn't blonde.' Claudia paused and stroked her tress of hair. 'Chestnut, it was. But I had these *assets* – you wouldn't know it now – that were very attractive to men. A shock to me, I have to tell you, but I was compliant because it was really the only way I knew of relating to men. I suppose I became *addicted* to sex as a measure of my worth. So, you see, I knew what I was missing in my marriage. I spent years consumed by a hunger I'm ashamed to describe.' Claudia leaned forward and dropped into a formidable stage whisper. 'I tell you, I would have done it with a horse!'

Heads at the next table swivelled but Claudia clutched at her face and continued more quietly.

'But that was not necessary. Dearly Beloved had students come regularly for tutorials. I had my studio at the bottom of the garden – a darling little shed, all electric, where I scribbled away at my drawings. You can see where this is going? Quite a few students were persuaded to take an interest in my illustrations. I was shameless, Naomi! I would waylay them in the shrubbery before they reached the gate. Not really the thing for a professor's wife.'

Naomi grinned. 'I like it. Must have taken some courage.'

'I was just desperate.' Claudia paused and broke off a piece of Eccles cake, licked her fingers.

'It all worked fine until Stephen came along, Will's father. We fell in love. Nightmare.' She clutched her face. 'Bliss and nightmare. Never meant to happen. He was a bright student. Had a good job to go to back home when he graduated. Not to mention a wife and two little girls in Nigeria.' Claudia gazed out of the window. 'He was just so beautiful.'

She poured more tea and gulped it down. 'The inevitable happened – obviously. Stephen graduated. He got a first and went back to Nigeria sad but triumphant. What with a job and the reunion with his family, I don't suppose he stayed sad for long. I was bereft. And pregnant. Definitely Stephen's child. He'd been the only one for over a year. I was totally faithful to him, never looked at any of the others again.'

Naomi could only think to say, 'Oh, Claudia.'

'So I told Dearly Beloved, who was not surprised. He said, "I'm not a fool." Then he said, if the child was white, it could stay, but if it was Stephen's child it would have to go. And of course, Stephen's skin could not have been blacker – no half measures. He wasn't prepared to be humiliated on his home ground. "It would ruin my reputation," he said.'

Naomi drew breath but Claudia was not to be stopped.

'Dearly Beloved said he would let me stay as his wife – let me stay! Of course he let me stay. He was fond of his food, I was a good cook, a clever hostess, an intelligent consort. Where would he find a better housekeeper?

'Huh!' Claudia munched on more of her cake as if she needed the sugar to keep going. 'I developed a mysterious illness that winter and went to a "spa" to convalesce. Dearly Beloved arranged it all. Will was born and no sooner had I fallen for him with a love even greater than I ever had for Stephen, he was whisked away and lost to me forever. For months after I returned to Oxford I wouldn't go out for fear that people could see the bleeding wound where he'd been torn away.'

Naomi grabbed Claudia's hand and held it tight. 'Did you have no say?'

Claudia looked long and hard into her tea. 'The truth was, I never expected to be in control of my life, weird as that might sound. And to be brutally honest, I didn't want a say. I was a coward, Naomi. You see, I never wanted to be a mother. Was never on my agenda. Didn't think I could be one.'

Naomi nodded. 'I get that. Not all women do.'

'I thought long and hard about it. I knew I could have done it with Stephen. But that wasn't an option. I tried to imagine doing it with Dearly Beloved. The two of us as parents, I mean. I had this picture of our eyes meeting above a baby in a crib – and it was bleak, terrifying.'

As Claudia looked up, Naomi held her gaze. The look of fear in her eyes was raw. Claudia not acting for once.

'I just knew he'd be a bad father even of a white baby and I would be powerless. So even if I had persuaded him, I absolutely knew I couldn't do this mother thing with him. And I absolutely knew I couldn't do it alone.'

Naomi started to speak but Claudia hurtled on.

'I was so naïve. No clue about how actually having a baby would change things. But by the time Will arrived, it was too late. Papers had been signed. Dearly Beloved was cunning. It might have been the seventies, but the place he sent me to was a Catholic mother and baby home still dealing in what were effectively forced adoptions. I crept back to the security of the Oxford house to lick my wounds. I told you I was a coward.'

Naomi grasped Claudia's hand again. 'Not at all. That's a terrible story. He took appalling advantage.'

'But you see, he wasn't lost forever, my darling Will. Five years ago he turned up. He'd found me through some DNA scheme. So there you are, dear one, that's my story. I try not to be sad for the lost years. I focus every day on the fact that he is here, now.'

'I just don't know what to say. Devastating. But thank you so much for telling me.'

Claudia was suddenly business-like. She pushed away her plate. 'I absolutely *don't* want sympathy, but now you know an important part of me.' She retrieved her bag from the floor. 'What I *do* need to know is – are we on for your house-warming? Is it all okay? The hot dogs, the soup? You're not taking offence?'

Naomi smiled. It had been slowly dawning on her that the house-warming wasn't just hers. Friends, the village were hijacking it. Why should she be indignant? Why should she not be pleased? 'Of course not. I'm hugely grateful, really I am, now I've got used to the idea. It doesn't have to be either/or. I'll just have my indoor chilli party a little earlier – before people come to see the bonfire.' She looked at her watch. 'And now I have to go and pack. Patrick and I are off on a mini break before the big day. Early start in the morning.'

'Oh, where? Do tell!'

'Lyme Regis.'

'Oh, dear one, you can play *French Lieutenant's Woman* on the Cobb.'

'No, not me. You'd be much better at that.'

'Nonsense! You've got the cheekbones.' Claudia leapt up, stroked Naomi's cheek, running her thumb along the edge of her cheekbone. Then she pecked her on the other cheek and was on her way. 'Have a wonderful time,' she said over her shoulder.

37 *Naomi*

As Naomi switched off the vacuum cleaner, the noise of its motor was replaced by the chug of an engine and rumble of wheels. More noise and activity than Mill End had seen in months. Naomi had taken great satisfaction in the physical effort of housework that was making the place her own – becoming familiar with the boards that squeaked and rocked, the tiles that were crooked and the dirty marks that wouldn't wash off. Now Big Harry and his son Little Harry had arrived with the furniture she was bringing from the bungalow.

Once these items had been distributed, tea had been drunk and news exchanged, the Harrys departed and Naomi sprinted upstairs to stand in the doorway of her room, which was to be bedroom and study. Was it right? Would it work? The table under the window looking out to sea was perfect. So was the small "thinking" armchair close by, with the plant stand to take her coffee pot. The bed, her own bed at last, was not too big, and the faded chest of drawers blended with the floorboards. But when she sat on the bed, she was overwhelmed by the wardrobe. It fitted neatly behind the door but it towered above her and seemed to suck up the light from the window. Too much bedroom, not enough study. It had to go.

She had manoeuvred it into the middle of the room and was eying the doorway when Meghan shouted from the kitchen. After some false attempts, they persuaded the wardrobe onto a rug and slid it sideways into the next room, where it settled against a blank wall, ready to be useful.

Meghan surveyed Naomi's room. 'What that space needs behind the door is shelves. For books, not clothes.'

'Perfect,' Naomi said.

'Now,' Meghan said, 'I have something for you. By way of a house-warming. Down here.'

In the kitchen she said, 'What's different?'

Naomi saw it immediately. The red chair was taking fourth place around the table. It caused a bigger lurch of dismay than the wardrobe.

'I thought it should come home. Now you're here. Makes up the set and you may sometimes need four chairs.' Meghan stalled and looked at Naomi. 'It is all right, isn't it? I mean, it is just a chair, right?'

Of course it's just a chair, Naomi told herself. But it was Wilson's voice telling her that, which wouldn't do. 'Of course. That was a lovely idea,' she managed. If only it had remained an idea.

'Here's my other offering,' Meghan said.

It was a picture. A tree with a pair of jackdaws cavorting on a branch. They were, of course, static – it was a painting – but the energy of the composition, the subtlety of light and shadow, and the almost effervescent colours of the feathers somehow conveyed movement.

Naomi was almost speechless. 'Stunning! I can't believe…'

Meghan grinned. 'Glad you like.'

'I have the perfect place. Toolbox. Where have I seen it? In the larder? Bring the hammer.'

They hung the picture in Naomi's room, between the chest of drawers and the window so that she could see it from the bed and from her thinking chair.

Meghan insisted on blitzing the bathroom and making up beds while Naomi cleaned the sitting room and filled the basket beside the newly installed wood-burning stove. They then went up to the bench on the headland for a well-earned breather.

'Do you think it's enough?' Naomi asked. 'Just to be here and write – or whatever it takes? Like I said, I want to make sense of it all.'

Meghan nodded. 'Yes, it's enough. It's what I do, have done for years. More than enough.'

'But you do other stuff as well. You're useful, you…'

'Only because I have to. If I could gaze at a tree all day I would.'

'Or a bird.'

Meghan laughed. 'Yes. A bird. In fact I have something to tell you about black birds. A bit of news.' She paused and the pitch of her voice dropped, heavy with some barely concealed emotional charge. 'Not real news, but potential. Geoffrey rang. He knows someone on the festival committee. Had a word, ran my idea past him. Apparently he sat up and took notice, which is Geoffrey's way of saying he was really interested.'

'That's wonderful…'

Meghan held up a hand. 'Except he then said, this guy is bonkers and likely to be booted off the committee by all the other old fuddy-duddies like himself who won't stand for it.'

'Rubbish, he's just saying that so you don't get your hopes up.'

'Saving face, more like.' Meghan shrugged. 'Won't know until the spring, anyway. Don't tell a soul.'

'Have you told Alex?'

'No.'

'Win her respect, involve her? She'd like to be part of a secret.'

Meghan leant over and gave Naomi's shoulders a squeeze. 'You're probably right, my wise friend.'

'Not necessarily wise. It's up to you.'

'There was one thing that gave me hope.' Meghan gave a twisty little grin. 'The rooks were onto it. While I was on the phone to Geoffrey, a great troupe of them swooped down over the garden, all clattering wings and squawking, having some dispute. Then they were gone again. But when I hung up and went outside, there was Rocky on the fence, eying me as if to say, *How was that for a performance? And don't I get an apple?*' Meghan laughed. 'I know, I'm a mad, superstitious old…'

Naomi shook her head. 'Not at all. Just a bit of a witch. Definitely an omen.'

Meghan nodded. 'It did seem like it. We'll see. But, right now, it seems enough, doesn't it, to be sitting here staring out at that.' She gestured at the ocean with a wide sweep of her hand. 'Letting it in. The endlessness of it. In fact, come to think of it, the world could do with a lot more people doing just that. You can be one of them.'

'If you say so.'

'Anyway, ironically, I've got to get Rita's car back to her. I'll leave you to contemplate. Patrick coming tonight?'

'No, first night has to be solo – but he's coming tomorrow. Little house-warming.'

*

She didn't notice the dog at first. Picking her way over and between boulders, pausing to pocket a pebble, she became aware of a sound audible above the swirling of the incoming tide.

The creature blended with the rocks where it stood, panting heavily, tongue lolling, fur scuffed up in the breeze. A scrawny, raffish animal with lop-sided ears. She looked about for the owner. The dog seemed to be doing the same, surprised that no one materialised. It jumped down onto the only small patch of flat sand and flopped at full stretch.

Naomi continued to the water's edge. The tide had covered the reefs and in the nearest rock pool she could see anemones opening to the flood and small creatures emerging from crevices. A whole world between land and ocean. She looked out to the horizon. Earlier, the pewter sheet of the sea had been spangled with light, but now clouds covered the sun and there was a chill in the air. As she left the beach, she noticed the dog had gone. The owner had presumably caught up and they'd continued on their way.

She was hungry and would eat early. Back at the cottage she lit the wood-burner and made herself an omelette. It was liberating that there was no need to consult Patrick. Not that he would mind. But it would be rude not to consult. Rude and unloving. Consulting didn't come naturally to her. Did that make her unloving? Before she'd moved, she and Patrick had managed a pattern of being apart and together, which had flowed pretty easily.

There was every sign this could continue. For Patrick's first visit to the cottage had gone better than she could have imagined. He showed no sign of criticising or finding fault, made no attempt to tidy her slightly messy kitchen and had been generally enthusiastic. They had happily christened her new bed and she had woken to smells of bacon and coffee.

Patrick confessed to worrying about her being alone in such a remote location. 'I know that doesn't worry you,' he said over the toast and marmalade. 'I'm doing my best to be philosophical. Believe that no harm will come to you.'

Naomi sat back in her chair. 'I just feel so sure of that. Maybe it's foolish.'

'To be honest, it's probably mostly because I miss having you next door. The sense of you, right there. Not that you're so far away. I can still reach you – it'll take twenty minutes instead of twenty seconds, that's all.'

Naomi had admitted that she too missed the close proximity they had shared. She appreciated his concern and appreciated even more that he was not making it into a big issue. Yes, she had felt a tinge of regret, a sense of being abandoned, when he drove away later that morning. But still she loved the solitude. It was what she wanted. And now she had it in abundance.

In the days that followed, there had been no time to write or think or stare at the sea. She was busy unpacking boxes, arranging everything as she wanted it and finding a carpenter to build the bookshelves in her room. The only thing that jarred in the whole cottage was the red chair. It occupied the side of the table opposite the most useful work surface and was often, quite literally, a stumbling block. It's only a chair, she told herself and considered painting it to obliterate the red, but it would still be a nuisance whatever its colour. Eventually, in exasperation, she had moved it into a corner of the larder. The kitchen had seemed to positively expand into the space it freed up.

Now, as she sipped the last of the wine she allowed herself with her omelette, she reflected on the last few days. She had wondered how she would cope with images of Wilson and Gordon appearing in the rooms of the cottage, but this hadn't happened. Wilson hadn't featured at all, and memories of Gordon had come free of context – his laugh, a phrase or a familiar gesture. Nothing to trouble her. She wasn't being haunted by the tall, thin house either. Maybe the tedious sessions of thinking herself through the past on rocks, headlands and the hotel bed had served their purpose. While the story-telling with Meghan and Patrick had given her a better sense of perspective. Whatever story she now had to tell might be the better for that. Or maybe she could put it all behind her and immerse herself in the present and find some peace in that.

Contentedly, she looked around the room and opened her book. She was getting used to the best way to stoke the wood-burner, and it was throwing out a comforting warmth. She might ring Patrick later, but just now he was probably making his own supper.

You knew immediately, didn't you, when you heard the gentle scratch on the door? You were washing up, noticing your reflection in the window becoming clearer as it grew dark outside. The nights were drawing in, time to shut down for the evening. You felt a quiver of anxiety about who might be looking in. No one, of course, but you wiped your hands on your jeans and pulled the curtain across. Then came the scratch, accompanied by a whimper. Nothing as pathetic as a whine, nor as demanding as a bark. You'd almost been expecting it.

You opened the door and the dog looked up at you. Hopeful. Waiting. The wind was getting up, rain not far off. The animal was shivering. You, who cared nothing for dogs and had met more in the hotel bar than in your entire previous life, invited the creature in.

Connor, you said, reading the disc on the dog's collar. I'm Naomi, you said and were charmed when he put a paw into your offered hand. You remembered the tin of corned beef at the back of the cupboard, a legacy from Gordon. Once in a dish on the floor, it vanished faster than you could believe – the first revelation.

Overcome by your own generosity, you thought fleas, mud, hairs, and decreed that Connor should stay in the kitchen, indicating the rug and telling him to stay. There was no doubt he understood. That was the second revelation.

As you settled to read by the fire, your mind was not on your book. What happened next made you laugh out loud. First a gentle patter of paws on the slate floor in the kitchen. Then silence, before a grey shape insinuated itself, sidling towards the fire, pretending to be part of the carpet. When you laughed, he put his head on your knee.

'Oh, Connor,' you said. And a friendship was formed.

Naomi went to the police to see if Connor had been reported missing, only to discover that he was well-known in the area. Evidently his owner worked abroad and had a casual attitude to dog ownership, leaving the animal to the care of his neighbours when he was away. This had worked reasonably well, but now the owner had emigrated to Canada and the neighbours were not keen to take permanent responsibility for the dog.

'Who can blame them?' the duty sergeant said.

Naomi stepped aside to phone Patrick, who was extremely dubious at the prospect of taking on a stray dog.

'He sounds very scruffy. What is he?'

'Connor, so Irish, I guess. So, wolfhound possibly.'

'But they're huge!'

'Yes. Quite tall, up to my hip, maybe.'

Patrick might think Connor was too big, too scruffy or too skinny, but the more he objected, the more Naomi realised that her mind was made up.

She promised Patrick she would take Connor to a vet and turned back to the police desk. 'So, what if I took him on?'

The duty sergeant beamed. 'I would venture to say, that would suit everyone, ma'am – including us. We wouldn't want to be rounding him up for the dog pound. Such a good-natured animal, never been known to go after livestock, gentle, reliable and amazingly self-sufficient.'

It sounded like a character reference for a personal secretary.

'One thing, though, maybe we could agree upon?' the sergeant continued. 'That, when he goes AWOL, as is his habit, you won't report him missing. In return, we won't round him up, in the knowledge that he will always come back to you. He may be independent but he won't pass up a warm fire and easy food for long.'

It had all been surprisingly straightforward. Before she knew it, she was officially a dog owner. Except that, in Connor's case, owner was an inappropriate word.

The next time Patrick came for the evening, Connor warned of his approach with throaty growling and burst into full-blown barking as he reached the door. It was the first time Naomi had heard his voice. Patrick was impressed. He was further impressed at the way Connor stood guard over Naomi and took some time to be won over by charades of biscuits before he was willing to accept Patrick as a friend.

'It's a great relief, really,' Patrick said, scratching Connor behind the ear. 'Knowing you have protection.'

'And company.'

Patrick looked down at Connor as if assessing his talent for providing company. He grinned. 'Yes, and company, but not too much competition.'

Over supper that evening, he grabbed her hand across the table. 'You know why I feel so very lucky?'

Naomi waited, wondering what was coming.

He grinned. 'To have fallen in love with a woman who makes the best chilli in the world.'

'There's romantic.'

Later, as they curled up with the crossword on the saggy old sofa in front of the fire, Naomi was thinking, domestic bliss, and voiced the thought.

'Hmm,' Patrick said. 'Apart from this horribly uncomfortable sofa and the draught round the back of my neck.'

'Oh, not bliss at all! Must get some newspaper to stuff into that window.'

'Darling, the windows all need double-glazing.'

'Perish the thought! That's not going to happen.' Her tone was so indignant that Connor raised his head and looked suspiciously at Patrick.

'Anyway, can we go to bed before my back seizes up?' He grunted and shifted position. 'And, just for the record, if you're ever ill, you get looked after at my place. I love this cottage because you love it and it suits you so well, but to actually live here – a step too far.'

'And you don't have to! That's the joy of it.' She shut down the wood-burner. 'And being nursed by you at your place would be luxury. It's a deal. Let's go up.'

Patrick eyed Connor. 'Where does he sleep?'

Naomi laughed. 'No worries. He's a downstairs dog. Happy as Larry by the Aga.'

Patrick stretched and relaxed. 'Thank heavens for your really comfortable bed.'

She could almost hear him thinking that he'd be off home to civilisation in the morning, and it didn't worry her one bit.

38 *Naomi*

It was the chilli party. It was really happening. Naomi was hardly able to eat. She looked round at the faces of her friends, lit by flames from the wood-burner and Claudia's fairy lights. They were all crowded in, on sofas and stools, perched on arms and the window ledge, tucking into bowls of chilli – her own, very hot, Meghan's medium and vegetarian and Patrick's mild for the sake of Alex and the unborn baby. All those faces, more friends than she'd ever had at any one time in her life. How had that happened in the space of six short months?

Patrick read her thoughts and leaned forward to whisper in her ear, 'They're all here for you.'

She felt her eyes watering and was glad of Rita's Harry booming across the room. 'With chilli this hot, your house will always be warm.'

Rita gave him a look, but laughter and toasts followed and the discordant note was drowned out. One day, maybe, Rita would accept her. She wasn't holding her breath. Meanwhile Meghan remarked to Alex that Naomi's chilli might be just what she needed if she went over her due date.

'Nothing like it for getting a few contractions going.'

'For God's sake, Mum.' Alex shuddered and dropped her fork. 'I'd rather let the hospital take care of that, if you don't mind.'

Will frowned and looked up at Alex, shaking his head, but was distracted by the unfamiliar sound of tramping and running feet on the path outside. Everyone scrambled to their feet, hurrying to climb into wellingtons and take their part in the next phase of the evening.

Naomi had wondered how Connor would cope with the influx of visitors, but he had ignored them all, completed his usual clean-up of the kitchen floor and flopped in front of the fire. Now he'd gone out with everyone else. A dog who knew his own mind. She shut down the wood-burner, pulled on her coat and followed Meghan, holding the door for someone behind her. It was Rita, who shook her head. 'I'll stay for a bit. Be with you later,' she said, addressing Meghan.

Naomi shut the door behind her, trying not to have the unworthy thought that Rita might fancy a nose through her things. What if she did? Forget Rita. Stepping outside, she inhaled the aroma of frying onions and was surprised to see a sizeable crowd had gathered on the headland around the bonfire, some already munching hot dogs. Claudia had positioned herself at a table and was handing out sparklers to the children. At Claudia's feet, Naomi knew, was a box of her "signature" toffee apples – *my pièce de résistance, darling* – but those were for later.

Gordon was still never far from her thoughts. He'd have approved of the wood-burning stove, but not of Connor, who would have taken off to avoid being kicked. She imagined him now, good old Gordon, stomping round the bonfire with his hipflask, shouting unhelpful instructions and asking why the hell they didn't get on and light the damn thing.

Now was the moment. A shout went up and a round of applause greeted the whoosh of flames as Will set light to the pyramid of branches, brushwood and other vegetation. As they stood watching the fire take hold, creeping up to envelop the whole towering structure, Meghan dug her sharply in the ribs. 'It needs a guy,' she said.

They stood for a moment looking fiercely at one another. Then Meghan turned. 'Are you thinking what I'm thinking?'

She started running, and by the time Naomi reached the cottage, she was coming out, carrying the red chair.

'I saw you'd relegated it. Wasn't right, was it?'

Naomi shook her head. 'No, I couldn't cope with it. You're not offended?'

'As if. Maybe this is why I gave it to you, anyway. Come on, let's get it up there.'

Will frowned when he saw the chair and muttered about the paint not being environmentally friendly.

'I know,' Meghan said. 'But just for once? Will, please! There's very little of it, this is really important. Please?'

Will shrugged, gave Naomi a quizzical look and gathered his gang.

She and Meghan stood clutching each other round the shoulders as the men considered the task.

'Guess what?' Meghan said. 'When I fetched it just now, there was Rita, just finishing the washing-up. All done. Tidy kitchen.'

'Rita? Why would she? Of all people.' Naomi felt even more ashamed of her earlier uncharitable thoughts.

'Reckon it's her way of making the peace. She'd never *say* anything. But now you know who to thank. Ooh, look, here we go! It's on its way!'

They watched the chair's progress as the men hoisted and prodded it onto the top of the fire. At last it balanced, the legs a scarlet scaffold silhouetted against the night sky. The red paint bubbled up and dripped into the heart of the flames and a roar went up from the crowd.

People were dancing round the fire, made into other-worldly creatures by the flickering flames. Claudia was busy handing out her toffee apples and had produced a canvas chair for Alex. As Naomi watched, Will appeared, bringing Alex a beaker of soup, bending over her, making sure she was comfortable. Not long now to the baby. That would be the next excitement.

Patrick materialised out of the darkness, his face lit by a shower of sparks. 'There you are, my two favourite witches,' he said. 'I'm not going to ask why you're burning a perfectly functional chair.' He put his arms round them both. 'I'm sure you have your reasons.'

'Let's just say, it's served its purpose,' Naomi said.

She pulled Meghan and Patrick closer to her, gazing up at the stars, treasuring the moment. Close behind her was her cottage, snug in the valley, and beyond it the sheltered woodland track leading inland to the village. To her left, the stream hurtling itself continuously over the waterfall to meet the sea – *Mother Earth carry me, child I will always be.* To her right, the vast haunch of the hill, giving protection from the northerly gales. Above her head, the arc of sky meeting the unseen horizon, and beneath her feet, the well-trodden earth of the headland. All the elements. All the vital conditions for her solitude. But most precious was being contained by the warm bodies of Meghan and Patrick on either side of her.

While the three of them stared up, spark showers flew in all directions as the chair toppled backwards into the white-hot heart of the blaze, where it continued to burn, consumed by tongues of flame like an animal licking its wounds.